Unable to sit still witho[...] found romantic fiction [...] the deadly dull knitting [...] pages of her grandmoth[...] was born! But it wasn't [...]g, not summer, after completing her first degree in English Literature, that she fell upon the legends that are Mills & Boon books. She has occasionally lifted her head out of them since to do a range of jobs, including barmaid, financial adviser and teacher, as well as to practise (but never perfect) the art of motherhood to two almost grown-up cherubs. Bella lives a very energetic life in the UK, but tries desperately to travel for pleasure at least once a month—strictly in the interests of research!

Amanda Cinelli was raised in a large Irish/Italian family in the suburbs of Dublin, Ireland. Her love of romance was inspired after 'borrowing' one of her mother's beloved Mills & Boon novels at the age of twelve. Writing soon became a necessary outlet for her wildly overactive imagination. Now married, with a daughter of her own, she splits her time between changing nappies, studying psychology and writing love stories.

THE TYCOON'S SHOCK HEIR

BELLA FRANCES

ONE NIGHT WITH THE FORBIDDEN PRINCESS

AMANDA CINELLI

MILLS & BOON

First Published in Great Britain 2018
by Mills & Boon, an imprint of HarperCollins*Publishers*
1 London Bridge Street, London, SE1 9GF

The Tycoon's Shock Heir © 2018 by Bella Frances

One Night with the Forbidden Princess © 2018 by Amanda Cinelli

ISBN: 978-0-263-27326-7

MIX
Paper from
responsible sources
FSC® C007454

This book is produced from independently certified FSC™ paper
to ensure responsible forest management.
For more information visit www.harpercollins.co.uk/green.

Printed and bound in Spain
by CPI, Barcelona

THE TYCOON'S SHOCK HEIR

BELLA FRANCES

To my son, Harry.
With all my love.

CHAPTER ONE

FRIDAY AFTERNOON. BEST TIME in the world. Working week wrapped up and the party just about to start. And, with the news he'd just heard, Matteo Rossini knew it was going to be some party.

He stepped out of the car, loosened his tie and took the steps into his jet for the last task of the day—the short flight from Rome to London and a call to the Executive Director, Signora Rossini herself. Mamma to him.

He walked through the cabin and sat at his desk, ready to sink his Friday beer. It wasn't there.

He slung his bag on the empty chair and looked around. Neither was his assistant David. Strange. They had this routine down—the beer, the call, some water, some press-ups, shower and change, the car ready in London, sometimes a woman, sometimes not. Tonight was definitely a 'sometimes not' night. Tonight was boxing, a little gambling and all-male bonding—as soon as he delivered the news.

He sat down and keyed in the number. Drummed his fingers. Looked around again for David. Where *was* he?

At the sound of a beer being opened he turned, just as the call connected. He noticed the legs first, then the red dress. Definitely not David. He frowned and swivelled away from the sight as the bottle was placed beside him. Someone had some explaining to do.

'Hey, it's me.'

'Matteo! Good. I was just going to call you.'

'Well, here I am. With some news.'

'OK? You first, then.'

His heart raced. This was it.

'Arturo is finally selling. And we've got first refusal.' He touched the beer bottle, waited to hear his mother's response.

'Seriously? After all this time? That's incredible news.'

Matteo allowed his fingers to close round the neck of the bottle. Indeed it was.

'How did you find out?'

'It wasn't hard. I heard a rumour and did a little digging. Word is he's had enough. He wants out and we're the only ones in the running…'

He let the sentence dangle in the air. Even over the thousand miles that separated them he could imagine the mixture of heartache and hunger on his mother's face.

'You're absolutely sure about that?'

He paused. There was no point in pretending.

'We're the only ones properly in the running. I heard Claudio's going to throw his hat in the ring. But he's poison. His reputation has travelled to Switzerland, I guarantee it. He hasn't got a chance.'

'Matty, I don't want you to get involved.'

Her tone sank further than the ground beneath the plane.

'Mamma. You know this is the one that matters. Claudio walked away with half our clients and now I'm going to get them back. If we merge with Arturo we'll be unstoppable. I can do this. I promise you.'

'I don't want you to promise anything, Matty. I don't want you losing your mind the way your father did. It's not worth it. Nothing's worth it.'

He sighed and released his hand from the bottle. He had known she'd feel like this and he couldn't blame her, but they'd never get another chance.

'I can't let it pass—you know that,' he said quietly. 'Come on, Mamma. For Dad. We can't let Claudio get one over on us again.'

He waited for her to speak, but the plane climbed through silence. He could imagine the worry knitting her fine brows, twin tracks of loss and anguish. The look that had haunted her for years.

But she was Coral Rossini. And he was her son…

'You're right. We can't let that happen,' she said finally. 'We can't sit back and let him walk all over us again.'

'Exactly,' he said, letting out a breath.

'But you have to promise me that if he tries to do anything you'll walk away. Matteo. Promise me. I can't lose a husband *and* a son.'

The image of his father lying across the dashboard of his car flashed through his mind and he clenched his jaw so hard he could almost taste metal. Metal that he would use to grind Claudio's bones to dust. One day.

'You have nothing to fear, Mamma.'

'I have everything to fear. I couldn't bear anything to happen to you.'

The break in her voice killed him. She had more strength and resilience than anyone else alive. The fact that they could even say the name 'Claudio' in a conversation now was testament to how far they'd come.

That man had been closer than family, his father's best friend, his trusted lawyer then partner, and he'd sold them out—right under their noses. No one had been able to believe he'd set it all up and got away with it. And the rest. The unspeakable dark shadow he'd cast over their lives.

All they could do was put one foot in front of the other and try to salvage Banca Casa di Rossini—the two-hundred-year-old private bank of the Italian super-rich.

'Nothing's going to happen other than us taking the bank back to where it should be. Even if we don't get all of Arturo's clients we'll outrank Claudio. And that's all that matters, isn't it?'

The plane hit a patch of turbulence and Matty looked out at the thick grey cloud wrapping itself over the Italian countryside, Not even a thunderstorm was going to dim his spirits. Not with this rainbow on the horizon. Handing their crock of gold back to his mother had been his dream for years.

'What about the name? We might need to change the bank's name. Have you thought of that?'

'I'm ahead of you. If it comes to it, I'll do it. BAR. Banca Arturo Rossini. How does that sound?'

'Oh, Matty...'

He heard the wistful note in her voice. He felt it too. The bank went back generations, was respected the world over. But it was live or die. There was no third way.

'It's not what I want, but if it's the only way... We really do have a chance with this, don't we?'

Matty looked up as the woman in red walked past him down the aisle, the satin of her dress catching the light with every slow, steady step. His eyes zoned in on her legs again. They were quite something. And the way the skirt swished gently above her elegant calves with every step she took triggered a strong response. An unwelcome response.

'Matty?'

'We've got a really great chance,' he said, refocusing. 'There's no other private bank that reeks of old money and old values like ours. Claudio has turned his bank into just another sales-driven call centre. There's nothing sure and solid and *honest* about it. We're unique. Second only to Arturo in terms of stature.'

'I know. We just have to hope that stature and honesty are what he's looking for.'

'It's going to be all about the chemistry. And the fact that we've still not floated on the stock exchange. That's why we're ahead of Claudio—no matter what kind of offer he makes Arturo. I'm sure of it. In fact, I'm so sure I'm going to bet you that I land an invitation to Arturo's villa when we're at the Cordon D'Or Regatta. It's going to be a slow burn, but that's where I intend to start.'

He turned at the sound of water being poured. A squat crystal glass was placed down. He saw long, elegant fingers. Long, slim arms bare in the strapless red dress. And beaming down at him the dimpled smile of an angel.

'Thanks.' He frowned, automatically turning his head to watch her walk away. Mistake. His eyes narrowed on the smooth white skin above the red bodice of her dress, the delicate bones and long, swanlike neck. She was absolutely beautiful.

He was far too busy to allow himself any distractions. What the hell was David playing at?

'That'll be a start. But it'll take more than a little corporate hospitality at the Cordon D'Or to win him over. He's the last of the old guard. You'd better make sure your social media profile is squeaky clean. If there's a hint of any more scandal he'll pull up his drawbridge before you get within a mile of it.'

'There won't be any more. You can rely on that.'

He bitterly regretted there being any at all. And the timing was a disaster. He drummed his fingers on the window, traced the water droplets as they shook their way across the glass. His media presence had never been an issue before. Not until his most recent ex, Lady Faye, had started to feed the story of their break-up to the press. Now he was the 'City Love Rat', destroying the life of any woman who got close, stringing her along with promises of marriage and then dumping her disgracefully.

The truth was nothing like that. He never promised anything beyond the first date—as every one of his ex-girlfriends could testify.

Over the years he had carefully developed the symptoms of full-blown commitment phobia—the best possible illness for any confirmed bachelor to suffer from. Married to the job. Workaholic. Unashamedly, indubitably *yes*. He didn't commit to anything he couldn't see through to the end and he would never, ever commit to a woman the way he had once committed to his first love, Sophie.

He had lost his dad, lost his path in life and then lost her. There would be no more loss. He'd never be that vulnerable again.

'I wish you'd let David handle it. We could have done some damage limitation at least.'

'It's not my style. I refuse to play the games those trashy media sharks want me to play. And I won't get involved in any tit-for-tat about something that is no-body's business. Faye was ill. That's the only explana-tion. She believed something that wasn't real and then when it didn't fall into place the way she imagined she took it to the press the way she did with everything else. If she wasn't minor royalty no one would have cared, and me weighing in with "my story" would have been the last thing to make it better. That would have just prolonged the whole sorry mess.'

'I know that. But because you refused to even make a statement people think you're some sort of pariah. I hate anybody to think badly of you when I know what you're really like. It upset me reading that stuff.'

'So do as I do and don't read it.'

He heard her sigh and it cut him. It was easy for him to brush it off. What did *he* care what a bunch of people who didn't know him thought? It was ridiculous, wor-rying about stuff like that. But his mother was differ-ent. She cared. Deeply. About him and the bank. And everyone else too. She cared too much.

'I'm sorry, Mamma. But I can't turn the clock back. It'll all blow over and then it'll be some other poor sod's turn to be vilified.'

The woman in red was reaching up to put linens in the cupboard. Her arms were as slender and pale as long-stemmed lilies, her moves graceful and elegant. Her hair hung in a dark ponytail down her back, shiny and thick and long. She turned to glance at him, her dark eyes coy and unsure. He knew that look. He knew where it could go...

'Hang on.' He walked to the bedroom at the other end of the cabin and closed the door. 'Have you heard from David? He's not here and some woman is in his place. It's totally out of character for him just to send in agency staff like this…'

'Ah, I think you must be talking about Ruby. What do you think? Isn't she lovely?'

His mother had that excited tone in her voice that made him instantly aware…

'That's not in dispute,' he said. 'But I was hoping David would be looking after things for me until I said otherwise. What's going on?'

'Don't get upset, Matty. I'm up to my eyes and I needed David to finish off the branding work with the new advertising agency. No one knows our business better than him.'

'You've pulled rank and left me with a newbie?'

'I met Ruby,' she said, ignoring him, 'and I was very impressed. She's a fast learner—I think you two will get along fine. And you'll have David back on Monday.'

His mother was still holding something back. He was sure of it.

'You know she's dressed in a cocktail dress? A very nice cocktail dress, but it's not exactly work wear. Is there something else you've forgotten to tell me?'

Like last month, when she'd only remembered to tell him he had to make an after-dinner speech at the International Women in Finance dinner an hour before the canapés were served. Or the time when he'd had to present a prize at a kindergarten they sponsored on the way home from the casino. It was getting to be a bit of a habit, her asking him these last-minute 'favours' now that she was neck-deep in charity work.

'Ah. Now you mention it…'

Here it came.

'I'm afraid I'm still in Senegal, and there is one *tiny* engagement that needs to be covered tonight. You're in

London anyway—so it's right on your doorstop. And who knows? Maybe you'll net some good press coverage from it too! Wouldn't that be lovely? Matty? Are you still there?'

Matty's fingers slid down the veneer of the door as one by the one all his party plans burst like bubbles in champagne.

'It's for charity, darling. The underprivileged.'

Of course it was. It was what she did. While he took care of the nuts and bolts of the business she got on with all the charity and philanthropy. She was amazing at getting the rich and famous to part with cash and favours for the various charities the bank sponsored. It worked perfectly well—if only she would remember to tell him when she needed him.

'OK. You've guilt-tripped me. I'm in.' He sighed. 'What's involved?'

'It's an arts benefit premiere at the King's.'

'As long as it's not dance. You know I can't stand men in tights.'

'Did you say dance? Yes, it's my favourite company—the British Ballet. Don't groan, darling. All you have to do is a quick photo-call on the red carpet and shake some hands afterwards. Everything is arranged. I know you like to be prepared, so I've asked Ruby to look after things. She has your itinerary, and there's nothing she doesn't know about dance. She's one of the British Ballet's soloists, but she's recovering from injury at the moment—a dreadful year she's had, poor thing.'

He opened the door into the cabin and right on cue the gorgeous Ruby appeared. So she wasn't agency staff—she was a dancer. Well, that checked out. Her posture was perfect...her body was perfect. But why on earth was she serving him iced water at twenty thousand feet?

Suddenly it all became clear.

He went back into the bedroom and closed over the door.

'This is a roundabout way of saying that you met someone with another hard luck story and took her under your wing.'

'I know what you're thinking and I'm not going to lie. Ruby's had a tough time, but she's not a victim. This isn't all a one-way street, so you can relax.'

'Well, what is it, then?'

His mother was always feeling sorry for some waif or stray, and they didn't all have the best of intentions. He'd had years rooting out the swindlers and the chancers from the genuinely broken people who seemed to flock towards her. For all she was a shrewd businesswoman, she was also immensely gullible when it came to anyone with a hard luck story.

'Matty, there is nothing for you to worry about! Ruby is not going to trick me out of my millions. She's completely dedicated to the British Ballet, but she's off with an injury so this is her way of keeping involved. But if you'd rather have one of the men in tights I'm sure that can be arranged…?'

He shook his head in disbelief. Once again she'd twisted him around her little finger. How could he resist anything his mother said? After all she'd done for him, holding it together all these years. They were tight—a unit. They had been since his father's death and always would be. It was that simple.

And if ever he had a moment when he doubted anything he heard his father's voice—his conscience, whatever—whispering in his ear. There was no way his mother's wishes would go unheeded. Ever.

'OK. As long as she doesn't get the wrong idea.'

'That part's entirely up to you, Matteo.'

He caught the slight note of censure in her voice—and the double meaning. She knew his vices as much as he did himself. The fact that he didn't want a long-term relationship didn't mean that he wanted to spend his evenings alone.

'OK, Mamma. I didn't mean with me, but we'll let that pass.'

'I'm sorry, darling, I don't mean to have a dig. But it upsets me that women are so disposable to you. I know you could have a happy life if only you'd let yourself settle down with someone. At the end of the day I'm your mother, and I only want what's best for you.'

'What's best for me is what's best for the bank. That's all I'm interested in. Not settling down with a woman. I'm not saying that I'll always feel this way, but for now, until I've got past this hurdle, the bank is all there is.'

The words were out. As plain as numbers on a balance sheet. Irrevocable. No room for misinterpretation. Profit. Loss. Black. White. No shades of grey, no emotion colouring things. Just following the dream. His father's dream. And now it was his. Like it or not.

CHAPTER TWO

FLIGHT AT SIX, land at seven-thirty, less an hour for time difference. Half-hour to get to the theatre. It would be a miracle if she pulled it off without a hitch.

Ruby stood in the middle of the cabin and stared—left to the cockpit and right, all the way to the firmly closed bedroom door, where Matteo Rossini, company sponsor, heart-throb and all-round Love Rat was still taking calls while the minutes ticked past.

She shook her head and stared down at her arms, where blotches and hives were beginning their stress march across her skin—a sure sign that she was out of her comfort zone.

It was bad enough that she'd been on the bench for months, waiting for this ligament damage to heal, but now she was hurtling towards London, and the world premiere of *Two Loves*, with the job of convincing their sponsor that the British Ballet was worth every penny of the money his private bank channelled their way.

So much responsibility—and she was the last person they should have trusted to do this.

If it had been Coral Rossini herself it would have been fine. She was the Grande Dame of Dance. She'd been a massive support to the company for years. She was loved and gave love in return, supporting them at every premiere. But not this time. This time her second-in-command was stepping in.

And when the director had passed Ruby that note, with a *Who's the lucky girl?* look on his face, it had been all she could do to stop herself from groaning aloud, *Hopefully not me...*

She'd read Coral Rossini's note.

So lovely to meet you again yesterday!

I've suddenly realised you would be the ideal person to look after my son Matteo at the benefit on Friday. He's not the biggest fan of dance but I'm sure you'll work your magic.

I have taken the liberty of sending some things for you. And some things for Matteo to wear too.

Don't worry if he puts up a fight—he's a pussy-cat really!

Ciao!

Coral x

She'd stared at the note, her heart tumbling into her stomach, and then opened the bags and boxes of clothes, all beautifully wrapped and folded in tissue. There had been the red dress—a froth of satin and petticoats—a wrap with a beautiful Chinese poppy print, beige court shoes and a little matching clutch. Then she'd found a red tie and pocket square for Matteo to wear, and tucked into an envelope was a cheque for a thousand pounds.

A thousand pounds! That had made it even more impossible to say no. No one could afford to turn her nose up at that kind of money. But for *this*? She just wasn't cut out for schmoozing with the people who hung around the fringes of the dance world. She couldn't care less who was famous or rich or both.

The director had been quite up-front about it.

'I can trust you to do it. Some of the other girls might get a bit carried away, but you've got your head screwed on. You'll not let us down. Or yourself...'

He was right about that. She'd been with the British Ballet longer than anyone else—it had been home and school and friends and family to her for years. She'd come up through the ranks from eleven years old and she had no ambition to go anywhere else or do anything else. She was safe there. It was all she knew. And all she wanted to know.

Others came, made friends, found lovers, moved on. They had lives outside of the studio and the theatre. They went to parties and spoke about their families. They knew not to ask her about hers. She knew they were curious, but they accepted her silence. Who'd want to talk about that, after all? The gap year father who just kept on travelling, and the teenage mother who hadn't been able to accept the curfew demanded by a newborn baby.

Thank God for dance. That was her silent prayer. Without dance she would still be the millstone around her mother's neck or the fatherless obsessive—scouring the internet, searching for his face in the crowd, dreaming about reconciliations that would never happen...

'Hi. I'm Matteo. Good to meet you.'

She startled at the sound of his voice and dropped the bag of peanuts she'd been about to open.

Deep breath, big smile, and turn.

'Ruby. Hello.' She smiled as she neatly grabbed the bag and extended her hand.

She had to admit he was even more of a heart-throb up close—and so *tall*. His tie hung loosely, like a rope on the wall of his wide chest. She gazed up past thick broad shoulders to a blunt jaw and a full-lipped mouth. His nose was broad and long, broken at the bridge, and his eyes, when she reached them, were sharp brown berries, tucked deep into a frown.

He shook her hand. Warmly…firmly. Then dropped his hand away. She found herself staring at the half-smile on his lips, noticing how wide and full they were, and thinking that with his longer-than-collar-length hair he looked more like a romantic poet trapped in a boxer's body than a boring banker.

'Everything OK?'

Bang, bang, bang. Words were fired out like bullets at a target, and his eyes were taking in everything. *Every. Thing.* They darted all over her face and swept up the rest of her—and maybe it was the close confines of the plane, or the fact that he had such a *presence*, or the fact that she was not used to standing in heels serving drinks to a total stranger at twenty thousand feet, but her footing faltered and she had to reach out to hold the back of a seat for balance.

'Yes. I—I was just going to pour you another drink and find some snacks and…'

'No problem. I'm fine for drinks and snacks. But apparently I'm heading to the ballet now, which is quite a turn of events.'

'Yes,' she said, regaining perfect balance and poise. 'To see *Two Loves*. The premiere. We're so excited. It's an amazing production.'

And it was. And she'd have given anything to be in it. But because of this hideous injury she wasn't even in the corps. Instead she'd had to pack her day with teaching junior classes and attending physio. And serving Love Rats…

'And you're the face of the British Ballet. That's

good. That's really good,' he said, scanning her again and nodding as if in fact it was really bad. 'Done your homework, I take it? I'll need to know the names and the bios of the people we're going to see.'

He moved around the cabin now and she stood there, not quite sure if she was supposed to follow him, reassure him, or disappear off the face of the earth.

She watched him turn on a screen that flashed stock exchange numbers. He glanced at it, then changed it quickly to sports. He folded his arms and stared at the screen as a commentator's voice rose to a crescendo over the roar of a crowd. She looked to see what it was—men charging into one another, with mud-splattered thighs as big as tree trunks, ears and noses like Picasso paintings, all grabbing for an oval shaped ball as if it was the Holy Grail. Rugby. *Yuck.* How could anyone get excited about that?

'Come on!' he grunted at the players on the screen as he moved towards it.

Obviously Matteo Rossini did. She waited...and watched, but it was as if she had become a part of the furniture, as incidental as the beige leather chairs. He might have the looks, but he had none of his mother's charm.

Suddenly he turned, caught her gawping, and frowned. He pressed the remote control 'off' and tossed it down on the chair.

'I have plans for later, so I'd like this to be all wrapped up by ten. Shall we make a start?'

He nodded, indicating the little lounge area where four leather armchairs were grouped around a coffee table. He lowered himself down, comfortable, confident and totally composed, while she perched carefully, straight-backed, knees locked, smile fixed.

'OK. Basics first. You're a dancer with this ballet company, but you've "volunteered" to take on this PR role just for tonight.'

'Something like that,' she said, ignoring the air quotes he made with his hands.

'So what's Ruby's story? Why you?' he said, narrowing his eyes and steepling his fingers.

'You want to know about me? There's not much to tell. I've been with the BB since I was eleven,' she said, realising that she was now being interviewed for a job she didn't even want. 'I'm not dancing tonight, so I think I was the obvious choice.'

'The BB is the British Ballet?'

She smiled at his stupid question.

'Yes. The company's fifty years old. I've been in the school, the corps, then a soloist and hopefully one day a principal. So I know everything there is to know.'

'What about the other side of things? There will be political points being scored here tonight. You know everything there is to know about that too, I take it?'

As she stared at him she suddenly remembered the notes. Had she brought them? Pages and pages of silly handwritten notes about all the other stuff she was meant to tell him. She'd been writing them out in the kitchen, she'd numbered them, she'd stacked them... And then what had she done with them?

'You're prepared, right? One thing you should know about me is I'm not a big fan of winging it.'

Neither am I, she wanted to answer back. Which was why she had spent so long making notes about things she didn't find remotely interesting. But being rude to the sponsor was not an option—not with all that revenue riding on it. Her own scholarship had been funded through the generosity of patrons like Coral Rossini, the Company Director had been quick to remind her.

'I'm sure you won't be disappointed. Mrs Rossini was confident I was right for the job.'

'Yes. I'm sure she was,' he said, in a tone that buzzed in her subconscious like an annoying fly.

But where *were* the notes? In her bag? Or could she have stuffed them in her pockets? Left them on the Tube?

He tipped his head back, scrutinised her with a raised brow, looking down the length of his annoyingly handsome nose, and she wondered if he could read her mind.

'How long have you known my mother, incidentally? She seems to have taken quite a shine to you.'

'She has?'

She'd definitely had the notes just before she got in the car…

'Yes. And you wouldn't be the first person to want to be friends with my incredibly kind, incredibly generous mother.'

What was he talking about? Did he think that she wanted to be his mother's friend? Did he think she actually *wanted* to be here, doing this?

'I'm not here to make friends with anyone. I'm here because I was told to be.'

And then she stopped, suddenly aware of the dark look that had begun to spread across his face. She'd gone too far.

'You were *told* to be?' he asked as his brows rose quizzically above those sharp sherry-coloured eyes.

'Someone had to do it.'

He sat back now, framed in the cream leather seat, elbows resting on the arms of the chair and fingers steepled in front of his chest. They were shaded with fine dark hair, and above the pinstriped cuff of his shirt the metallic gleam of a luxury watch twinkled and shone.

She kept her eyes there, concentrating on the strong bones of his wrists, refusing to look into his face as the jet powered on through the sky.

'And you drew the short straw?' he said, lifting his water.

She caught sight of the solid chunks of burnished silver cufflinks. She'd never even known anyone who wore cufflinks before, barely knew anyone who bothered to wear a shirt and tie, and she wondered for a moment how he got them off at night.

'You'd rather be anywhere other than here?'

His voice curled out softly, quietly, just above the thrum of the engines, and with the unmistakable tone of mockery. Was he teasing her? She flashed a glance up. He was. The tiniest of smiles lurked at the corner of his mouth. Did that mean he *didn't* think she was trying to stick her claws into his mother?

Maybe.

She shifted in the chair, used her core muscles to keep from slipping further down into the bucket seat. He sat completely still, and with all that *body* sitting across from her it was impossible to concentrate.

'I'd rather be performing,' she said. 'Nothing matters more to me than that.'

'That I understand,' he said quietly. His face fell for a moment as some other world held him captive. He opened and flexed his hand, turned it around and she saw knuckles distended, broken. 'I understand that very well.'

She looked down at her own hands, bunched up on her lap in the scarlet satin, and waited for him to speak. He didn't. He crossed his leg and her gaze travelled there. And all the way along it. All the way along hard, strong muscle. She knew firm muscle when she saw it, and he was even better built than a dancer—bulkier, stronger, undeniably masculine. She could make out powerful thighs under all that navy silk gabardine, and the full force of the shoulders stretched out under his shirt. He could lift her above his head, and spin her around, lay her down and then…

He laid his hands on the armrests and she glanced up, startled out of her daydream.

'Sorry. I— Let's get back on track.' She cleared her throat. OK, time to remember her notes. 'The performance tonight. You want me to give you the details now?'

'Please do.' He nodded.

She frowned. She could repeat every dance step, but that wasn't what he needed to know. Details. Names. Dates. All in the notes, in a pile, on her kitchen table—which was at least five hundred miles away.

'*Two Loves* is based on a poem.'

'A poem…? Anything more specific than that?'

Yes, there were specifics. Loads of specifics. She'd written them down, memorised them, but fishing them out of her brain now was a different thing. As if she needed any more reminding that the one single thing she could do in life was dance. She was completely hopeless at almost everything else.

'It's…really old,' she said, grasping for any single fact.

His eyebrow was still raised. 'How old? Last month? Last year? Last century?'

'Ancient old,' she said, an image of the poet that the choreographer had shown them coming to mind. 'Like two thousand years. And Persian,' she said happily. 'It's all coming back. He's a Persian poet called Rumi, famous for his love poems.'

'Ah yes. Rumi. *"Lovers don't finally meet somewhere. They're in each other all along..."* And all that rubbish.'

'Yes, well. Some of that—"rubbish"—has made this ballet tonight,' she said, pleased that she'd remembered something, even if he sounded less than impressed.

'OK. Though, since its unlikely I'm going to be shaking hands with the poet Rumi tonight, do you have any facts about anyone alive? There's normally a whole list of people I need to thank.'

'Yes,' she said, staring into his unimpressed face. 'That's all in my notes.'

'Right,' he said, standing up and staring at his watch. 'We land in thirty minutes. You get your notes and I'll grab a shower and get into my tux.' He looked at her and nodded. 'I think we're both agreed that the sooner we get this over with the better.'

CHAPTER THREE

MATTEO ROSSINI WAS sacking off boxing and the casino to go to the ballet? Was he for real?

He could hear the boys howling down the phone as they all raised their glasses in a fake toast. At least someone found it funny, he thought as he hauled his third-best tux out of the wardrobe and laid it out on the bed.

He'd been looking forward to this night for ages. A chance to really blow off steam after the disastrous media circus he'd lived through with Faye. And learning of the juicy prospect of tucking Arturo Finance into the back pocket of the bank was going to be the icing on the cake.

He felt he was almost on the home straight already.

But all that would have to wait while he went to the ballet.

He dragged the towel across his damp shoulders and chuckled, realising he wasn't nearly as down about it as he'd been half an hour ago. And it didn't have anything to do with a new desire to watch people flounce about the stage. All the charm of the evening was wrapped up in one beautiful little package called Ruby.

She might well have designs on his mother, but he wasn't getting that feeling from her—he wasn't picking up that sycophantic thing that most people had about them when they met him for the first time.

She was refreshing, and he was in the mood to be refreshed, and since there was no choice in the matter for the next couple of hours he might as well enjoy what he could.

He stepped into his trousers just as there was a knock on the door. He listened. It came again. Two tiny little raps—one-two. Quiet, but determined. Business not pleasure, he thought, registering with interest a slight sense of disappointment.

He fastened his flies and lifted his shirt, then opened the door and there she was. All eyes, lips and lily-white slender limbs.

'Hello, there,' he said, stretching his arms inside his shirt. 'Everything OK?'

By the look on her face everything was *not* OK. Her eyes had widened to coal-black circles and her mouth was in a shocked red 'O' as she gawped at his chest. He stifled a smile as he turned to spare her blushes and started to button his shirt.

'I'm so sorry to bother you,' she said, tucking her eyes down, 'but I was meant to give you this to wear.' She held out a little parcel, kept her head turned away. 'From your mum.'

He continued to fasten his buttons and stared at the little parcel.

'Want to open it for me?' he said, now walking to the table for his cufflinks.

Her eyes flicked up, then down, but not before she took a good long look. He couldn't help but smile broadly. *Game on.*

She pulled open the package and held out a red bow tie and pocket square.

'Is everything OK?'

'What?' she said. 'Yes, of course everything is OK. I was just wondering why you bother with those things.'

He paused, his collar up, considering her carefully. That was not what he'd expected to hear.

'Pardon?'

'Cufflinks. What are they even for? Why not just use buttons? I don't get it.'

'Has anyone ever told you you're quite forward?' he said, clicking the cufflinks together.

'I say what's on my mind. I'm not trying to cause offence, but I've never seen anyone use them.'

He finished and tugged at his cuffs, checking that his sleeves were perfectly straight, watching her watching him carefully. He was warming to her more by the minute.

'They make my cuffs sit nicely. I like the look. A beautiful shirt deserves beautiful cuffs. And, since you're looking unconvinced by that answer, I'll also add that these were a gift from an ex-girlfriend. After we split up.'

He turned them in the light and smiled.

'I'm not all Mr Bad Guy, despite what you might have read in the press.'

'Oh,' she said. 'Right...' with a tone that was flat and disbelieving.

He raised an eyebrow and tied the bowtie in place.

Well, what did he expect? he thought, turning away to get his jacket while his mind ran to the stupid pictures his friends had texted him and those quotes about being emotionally stunted.

He hadn't bothered to read them properly. Anyone who knew him well knew the truth. And anyone who knew him well knew that all his stunted emotions sat with Sophie. The only thing he was sure of in his life was that there would never be another Sophie...

They had been the Golden Couple all through university—she with her long blonde hair and he a rising star of the rugby scene. He'd never been happier. The whole world had been spread out before him. His degree in sports science, his imminent career as a rugby player, playing for his country... Would it be Italy or England? When would he ask Sophie to marry him? Where would they live?

Those were the kinds of decisions he'd faced. Until the night he'd got the news that his father had died. Like a great oak being ripped up from the roots, his strength, his confidence had been sapped. He'd felt the world crumble under his feet, felt himself spinning in space. He'd thought his father sure and solid and strong. He'd had all the answers. He'd been wise and clever and honourable and he'd loved his mother—and Claudio had been his best friend.

They had been almost inseparable—closer than brothers. The only thing that had ever came between his parents had been Claudio's suffocating presence in their lives—until something had happened and everything had changed.

Matteo had once suspected that Claudio had made a move on his mother and his father had found out. It had to be something like that for the schism between them to have been so deep. How wrong he had been.

His father's fight to save the family bank had been epic. He had worked tirelessly for weeks, but so much of it had gone. People with lots of money wanted lots more. Loyalty was too expensive. Especially when Claudio had offered a fast dividend and people had been too greedy to care how it was made.

But it had been his father's death more than the losses to the company that had devastated Matteo's life. His mother had been inconsolable—the thought of her anguish still made him wince with pain. He had gone to her side, nursed her and taken charge as he knew his father would have wanted. A stream of people from the banking world had arrived—all firm handshakes, sober suits and quiet conversations.

All of that he had lived through, knowing that it couldn't get any worse. Knowing that Sophie was there for him.

And the knowledge of her warm, loving body had driven him one night to take a flight north to university, then a two-hour taxi ride from the airport to the cold, stormy coast of St Andrew's, where he'd known she would be just about to wake up. Maybe he'd slip into bed beside her, feel the love in her arms and bury himself and his pain...

How many times must he relive those moments? The crunch of the gravel, the lightening shadows of the morning and the frosted cloud of his breath. The cold, metallic slide of his key in the lock, lamps still burning in the hallway, the TV on, glasses on the table.

Like an automaton he had turned to the sound of the shower.

And then had come the sight he wished he could burn from his eyes.

His beautiful Sophie, naked and wet, her legs wrapped around another man. And the other man had been the national rugby coach, come all the way to Scotland to ask him to play for his country.

Was he emotionally stunted? All day long. And for the rest of his life.

'Most people don't believe what they read. I never do, if it's any consolation.'

His eyes tracked round, following the voice that had split through the sick daydream. Angel-faced Ruby, with those huge brown eyes and wide red lips was looking up at him with something that might be described as concern. How sweet. But if it was concern, it was wasted.

'Please don't worry about me,' he said, fastening the last button on his jacket. 'I'm a big boy. I can take what they dish up and swallow it whole.'

He winked. He smiled. He put one hand on her shoulder. Her delicate, silken-skinned shoulder. He stepped a little closer and watched as her eyes did that widening thing that women always did—usually just before he leaned in for his first kiss...

And wouldn't a kiss be the perfect way to start his evening with Ruby? Those gorgeous lips, that ivory skin, her lustrous hair... Hadn't he been tempted from the moment he'd seen her? Hadn't she shown that she was tempted too?

This could turn into the perfect night after all.

Oh, yes, he thought, and the stirring and hardening in his groin were now very obviously happening. There was only one thing left to do.

'But it must hurt your mother—reading that,' she said, turning her head.

He paused in mid-air, correcting himself and exiting the move swiftly. He'd been rebuffed. Well, well, well...

'What my mother feels is no concern of yours or anyone else's,' he heard himself say. 'I wish people would leave well alone.'

Colour rose like a scarlet tide over her cheeks and he instantly regretted his sharp tone.

Damn, that had been too harsh. Ruby didn't seem

like the gossipy type. And she was only being kind. And, worst of all, she was right. He knew his mother had been hurt by the press, and he knew he had no one to blame for that but himself.

But why couldn't people worry about their own lives instead of raking all over his?

He reached out a hand—an involuntary gesture—but she muttered an apology under her breath and was already making her way back through the cabin. He watched her walk carefully, the red satin billowing out above her calves, swishing gently with each step, until he was almost hypnotised by the sight.

And then the plane bumped and dropped. And she stumbled. She reached out to grab at the nearest chair and held on to it for two long seconds. He could tell she was holding herself in pain. She didn't utter a sound.

He rushed to her.

'Are you OK?'

'Perfectly, thanks,' she said, keeping her eyes ahead and fixing that smile in place as she started to walk again.

'I saw you stumble there. Is it your injury? I know that's why you're not dancing at the moment. Is everything OK?'

She raised her eyebrows and flicked him an *as if you care* glance. He deserved that.

'I'm fine, thanks. I'm going to sit down now, if that's OK.'

'Ruby—hold up.'

She sat carefully in the seat, straightening her spine, and her bright smile popped back into place. He recognised that—smiling through pain. Everybody had a mask.

He sat in the seat opposite her. She tucked her knees

to the left and pressed them together, sitting even straighter—a clearer Keep Back message he'd never seen.

'What is it? Hip? Knee?'

'It's no big deal. It's nearly healed.'

'What happened?'

'A fall. That's all.'

'Must have been some fall to have taken almost six months to heal.'

The bright smile was fixed in place. At least it looked like a smile, but it felt more as if she was pushing him back with a deadly weapon.

'You know, I've had my fair share of injuries too,' he said, when she didn't reply. 'I played rugby for years. I know that you might never have guessed, thanks to my boyish good looks, but I was a blindside flanker at St Andrew's—when I was at university.'

He tilted his head and showed her the mashed ear that had formed after too many injuries. Luckily that and his broken nose were his only obvious disfigurements, but he'd lost count of the fractures and tears tucked beneath his clothes.

'Blindside flanker…' She looked away, sounding totally, politely uninterested. 'Sounds like rhyming slang.'

'I was about to be capped for England,' he said, grinning through her cheeky little retort.

'Really?'

At least that merited a second glance. He smiled, nodded, raised his eyebrows. *Got you this time*, he thought.

'About to be? So what happened?'

'Long story. Doesn't matter. So, what exactly is wrong with you, may I ask?'

'It's complicated.'

'I'm sure I'll be able to follow. I've been heavily involved in most sports, one way or another, and I know the pounding bodies take. Ballet is tough—I know that. It might not be my cup of tea, but I respect what you guys do.'

He could see her pausing for a moment, hovering between cutting him off again and continuing the conversation. The smile had dropped and she was watching him carefully, but her body was still coiled tight as a little spring.

'I've not always been a boring old banker. I wasn't born wearing a pinstripe suit,' he said softly. 'Give me a rugby ball any day of the week.'

'So what happened?' she asked. 'Why didn't you follow your dream?'

'Tell me about your injury first,' he countered.

'Cruciate ligament,' she said after a moment.

'Anterior? Posterior? Don't tell me it was one of the collaterals?'

'It was the anterior. I had to have surgery. Twice.'

'Painful,' he said, sucking his teeth. 'You'd better be careful. That can be the end of a beautiful career.'

'I'm well aware of that.'

'I imagine you are. Must be on your mind all the time. One of the players in my uni squad had a terrible time. Had to jack it in eventually. Pity. He had a great future ahead but the injury put paid to all that. I've no idea what he's doing now—he was a bit of a one-trick pony. I don't think he had a Plan B…'

And then suddenly the mask slid down and her brilliant smile slipped and wobbled. Her delicate collarbones bunched and the fine muscles of her throat constricted and closed. She was visibly holding herself in check.

'I'm sorry,' he said. 'That's not what you want to hear right now. Dance is your whole life, isn't it? I totally get it.'

'How can you until it happens to you?'

She shook her head and twisted away from him, staring out over the twinkling yellow lights of London.

'I really do understand,' he said, cringing at his thoughtlessness. 'Rugby was my whole life. As far as I was concerned banking was what my father did. And then—*whoosh*—he died and the carpet got pulled from under my feet. And here I am.'

He looked round at the jet, at the cream leather, the crystal glasses, the plasma screen flashing, the numbers and money, wealth and success. For all the Arturo deal would be the icing on the cake, he still had a pretty rich cake.

Her face told him she was thinking exactly the same thing and he couldn't blame her for that.

'It's not exactly the same, though, is it?' she said, with a note of wistfulness that rang like a bell in his consciousness. 'You had a Plan B. I've got nothing else. Only this. My whole life has been preparing to be a principal dancer. I'm not good at anything except dancing—I barely got myself together to do this.'

She held out the skirts of her dress and looked right into his eyes with such an imploring look that he thought how easy it would be to fall for a woman like her. She was strong, yet vulnerable too—but all he had to do was dive right in and before he knew it he'd be scrabbling for the banks of some fast-flowing river or, worse, being dragged under and losing his mind along the way.

He would not be diving into anything. Arm's length was the only safe distance with any woman—especially one that looked like this—because even when he was crystal-clear it always ended up the same way, with her wanting more than he could give.

Relationships: the rock he was not prepared to perish on again. No way. The skill came in avoiding crashing into that rock by keeping it light, keeping it moving along, keeping it all about the 'now'. Worrying about the future…that wasn't such a great idea.

He turned to Ruby, lifted her chin with his finger, the lightest little touch.

'You're doing a fine job. You've nothing at all to worry about,' he said, hearing himself use his father's gentle but firm *pull yourself together* tone.

But she shook her head and lifted those doe eyes.

'I'm not. I'm useless. I've left the notes I wrote out at home on the table. And I spent hours writing them—in case I forgot something. I can't hold things in my head, other than dance steps, and it's been months since I've danced. I'm terrified that I'll have even forgotten how to do that.'

'Well, one thing at a time, yeah? You've been brilliant so far. I had no idea I was going to see a ballet based on a poem by Rumi, who I used to think was an amazing poet—back when my head was full of mush. Maybe I'll see the error of my ways. Who knows?'

'You really don't mind that I've been a bit of a disaster so far? I don't want to spoil your evening.'

'It's certainly different.'

'You're really going to love the ballet. I promise you.'

She smiled. Wide and fresh and beautiful. He wondered if she knew it was her deadliest weapon. She had to. She might say that she was no good at anything except dancing, but he would wager she could wrap pretty much anyone, male or female, around her little finger with just a flash of that smile or a glance from those eyes.

The plane touched down and rolled along the runway. This was shaping up to be quite an evening—the last before he turned all his attention towards netting Arturo. So he might as well enjoy it.

The game was definitely on.

CHAPTER FOUR

SO, THE LOVE RAT wasn't so much of a rat after all.

He *could* have gone to town on her for messing up with the notes, but he'd let her off the hook and he'd actually been quite kind when she'd almost started blubbing like a baby.

He wasn't just a boring banker. He was smart. And handsome. Even with a broken nose and a flattened ear he was built like a man should be built.

She glanced down at his thighs and his biceps, pushing out the fabric of his tux as they waited in the back of a limousine to take their journey along the red carpet. He was prepped and primed to play the role of patron, and all the doubts she'd felt that he was just a surly shadow of his mother were gone. He could dial up the charm as easily as she could.

Or down. He was no pussycat either. He'd grilled her when he'd first met her, and that had been no party, but she could see why. He was only trying to protect his mother, and who could blame him for that? In his place she'd have been exactly the same—though of course that was never going to happen. The last person that would need any defending was her mother... except from herself.

The car door was opened. It was time to go. Matteo

turned to her, gave her a wink and a smile and stepped out, walking off towards the entrance with lithe grace, light-footed.

It was just like stepping on stage without the dance steps, she thought. Her stomach flipped. She took a breath and popped her smile into place. Then she followed him past the flashing cameras, pausing beside him as he chatted in the foyer, breathing in and out and beaming for all she was worth.

With moments left until curtain up they went on into the auditorium, where the air above the velvet rows bubbled with excitement. Heads turned everywhere as they stepped out into the royal box. Ruby stared straight ahead, the interest of so many people feeling like hives on her skin.

She moved to sit down in the row behind his, but he indicated with a smile and a gracious gesture that she should sit beside him.

He leaned close as the lights dimmed.

'You're sure this is going to be as good as you say?'

'If it isn't you can always ask for your money back.'

The music struck up. A penetratingly beautiful note was sung in the unmistakable voice of an Indian woman, cutting through the atmosphere of the theatre like a sabre through silk. The audience gasped.

Matteo's eyes held hers. A shiver ran down her spine.

'Or I can take recompense another way,' he said.

Slowly his eyes swept over her bare shoulders and décolleté, down to her mouth and then back to her eyes. She felt it in every tiny pore, every nerve, every fibre of her body. His mouth curled into a smile…some promise of what he would take. With each second she felt the charge of attraction flare between them. Her whole body reacted as easily as if he'd flipped a switch. She wasn't imagining it.

She sat back in her seat, blind to the emergence of the principal dancers onto the stage. Some part of her knew that they were dancing—striking buoyant and beautiful poses, their costumes flowing and extending the elegance of each step, the hauntingly beautiful song telling the story of the stirrings of early passion between the dancers—and some part of her watched. But most of her was alive to this totally new sensation.

'Having fun?' he whispered.

Yes, she wanted to gasp out loud. For the first time in months she felt she was actually living. The dance, the theatre, the interested crowd and, despite knowing the dangers, the magnetic draw of this man.

'I'd rather be on stage with them,' she said, for the first time in her life doubting it was actually true.

'I'd love to see you dance.'

He leaned further into her space. His voice, close to her ear, was thrilling. It was that even more than the dance that set her nerves on edge, dancing their own feverish path across her skin.

'I imagine you'd be amazing. Maybe one day...'

For a moment she thought he was going to touch her—his hand hovered and then landed again on his own leg. She stared at it, and then risked a glance to the side, where his profile was outlined in a sleek silver line from the stage lights. He stared straight ahead, rapt, but she could feel something between them, a strange energy that made her suddenly aware of her bare flesh, her braless breasts under the bodice of the dress, her thighs as she crossed and uncrossed her legs, her feet in tiny straps and pointed heels.

Her body was what she used to express herself. It

was her language, her vocabulary. She could read and sense others through their wordless actions too. How they held themselves. She could see how nervous or confident they were in the tilt of their head or the curl of their shoulders. And the language he was speaking now was as sensual as any lovers' *pas de deux*. She was aroused by it. She was aroused by him.

She strained forward, facing the stage as the dancers drew pictures of their anguished love, their bodies twisting and writhing with pleasure and pain. And in every move she felt the exquisite pleasure of physical love. And she saw herself with him as the hero lifted his lover and then let her slide down his body, his hands skimming her waist, her ribs, her breasts, before clutching her face and holding it close against his.

She had danced and felt hands on her body—all dancers had—but she had never, ever felt the way she was feeling right now, simply sitting, watching. Waiting.

It was electrifying. And he had to be feeling it too?

'What do you think?' she whispered in a voice not even her own.

'I think I'm hooked—I think I might just have found my newest passion.'

His expressionless face told her nothing, but the effect of his words sent another searing flash of heat to her core. She watched the final scene in the dreamy haze, felt his hand brushing hers, his foot touching hers— tiny little accidental movements that made her skittish.

Finally it ended. There was uproar from the audience, people yelling 'Bravo!' and stamping, up on their feet. She sat there, stunned, beside him. Although she faced forward all her vision was from the corner of her eye—his thigh, his hands clapping in front of his chest, his secret smile as he turned to her.

'So now, I take it, I have to meet the dancers?' he said. 'And then...'

He speared her with a dark look that thrilled her to her core.

She turned back to face the stage, clapping her hands, trusting herself only to stare at the line of dancers taking their bows. He stood beside her as the dancers looked to the royal box. He beamed down at them, waving a salute and applauding once more.

Ruby stood up too. Her legs shook. The theatre lights came up and the crowds began to move. Security appeared, opening the doors and leading them out. She followed Matteo's back, his sure stride, out and down through the theatre to the back of the stage, people parting like waves before them.

Post-performance adrenaline was pulsing through the air as they walked the line-up. Glittering eyes shone through smudged make-up and gleaming, sore bodies. She felt almost as exhilarated as the soloists and principals as she introduced them.

She could see their raised eyebrows and wide-mouthed smiles. She knew they were watching her closely, would be gossiping excitedly. *Ruby the weirdo, who never put a foot out of line, was flirting with the patron.*

Let them. It didn't mean she was going to let herself or anyone else down. She had her head screwed on.

Round the room stood tables laden with drinks and food. She felt a hand on her back, guiding her towards them, and her body tensed and melted. Matteo.

He raised his eyes and smiled indulgently, as if to say, *More delay*, and she had no thirst for the champagne that was thrust into her hand. She could barely concentrate as she tried to resist being buffeted by the waves of her physical attraction to Matteo as close-eyed scrutiny lapped like the tide where she stood.

When he leaned his ear over his right shoulder—a sign that he wanted more information about someone or something—she happily stood on tiptoe, letting the moments when she whispered names take longer. She lingered there, enjoying the sensation. He placed his hand on her waist, splayed his fingers, tugged her close, and she let her lips brush the side of his cheek.

His skin was soft, but grazed with stubble, and his scent was incredibly subtle. But his aroma, his essence, was magnetic, irresistible male.

'Say that again,' he demanded as she delivered him someone's name. As she tried to pull back a waiter came into view with a wide tray of canapés lifted high on his shoulder. Matteo sidestepped to let him pass and tugged her close to his body. She stood without moving, her breast and hip completely against him, pressed flush. Desire curled—hot and heavy and low in her body.

She knew she should move but she couldn't seem to do anything other than stand with her body against his, loving the mixture of sure, solid sensation and the sweet yearning to feel closer. Blood was rushing all around her, and she was feeling lightheaded as the noise of the party bubbled higher.

People bustled past, but what did she care…?

The waiter passed again and finally they stepped away.

'Who is the blonde woman in green, walking towards us with your director?'

Ruby flicked her eyes away and looked down quickly as a wave of guilt washed over her. Her director had trusted her to show Matteo around. She was the one who had her head screwed on. She couldn't bear it if she disappointed him.

'Dame Cicely Bartlett,' she said, focussing. 'The actress turned politician. She's going to make a political point about under-funding for the arts…'

'I'm impressed. You really *do* know everything about your world. With or without your notes.' He stepped closer to her again. 'Are you all right? You look pale all of a sudden.'

He took her hand in his, rubbed his fingers over the back of her wrist, and words died in her throat. She fought to keep her head from rolling back. She was sick with desire, weaker with every passing moment. She had to stop this before it got out of hand.

'If you don't mind, I think I need to sit down. I've had a bit too much champagne.'

He manoeuvred her into a chair.

'I'm so sorry. What was I thinking? As soon as I've finished with Dame Cicely we can go to supper.'

Supper? He didn't really mean that, did he? He meant sex.

The thought sent her stomach flipping through her ribs. She couldn't go through with this. Who was she trying to kid? She would end up back at his place and then the kissing would start. And then the touching. And then she'd realise that she'd changed her mind. She'd want to get away, then he'd look baffled and wonder what was going on. She'd call a cab and go. It was the way it always ended.

And that would usually be fine because she'd never see them again. But Matteo Rossini was their patron, and she couldn't make a fool of herself with someone like him.

'I don't think that's such a good idea.'

'What's wrong?' he said, stepping close enough for her to see the tiny indentations of his chest hair through the silk of his shirt, the hollow of his strong throat above the collar, the curl of those lips that had grazed her cheek, her jaw, her ear, that she so desperately wanted to feel against her mouth. He stood there and she felt the might and allure of his body pounding down her flimsy defences.

Maybe this time would be different? It felt different...

'Ruby, it's a *very* good idea,' he said softly.

'No, honestly. I'm really tired. I should go home.'

He was scrutinising every inch of her face, staring into her eyes as if he was seeing right inside her head.

'You're not tired. You're nervous. You're worried that people are judging you.'

He nodded, then looked over her shoulder, frowning. 'Wait here. Don't move.'

He moved away and she stood alone in the thinning crowd. She felt as if night had fallen and she was left alone in a moonless sky. She wanted more of him... more of his light.

'Right. That's the bank committed to support Dame Cicely's dance graduate programme. Your director is delighted and he told me to pass that on to you. So my work here is done. We're going for supper and I'm not taking no for an answer.'

The impact of those words lit her up, smashing the last of her resistance.

'OK,' she said. 'Supper would be lovely.'

He took her hand and she didn't pull away. In minutes they were winding through the remains of the throng. People approached with open smiles and hands outstretched to say goodbye and he smiled, shook their hands and smoothly swung past them, patted them on the back and moved on.

The exhilarating rush of what was to come overpowered her every other sensation.

Security men stood at the door, eyeing everything. Matteo nodded as they walked past them, along a passageway and out onto the street. At the car he stopped, turned, gave her the most heart-stopping smile.

'Ready?' he said.

'As I've ever been,' she whispered.

The car door was opened. She slid inside.

CHAPTER FIVE

'CAN'T THIS WAIT, DAVID? I'm right in the middle of something.'

Matteo nodded to the driver to go and lifted Ruby's fingers into his hand. If it wasn't for this call he would have been lifting them to his lips.

'Of course. I can wait until tomorrow morning to tell you that Claudio has approached Augusto Arturo about a merger, if that's what you'd prefer.'

'That's not news. I already knew that. He hasn't a chance.'

He put his arm around Ruby's shoulders, tucking her close, sliding his fingers down her silken flesh as the car rolled through night-time traffic.

'Apparently there's a been a change of heart. They were spotted at lunch in Cannes.'

Matteo's stomach lurched. He sat forward. Lunch meant that they were starting to explore things informally. That was not good news at all.

'What? Are you sure? Where did you find this out?'

'Interestingly, Claudio posted on social media. Shall I read it to you? *Looking forward to catching up with old friends and new in the French Riviera this summer. Obligatory Cordon D'Or Regatta and then a weekend in Tuscany with the irrepressible Arturo Augusto.*'

'You've got to be joking. What does he think he's playing at? "Obligatory Cordon D'Or"—he's the last person I want to see there. And name-dropping Augusto? That doesn't prove anything.'

'It proves that he knows how to wind you up.'

Matteo sat as still as his bursting blood vessels and pounding heart would allow. He would *not* overreact to this. He knew Claudio and he knew how he operated. There would be nothing to gain by getting himself in a tailspin over something like this.

'You're right. Claudio knows how important this is to us. It doesn't matter a damn to him if he gets Arturo or not. He doesn't need those clients—it's hardly even worth his while. What do you think he's really up to?'

'In my view, I think he's trying to provoke you. Get you to react to his message. He'll have seen all the recent publicity about you and maybe he thinks you want to play it out publicly. That's my best guess. As you say, turning up at Cordon D'Or would be a new tactic, to say the least. I'll step up security just in case.'

'I didn't see this coming. I really thought he'd have bigger fish to fry.'

The anger he felt was as much anger at himself for being so damned naïve as at Claudio. He should never have made assumptions about anything involving Claudio Calvaneo. It was if he was determined to erase every last trace of Banca Casa di Rossini and all it stood for.

'That may well still be the case. The only thing we can be sure of is that Banca Casa di Rossini is a much better bet for Arturo than Calvaneo Capital. Even if Claudio decides he wants it, there's no reason to suppose he can make it happen.'

'At best it's his sick little way of needling me. At

worst it's the start of a full-blown attempt to merge or buy. Either way, there's nothing I can do about it now.'

'I hope it hasn't ruined your evening, but I thought you'd want to know—just in case.'

Just in case. Matteo knew what that meant. There was a time when he might have done something stupid—he'd have given his right arm to do something stupid, to see Claudio sprawled out in front of him, begging for mercy, to see him confessing his crimes, to see any kind of justice at all.

But it wouldn't happen that way. He knew his physical strength—and his weaknesses. He could take Claudio out with one punch. But then where would they be? With him in jail—his mother's biggest fear. He'd grudgingly had to accept that it was possible, and had stayed well away for years.

But now this? His gut was telling him that soon they would be coming face to face in the showdown that would decide the fate of Banca Casa di Rossini. And Claudio was going to play it out like a boxing match—making cheap gibes to goad him.

He had to rein it in, bide his time, keep his head clear.

'Thanks, David. I appreciate that. I'll sleep on it. Let's catch up tomorrow.'

He sat back, his mind racing as it always did whenever Claudio butted his way back into his life. But he had to get it into perspective. There was nothing he could do until he met with Augusto Arturo himself. He couldn't control who the old man had lunch with. He could only control himself.

'Is everything all right?'

He looked round. Ruby stared at him with wide, almond eyes.

'Absolutely, sweetheart.'

If there was anything at all that was going to help him get through the next twenty-four hours it was this woman. He was going to give them both a night to remember.

'Just work. Nothing for us to trouble ourselves over.'

'Hmm…if you say so.'

'I say so,' he said. He reached for her. 'I've got to keep my phone beside me, but I don't think we'll be disturbed now. And here we are…'

The car rolled to a halt outside Luigi's, one of his favourite restaurants, where the food was amazing and the staff were fast and friendly.

He got out and stood on the pavement, rolled his tensed shoulders and willed himself to clear his mind. He breathed deeply, inhaling the sultriness of the evening, the dense, heady scent of the jasmine planted on either side of the restaurant entrance.

Ruby emerged from the car. Just looking at her was like a sip of summer wine, full of promise, easing him into a better place.

He hoped.

Just one more detail to be sure of before he could completely relax with her…

Minutes later they were settled in a subtly lit corner of the restaurant, where shadows licked at Ruby's delicate throat, her fine-boned chest and long slim arms as they rested on the white tablecloth. He so badly wanted to reach across the table and take hold of her hand, trail his fingers along her collarbone, absorb the softness of her skin.

But control was all. Control and then controlled release. Like exercising a muscle.

'You were amazing tonight,' he said. 'I couldn't have

asked for a better assistant. You know your world inside out and you didn't need any notes. I'm impressed.'

'It's easy when it's something you care about.'

'It's not just dance, is it? You care about the company, too. It's obvious how much those people mean to you.'

He thought of her face, shining with pride as she introduced him to her colleagues, how they'd embraced and smiled happily together.

'They've been my family for years. I've been very lucky.'

'You mean that in a figurative sense, of course?'

'I mean that since the age of eleven I've been with the British Ballet as a boarder. So they really are my family. My mum and her boyfriend moved to the south coast when I was twelve, but I was able to stay here. I'm in with the bricks,' she said brightly, ending the sentence with a fake note of joy.

He was beginning to recognise her little signatures: the overly bright smile, the wide-eyed stare, the *happy to help* tone in her voice. Those little idiosyncrasies could pull a man under if he wasn't careful.

'I'm sure everything will work out for you, Ruby,' he said. 'Even if it's not performing on the stage there must be other things you can do with the company— assuming you want to stay with them? Education or... I don't know, maybe you want to see a bit more of the world? Aren't there jobs in other companies?'

'Of course there are, but I'm not exactly in a position to plan anything yet. It all depends on what my consultant says next month.'

'And if you get the all-clear would you move? Is there anything—or anyone—holding you here?'

'I don't have anyone special in my life if that's what you mean?'

'That's exactly what I mean.'

She screwed up her face. 'My track record with men isn't exactly my strong suit. I've never been much for socialising, and this injury has completely drained me—so, no, there's no one special in my life.'

'My track record with women isn't exactly *my* strong suit either.'

Her lips curled into a mocking smile. 'For completely different reasons.'

'So the press would have you believe,' he said, grateful for the arrival of the waiters. He didn't particularly want to go into any of his relationship back story with her. Nor did he want to know hers. Sharing all that stuff gave out the wrong signals—as if he cared, as if there was going to be a future between them.

They sat silently at the circular table, watching as napkins were flicked and laid over their laps, as platters of cheese and meat, olives and artichokes and glistening melon were laid down and wine sloshed gaily into their glasses.

All the while her eyes widened, and in the candlelight the hollows of her cheeks seemed to deepen and the column of her throat lengthen as she sat forward to stare at each plate.

Finally the waiters bowed and left.

'Tuck in,' he said, steepling his fingers and watching as she began to eat, cutting cubes of melon and ham slowly at first, swallowing delicately, then devouring them and washing it down with sips of wine.

It satisfied something deep within him that he was able to provide food for her. He'd taken dozens of women to dinner, and never once before had he ever taken such pleasure in watching anyone eat. She was fresh and new and lovely and she didn't care about what the all the others cared about. She hadn't shown any interest in the jet or the car, or the people who clambered all over him to get their picture taken. She genuinely wanted to make him like the ballet and the dancers. She cared.

He knew that feeling. It was buried deep inside him. The passion for his game, the hunger to train and win. The drive to get better and better and then the ultimate payback: the chance to play for his country.

He would never forget that soaring feeling of joy when the coach had pulled him aside and told him he was under consideration. He hadn't even told his parents—only Sophie. She'd been the only one he'd trusted, the only one who had known what it meant to him.

But that was all in the past now. Even if he hadn't had the heart ripped out of him, he was never going to be able to dedicate himself to rugby again. Not with a widowed mother and a bank to pull back from the brink. His family pride as well as billions in sterling, euros and Swiss francs were in the balance. There was no possible way he could turn his back on that and run out onto a muddy field.

Sometimes money sickened him. Greed climbed inside people's souls and turned them black. Like Claudio. The man had always been rich in his own right, but he wanted even more than money. And look where that had got them all.

He looked up to see Ruby sitting back from the table with a happy, sated smile.

'Is that better?'

She beamed, revealing her dimples to him. 'Oh, yes, thank you. It was delicious.'

'That was just the starter. You've got space for

more?' he asked as the table was cleared and restocked with all sorts of sharing plates of pasta, fish and salad.

'Maybe a little,' she said, her eyes widening over the next load of steaming dishes. 'I don't normally eat a lot. Well, that's not strictly true—I normally stuff my face. But not recently. Not since I've not been able to dance.'

'Don't they pay you?' he asked. 'Don't they see you as an investment?' It was none of his business but the injustice of it puzzled him.

'Of course they look after me—but if I can't dance I can't dance.'

She turned her head to the side and twirled her ponytail through her fingers.

'Anyway, all you need to know is that I've been on a bit of a tight budget recently. Normally I'd pay my share if I was on a date, but I'm a bit broke until my cheque clears.'

'Is this a date, Ruby?'

The forkful of pasta she had stabbed and was drawing up to her open mouth was placed down carefully. She looked up and the flickering candlelight licked the hollows of her huge almond eyes. He didn't think he'd ever seen a more beautiful woman.

'I… I don't think so.'

'We've already established that there's something interesting going on between us. Wouldn't you agree?'

'Is this how you normally seduce women?' she asked. 'I thought you'd be a bit more subtle.'

She picked up her cutlery again and continued eating, her eyebrows raised like two black birds, mocking him. He couldn't help but smile at her quick-on-the-draw retort, but he wasn't going to let her off that easily.

'I didn't think we were working on the premise of

"subtle". I thought you were quite clear that you found me sexually attractive.'

She put her hand to her chest. The solid line of her dress cut right across the shadows of her small breasts and his eyes fell there. She was exquisite. And he allowed himself the luxury of imagining what those small breasts looked like, what those rosy nipples would taste like rolling under his tongue.

'What? You're shocked that I would call you on that?'

'I'm shocked at your double standards. *You're* the one who's been putting it out all night.'

'Ha! Oh, really?'

'Absolutely. Every time I had to say something to you, you were well inside my personal space. I couldn't move so much as an inch and you were right beside me, hands all over me.'

'Is that right? Hands all over you?' He could barely contain his chuckle. She was making him more and more aroused with every second. 'Well, I have to apologise. I didn't notice you pulling away or asking me to back out of your "personal space". In fact, as I recall, in between your breathy little whispers, you liked to linger in *my* personal space much longer than a person would normally take to move away. In fact I'd go so far as to say you were almost rubbing yourself against me. Maybe that's something that you dancers think is normal, but for the rest of us—I'd say that that was provocative.'

As he spoke he watched her face react. Her eyes widening and the trouble she was having swallowing. It was pure, unadulterated pleasure—just what he needed.

'That was *you*! You were provoking me!'

'And I happen to know just how sensitive your ears and neck are.'

He looked there now, watching the soft pink flush that was travelling all over her cheeks, imagining how she was going to react the next time he touched her.

'You could barely stay upright when I had to ask you a question. If I brought my lips anywhere close to your ear you practically melted in my arms. You have a very responsive erogenous zone.'

She rolled her eyes, as if he was talking rubbish, but she couldn't disguise her smile or the deepening of her blush. She was playing for time, and every second thickened the hot, heavy, sultry air between them.

'I was only doing my job,' she said, looking up at him coyly. 'It's not my fault if you read more into it than was actually there.'

'Ah. I *see*. I was imagining things.' He knew women. He knew what he was and wasn't imagining. 'I'd certainly like to revisit my poor judgement over dessert. If I'm wrong, you'll have my full apology. If I'm right...'

'We'll see,' she said, and she gave a tiny shrug, the twin hollows of her perfect collarbones softly shadowed in candlelight.

But with each second he could see her reaction deepen. He could feel it. Unless he was completely off his game, this was shaping up to be a night to remember.

He leaned forward and took her hand, secretly thrilled when she didn't try to pull away. He traced the fine veins that lay across her wrist, circled them over and over with his thumb. Her eyelids fluttered and her lips parted.

'Indeed we will.'

He brought her fingers to his lips softly, gently. Her eyelids dropped. He smiled and ran his fingers up and down the smooth skin of her forearm. She was visibly melting under his touch, but still she held something back.

'I missed an evening at the casino tonight, but I'm willing to bet that I'll have discovered every last one of your erogenous zones before dawn.'

'I'd better warn you: I'm not really into sex,' she breathed through a heavy-lidded smile.

He tipped her face towards him until her mouth was at the perfect angle. He looked into her eyes, and in that moment he saw the wariness of the little girl she must once have been, but quickly it was gone and desire swept her lids closed.

He angled his mouth and placed one slow, soft kiss on her lips. And then he slowly drew back.

'That lengthens the odds, but I'm still willing to take the risk.'

A smile broke across her full, kissable lips. Her eyes opened slowly.

'You're on,' she said.

CHAPTER SIX

RUBY STEPPED OUT onto the terrace and walked to the wall that separated Matteo's penthouse apartment from the rest of the dazzling London skyline. Below her the glow of a thousand lamps lit up the Thames embankment. Boats glided this way and that on the mottled surface of the river, which rolled along under a clear night sky.

A tiny light breeze wafted over her bare skin and she touched her arms, holding herself close. She looked at the champagne flute, half full and balanced on the wall, and listened again for the sound of Matteo's voice, rumbling low within the apartment—the third call he'd had to take this evening so far.

The life of a corporate exec.

She'd had no idea that people lived like this, in surroundings like this, on call day and night, and for a moment she let herself imagine becoming part of it. The money, the views, the parties. The meetings in boardrooms with demanding clients and hungry shareholders. She imagined him delivering a presentation in a glass-walled office, all eyes watching him, thought how impressive he must be in his world. How different that world was from hers.

The shadowy shape-shifting future that she'd always

imagined only ever featured herself—alone. It was a world on-stage, pushing herself to her limits, twisting her body into the shapes that she had practised over and over in rehearsal, presenting to one audience after another, relishing their thrilled excitement and basking in their awe as they rose to their feet, applauding.

There was never any 'afterwards'. No handsome husband to share the cab ride home with. No children waiting to say goodnight with the nanny, sleepy-eyed and pink-cheeked. No mother on the phone gushing with pride.

She'd never seen those things in her future, and until this moment she had never even known they might be missing. Her dream had been the same since the moment she could remember. Since her first ballet lessons at the church hall and the surprised pleasure of the teacher, telling her mum that her daughter was *very talented*. She'd danced everywhere she went—the bus stop, in the supermarket—and people had beamed at her, filling up that achy dark spot inside her with their happy smiles.

She would turn to her mother, expecting to see the same happiness, but it had hardly ever been there. She had been deep in her own world, her mobile phone never far away, her own heart broken and never healing. Not until she'd met George. And then it had all been decided.

In her mind it had felt like coming to the top of a road and seeing two paths going in totally different directions. The promise of a 'new life' in Cornwall, with Mum and George. New school, new friends. She would still dance. They did ballet in Cornwall for goodness' sake. But Ruby had known—she had known what that new life would really be like. It would be all about

George. There would be no dance—not like she'd had before—and there would be even less of her mother's love...

She snapped out of her memories as Matteo finished his call and walked across the wooden floor. Her heart began to skip and her stomach flipped again against her ribs. He had been the perfect gentleman since they'd left the restaurant. Faultless. *Too* faultless. Attentive and caring and kind. He'd asked after her knee...asked was she still hungry? Could he prepare her some food? Bring her some wine? Could he kiss her here and here?

He paused in the doorway, his white shirt unbuttoned at the neck and the dark shadow of hair and muscle excruciatingly close and alluringly touchable. Once again she felt that deep tug in her core. But she didn't fight it—she couldn't. The battle was well and truly lost.

'I'm sorry about that,' he said, walking up to her and circling his arm around her waist.

He delivered another soft, leisurely kiss to her lips and then pulled back and smiled at her. Just as he'd done several times already in the past hour.

'I hope you don't mind. But that should be the end of it until tomorrow morning.'

'I guess there's never any real downtime in your world. There's always someone's needs to take care of. High net worth people must be very high maintenance.'

'You're right. And I can't pretend that that's my favourite part of the job. You know, in the summer I'll be on the Riviera most weekends? We host a regatta for charity. All the big names come. Sounds amazing, yes? But it'll be full-on. Entertaining can be draining.'

'Yes—so I witnessed tonight.'

'But you were the best possible antidote,' he said, leaning in for another kiss. 'I'd never have thought I'd hear myself saying I had a great time at the ballet. But I did. He tugged her close and started to trail kisses on her neck. 'Thanks to you...'

Once again she felt herself melt into his arms, felt those overwhelming urges rise up within her. She turned around in his arms, aching to feel his lips on her mouth, his hands on her body, but every time she thought he was going to finally lead her off to bed he cooled them down again—like the conductor of an orchestra, setting the beat and the heat of their passion.

She'd never had an experience like it.

He walked to the wine bucket and lifted the champagne bottle, topped up her glass and handed it to her, looked around for his own. The tray of *petits-fours* and strawberries lay untouched. She sipped the champagne, but truly she only had an appetite for Matteo now.

'What do you think of the view?' he said, leaning beside her. 'Isn't it spectacular? I never tire of this city. Even Rome doesn't do it for me the way that London does. And Rome is in my blood.'

He hooked his arm around her shoulders as they stared down at the river. Two party boats, illuminated and booming with the deep bass sounds of dance music, sailed past one another in opposite directions, while on the bridges above them traffic rumbled back and forth.

'Honestly? I've never seen the city from up high before. This is a totally different place from the London I know. Even though we're only a few miles apart. You see those buses down there? That's usually me on one of them, while you're up here—or up there. Do you have one of those?'

She pointed at a helicopter hovering above the roof of a nearby tower block.

'Not at the moment, no. But where is your world? Can you see it from here? Show me.'

He circled his arm around her waist once more and laid his hand on the wall, tucking her close to his body.

'Way over there is Croydon. That's where I grew up. Before Mum moved away and I became a boarder at the British Ballet.'

She paused, expecting him to ask her for more details. It was a subject of great interest to most people—how her mother had moved three hundred miles away with her boyfriend and started a new family, conveniently forgetting the child she already had. She barely understood it herself, but she didn't blame her mother.

She'd started with good intentions, but it had all fallen apart after a year or so. There had been visits and phone calls during which Ruby had forced herself not to cry. Because she had known that if she'd cried she'd have had to leave ballet school and move to Cornwall. And be eclipsed there for ever, in the shadow of George and the twins that were about to be born.

They were sixteen now, she thought suddenly. Sixteen—almost adults themselves—and still no sign that she was ever going to get along with them. The awful thing was she just didn't *feel* anything for them. It was terrible to admit it, even if only to herself. Was it because they didn't look like her? They had their mother's blonde hair, George's sturdy build, while she was dark, slight...

She looked out across the river, at the moonless sky, the endless inky horizon. Somewhere out there she had family who looked like her. Uncles, aunts, cousins. Brothers, sisters. People with features like hers, minds like hers. Maybe dancers like her...

Her mind conjured up her favourite daydream. She

was dancing on some foreign stage—the performance of her life. A man stood in the audience—her father. He called her name, pushed forward to see her, She shielded her eyes and then she saw him. *'Father,'* she cried...

Her heart leapt into her throat and her eyes burned. Beside her, Matteo moved closer and she tensed. For a moment she was still lost on that dark stage, searching for that face.

'You must have been a very gifted child,' said Matteo through her dream.

She felt his fingers cradle the back of her head. She let her head rest there, grateful for the warmth, the strength, the masculine grasp. She didn't fight it. Emotions were surfacing tonight that she'd kept buried for a long, long time. Maybe it was the champagne. Maybe it was the soft touch of his fingers on her skin, being held close...

She turned in his arms. Another kiss—gentle, soft. The slide of his tongue dipping into her mouth. She accepted it gratefully, eagerly. He pressed closer, his arms encircling her at the wall.

'Something like that,' she said on a sigh, relieved to be pulled from her memories as her head fell back and the ache between her legs grew hotter and heavier.

'I really can't wait to see you dance,' whispered Matteo as he hooked his other arm around her and drew her into his sensual world.

He placed tiny little kisses on her neck, which had her extending her head to give him more access. She sighed and shifted against him and he pulled her closer, his hands holding her possessively. She relaxed against his broad, strong chest and felt the urgent ridge of his desire. His kisses travelled to her ear and she shivered as a huge spasm of desire ricocheted through her.

'Matteo, please...' she moaned.

'You like this, don't you?' he murmured. 'Your secret exogenous zone. And we still have all the others to find too, before dawn.'

He kissed her again, nibbled and suckled at the edge of her earlobe, licked and kissed and nuzzled her neck. She was tired of holding back. Tired of striving so hard for so long and there being nothing to show for it. She was tired of feeling hungry for life, of starving herself of pleasure, fun. She'd worked so hard to get here and the exhaustion of keeping it together was lapping inside her now like the relentless dragging of the tide.

Her own private rules—training and abstinence, working until her body was exhausted to be the best, to please—had been her whole life as far back as she could remember, with little time to relax because it was too terrifying to stop.

She deserved this night. She needed it.

Under her dress her nipples throbbed in tight buds and she felt almost unbearably aroused. She pressed even closer to his body, the full skirt of her dress swishing noisily as she ached to feel his lips on her mouth and his hands on her body.

He held her head in his hands, kissing her mouth until it opened, his tongue plundering deeply inside. She kissed him back and pressed herself closer, desperate to free herself from all this red froth, to step out of it naked and feel his hands on her body.

She wanted to feel the way she knew he could make her feel.

'The bet's off. Take me to bed,' she breathed.

The words spilled from her mouth into the hot heavy air between them and he stopped. She looked up into those chestnut eyes, willing him to take control now that she had relented. Willing him to do what she trusted him to do—give her the oblivion she sought.

She reached up and traced her finger around his mouth, feeling the graze of stubble, the soft pad of his lips, then she slid her fingers inside his wet mouth. Her head fell back as he sucked her fingers.

'Exactly what I plan to do.'

He took her hand and led them back indoors, past the discarded champagne and the twin palms on either side of the French doors, nodding in the breeze like benevolent sentries. In through the lounge, where her clutch lay like a red silk flag against one dark leather couch, and where its reflection, his red tie, lay across another. Her skirt swished brazenly with every step she took.

Through an open doorway she glimpsed a solitary silver bowl, overflowing with fruit—the only sign of life in a gleaming, sterile kitchen. In the shadowy hallway a wall of photographs faced another bare of anything other than lamplight. She caught the face of his mother, smiling on the prow of a yacht, her hair blowing in the sea breeze, and felt a momentary jab of discomfort, a whiff of disloyalty that made her footsteps falter.

He must have sensed it for he turned and caught her eye, holding her steady with his gaze. He cupped her jaw and placed a hot, demanding kiss on her mouth. She felt the brand of his desire.

He walked to a door and opened it into a bedroom. *His* bedroom. Acres of pale carpet spread out under rugs and various pieces of furniture, lit only by the spill of lamplight from either side of a wide, low bed.

She stepped inside. This was it. This was where she was going to be seduced.

Her heart thundered in her chest as she looked

around, and there in the mirror Matteo stretched out an arm towards her.

'I've been admiring your dress all night,' he said as he trailed a finger along her collarbone. 'Wondering what you looked like under all this…'

His finger traced the line of her bodice from left to right, lightly brushing the skin of her décolletage. She shivered uncontrollably and closed her eyes as he traced the line down the middle of her chest to where the skirt of the dress flared out. Then he placed a hand on either side of her waist and pulled her towards him for a kiss.

Kiss me and never stop, she thought, loving the sensation of his tongue expertly licking and probing, stoking the fire higher. How could she have denied herself this pleasure…so much pleasure?

Her own greedy fingers pressed against his chest. She could feel the spring of hair under her palms and rubbed tiny circles there, loving the sensation of his firm muscle, loving the groans of pleasure she was making him deliver.

Fumbling, she undid his shirt all the way down to the waist, until the twin panels of fabric opened to reveal a golden chest dusted with hair that narrowed down into a single dark line, swallowed up by the waistband of his trousers. She pulled the shirt from his trousers, her eye landing for a moment on the huge hard ridge at his groin, and she bit back a groan of anticipation.

She had seen countless male bodies—men at the peak of physical fitness, slick with sweat and shaved clean of hair. But none of them had proclaimed their masculinity like Matteo as she pushed his shirt from his shoulders and drank in the sight of his magnificent naked torso.

She bit her lip and then looked up at him, smiling a dark, devilish smile.

'What's going through your dirty little mind?' he whispered, leading her to the bed and pulling her down on top of him.

She pulled her skirt up round her waist and sat back on her heels, straddling him. 'You,' she said, rocking slightly back and forth.

His erection throbbed between her legs in response. Her panties were thin and the sensation of his arousal was almost too much to bear. She rocked against him again. It felt heavenly. He watched her closely, and the thrill of seeing him and feeling him sent wave after wave of pleasure through her.

But as he reached his hands up to touch her she stilled his wrists. 'Don't move,' she said.

She closed her eyes and rubbed again. She was *so* close to orgasm.

'Please don't move.'

He didn't move a muscle but he grew harder.

'You dirty, dirty girl.'

She stared down at him…at every gorgeous masculine inch of him She rocked again, staring into his eyes.

'You want me to lie here between your legs and not get to touch you, but you can pleasure yourself against me until you come? Is that what's going on here?'

She threw her head back and rubbed harder.

She felt his hands close around her arms. 'There will be hell to pay for this, Ruby.'

'Yes—yes!' she cried, rubbing herself harder still.

In the quiet of the night she could hear the rustle of her dress and feel the friction of her bare feet on the smooth cotton sheets. And she heard the sounds of their flesh touching, hot and wet and insistent. And his breath. And his passion. And the knowledge that she could do this.

'Come for me Ruby. *Now.*'

And she did.

The huge, hot orgasm burst forth, and she was aware of him lying there, telling her to keep coming.

Then she collapsed on his chest. His heart was pounding. A cry had died somewhere in her throat. His hands soothed her back, coiled round her hair, and then in a heartbeat he had flipped her over.

'Glad I could be of some assistance there. And, now, if you don't mind...'

His fingers hooked around her back and instantly found the top of the zip. With one hand he tipped up her chin and held her gaze, and with the other he slowly drew down the zip, all the way to the waistband.

Then he bent forward, kissed her lips, and with a final tug pulled the dress all the way down. She lay there, warm in her post-orgasm glow, naked apart from her black panties and her shameless desire. And it felt good. It felt wonderful to know how much he was loving her body and how much she was loving his.

'You know you're even more beautiful than I imagined,' he whispered, unfastening his trousers and slipping them off.

The sight of him sent flames dancing all over her skin. She reached up to touch him but he grabbed at her wrists and gently pushed her down.

'Oh, no. It's my turn now.'

In seconds she was warm in his arms as his head dipped to place kisses on her mouth and then in a trail down the centre of her chest. Her back arched as she thrust her aching breasts forward, desperate to feel his lips there.

'Please, Matteo…' she breathed, staring down at his dark head outlined against her white skin.

He looked straight at her with devilish intent, holding his mouth in place for long, excruciating seconds as she tried to jerk her breast towards him.

'Now, now…you've got to learn patience,' he said, and smiled as he held her fast and then finally, slowly, brought his mouth down to hover over one pink nipple, his tongue dipping low until he finally closed his lips around it and tugged.

'Yes…' she breathed, her eyes scrunched up with pleasure, her back arching further towards him. 'Yes…'

'Oh, yes,' he whispered into her flesh.

He teased and tugged and suckled her nipple until he'd had enough and then moved to the other. Instantly the cool air clenched around her damp skin and she looked down, held his head in place as he drew more and more pleasure from her with his lips.

In seconds he'd scooped his hands under her shoulders and lifted her gently further back onto the bed. 'Do I have to be careful with your knee?' he whispered. 'I can't hurt you, can I?'

She shook her head vigorously. 'Only if you throw me across the room or drop me.'

'I don't plan on that. I've got much better ideas.'

'Like what?' she breathed, loving the way he was dipping his head to take care of one throbbing pink nipple and then the other in quick succession.

'You've got too many clothes on,' he said, kissing his way down to her navel, putting his hands under her bottom and holding her up like some sort of precious object.

'I'm a feminist,' she said, hooking her hands around

his neck and pulling him down on top of her. 'What's good for you is good for me.'

'You *are* strong, aren't you?' He smiled, circling her arm in his hand. 'I probably wouldn't mess with you.'

'We can arm wrestle later,' she said as she ran her hands over the satiny skin of his back and down to his shorts and began to tug them off. 'Let's have more fun first.'

But before she could grip them he'd rolled her onto her back and they were kissing. And kissing. And kissing.

More than anything else she wanted to feel every inch of him. With expert hands he pulled off her pants and his, and reached into his bedside table for a condom. She lay back on the bed watching as he held himself in his hand. He was long and thick, and she bit her lip with longing.

'Open your legs for me.'

His voice was almost hoarse, and she could see just how close to the edge he already was.

She lay back and stared at the ceiling, feeling the seconds slip past, but he was there, cradling her in his arms as he moved her exactly where he wanted her. Then, with his lips on hers and his hands on either side of her head, he positioned himself and slid deep inside her.

CHAPTER SEVEN

RUBY WOKE IN the night. She was in a strange bed, in a strange room, and every single fibre of her body tensed in alarm. She was in complete darkness, silent apart from the breathing near her face, Matteo's breathing.

Matteo Rossini, CEO of Banca Casa di Rossini, Love Rat, sponsor of the British Ballet. The last man on earth she should be lying beside.

What had she done? What on earth had she done? How had she ended up here in his bed?

Her mind sped through the events of the night, landing on the moments that had led to this. There had been too much emotion, too many memories unwrapped and unravelled. Far too much champagne and wine. Definitely that was to blame.

She tried to remember how many glasses she'd had. Two? Maybe three? Half a glass when she'd got here?

Was it really the booze that had done for her?

This felt worse than any hangover.

There wasn't any point in lying to herself.

She should never have agreed to stay the night. She felt as if she'd given something away that she'd never get back—let the genie out of the bottle, let herself down. She knew the other dancers thought she was weird because she made a point of setting herself apart. But it wasn't because she thought she was better. It was because she was afraid she was worse...

She had to get out of here—*now*. She couldn't face herself, never mind anyone else.

But suddenly the strong, heavy weight of his arm landed on her waist.

The urge to roll over and slide out of bed was almost unbearable, but she didn't move. She lay still. She had to stop and think—not bolt for the door.

Waking up in a man's bed was not the worst thing in the world. Other people did it.

But his arm was so heavy and he was so close. She could scent their night together—feral and musky. She breathed deeply, feeling her chest fill with air and then slowly empty. What a night. She'd done things she'd never done...feeling and giving pleasure until she had fallen into a deep sleep.

And hadn't he been every bit as amazing a lover as she had thought he would be? And considerate. And kind. She didn't have much to compare him with, of course, but she knew that she'd never been made to feel this way before.

The memory of him finding his release inside her sent echoes of pleasure pulsing through her body and she gave an involuntary sigh. Beside her, Matteo gave a sleepy grunt in response, and once more she had to stifle the urge to move.

Why was she like this? Why couldn't she just lie there in a post-orgasmic glow like everybody else and enjoy it? There was something wrong with her—she knew that. She'd been told by both the men she'd slept with. She could have sex—just about—but staying the night was a complete no-no, and had been the undoing of each of her previous relationships.

I need to get an early night. Her get-out clause of every situation.

But to slope off out of Matteo's bed? After what they'd shared that seemed—*wrong.*

In the darkness of the room gloomy shapes began to form and make sense—a chair here, a table with the round glass vase, the edge of a huge photograph of an island.

The slash of light from below the doorway spilled a silvery glow onto the discarded clothes on the floor. She could just make out the scarlet dress where it lay draped over a chair, its stiff petticoats giving it an air of waiting impatiently to be worn again.

She had enjoyed wearing it last night. Had had so many compliments about how it suited her. But when was she likely to wear a dress like that again?

Matteo would be off soon, back to Rome—more hosting, more guests, more fancy clothes and fancy people.

Her mind wandered, imagining how he would look, what he would wear and who he would meet.

Lady Faye and others like her.

She racked her brains. Had he mentioned her or any of his exes last night? She didn't think so. He hadn't really said much about himself at all. Only the stuff about rugby. He hadn't mentioned any women and had closed her down fast when she'd mentioned his mother.

But all those women in his life, said a little voice. That wasn't such a great character trait. And those were only the ones who'd been photographed. There were bound to be even more—the one-night stands. And now she was one of them...

A sickly sense of unease rolled through her. She

could be lying in exactly the same place as countless women before her. That was not a good feeling.

Matteo groaned quietly. He was coming closer to the surface. But if she lay still he might go back under, and then she could slip away—no small talk, no awkward glances, no shame.

His breathing steadied and deepened again and she took her chance, easing out from under his arm, sliding one leg out into the cool of the room, then another, gently shifting her weight, pausing to make sure his breathing hadn't shifted, then easing out further.

Finally she put one leg down on the floor and backed away from the bed and his sleeping form. She felt over the carpet for her shoes, grabbing them up into her hands, then taking her dress from the chair.

She tiptoed across the room, put her hand on the door and eased it open, pausing suddenly when it began to squeak. But Matteo's slow, steady breathing carried on as daylight pushed forward, letting her slip out into the hallway.

She needed to phone a cab and get out of there as quickly as possible. She pulled the door open and paced along the wooden floor, past the photographs of skiing trips and yachting trips, past his mother's beaming face and along the hallway to the kitchen.

There was her bag, and there through the glass was the ice bucket, the strawberries, and her wrap discarded over a chair. Midnight's debris dressed in daylight's accusing glow.

She tugged open the patio door and lifted her bag— but when she turned there was Matteo, framed in the kitchen doorway, tall and bronzed and looking murkier than the Thames on a winter's day.

'Hey,' he said, and his voice was a growl, rough with lack of sleep. 'You're up already.'

He tugged at the waist of his boxers as he walked into the room and she watched as his fingers trailed along the red, raw-looking marks on his stomach. Marks that she had made with her nails.

She looked away. 'Yes. I thought I'd get going. I've got a lot to do.'

He was at the sink. She heard the tap running and the sound of water filling a glass.

'You should have said,' he said, drinking thirstily. 'Could have set an alarm. Want some?'

He wiped water from his mouth with the back of his hand and it was completely mesmerising. Just looking at him made her mouth water, but she shook her head and turned her face away.

'No, thanks. Just call me a cab, please.'

He filled a pot with coffee and water and set it on the hob, looking at her over his shoulder as he did so.

'A cab?' he said. 'You don't want to stay for breakfast? I can order whatever you like. You had a great appetite last night...'

'I'm in a bit of a rush.'

At that he looked up. His eyes flashed with something, but it was too fast to see what before his face smoothed out into rock.

'I didn't catch on to that last night—apologies. I'll not keep you back if you want to go.'

'Yes, I should have said I had to leave early—sorry.'

'It's no problem.'

He paused, and the silence and his accusing stare were like a toxic cloud, mushrooming between them. She tried to find words—but what could she say? It was like corpsing on stage. Sentences were dying in her mind, not even making it to her mouth.

Please let me off the hook, she thought. *Let me go.*

'I thought we had a lovely night, Ruby,' he said finally. 'An amazing night.'

'Yes, we did. Thanks.'

He put his hands up.

'*"Thanks"*? I'm not completely clear what's happening here. I thought we might hang out a bit longer?'

He walked towards her, stretched his hands out as if to rest them on her shoulders. She side-stepped that neatly.

She stared down at a corner of the kitchen worktop along which his mail was arranged in two neat rows. Bills and official-looking stuff in one, and cards and invitations to parties in another. She could see his name emblazoned on one in cursive font and the name of the world-famous hotel it was to be held in. He was probably out every night of the week at some thing or other. Meeting women…having supper afterwards.

That bed was probably never cold.

She turned. Looked at him. At the navy stretch of his boxer shorts as they cut across his perfect stomach, the bump of each muscle and the dark arrow of hair. His wide, hard chest, its bones extending out, broken and uneven on one side, perfect on the other. The wide trunk of his neck, his stubbled jaw, hair messed up and framing his cool morning-after face.

For a split second she hovered. The urge to jump into his arms and wrap her legs around his waist, to bury herself in all that man, glory in the kissing and hugging and sweet, dirty loving they had shared was as tempting as her next breath.

But she didn't move a muscle. Because she couldn't

unwrap herself all over again. She'd get away with it once, but not another time. Not now that she had bound herself back together again.

She shook her head vigorously.

'I can't. I have to go. I'm sorry—I need to…to get things done.'

He was looking at her carefully, warily, and then he put his hands down. 'Fair enough. You don't need to explain anything. I've got a lot on too.'

'Yes, I hope it goes well. So, can you call me a cab, please?'

He looked at her, then lifted his phone. 'Send the car,' he said.

He stared at her, his brown berry eyes now glassy and hard. The coffee brewing on the hob began to splutter and spill out of the spout.

'It won't be too long.'

The lid of the coffee pot rose up as steam and coffee broke free. Matteo reached for it and casually lifted it to the side.

'I can wait downstairs.'

'If you like.'

She strode through the hallway, her heels clicking on the tiles, the faces on the walls grinning like clowns now, mocking her desperation to get out of the apartment, onto the street and out of this stupid dress.

She stared at her scarlet reflection in the hallway mirror, and the agony of waiting was accompanied by the sonorous bell as the lift slowly climbed closer.

'Wait,' said a voice, and then Matteo too was in the mirror, hopping towards her, pulling on a pair of joggers, his big body loose and powerful, his face smooth, his lips closed.

The lift doors opened and she rushed gratefully inside, willing the doors to close before he could come in. But in he came, utterly consuming the air, the space, her line of sight—everything.

She stared straight ahead at their twin reflections, blurred lines in the glass: her in last night's dress and him broad, bronzed and bare-chested.

She bowed her head. 'You don't need to do this.'

'I'll see you into the car.'

The rest of the trip down thirty floors was silent but for the whoosh of the lift. She stared at her shoes. The satin toe of one was scuffed. His feet beside hers were bare. She turned her head.

With infinite slowness the lift finally bumped to a stop and the doors eased open. She stepped out into the plush, hushed reception area. Ahead, the glass doors screened the city—the world she knew, the world she was desperate to reclaim. Anywhere but here.

'This doesn't feel right,' he said, suddenly grabbing her hand. 'This doesn't feel right at all. Did I say something? Or do something?'

They were almost at the doors. A round glass table laden with fruit stood in their way. A car rolled into view.

He swung her round and she looked up into his face. She memorised the lines of his eyelids, the crooked bridge of his nose, the soft pillow of his lower lip. She'd never see them again.

'I'm sorry,' she said. 'You're just not my type.'

He winced as if she'd slapped him and stepped back.

A doorman loomed into sight through the glass. The doors were opened. She looked at the roll of burgundy carpet spread out before her, ending at the gutter.

The car door was opened. She stepped inside.

'Nobody is,' she whispered as the car sped away.

CHAPTER EIGHT

THE WAITING ROOM at the clinic was light and bright and cheerful. Magazines lay neatly stacked in a wall rack and a water cooler offered its shimmery blue contents silently beneath.

Above the sofa opposite a screen flashed news from an announcer as a tape of stories ran underneath. To her left the white-uniformed staff competently filed and welcomed and attended to various other things.

Ruby sat alone. Upright and alone. Her knees were locked together and she gripped the edge of the chair—waiting.

She glanced up at the staff, wondering when she would hear her name. And then she did. And she jumped so suddenly people turned to stare.

A uniformed, clean-faced woman holding a clipboard raised her eyebrows. 'Nobody with you?'

Ruby shook her head. When would people stop asking her that?

The woman softened slightly, cast a glance over her. 'Follow me.'

Ruby placed her weight carefully on her feet and stood. There was no pain. It was fine. It was all going to be fine. She followed the woman through a set of doors. A long corridor stretched ahead. She'd never been in this hospital before. The medical team normally came to the studio. But her physician had a clinic here and had specifically told her to come to the hospital for her final meeting.

Since she'd learned that her mind had run and her stomach had lurched. This incessant scrolling through every spinal, disc and musculature injury had got out of control. It didn't necessarily mean it was bad news, just because she wanted to see her here. Maybe she preferred to do her consulting here. Maybe all sorts of things might explain the gnawing aches, the awareness she had that she didn't want to listen. Maybe it would all be nothing.

But she had been through all the maybes in her head. It wasn't going to be good news. No one else had been asked to come here. She could only hope it wasn't really bad news.

'Come in, come in,' the consultant said, standing up when she opened the door, then nodding to the nurse. 'Have you brought anyone with you?'

Ruby stifled the urge to snap at her and shook her head instead.

The room was a square sterile box, with a window at the back and a desk facing the wall. She stared closely at the paper files on the desk, at the slice of computer screen she could see angled away to one side. She sat down on the chair she was offered—carefully. There was no twinge of pain. She was going to be given the all-clear. She could go back to rehearsals. It was going to be OK…

'Your knee,' said the doctor. 'How has it been?'

'Since the brace came off—nothing. I've been incredibly careful. All the physio and hydrotherapy—

that's made a difference. My diet—I've followed every instruction. I can't wait to get back.'

'And the other pain?'

'It's almost gone, I think. I barely notice it.'

The doctor nodded. 'We did some blood tests, as you know, after you mentioned this new pain in your back.'

She knew. She'd been feeling so tired, so lethargic. She pressed her knees together and sat up as straight as she could. She angled her chin and stared ahead, ready to hear the next words. She'd heard those kind of words before—that was all they were. Words. There was always hope after the shock.

'Is there anything you want to tell me?'

The consultant had turned to read the screen, scrolling through the notes.

'No? In that case, I should tell you we screened for pregnancy as well as other things. I don't know if you're aware of that?'

A hammer fell in her head. Why was she saying that word? *Pregnant.* What did that have to do with anything?

'It's routine in medicine. With women of child-bearing age it's always a consideration.'

That hammer fell again as another thought forced its way through. The tiny voice that had been talking to her, whispering it.

Pregnant.

She'd refused to hear it, had blocked it out.

The hammer crashed the barrier down and suddenly she could see what she had known was there—the hideous thought that had been lurking in the shadows of her mind.

The whole world spun into a sickening swirl as a wave of nausea from low in her tummy rose up.

'I think that would explain all your other symptoms too. You know—the low blood pressure. That can happen. And back pain can be a symptom for some women. I wasn't sure if you already knew.'

'But I'm a *dancer*.' She looked into the pleasant face of the other woman.

'Dancers have babies,' she said, as if that was the most obvious and delightful thing in the world.

'But I *can't* have a baby.'

'Is there a reason why not?'

Her mother's face swam into view—frowning, angry, tearstained. Ruby was sitting beside her on a park bench as a little girl, putting her hand on her mother's leg to comfort her—she had long, slim legs, like hers. She jerked away, stood up.

'Are you OK, Mummy?'

'No, Ruby—I'm not. I'm not OK. I hate this life! It's so unfair...'

She'd never said what fair would be, but Ruby knew it wasn't this. She'd never smiled when it was just them. But she'd been happy when someone else was there— she would light up, laugh and sparkle. And then she would like it when Ruby would dance.

'Come and dance for us, Ruby.'

They'd all smile and everyone would be happy, and the coldness and fear would slide away because Mummy *liked* it that she could do this for them. Mummy loved her then.

And that was all she'd wanted—to see her mother smile, to make her happy. But the music would end, the people would go, and they'd be left alone again. That aching, empty sadness would fall around them.

She'd lie in her bedroom, listening to the sounds of her mother, knowing that Mummy wanted to be out with her friends, praying that she wouldn't leave her alone again. The house was so dark, so quiet, so empty… She'd hear her own heart beating, hear the fear creeping through her, hear every single sound in the house.

The ping of the kettle was good, and the striking of a match to light a candle, the lights being turned off and Mummy's feet on the stairs. But sometimes she'd hear other sounds—the slide of the cupboard door, the rustle of a raincoat, the drag of keys along the shelf, the pause, the whoosh of the world outside, the silent click…

No, she couldn't have a baby because she couldn't have that world again. She couldn't look after a baby and give it everything it needed. She couldn't cause that pain. She could only keep her own pain at bay by dancing and rehearsing over and over and over. She couldn't be responsible for another living soul.

'I understand it's a shock. There's help available… I wasn't sure if you knew already. I can arrange for someone from the ballet company to speak to you— your mentor? Or there are services here. Is there no one close at hand? The father?'

The father. Matteo Rossini. What on earth had she been thinking? His face. His smile. His body. His never-ending stream of women.

This is what happens when feelings are given space. This disaster!

He was the worst possible person she could have let her guard down with. The very worst. She'd thought he might, just *might* get in touch with her—but, no. There had been nothing. He'd have had another whole troupe of women in his bed since then.

Would he even acknowledge that this had happened? He had been extremely careful with contraception. She had been reassured when he'd taken care of it so well because she knew she couldn't afford to get pregnant. She couldn't be a mother...

She put her hand out into the space that swam around her. Seconds, days, years suddenly spun ahead of her, showing her a different world that she could never in her worst nightmare have imagined would be hers.

'Let me get you some leaflets. We can talk about options.'

She couldn't talk about options. There *were* no options. He would have to take responsibility and let her get on with her life. There was only that. She couldn't mother anyone. She couldn't and wouldn't do that.

She breathed in, filling her lungs with air, willing her legs to be still, praying for the strength to stay calm and cope. Focus.

She stood up. 'So, just to be clear,' she said slowly. 'I am ready to go back to work. The ligaments are fully repaired and I won't be risking doing any damage. You're sure of that?'

'Your body will start to change during pregnancy, but you'll get all the help and advice you need.'

Her body would change? Her body was her only weapon in this world. She needed it to work.

Her throat closed over a new wave of fear.

Focus. Focus, she told herself, refusing to let it wash her away. *You've come so far. You're nearly there. It's just like those early calls to Mum. Focus on the good parts—ignore the rest or it'll pull you down.*

She swallowed again. 'My blood tests were clear? I'm in perfect health?'

'Ruby, you're pregnant. I can see that this is quite a shock and I'm here to help and advise.'

She lifted her bag onto her shoulder, looked inside

it—her purse, her phone, her keys. One, two, three—all there. Everything was there. Time to go. She checked her watch. Eleven-thirty. An empty day ahead. But soon her days would be full again.

One step at a time.

'Thanks. I'll let you know if I need anything. What a beautiful day,' she said staring past the doctor's head to the trees and the sky outside.

She retraced her steps along the corridor, past the nurses' station, where their chatter was bright and chirpy, past the television and the blue water cooler, past the automatic doors and out into the warm sunny morning.

She could go back to rehearsals now. That was amazing—the hugest relief.

You're going to have a baby.

She should call someone to tell them the news. That she was able to dance. She should call someone and not think of anything else. Her mind whirred. Her heart pirouetted in her chest. They were about to start rehearsals for the winter season. She had a good chance of getting a principal role.

December.

Her heart sank. What size would she be? There was no chance of her being cast in any role, in any performance. There wouldn't be any point until after the baby was born.

And what was she going to do until then? More coaching and more watching? And then—childcare? She could never afford that. Not on her salary, in London, alone.

Her feet were moving—left, right, left, right. She was at the underground station. She went down the steps. People thronged past her. She walked to the platform, felt the unbearable heat surround her. The noise of a train rumbled in the distance. People flicked their eyes at the information screens, fanned their faces in the stifling heat.

Like a dragon roaring closer and closer, the train finally loomed into view, lights like eyes blasting through the trapped turgid air.

There really was only one thing she could do.

CHAPTER NINE

MATTEO FASTENED THE cuffs of his shirt. He buttoned the single button on his suit jacket and straightened his collar. Tie or no tie? No tie. And no pocket square either.

He checked his image in the mirror one last time. It wasn't great. His hair needed a cut, but he hadn't had time, and he'd nicked his cheek shaving.

At least his lack of sleep was hidden under a midsummer Mediterranean tan. And it had been worth those two days on a yacht, convincing some of the wealthiest men in Europe to become part of the bank's youth sponsorship programme. That had felt good. And it didn't do any harm that it would *look* good—this was a week when appearances mattered.

He walked to the dressing table, collected his keys and phone. He pressed the screen, opened the contacts, scrolled until he found the one he wanted: *Ruby, Ballet*. It was time he deleted that number. He'd been right not to chase her—she was too much trouble. He'd barely been able to concentrate since that night, and there was no time or space for that right now. He'd had a lucky escape, truth be told.

He tugged his cuffs down one last time and walked through the immense French doors to the grand terrace of the Château de la Croix.

David had done a brilliant job. He'd really pushed the boat out arranging the Cordon d'Or Regatta this year, leasing this fabulous former home to royalty and movie stars from days gone by. There was nowhere finer than the Bastion St-Jaume, and no better event in the entire social calendar of the Riviera. Tonight the high-rollers and big spenders would descend. And the die would be cast.

Outside the finishing touches were being set. Three huge marquees dotted the immaculate lawns that ran down from the swimming pool through densely planted palms and onto the beach beyond. Already the château's tiny harbour was filling up with launches as people journeyed in from ships anchored further off shore. Above, the sound of rotors slicing the air announced the arrival of the media, here to set up camp to get the very best shots of the A-list as they arrived.

And among them would be the sedate and conservative, deeply pious Augusto Arturo and his wife Marie-Isabelle.

Matteo walked through the sea of white-linen-covered chairs and cotton-draped tables to where the local media were setting up their shots. Huge gold ribbons encased each area, along with banners of golden silk. Bouquets of white roses were draped artistically across the tables and around the arches. Under one of these, the first guests to arrive had gathered—the kids who had sailed in the Medaille d'Argent that morning and were already toasting their own bravado.

He envied them their carefree youth. He'd been that naïve once, imagining his life could be built on his passions instead of being the pure, hard slog it had become.

'Looks like it's shaping up, David,' he said as he took

a beer from his assistant and turned to walk with him. 'Everything going to plan?'

'So far so good. Arturo and Marie-Isabelle will arrive in half an hour. I'll hold back all the other guests until they're safely inside. Couple of pictures and then you can take them onto the west terrace. The sunset will be beautiful. You'll be irresistible, I'm sure.'

'And Claudio?' he said. 'Do you think he'll try and pull off any more dirty tricks?'

'Well, the montage of your exes on *The Finance Report* last night wasn't exactly helpful, but what else has he got?'

Matteo paused. What else *did* he have? Someone was drip-feeding the media with stories of his former girlfriends, trying to raise questions about his ability to lead the bank, never mind his morality.

'Nothing that I'm aware of, but that doesn't mean he won't try. He might claim he's got bigger fish to fry and we still need to cover every angle. I don't want a single drop of his poison to land on this.'

'I've analysed it from every single angle and back again. I can't see anything coming at you now that we're not prepared for. We've lived through Faye-gate, after all. Could it get any worse? Nothing came of those pictures of you with that dancer at the ballet premiere, despite how they tried to paint it.'

'That's true,' he said.

They'd reached the edge of the lake. Matteo stared across the dark green water, his mind filling with images of a beautiful woman with fear in her eyes.

He thought he knew women, but that morning he'd come to realise he knew nothing. He'd been all set to make a commitment as far as a second date, when—*bam!*

'You're not my type.'

He might not know women, but he knew a lie when he heard one.

He shook his head, shook her image out of his mind, and turned to look back up at the château. It was already aflame with stars of the media and finance, locals and internationals. People came here to have a really good time and then go on to have an even better time somewhere else.

Well, not he. He had traded in those chips. That night with Ruby had unsettled something in him and he hadn't chased anything since, no matter how hard his friends had pressed him.

He pulled out his phone, checked the time—less than ten minutes until curtain-up. Time to get back in the zone.

It was all hanging on him tonight. His mother had pulled back even further from the daily grind of the bank. It was as if the closer he got the further away she went. But it was good that she was feeling fulfilled, working with her kids in Africa. He'd never heard her happier since Dad died.

God, he missed him. He missed him so much.

He touched his wrist with his right hand, wrapped his fingers around his father's watch—the one thing that had survived the crash. He ran his thumb over the ridges of the dial, feeling the imprint of every etched line, remembering the times he'd cursed that watch because it had survived, ticking on while his father perished.

They would never be able to prove that Claudio had caused the accident. No one could accuse him of opening that bottle of whisky and pouring it down his father's throat. But he was the one man who had known about his alcoholism—the one man who'd been there with him when he'd battled it and won.

He'd been the man to drive him back there, too. He and his father had had a fight and the next thing they'd known he'd stolen his clients, started his own bank and then walked back into their lives goading them and gloating over his victory.

The day of the funeral—that fateful day—things had risen to the surface like so much toxic oil. Claudio had walked towards him, arms outstretched. All the signs of *Let's bury the hatchet for your father's sake.* And Matteo's urge to be comforted, reassured, had been huge. Here was his father's best friend, full of remorse, come to console him. He'd wanted it so badly. Despite everything he knew about Claudio he'd wanted to keep something of his father alive—even a corrupted friendship.

He'd been ready to forgive until, deep in Claudio's embrace, he'd heard those words.

'Get your hands off my son.'

And he had seen his mother, white-faced, grief-stricken, standing alone behind him.

'Don't you touch him. Don't you dare come here to start your tricks again...'

And then he had known. The suspicion that had wormed black holes into his brain had taken hold and a sickening rage had fallen. It was his *father* Claudio had loved—not his mother. That was the reason for his presence that had shadowed their lives for years.

His father—his hero, his rock.

Who was the man they'd just buried?

Ashes and dust and the truth gone with him. And Matteo's own world had crumbled and died too.

His paralysis had been broken. He'd lunged forward and bone had met flesh. His mother had screamed. Vases full of flowers had crashed to the ground. Women had shrieked and men had jumped forward. Hands had heaved at him, pulling him back as he'd struggled to get his hands on him. But Claudio had stepped away, clutching his jaw, spitting through the blood.

'Get out of here! Get out of our house or I'll kill you!'

He remembered his own roar. He remembered the words. He remembered the faces of the police officers as they told him they weren't going to charge him for assault but that he was lucky. And that he'd better give up on the idea of blaming anyone for his father's death. There was no way he could prove that the alcohol in his bloodstream was the responsibility of anyone but himself.

His mother had been inconsolable, sobbing. Words she'd never dreamed she'd say had finally tumbled out, confessing her secrets while he'd held her grief-wracked body close.

He learned that his father's relationship with Claudio had gone further than friendship.

They'd battled it together. She'd stood by him once, but she would not do it a second time.

And then that journey back to St Andrew's. The urge, the yearning, the need to see Sophie, to see her smile and feel her arms and let himself go, let it all out. But he hadn't been able to do that, because she had stood there naked, with another man. Betrayal had been everywhere he looked. Nothing had been safe, nothing sure. Love was worthless.

'Matteo?'

David's voice.

'Hmm…?'

'Maybe you should head up and start hosting. Things seem to be hotting up already.'

He was here. It was now. His father had done what he had done. He was never coming back, but after years of work the bank might just make it back to where it had once been. He might just pull this off. He might just be able to feel as if Claudio's dark shadow wasn't going to hang over them for ever.

He stared at the crowd of youngsters who'd now dispersed and were wandering through the rose bushes at the edge of the steps, with a photographer snapping them here and there as they moved.

'Let's go,' he said.

He strode up the lawn. People turned to stare. He could feel the interested glances of women and their light-voiced laughter like torches lighting his way up the path.

White marble steps appeared. He bounded up them. At the top were more of the young men and women who'd won the Medaille d'Or that afternoon. Bronzed and happy and on their way to a good time. He shook hands and kissed cheeks, walked on through the throng.

Faces swam before him—bright, smiling faces, so much happiness. The bank's brand was really on the rise. It was just what his father would have wanted. They were finally back in the big league.

He took all the praise with a smile, but it still felt undeserved. Until they had those extra clients from Arturo Finance he wouldn't feel back in the black.

He walked across the terrace, putting his empty water glass on a tray and stretching out his hand to shake that of the man coming towards his—the town's mayor, with his wife.

Wasn't it a marvellous event this year? So exciting!

He introduced the mayor to the winning team, photographs were taken, and they shuffled indoors as the next guests arrived. An actress and her boyfriend, fresh from Cannes.

She was looking as exquisite as ever! Was she showing at Cannes?

He listened to her reply as they too swung round for pictures. Over her shoulder David signalled Augusto and Marie-Isabelle's arrival.

Matteo felt grim determination clutch at his heart. There was no reason to feel anxious about this and every reason to feel confident. All the signs were there—this was the delicate first step in talks towards a merger. Arturo wouldn't have come if they weren't going forward. But it was the old-fashioned way. Private talks to build the relationship, get the chemistry right, and only then would the lawyers be given clearance to tidy up the deal.

He watched Augusto Arturo exit the car, saw the care the old man took over his wife, waiting while she adjusted her dress, offering her his arm as they looked up and smiled and began the slow climb to meet him.

And then, out of the corner of his eye, he saw the flash of something red—something that was burned deep on his subconscious. His heart thundered. His groin tightened.

He turned back to see Augusto and Marie-Isabelle, heads down, still climbing up. He swung his head to the left to see David. His assistant's face had changed from looking composed to a full-blown frown. He saw cameras begin to flash and felt a wave of interest pass over him and the others on the steps in the direction of the figure in red.

He turned now—fully stared. And there between two security guys, eyes fixed, wearing the same cherry-red, wide skirted dress, was... *Ruby?*

He stalled for a second, framed by guests and cameras, on the cusp of the most important moment of his business life. His heart crashed into his throat. Not another woman come to make a scene? Not now. Surely…?

But there was no mistaking it was her, and in a split second he read the situation. The two security were doing their, job checking to see if she was welcome or not, but they stood back respectfully, awed by her bone-deep beauty, her consummate elegance, her spirited challenge.

As if the rest of the world had dissolved he saw her she looking at him steadily, imploringly, with some deep, dark message, and he knew something was up. Something really big.

In a second David was at his side. 'You want me to take care of this?' he whispered as he slipped behind his shoulder.

Matteo's hand automatically reached for David's arm, holding him in check.

Augusto's sharp eyes watched everything even as he held out his arm for his wife, who was mounting the last step. Matteo glanced back at Ruby, then to Augusto, who now approached with his wife on his arm.

They were only a metre apart.

This was his moment. The tone, the chemistry of their welcome had to be right. He had to pull this off without a hitch or everything else would fall like a house of cards.

Around him people sensed the tension and began to crowd closer. David hovered expectantly.

Whatever she wanted, she would have to wait until they were safely settled away from cameras.

He stepped towards the couple, arms outstretched. 'How lovely to see you both. I'm so glad you could come.'

From the corner of his eye he saw the solitary red figure step closer.

'Can I speak to you, Matteo, please?' she said, her voice as clear as a midnight bell.

For a second he froze. The world was here—watching, waiting. He was swimming in a sea of staring faces with only one lifeline.

'*Darling* Ruby. You're *here*!' he said, hating himself. But he would not drown—not now.

They all turned to look at her. Marie-Isabelle was happily curious, but Augusto was no fool. Matteo's heart thundered faster. David's eyebrows shot up. And Ruby stood there, her dark eyes burning with a story he didn't yet know and couldn't risk hearing in front of this man.

Because she could ruin him. With a single phrase she could lay months of work to waste, destroyed. Another untrustworthy woman…another disaster ahead.

He kissed Marie-Isabelle's powdery cheek and dipped his head respectfully. 'If you'll excuse me for a moment. David will take you straight through to the terrace. I shouldn't be long.'

He turned just as Augusto's shrill voice cut in. 'Please invite your lady-friend to join us. The lovely young lady in red. Isn't she the dancer you were photographed with in London last month? We saw the feature in the press. I would be *delighted* to meet her. Wouldn't you, my dear?'

Marie-Isabelle smiled graciously.

'What a lovely idea,' said Matteo, and with a slight nod he took two paces across the carpet, past the curious faces, and lifted Ruby's hand into his.

He didn't pause to look at her or at anyone else as they moved off together, as if to the music of some practised *pas de deux*.

Away from the guests, down a short flight of steps

and through some huge French windows, he led her into a drawing room full of nothing other than heavy antique furniture and vast windows that lent no privacy.

'Whatever you've come to say, you'll do so in private,' he said, moving briskly through the hallway, scanning the area for signs of listening ears or probing cameras.

'That depends,' she said.

Her fingers were snug in his hand. He felt a certain satisfaction from that, even as her words put him on guard.

'How did you know I was here?' he said as they breezed through the house and up the wide staircase.

Staff bustled about everywhere. Rooms all over the house were being used to interview the various stars who were due to arrive.

'You're not exactly hard to find,' she said, and he tried to hear in her voice the emotion that had caused her to come. There was an edge, a steely forceful tone through her words that put every nerve in his body on guard.

'Of course,' he said, thinking that she, too, would have seen the photographs of them at the benefit.

He wondered if she'd felt any of the yearning he'd felt as he'd scanned the press coverage of that night. Discretion hadn't been top of their list, he'd realised.

'You'll have seen, then, that this is the biggest Regatta we've ever attempted. And my mother's still in Africa so it's just me this year—and the biggest A-list donors we could find.'

As well as the start of talks with Arturo. Did she know she was exposing him to gossip just by being here?

The stress hormones in his blood were pumping

higher and higher as he hurried them along silken rugs, down a high-ceilinged corridor flooded with light from an immense circular window at the end, right above the terrace where—please, God—David was keeping Augusto and his wife quietly entertained.

'In here.'

He opened a door on the left and led them into a bedroom, then paced around opening doors into cupboards and an en-suite bathroom. With microphones and lip-readers everywhere you couldn't ever be too sure, but it seemed safe.

He walked back across to where she stood—a vision in red that he would never forget.

'How is your knee?'

She closed her eyes, and the sweep of those eyelashes tugged at the memory of that night, that beautiful night...

She nodded. 'Fine. All clear. I'm back dancing full-time. For now.'

'Good...that's good.' He nodded.

For a second a smile lit her up, then vanished into the sorrowful beautiful hollows of her face.

'You look well. You suit this dress very much.'

'It's the only one I have. I thought I'd better make an effort or they might not let me gatecrash your party.'

'There was no need for you to gatecrash anything. You could have said—'

'I'm pregnant,' she blurted.

'You're what?' he said.

An instant image sprang into his mind—Ruby, plump with child. Her figure full and soft and feminine, rounded and abundant with life.

But not his—surely not his? It *couldn't* be his. But she was here. She'd tracked him all the way to France...

'It's yours.'

The words he most dreaded punched him in the stomach like two fists.

'No...' He started shaking his head. 'You can't be. It can't be— Are you sure? *Pregnant?*'

He sank down into a chair. His hands were in his hair, on his face, He stood up, staggered around. She stood staring at the space he'd been in, her own face a complete mask, showing nothing.

He strode over to her. 'How can you be? Didn't we...? Weren't you...? When did you find out? Oh, God...'

He paced again—to the bathroom. He opened the door and turned on the tap, let cold water gather in his hands and splashed it on his face. He stared at himself in the mirror.

Pregnant? He was going to be a father. No, no, *no*.

A *father*? This wasn't the face of a father!

He wasn't cut out for that. He wasn't even cut out for his own path in life—he hadn't led the bank back to glory yet—never mind starting a family. He could never be a father—not now, like this.

He walked back out. She was still there, standing exactly as he'd left her.

Her shoulders were straight, a delicate blend of bone and muscle and satin skin. Her slim arms were folded at her waist. Her wrists lay crossed over her tiny stomach. Her chin was high and proud. This woman he had spent one single night with was now bound to him for life. The path of his life had just taken another unforeseen fork.

Dear God—what had he done?

He thought of the château, the guests, the Arturos waiting. He thought of his mother's face, his father's smile, the mess he'd made of his life, of his one chance to get the bank back to where it should be.

And he thought of this woman—this beautiful creature standing before him, creating a life with him.

What the hell had he been thinking? Why couldn't he have been more careful?

Augusto. He had to get downstairs, manage this, calm everything down and then salvage the situation. He had to steer the ship away from the rocks.

'Who have you told?' he asked. 'Does anyone else know? I need to know what I'm dealing with here. When will it hit the press?'

He reached for her, felt the perfection of her limbs, the warmth of her skin and the silken twist of her hair against him. But instantly she pulled away.

'The *press*?' she said, her voice strained and shrill. 'Is that all you can think about?'

'Of course not. But they're here. They'll have a field-day if this gets out.'

'It's going to get out sooner or later. And if you don't stand by your responsibilities—*that's* when you'll need to worry.'

'I'll stand by my...*responsibilities*. There's absolutely no question of that.'

But he had other responsibilities right now. He had to get back to the Arturos. He had to calm this down, give himself some thinking time and then come back to it.

'You're right—you will. I didn't do this by myself. I need guarantees that you're not going to disappear and leave me to bring this baby up alone.'

Panic laced her every syllable and as he stared at the fear in her eyes he realised she had been dealing with this for weeks, while he was still running to catch up with the news. But the fact that she'd come here to tell him in person, choosing a moment when she knew he was under the spotlight, worried him. He had to keep this under control or he would lose his mind, and everything else with it, right in front of the world's press.

'Hang on. One step at a time. I'm still getting my head around it. I've got the deal of the century on hold down there and you think you can drop a bombshell like this and it's all OK?'

'*OK?* I don't think *any* of this is OK. I was just getting back to work—this is a complete disaster for me. I can't train… I can't perform. I'll miss the winter season and then what happens after that? What do I do?'

She threw up her hands and looked around wildly.

Matteo spoke again. 'We need to sit down calmly and talk it through. But there's plenty of time for that…'

'I never wanted children. I never even wanted to sleep with you. And now I have to have a child with you. This is the worst possible thing that could have happened to me.'

'Ruby, I'm sorry,' he said, choosing his words as carefully as his pounding heart would allow. 'But that's not how it was. You absolutely did want to sleep with me. You can't pull that excuse now and turn this into something that I *made* you do, as if this is all my fault.'

Her face twisted wretchedly. 'I still can't believe it. I still can't believe my whole life is over because of one stupid mistake.'

A burst of pride flared up in him. He'd never heard a woman describe him as a 'mistake'. Since Sophie, he'd been damned sure to keep women where he could manage them. The only stupid mistakes happened when he didn't.

'Your life isn't over,' he said coldly. 'This is a child we're talking about here. *My* child. But there are people waiting downstairs for me. I still have a business to run and I really need to go and sort it out. I'll come back and discuss this with you afterwards. Like adults.'

'Don't patronise me. Don't you think I *know* we're talking about our child? But you'd rather go and discuss business—that says it all.'

His phone vibrated in his pocket. He stared at her. Almond eyes, blurred and wild. Outside the band struck up another tune...a wave of laughter rolled in through the open windows.

'I will stand by you,' he heard himself say. 'My family means the world to me, and if there's going to be another part of it then I will do the right thing. There is no question of that. But this isn't the only thing going on right now...'

The phone continued to vibrate. It could only be David. The Arturos... He pulled it out.

'It was the *west* terrace, Matteo...?'

'On my way.'

'I have to go down there,' he said, slipping his phone back in his pocket. 'I know this is the worst possible timing, but David will come up and make sure you're comfortable. We can work out the other arrangements as soon as this is over. Just give me some time.'

'Do I have any choice?'

'No.'

He couldn't look at her face, but those dark eyes burned all the way to his heart as he strode to the door and out into the hall. The sounds of the party rumbled up to meet him. There were people smiling, posing, cameras everywhere. He pushed back through them, some sort of smile fixed on his face, giving a white-knuckled handshake to the people who stopped him.

He made his way to the west terrace. There they

were. Marie-Isabelle was sitting on an elegant wicker chair, with a glass of champagne and a beatific smile. Augusto stood over her, and both were staring out over the marina to where the dipping orange sun was sinking low on a slick indigo sea.

'Ah. You've found the marvellous sunset,' he said, hearing words that meant nothing dripping out of his mouth. 'The best night of the year so far, don't you think?'

'Indeed… A night to talk about love, not money,' said Augusto. 'Where is your young lady? You should be spending time with her, not sitting with a pair of old fogeys like us.'

Matteo looked at him sharply, guilt settling in his stomach like acid. Augusto couldn't possibly know that he'd left his 'young lady' abandoned upstairs with her terrible secret. He had to swallow it down and get on with the job in hand, even though he felt it was already slipping out of his grasp.

He'd just put the whole Lady Faye nonsense behind him and now along rolled the next situation to deal with. The heavy yoke of his life suddenly felt like iron around his shoulders. He couldn't take much more, and now there was a child on the way, and Claudio would be standing and watching, waiting for a single slip-up so that he could come over and trample what was left of his family into the dirt.

He looked around at the sparkling boats on the marina, at the couples wandering on the grass, at the dance floor pulsing with bodies, the terrace, the long sweep of the driveway where cars were still coming and going. People with nothing to worry about other than having a good time.

For a moment he saw only the cloudless skies of their

liberty, and jealousy rumbled like thunder in his heart. He'd never asked for any of this. This bank...this life. He'd never been given a choice.

What if he were given a choice? What if he turned his back on his duty? What was the worst that could happen? The bank would be sold off. But money would still move about from London to New York to Geneva. Everyone would be all right. No one would die.

'The party is going very well. The youngsters who won the Medaille are in fine spirits, don't you think?' asked Augusto.

He swallowed, focused. The effort to answer was almost too much. Words were there, but dredging them to his mouth, saying them—what was the point?

He stared ahead.

So many people. His mother, abroad, relying on him. David—long-serving and loyal. All the employees of the bank. A whole endless stream of people who needed him to keep going. And now his baby—his child. And the woman who had lit a fire in him that he'd thought dead, and then left him cold in his bed before the sun had risen. The woman he was going to be tied to for years and years to come...

'Indeed. It looks like they're having the time of their lives.' Slowly he managed to whisper the words from his dry and dusty throat.

'You were a sportsman once—is that right?' Augusto asked, fixing him once again with his bright-eyed stare. 'There was talk of you going professional. You weren't always going to follow your father into banking?'

Matteo frowned. How did he know that? He must have done his homework. The old fox was as wily as his reputation. This was an interview, right enough. The game was still on.

'I was a rugby player. But it's been a long time since I played.'

'But you are quite sure that it's banking that is your passion now? Your world? You cannot lead well in any field without feeling passion. Otherwise you'll only ever be a manager.'

From the corner of his eye Matteo looked at Augusto's crinkled skin, the liver spotted hands, the sharp, inquisitive eyes.

How did he know? How was this old man he barely knew able to say words that cut to the core of who he was? How could he see the gnawing worry that he just didn't care enough and that was why the bank had never fully recovered?

Matteo fixed his gaze to the bunting fluttering in the evening breeze. He could not look round. He could not even speak. He couldn't trust himself.

Augusto spoke on. 'Because we both know that the person who takes my bank on will be more than that. I need someone who believes in what they do—not just someone who'd be going through the motions. I have no time for that.'

The moment was here. Matteo could feel it. Time was waiting, and from this moment all would slide along one path or another. He had been given the choice. It was up to him now to shake his head and walk away or step forward.

'With every breath in my body I want to make Rossini into the bank it should have been. And I am convinced that our two brands are unique in what we offer. What I want is to talk it over with you.'

The old man's penetrating stare was deep and long, and Matteo battled to keep his raging emotions under control as he gazed back. He would not lose yet. He readied himself to keep going—to say whatever it took to convince him to give him a chance.

Finally Augusto nodded. 'We'd like that too. Come to the Lake House. In a fortnight.'

The heaviest weight fell from his shoulders—so hard he almost slumped in relief.

'And bring your lovely young lady. It's important that we meet her too. My dear, I think we've spent enough time with the youngsters for one evening. Shall we?' said Augusto, lending his wife his arm.

'It will be our very great pleasure,' Matteo replied. 'I'll tell her straight away.'

'We're old-fashioned, though. You're not married yet, so please don't be assuming any privileges under my roof.'

Matteo smiled and shook the old man's hand as warmly as his chilled face and frozen heart would allow.

Marriage...

Pregnancy...

This whole situation was unravelling faster than he could ever have thought possible. Almost out of his grasp. Almost lost.

But not quite. Not yet. All he had to do was convince Ruby to play along.

He watched the Arturos settle into their car and drive away. Then he turned on his heel. He had business to get on with.

CHAPTER TEN

It had to be done. There had been no other way. She'd tried to call—lifted the phone a hundred times. But she simply hadn't been able to get the words out of her mouth to say so much as his name to the elite-sounding voice that had answered at Banca Casa di Rossini.

What if he wouldn't take her call? What if he denied it? Men with money like him—they could do anything they wanted. He could lie to the police, get a restraining order on her—anything was possible. Her own father hadn't had two pennies to rub together and *he* had managed to disappear off the face of the earth, shirking his responsibilities, pretending she didn't even exist.

So, until she had made up her mind as to how to approach him, all she'd been able to do was stalk him in the virtual world.

It had become a routine since the day she'd walked out of the hospital. Who *was* this man who was going to father her child? She had no idea. She barely knew his name.

She had traded in her whole world—her career, her childhood dream about to come true—for one night with him. Just because he'd made her smile and laugh, and kissed her and made her body come alive, made her want to do things she'd never wanted to do before, made her want to lie beside him long after she should have slipped out and away,

She had no doubt that was when it had happened—in the depths of sleep, when they'd found one another in their dreams and the fire had burned and engulfed them.

Making a baby was as easy as that. And two lives were changed for ever.

The horror of it clutched at her heart every time she opened her eyes. In the mornings she'd lie awake in bed, waiting for the hideous nightmare to creep over her again like a dead woman's shroud. Her career was over. She couldn't dance for the best part of a year. And, despite all her best efforts, her money was dwindling away.

Memories of the days before her mother had met George would rise like ghouls from the depths of her mind. Wintry mornings in their freezing council flat, painting pictures on the damp windows between the mould-mottled frames, longing for breakfast before school but too afraid to ask her mum in case it made her cry or shout or—worst of all—storm off and leave her.

That fatherless world. The shame of school, where everyone else had pictures to draw and stories to tell of dads who taught them how to swim and ride a bike. Where playground voices had risen in competition: *'My dad says...' 'My dad does...'*

She had known nothing about him. He had been just a man who *'lives far away and can't come back'*. Ignorance had been bliss—until the dreadful night she'd overheard her mother's slurred voice telling someone how *'Everything was fine until Ruby came along. If it wasn't for that kid I'd be in a different world right now.'*

She'd stopped asking about her father after that, and tried to bury the sickeningly shameful secret that she'd

driven him away. Then she had found dance and her
mother had found George and it had been as if she'd
lost her mother too.

The only thing she'd had in her world was her body
and the music and the steps and the shapes and the
struggle to be perfect. If she hadn't found dance she'd
never have made it this far.

Dance had given her confidence. And hope. And finally an understanding that a baby wasn't responsible
for anyone's actions.

But now she had done *this*. She had turned off her
own life supply and turned on another. This new life.

She would lie in the watery morning light, put her
hand on her stomach—still flat and hard with muscle—
and wonder what lay beneath. What little life was in
there, burrowed away, safe until it was ready to be born?
How was she ever going to give it what it needed? What
chance did she have of being a proper mother when her
own life hadn't begun until she'd become a boarder at
the British Ballet? They were her only family. And now
she'd let them down too…

That thought would make her heave herself out of
bed before she was sick. She'd clean up, then lie on the
cold floor between her tiny bathroom and tiny kitchen
and torture herself with fear. What if she was left alone
with this? What if Matteo had already met someone
else? What if he refused to see her? What if he denied
that he'd ever met her?

A phone call to her mother had proved once and for
all that being left alone was a very real possibility—
because relying on her for help wasn't an option. Oh,
yes, she'd said she'd come to London when the baby
was born, but as Ruby had ended the call, and felt the
sorrowful finality of her whispered 'goodbye', she had

known that *See you soon* was the last thing in the world that would actually happen.

No, there had been no other way. She'd had to try and see Matteo face to face as soon as she could.

So she had followed him on social media and in the press until she knew almost everything about him—including the fabulous annual Cordon D'Or, which ten weeks after she'd left the clinic, was exactly where he was going to be this weekend.

It was perfect. She still had her Banca Casa di Rossini ID badge and she still had the dress she'd thought she'd never wear again.

With the hugest reluctance she'd dragged it out from the bag at the bottom of her wardrobe and had it cleaned and altered. A few centimetres at the waist was all she'd needed to allow the zip to close. She'd bought her first ever strapless bra, put on her make-up, and then, with no luggage other than her passport and her handbag, her stomach heaving with hormones and nerves, she'd climbed aboard a budget airline flight to Nice.

With cameras everywhere, there would be no better place to do it. He couldn't say or do anything bad to her with the world watching. She'd jumped in a taxi, pulled up to the château gates, flashed the badge and made her way through the crowds, over the lawns, and up the marble steps to where the rich and the talented had been kissing their hellos.

Her heart had lurched at the sight of him. The same tall, broad frame, the wide, sure stance. His hair had flopped over his brow and his head had been down like a panther about to pounce. He wore a dark suit and pale blue shirt, open at the neck. And, damn him, he'd looked even more handsome than she remembered.

She'd walked along the path, never taking her eyes

off him, fully intending to blurt it out, right there on the steps, but as he'd turned and seen her, and shock had filled his eyes, something had held her back. Something in that look had held her in place, told her not to say the words yet. Some desperate warning that, miraculously, she had decided to heed.

But it was all about a deal.

As soon as he'd learned he was going to be a father he'd upped and left, gone back to his party. The deal was clearly more important than learning he was going to be a father. But what else had she really expected? And now she'd lost her chance to shame him in front of the world.

She walked to the window and stared down at the party.

The elderly couple were pulling away in their car. She saw Matteo raise a hand to wave them off and then he watched them go, standing still as the marble pillars on either side of him that held the roof aloft.

'That's your father,' she whispered to the baby growing silently within her. 'Your father that I barely know. I'm sorry...so sorry, my angel. I never meant this to happen. But whatever is best for you I will do it. I will fight for you—and I will make sure he does not abandon you.'

As she stared down at the top of his head he suddenly turned and looked up at the window, as if he'd heard her words. She met his eyes, and again that arc of something deep and strong sprang between them. He turned around fully now, as one, two, three more seconds ticked by, his steady gaze so powerful that it made her want to reach for something to hold on to.

Then he bowed his head and was gone.

Her heart began to thunder and her legs began to move. She wasn't going to stay hidden away up here a moment longer. She was going to go down to the party and find him—before he got tangled up in some other business conversation, or some woman threw herself all over him and she slid even further down his list of priorities.

She would not disappear because it didn't suit him to have a child. *Never.*

She moved across the room, put her hand out to push the door—but it landed instead on the wide, warm chest of Matteo.

Without missing a beat, he put his hand over hers and spun her around with him.

'Now we can get out of here.'

Her feet barely touched the ground as he sped them along the hallway, now flooded with late-evening sun and the faint glow of just-lit lamps.

'David, I need a launch out to the boat. Set it up. Clothes, food... But above all else—privacy.'

He slipped his phone away and at the top of the stairs he turned. 'We'll use the servants' entrance.'

'For what? What's going on?'

His jaw was grim, his mouth pinched, but he looked at her with surprise in his eyes.

'You wanted to talk. So we talk—without anyone listening. Offshore. I don't want any distractions.'

His dark berry eyes gave nothing away, but she could feel the energy pulsing off him in waves. He was bullish. He was going to take this head-on—she could see that. He wasn't running away.

'Do you have anything with you? Anything you need back at your hotel?'

She shook her head. 'I wasn't planning on staying any longer than necessary. This is all I have.'

'Doesn't matter. If you think of something David

will sort it. OK—you ready for this? Because you'd better get used to it.'

He put his arm around her shoulders and steered them both out. She didn't raise her head above the trail of steps and gravel paths, the perfect lawns and flowerbeds, all the way down to the tiny beach and jetty where a sleek white motorboat was waiting.

He jumped aboard and the little boat bobbed with his weight.

'Take your shoes off,' he said as he held out his arm to help her aboard.

She stared at the slippery jetty, at its ridged surface, and then at the inky water and the huge gap between solid land and the boat.

'Come on,' he said, 'before we attract a crowd.'

He stretched his hand out a little further but she faltered.

'I'm a bit nervous of water. I can't swim properly.' It was a fact she hated to say out loud, but a fact nonetheless.

'That's totally OK,' he said, and she noticed with relief the lack of censure in his voice. 'You'll be completely safe—just do what I tell you. Take your shoes off first. Heels are dangerous on boats. Throw them to me and then put your arms out. That's it,' he said as she followed his instructions.

His strong hands gripped her arms, then her waist, and then, as she stared up into his face, she gingerly stepped into the boat. It moved slightly, but his body was like a rock and she found herself holding on to it with both arms, just for a moment, but long enough to feel an echo of that hunger.

He lifted a life jacket and helped her into it, his fingers swift and deft, face focused. Then he unfastened the rope and sat down, pulling her by the hand to sit beside him. The engine fired up and they began to nose their way through the bay between the other boats, berthed like huge chess pieces on a watery board.

Suddenly they reached clear water and picked up speed. As the boat bumped along on the waves and out to the sea, spray landed on her bare arms and face and the wind whipped at her hair. She looked at him but he stared stubbornly ahead, eyes fixed on the horizon.

'Where exactly are we going?' she asked, as they rounded the bay and a huge white yacht came into view.

He nodded. 'On that—where I'm pretty sure we won't be disturbed.'

They pulled alongside and waited as the water impatiently slapped the sides of the boat and her sensitive nose picked up the scent of salty ocean mingled with fuel. As the rope was pulled tight, men appeared from nowhere—all of them poised, it seemed, to help her on board.

'OK, I've got this,' barked Matteo, and they melted away. 'Ruby?'

She slid her hands into his as he helped her aboard with what seemed suddenly like something close to gentleness. Then they walked up through one deck into another and right into the prow of the ship, where tiny lights were draped around the wooden railings and a single table was set for dinner for two.

'Oh!' she gasped. 'Is this for us?'

Maids appeared with vases of white roses and domed silver platters.

'For you,' he said, pulling out her chair as if it was no big deal. 'And just one more thing...'

He reached out and pressed a button and the roof retracted, opening them up to the starry sky above. The ship's mast stretched high, and from the top fluttered a little flag. The distant sounds of the party rumbled behind them and all around a warming breeze stirred the trails of bunting that clung prettily to the ropes.

It was the most romantic scene she'd ever witnessed. She had been prepared for denial, a fight, maybe even a pay-off, but she hadn't been prepared for kindness or consideration or—*romance*?

Maybe it was Matteo's way of softening her up, lulling her into giving in to his will. She sat straight in her seat. She wasn't going to make any of this easy for him.

'OK. We're here now, and we've got a lot to talk about, but I suggest we take this slowly,' he said, easing his large frame into the seat opposite with the grace that, even now, she found irresistibly alluring. 'I don't want to rush into talking about things that are bigger than anything we've ever had to deal with before. We're going to take a little time to get to know one another again—you know, build up some trust. You OK with that?'

He poured water into her glass, his eyes concentrating only on that, his face registering nothing other than patience. But it wasn't patience that she wanted to see. She needed reassurance. She needed action.

'I'm OK with that as long as you understand that I'm not here for dinner and dancing. I'm here for one reason only and that's to discuss next steps.'

He put his glass down slowly. 'All right. If that's the way you want to play it I can't force you. All I'm saying is that we're asking a lot of each other if we don't take our time here. I never get into talks cold. It's a really dumb thing to do.'

'You think forcing small-talk is really going to make a difference to the outcome?'

'I wouldn't dream of forcing my small-talk on anyone. It's not that great. But I assume you'll want to eat and that you'll at least stay until morning. There's loads of space here, and you'll need to rest in...'

The steepled hands, the patient, soothing voice again. Instantly her hackles rose.

'Please don't patronise me by saying *in your condition*. I've survived the past few weeks of this pregnancy being sick in toilets, without your help, so I think I'm well aware of what I do and don't need.'

The silence with which he met her sharp words sat heavy and still.

'I'm sorry to hear that,' he said finally. 'I should have realised. It's not just coming to terms with being pregnant that you've had to cope with. It's all the physical things too. I've got a lot to learn.'

She looked sharply at him. This was not what she had expected. At all.

'Don't worry—the physical things only relate to the woman. You're quite safe.'

'OK, Ruby,' he said, obviously swallowing down on a chuckle. 'I know that I'm not going to be the one who actually goes through the pregnancy. I was only trying to say that I want to be part of this with you, and to do that I need to find out more about it. That's all.'

'You want to be part of this?'

He was *saying* the right things. He was making eye contact and acting concerned. But still...

'Yes, but, as I said, tomorrow is time enough for us to talk about all that. Why don't you tuck in? You must be hungry. And I know how much you like to eat.'

She lifted the dome from her plate to reveal a platter of ice and lemon and six fat oysters glistening in their shells.

'I can't eat these,' she said, looking up at him. 'I can't drink wine or eat soft cheese or lots of other things. And cream makes me sick. And soy sauce. Anything like that.' She pushed the plate away.

Matteo threw down his napkin, stood up and walked around the table. Startled, she tilted her head back to look at him.

'You see—this is just the sort of thing I mean. I need to know how to look after you.'

He put his large hands out and she slid hers into them. Like some stupid marionette, she allowed herself to be lifted to her feet. She could feel the heat from his body, sense the strength from his core, the sure, solid presence that she'd once buried herself in, guard down and heart wide open.

'Come on. Let me show you to your cabin and I'll get some food that you can eat sent in to you. Food that's not going to harm you or the baby.'

She could feel herself sinking towards him, the magnetic pull of his body offering and demanding in equal measure, natural as sunset and sunrise, just like the last time. But she couldn't afford that luxury again. She had to keep herself apart, head clear and mind sharp as a tack.

He was using her weakness against her—making her dependent. She shook her head, ready to argue, but the waves of tiredness were huge now. She'd been on the go for hours, hadn't slept well the night before, and stress and strain and emotion were all beginning to drag her under. She opened her mouth in a deep yawn.

'That's it,' he said. 'No arguments. I'm taking control here and you're going to bed.'

'I will not be ordered around,' she muttered stubbornly. 'I'll make my own decisions and...'

But she was engulfed in another yawn and the last of her energy evaporated.

'Make your own decisions in the morning. Make all the decisions you like. But right now I'm in charge. Let's go.'

He scooped her up, and just that—the sensation of his body around hers and his fierce directive—had her lost in the waves of her own fight. She caved, allowed him to hold her close, didn't fight the warm glove of his hand on her head. Didn't fight the steady beat of his heart on her cheek or the warm male scent of his chest. She didn't lift her head to check where he was going, or worry or wonder how she was going to get home.

She let herself melt.

When he opened the door of a cabin she saw subtle lights and soft fabrics in creams and pinks and lacquered wood. And she didn't resist.

He laid her down on the bed and she felt his hands peel down her zip and ease her out of her dress. And still she didn't struggle. She let it happen. She rolled over in her underwear, felt sheets pulled back, and then she was enveloped in the softest satin and her path into dreams stretched out ahead.

And she knew, as she drifted under, that she was here again, with Matteo, and that the hole in her armour was getting wider and wider.

CHAPTER ELEVEN

ON HIS EIGHTEENTH BIRTHDAY his father had given Matteo the fountain pen he now held in his hands. He ran his fingers along the onyx lacquer and tested the brass nib. The first time he'd used it was when he'd had to sign the lease for his flat at university. It had felt like a step into adulthood, symbolically marked by such a formal object. It was a lovely pen—now used for signing contracts and legal documents—but it wasn't what he needed right now.

He put the lid on it and tucked it away.

Right now he needed something much more current. Something with no trace of the past. Something he could use to write out his future. Because it was right there, in front of him, fast asleep on the bed.

He stretched out his legs and rolled his shoulders. The chair was comfortable enough for short people who wanted to take a load off their feet for a few minutes, but it was totally useless for a six-foot-three ex-rugby-player who'd been folded into it for the past five hours.

But where else would he be with all the chattering in his mind, the constant conversations he'd been having with himself since he'd closed the door on the Arturos, watched them roll off down the drive and then turned to see that vision in red at the window.

She had his mind—every corner of it.

He'd better get it back—and fast.

He opened his black notebook and took another fresh page. Lifted a sleek rollerball, made two lists. Things he was going to jettison and things he was going to adopt.

Booze. That had to go. Not because he had a problem with it, but because it was always there at the back of his mind that he might one day. His single Friday beer was his way of showing that he had it under control. But he'd still had too many nights on the tiles he'd regretted, and his father had seemed to have it all under control. Except he hadn't. And it'd killed him.

He looked at Ruby's face, soft in sleep. There was no way he was going to have anything around him that might do harm to her or their baby.

Next to go—gambling. That wasn't going to be hard: He couldn't care less if he never saw the inside of a casino again. But it was the boys he'd miss. He needed his friends. He needed the camaraderie, the bluster and fun.

And more than that he needed to feel that physical force, that competition. It was rugby he really needed— he still missed it every day. But this wasn't about him. This was about doing the right thing. This was the future, not the past.

Ruby moaned in her sleep and he sat up straight in the chair. She was dreaming, mumbling softly, and he leaned closer, watching. Her ebony hair was fanned out on the pillow, her bare arm as pale as the sheet it rested on. He saw the faint scar of a needle jab and a series of pale brown moles, but they weren't imperfections. All they did was made her look even more beautiful.

He had never felt such responsibility in his life.

He had to keep her safe, keep her healthy and keep her onside at all costs.

He went back to his list, made another column. Wrote down, in slow, bold strokes *Marriage*.

He stared at the word, at the letters and the shape they made. Even writing it made him feel that he'd aged ten years. It was a word of maturity, selflessness. It was weighted with responsibility and expectations. Those letters were both a mirror and a map—forcing him to see what a lightweight he'd been these past years. The playboy, playing fast and loose, the toast of all his friends because he would not let any woman tell him how to run his life.

Sophie's face flashed through his mind. The horror in her eyes through the steam of the shower. Those wounds had scarred him deeply, but it was time to acknowledge them and move on.

Sophie was ten years ago. Ruby was now.

And even though he didn't want marriage, could he bear his child to be brought up hundreds of miles away? By another man. Because if he didn't marry Ruby, someone else would.

Beautiful Ruby.

He checked his watch. She'd been asleep six hours. She was bound to wake up soon.

He wrote down *Home*. The answer to that word was going to depend a lot on the answer to the one above it. He'd ask her to marry him, she'd say yes, and they'd live in—London? Was that the best place to bring up the *bambino*? If he didn't ask her to marry him, could they live together? Where would that be? Would that work out better?

If they didn't live together the baby would be brought up in two homes. He'd need to stay more in London, or she'd need to come to Rome. He'd buy her a house, or move her into one of his. And what about her career? Didn't ballet mean touring and travelling? What then?

His own parents had led largely separate lives, he realised. But whatever his father's demons had been they'd stayed together, married, all those years. For the sake of him? The bank? His mother had loved his father—he knew that much. She'd fought for him. But at the end of the day Claudio had won. Whatever way you looked at it, marriage was a fake but probably necessary institution.

He put his head in his hands, ran his palm over his brow, felt the steady motion of the boat and the lure of sleep. The lure of sleeping beside Ruby. The thought of having her in his bed again—he'd tried hard to put it out of his mind, but who was he kidding? He hardened in response.

God, his mind was rammed with this and he hadn't even started to put the Arturo merger into the mix.

'What time is it?'

He looked up. She was propped up on her elbows, hair flopping all over her face, her cheeks pink and plump with rest and her eyes blinking awake in the soft light of morning. She looked sweet and vulnerable and his heart swelled.

He looked away. 'About six. Here,' he said, ignoring the pain as he stretched his cramped legs. 'I got you some tea and toast.'

She looked at him, then at the tray that had been sitting beside her for the past ten minutes.

'OK…thanks.'

'It's to prevent your morning sickness. I've been reading up about it. Have something bland first thing and it settles your stomach. So they say.'

'You've been reading up about morning sickness?'

'And other things.'

'Is that right? Anything else you found out?'

She sat up properly now, and as she moved the sheet dropped down, revealing her nakedness.

'Your breasts. They'll be tender. And getting bigger.'

She glared at him. 'That's none of your business,' she said, but she didn't rush to cover herself and he didn't rush to shift his gaze.

'I'm just stating a fact,' he said, taking in her softness, shaded in the morning light, as his voice deepened to a growl even to his own ears. 'And they're really pretty.'

Nothing moved but the steady rock of the boat and the solid beat of his heart in his chest. But all around his body his senses sparked to life. The air became hot as desire bloomed between them. Her chest heaved and she looked utterly undone already, with messy tendrils of hair hanging loose above the rosy pink tips of her nipples which, before his very eyes, were tightening into hard little nubs.

He hesitated. All he wanted was to grab her into his arms and fasten his mouth on hers. He wanted to mould her curves in his hands and tug them both into another sexual adventure. She was all he'd been dreaming about for weeks and she was right here, as ripe and ready for him as he was for her.

Not yet, a voice told him. *Not yet. Take it easy. She's vulnerable, and look what happened the last time.*

He needed way more than sex now. He needed her here, by his side, working things out together. This family, this merger, this life.

She reached for the sheet, pulled it up to her chest. 'If you don't mind…?'

He stood. 'Of course. Join me on deck for breakfast when you're ready. The shower's in there. David's delivered a load of clothes—just take what you want.'

He lifted his notebook, the pen. Took two steps and opened the door.

'As soon as you're ready we can talk.'

CHAPTER TWELVE

'OVER HERE.'

Ruby stepped out onto the deck into a brilliant blue-washed day, where sky met sea in strips of azure and indigo and shards of sunlight beamed like lasers all around. They were in the middle of nowhere. Literally not a speck of land was anywhere to be seen.

She looked up to see Matteo. He too had showered and changed. A tight white T-shirt stretched over his broad chest and light blue jeans hung low on his hips. Her eyes dropped automatically to the waistline and the erotic trail of dark coarse hair that disappeared into his groin.

He leaned over the railing, beckoned for her to join him at a table laid with breakfast things.

'You look lovely,' he said, reaching for her hand and helping her climb to the top of the ladder onto the deck.

For a moment she felt lovely too. Stepping into silk underwear and trying on summer dresses had helped to quell her nausea and for ten glorious minutes she'd felt like a little girl at the dressing up box, lost in a froth of pretty clothes.

'How was the toast? Did it work? Could you eat some more?'

She climbed the short flight of steps to the next deck

and there saw a table awash with fruit and yogurt and baskets of bread. Hunger battled nausea and won. She was starving, but she wasn't going to accept anything until they'd had a proper conversation.

'Where are we?'

'Boats have a habit of moving when you untie them.' He smiled. 'Just a little bit of privacy, Ruby. I wasn't going to hang around the Riviera to find myself the subject of any more gossip. This—' he held out his hands '—is private. There's too much at stake for me right now to have anything go wrong.'

So she was right. He was keeping this under wraps. Alarm bells started to ring.

'I'm not going to hide away, Matteo. You can't keep me on a boat for the next seven months.'

'I don't plan to hide you anywhere. But staying back there wasn't an option. You saw the press there last night—I don't want anyone crawling around in my private life and I'm sure you don't either.'

'My private life is an open book,' she said, as spiky hackles rose on her skin. 'I've got nothing to hide.'

'This isn't about hiding, Ruby,' he said calmly. 'It's about getting time together away from everything else. This is big. Huge. We need to get our heads around it.'

'It's quite simple. We're going to have a baby,' she said, hearing the shrill note in her voice and hating how desperate she sounded. But she *was* desperate. If he didn't play his part she was as lost at sea as if she'd fallen overboard.

He sighed. He smiled. He put his hands on her arms and pulled her towards the chair.

'Yes, we are. And from here on in we're going to be adult about this. What's the rush? We've got plenty of time to talk things through. And as soon as we're both ready we'll tell the world. Not before. I don't want this to overshadow anything. I've got other stuff on the go and I want some time. That's all. That's not unreasonable, is it?'

'I suppose not,' she said reluctantly, calming at the lull of his voice and the gentle slosh of the boat on the water.

There really was no rush, she told herself. He seemed to be accepting it. He hadn't denied it or accused her of sleeping around. He hadn't howled or beat his chest or simply disappeared. He'd sat by her bed through the night and he hadn't made a move on her.

She felt her shoulders slump and a slow breath ease out of her chest. The steady slap of water on the boat and the endless hazy day seemed to smooth her hackles, quiet her mind.

'Come on. Breakfast.'

The lure of glistening melon and hot rolls was too much, and she sat down and reached for some bread immediately.

He nodded, poured water. Didn't do anything else.

She watched him as she buttered bread and popped it in her mouth. He watched her back. A bowl of berries appeared before her, topped with fresh yogurt and seeds. It looked so good she gave in and tucked in greedily, flicking her eyes up to him between bites.

He sipped coffee.

'Aren't you going to have anything?' she said, as she popped another piece of fruit in her mouth and buttered another roll.

'I've eaten. And this is much more fun. It's like watching locusts.'

She made a face and looked around, still hungry. She helped herself to more yogurt, piling it high on her plate.

'It was like this the last time too,' he said.

'Last time?'

'At the Italian restaurant? Luigi's? Don't tell me you've forgotten our first date. It was an amazing night…'

She sipped water and sat back as his words hung between them. Wisps of memory fluttered up into her mind—the fun, the camaraderie, the intimacy—tugging her back into that warm embrace. And he, right there opposite her, looked as if he was sharing exactly the same thoughts.

'How do you think it happened?' he asked quietly. 'We took precautions.'

She steeled herself to look up into his face.

'Not every time. There was once…in the night… when we were both half asleep.'

He raised an eyebrow. 'Yes. But something certainly woke us up.'

She heard the slight tone of amusement in his voice and looked down at her plate.

'Come on, Ruby. There's no point in being coy about it. We had something special going on that night. And it feels to me as if that part of a relationship at least might work for us.'

She felt the tug of that night, in those hours before dawn, the warmth of his body, the pleasure of her own melting into his arms. Those hours when she'd lost her head and everything she'd ever stood for. It was as if she'd paused her life when she'd gone into that apartment—as if she'd thought some other life might be possible instead of the one she'd been striving for.

And being here with him now she could see how easy it would be to step into the honey-trap again, but this was far too important. She had to stay focused. He needed to understand that this was real. They were both in it for the long haul.

'Matteo, no.' She shook her head. 'This isn't about us.' She laughed at her own stupid phrase. 'What am I talking about? There *is* no us. There's only a baby without a family. And I need to know what we're going to do about it.'

She stared at his face for the optimistic signs that she wanted to see. Signs that he wasn't going anywhere...

'You're really in a hurry over this, aren't you? The baby's not even born yet. Don't you think you're getting ahead of things?'

'You said last night that you're going to accept your responsibilities,' she said. 'But what does that mean? I have a career. I can't perform when I'm pregnant, so I'm going to have work in the school, and then, when I'm fit again, I'll go back to dancing. But I can't do it alone.'

'You've had longer to think this through, Ruby. I don't even know what you've got in mind. You live in London. I live in Rome *and* London. We both travel a lot. How is this going to work?'

'Of course it can work. I want to get back to dancing as soon as I can. I can't afford childcare on my own—I assumed you'd want to employ a nanny, no?'

He frowned at that. 'How soon do you mean?'

'A few weeks after the birth. I don't see why not.'

'Weeks?'

Something in that judgemental tone made her antennae twirl even faster. She'd already had a lifetime of being judged. Everyone had an opinion.

'A few weeks after the birth?' he repeated. 'I can see you're not impressed with my question, but it's a perfectly reasonable thing to ask.'

'I'm not going to justify my decision to you or anyone else.'

He sat back in his chair, the only real sign that he was surprised. He touched his fingertips together and just that tiny movement caused the muscles in his arms to ripple and bulge. Arms that she'd trailed her lips all over, that had held her in the tightest embrace.

Arms that would cradle a tiny baby in a few months.

She could see it as clearly as if it had already happened—as if he really was lifting a crying infant to soothe and protect it. And she knew then that he was going to cherish it. He was going to be a real dad.

It was just a single second's realisation, but it was as intense and terrifying as standing on the edge of a cliff. Because she was terrified she wasn't going to be able to do the same. Her heart started thundering in her chest again. Her own childhood had been a disaster. She had a broken relationship with her mother, felt nothing for her half-siblings. She'd never wanted a baby—and now it was really happening.

'Ruby, we're not at that stage of decision yet. We're still at the stage of coming to terms with this. OK, *I* am still at the stage of coming to terms with it.'

He lifted his phone.

'I'm still fielding calls, trying to explain where I disappeared to last night. I have a bank to run that isn't nine to five and I have all this—this other stuff going on. My head is rammed, Ruby. I don't want to make any decisions until I've had a proper chance to think things through. Who knows how we'll both feel later on?'

As he spoke his phone vibrated on the table as if on cue. He glanced at it, sighed, put it down again and looked out past the deck, shaking his head slightly as if he couldn't quite believe the mess he found himself in.

Behind his head the long straight strips of sea and sky blended in a haze of blue. The creaking and whooshing sounds of the yacht's gentle bounce through the waves were all she could hear. She looked at him, and for the first time saw the exhaustion on his face. He had sat up with her all night, squashed into a chair, and even though now he was clean-shaven and showered his features were drained and drawn.

He had read up on pregnancy and morning sickness and brought her toast, and that was maybe one of the nicest things anyone had ever done for her. Because she didn't let anyone do *anything* for her.

He turned round to face her.

'I know you're looking at me, wondering what the hell I'm all about and if I'm going to stick around. All you've ever seen is the party side of me—at the ballet benefit and then last night. Or in the press. You're wondering what kind of guy I am who has this trail of women behind him and won't settle down. And I don't blame you for thinking like that. I'd be exactly the same.'

He leaned forward, his arms and shoulders and chest and everything about him telegraphing pure presence, pure strength. And she was right back there, in that Italian restaurant, gazing at him with a lust she'd never believed she could feel for anyone. The way he'd absorbed everything she'd told him and worked the room, the way they'd worked together, spinning the web of desire around one another until all her armour had melted away.

At least he'd been straight down the line. Then and now.

'You think I'm some kind of a flake who's going to leave you high and dry with a baby to look after, all on your own, and you're in a panic that maybe I won't even pay my way and look after things. I get it.'

'Yes,' she said. 'I am.'

But how did she tell him the rest—that she was more afraid of *herself*. She didn't want to let anyone into her life, to need or be needed by anyone. The only thing she needed in her life was herself.

He reached his big broad hand across the table and took hers, wrapping his fingers around it. She tried to pull it back but he held on.

'I'm going to do the right thing. I know you've no reason to trust me, but I want to help. I'm not the guy you think you know.'

And I'm not who you think I am, she thought. *I'll be no good at this. I'll let us down...*

Everything he said made her feel worse inside. She could see that he meant every word—and she believed him, she really did. But he thought she was like other women, wanting a baby and a family and all those things.

When they were the very last things she wanted.

She looked around the boat, a sudden sense of panic engulfing her like a blinding, heavy sea fog, even though it was the clearest, freshest day she could ever imagine.

'Ruby.'

She felt a tug on her hand.

'Ruby,' he said, tugging again and dragging her gaze around to him. 'Don't worry. I would never, ever leave you alone with this. That's not who I am. And we haven't spoken yet about your family—telling my mother, your mother. We can do that together, if it helps?'

'I've already told her,' she said woodenly. She poured some water into a glass, then pushed it away.

'And?'

She looked at him. 'And what?'

'Was she happy for you? Is she going to be around when the baby's born?'

She wiped her hand in the air as if she was swatting away his silly idea. 'Oh, you don't need to worry about that. She'll be caught up with her own stuff.'

'How do you two keep in touch? Does she come to London much? You said she lives in Cornwall, right?'

'We manage on the phone.'

She didn't need to look up to see the frown cross his eyes. She felt his judgement unfurl like a blow and kept her eyes on the horizon.

'Right... I see. I suppose it's quite a commitment for her to travel up, but we'll work around that—and you've met my mother, so you know she's not the average stay-at-home type, although she'll want to play her part. But, hey, there's plenty of time to work all that out too. More tea?'

She shook her head.

'She'll be all right about it, you think?' she said, an image of his mother coming into her mind. She wasn't the type of woman who'd let herself get into trouble. She was a super-powered, super-organised over-achiever whose every second seemed to be planned and executed with complete precision.

Coral Rossini was going to judge her too, and at best she would look like an idiot, at worst a scheming gold-digger.

This whole situation was getting worse and worse.

'Can we start to go back to shore now?' she asked, looking round. 'I have to get back.'

He stood up. The look on his face was something she couldn't quite read. Frustration?

'Sure,' he said. 'We'll stop at one of the little islands on the way. It'll only take an hour or so and they're so pretty. Seems a shame not to show you this part of the world while you're here.'

She opened her mouth to complain.

'No buts. You've come all this way. You're my guest and I want you to have a little fun before you go back.'

He walked around the table, his big frame and long legs somehow stepping gracefully between the chairs, until he was right beside her. She looked up, shielding her eyes from the sun until he stood directly in front of it, casting a shadow, close enough for her to see the creases in his T-shirt and the links in the strap of his watch.

'I'm not really in the mood for fun.'

He held out his hand. 'Come on, stop trying to punish me. I know you're mad at me—and yourself. But we had a good time. And now we need to manage the situation as best we can. We'll be fine.'

He pulled her to her feet. He encircled her in his arms. Held her close.

And she closed her eyes and let the sway of the boat and the heat of his body hold her still. Between them was the little life they had made, sleeping and growing, blissfully unaware, blissfully safe.

CHAPTER THIRTEEN

THE LAST TRACES of the Mistral whipped at the pines, sending green waves rolling across the tip of the island. Cicadas relentlessly announced themselves from bushes, and overhead the pealing calls of gulls carried tales of what they'd seen and warnings of what was still to come.

Matteo, sitting in a striped deckchair, put down his papers and raised his sunglasses for a moment, straining to see a yacht that was dropping anchor out in the bay. Tiny figures scuttled around, then one by one jumped into the dinghy that would take them ashore.

Ashore to this haven—the exclusive Ile-St-Agnes, ten square kilometres of verdant land, home only to teeming wildlife and the ultra-rich. Its single hotel, reached only by chartered yacht, was where Ruby had eventually agreed to come ashore, to have a little stroll and now to rest stretched out beside him, under a parasol on a fat-cushioned lounger.

It had been years since he'd been here—years since the annual holidays he'd spent there in his early childhood. He glanced at the little pool where children splashed noisily, and at the few people lying on loungers around the edges. That had been his parents once, with Claudio and his 'girlfriends'. Drinking martinis and smoking cigarettes, laughing and having fun together—the glamorous couple and their glamorous friends, the toast of the Riviera in their day, intact in their little bubble of happiness, years before the whole thing fell apart.

A waiter walked across the scene with a silver tray. He stopped to serve wine to an older couple on the terrace, sedately dressed, enjoying their lunch. Below them, on the loungers, a movement caught his eye—two women, sleek in their Saint Tropez tans. They'd been discreetly staring over at him, and were now doing it indiscreetly. They sat up provocatively, flirting, topless.

He turned his face deliberately away and looked at Ruby, who was watching with undisguised disdain.

'Friends of yours…?' she said, her dark eyebrows shooting up.

She scowled, turned her back and began to ease the red chiffon wrap from her shoulders, revealing a modest bikini beneath. Her waist was slightly swollen with their growing baby and her slim limbs glowed beautifully pale, obviously unfamiliar with hot sunshine. His heart surged with pride as he watched her.

'…they certainly look as if they'd like to be.'

He smiled at her snippy comment, watching as she squirted a dollop of sun cream on her hand and began to smooth it down her arms. As she attempted to rub her back the twin blades of her shoulders flexed accusingly.

'Allow me,' he said, reaching round and lifting the cream from her hands. 'And there's no need to sound jealous. I don't know those women and I don't want to either.'

'I'm hardly *jealous*,' she snapped back, 'It's nothing to do with me. I'm merely stating the obvious. They find you attractive and they're letting you know it.'

'You know what's attractive?' he said, as he pooled the cream in his hands and rubbed it over her shoulders. 'You being jealous and not admitting it.'

She lifted her ponytail and said nothing, compliantly allowing him to rub cream down over the twin blades of her shoulders and along the rim of her bikini. The fine bones and the ripple of muscle under her skin was a soft-strong combination he found completely seductive.

'Your skin is flawless,' he whispered in her ear.

'Hmm...' she mumbled.

He bent lower and smoothed all the way down her bumpy spine, fanning his hands out to cover her back.

'I'll be getting a lot more of it these next few months.'

'More beautiful, then,' he said, and he popped a little kiss on her warm cheek, lingering for a moment to savour the sensation of her hair and her ear as they brushed against him gently.

Oh, how he would have liked to linger there, he thought. But this was the exclusive Hotel St-Agnes, and she had already drawn her boundaries. Breaking them down was going to be a very enjoyable task.

He stood back and pulled off his T-shirt.

Twenty laps ought to cool things down for now.

He powered through the water, aware of the muffled voices of the children and the occasional snippet of conversation as he came up for air. Spending this time was a luxury he hadn't factored into this week. The aftermath of the Cordon d'Or was supposed to be spent tying up other bits of hospitality and calling in more favours.

He had some solid clients he needed to line up before he met with Arturo. Their influence would be crucial as he went forward with his negotiations. But all that was on hold because right now another plan was forming in his head.

Ruby was obviously pregnant. If he was lucky the media interest in him would soon have faded and no one would be any the wiser until after the event. But if he was unlucky, the ex-boyfriend of Lady Faye would still gather some mainstream press column space, and the last thing he needed was the media or the very devout Arturos casting aspersions on his character because of his pregnant girlfriend.

His mind was whirring with ideas and scenarios. His stress level was pumping higher and higher. He could feel it, buzzing around his body. All the while he was caught up with Ruby, who knew what Claudio was plotting down in Saint Tropez? It was enough to drive him slowly out of his mind.

He hauled himself out of the water and sat on the edge of the pool, feeling sunbeams hot on his shoulders. Ahead, one of the topless women sat up on her elbows and lowered her sunglasses to stare. To his right, a waiter served Ruby a glass of water. She lifted the glass and beamed her beautiful smile in thanks. His eyes fell again to her blossoming figure. Their child was there, growing. This on top of everything else.

The timing was like a torrent. Everything was coming together and he could sink or swim.

He had to conduct this like the symphony of his life. Save the bank. Keep Claudio at bay. And find the best possible solution for the new baby that would soon be in the world. Of everything, he felt this the keenest of all. Because he would not let the child down. It was unthinkable.

'Hey, come on, I'll teach you a little water confidence,' he said, leaping up and walking towards her, dripping water all over the terrace.

* * *

Ruby looked up from her daydream and saw the man who filled her mind. He was everything every woman would want. His body was protector and warrior and lover all at once. Water droplets were coursing down from his shoulders over his pecs in the way her fingers had that night—joyously, greedily. The hair on his legs hugged every building muscle in wet tendrils. His shorts were soaked, outlining him, and she could feel herself respond.

She wanted him. As fiercely as she had wanted him that first time. Yes, she was jealous of those other women, and probably all of the other women to come, but right now—today—he was hers, and she was going to claim him.

'I can't swim,' she said, staring up at him.

'Did nobody ever teach you? Doesn't matter—it's just confidence. Come on.'

He reached for her hand and tugged her gently to her feet and she walked with him, feet slapping on the warm tiles, over to the edge of the pool. Steps disappeared into the blue water and she stood, looking at them.

'Come on, dancer girl. Try it.'

'I'm not sporty like you,' she said, pausing. 'You seem to be able to swim and sail and play rugby. The only thing I'm good at is dancing.'

'The only thing you've *tried* is dancing,' he corrected, and he was right. 'There's more to life than ballet. Come on—trust me.'

He stood beside her, held her hand in his as she walked down into the water, her feet slipping slightly on the mosaic tiles.

'All you have to do is get in all the way up to your waist…'

They walked together into the empty pool. She started to laugh. Thankfully the little children had all gone for shelter from the harsh midday sun. Only a couple of sun-worshippers remained, toasting their bronzed bodies on the loungers.

'And keep walking until it comes up to your chest. Feel good?'

The water was gloriously cooling on her hot skin, and his hand round hers was rough and strong.

'Oh, yes,' she said.

'Feel the water drag at your legs. Now, let's walk in a circle...just get used to how it feels. OK, now hold on to the edge of the pool and flutter your legs up.'

She clutched on to the edge and stretched herself out, kicking hard against the water.

'And soak me too—that's no problem at all,' he said, laughing.

She turned to see him covered in spray from where she had splash-kicked.

'Oh, I'm sorry!' she said, and automatically let go of the side to reach for him.

As she did so she slipped towards him, and he caught her, there against his chest, holding her safe in his arms. Their bodies slid together, wet and smooth, and then it happened. Eyes met. She saw his mouth open for her kiss. She put her arms around his neck as he lowered his head down and kissed her. His wet lips and wet face found hers and it wasn't a gentle kiss—not for long. It was a branding. It was a demanding mark that said she was his.

She felt it deep within her heart even as her brain called a little warning. She was getting in way over her head again. But she couldn't fight it—didn't want to. Words formed and died in her throat as she let the

waves of passion pull her under, as she let his lips taste
and his tongue plunder.

'We have to take this somewhere else,' he whispered,
holding her close.

Her body was burning with sunshine and wet with
water and passion, and she had to hold on or she felt she
might slip out of his grasp and into the pool.

And then she was scooped up and into his arms, held
taut against his chest as he walked them out of the pool.

'I seem to have this overwhelming urge to carry you.
What the hell *is* this? I can promise you I've never lifted
another woman before, and yet I seem to have carried
you three times now. And counting.'

He waded out of the water and up the steps and she
didn't care if anyone was watching. It felt too good to
hold on, to be nestled against the wall of this man.

But when he didn't stop at their spot near the pool
she lifted her head. 'Where are we going?'

'We're going to take a little holiday, like I said. Beginning right now.'

They were inside the airy hotel foyer now. She could
feel the water cooling on her skin.

'*Madame* needs to lie down for a little while. In the
Presidential Suite. Arrange for our luggage to be trans-
ferred, please.'

Discreet staff opened doors. His footsteps sounded
dull and heavy on carpet. The light changed from bright
to soft. Sounds were muffled, then disappeared altogether as the door of the vast room closed behind them.

'Shower first,' he said, his voice a gravelly growl.

Still carrying her, he walked them through to the
bathroom. It was decorated as if from a previous century. Pale pink tiles and towels and white ceramics.
Brass feet and taps. The shower was over the bath, en-

circled in a white curtain, and it was there that she found herself standing as warm water began to drizzle and then pour over her body.

She looked at him, his dark hair drying in waves around his face, a smear of stubble on his jaw, and hunger in his brown berry eyes.

'You drive me wild, woman,' he said.

'Just how wild do you mean?' she asked, staring at his shoulders and his chest, and at the forest of hair that ran across it and down to his shorts.

And then he put his hands on them and tugged them down. She bit her lip at the sight of his magnificent arousal.

There was no way to stop now, even if she wanted to.

'*That* wild?' she said. 'May I?'

She dropped to her knees and held him in her hands. Water slid over her back and she slipped slightly on the surface of the bath in her rush to have the whole of him in her mouth.

He groaned aloud as she suckled him, her lips and tongue tugging furiously, somehow knowing just how to drive him on. Her other hand gripped his buttock and pulled him closer still. And she felt her power, was invigorated by it. Emboldened.

'Ruby, please. You have to stop.'

She pulled back, still licking and sucking, her eyes roaming up his fierce body to his dark tortured gaze. Then he reached for her and she was lifted to her feet. He undid her bikini top and released her tender breasts. Her nipples were erect and he put his lips to one, gently.

'Is this OK? Not too painful?'

She bit back a whimper and shook her head.

'Pain like this I can take all day long,' she said.

'Take these off. I want to see all of you. See if I had you right in my dreams.'

She paused as she shimmied out of her bikini briefs.

'You were dreaming about me?' she whispered mischievously.

He smiled that little half-smile and looked almost bashful.

She held his head in her hands, ran her fingers through the thick shock of hair, emboldened by each moment.

'Tell me. Were you dreaming about me?'

'Once or twice,' he answered, smiling up into her eyes. 'Probably not as much as *you* were dreaming about me, though.'

'I never gave you a second thought.'

He lathered soap in his hands, began to stroke all over her body, warming her and washing her.

'I didn't make much of an impression?'

She felt his hands slide over her tummy, her breasts, then gently in between her legs.

Her head fell back as he slid his clever fingers slowly backwards and forwards, rubbing exactly where she was swollen and longing for his touch. The sound of his hands slipping and sliding on her wet, naked body brought every bundled nerve screaming to life.

Then he cradled her in one arm and laid her over his lap. Her legs fell open and he slipped his fingers into the very apex of her thighs and kept up an insistent pressure while he lowered his head and thrust his tongue into her mouth.

And just like that she orgasmed—fully, powerfully, and with a suddenness that shook her to the very centre of her being.

She writhed and jerked and screamed. 'Oh, Matteo... oh, my God,' she called as the shock waves left her.

And then she was wrapped in a towel and carried through to the bedroom. Slowly he dried her, and kissed her drying skin, and then he knelt before her, proudly aroused and ready.

She sat up on her elbows, her mouth open in shocked delight.

'Is it all coming back to you now?' He smiled as he leaned over her, stretched his arms out, encircling her with his body.

'That you have the woman of your dreams at your mercy?'

He chuckled. 'You never give up!'

He nudged her legs open with his knee.

'I never do. I'm what people call "driven".'

'You're driving me insane right now, Ruby. That's for sure.'

And he thrust himself inside her and she watched as his face registered the pleasure. And then she felt it herself, as she hugged her legs around him and let go of all her cares and worries and fears as it became only her and him and nothing else.

CHAPTER FOURTEEN

'THIS PLACE IS AMAZING. I'd no idea these little islands existed. How did you discover them?' asked Ruby, sliding a forkful of delicious salad into her mouth and chewing happily.

It was dinnertime, and she was starving. They'd made love all afternoon and dozed until the sun began to dip and the light flooding into the sumptuous suite had turned from bright yellow to a gauzy orange.

His body was hers and her body was his. That was all she knew. She ached for him in a way she'd never believed was possible, but now, replete in his arms, she was aware of her mind starting to chatter its warnings. But she would not listen. She would not let those thoughts take hold.

Not yet.

She gazed across the candlelit table to where Matteo sat, lost in that world he disappeared into so often. His hair was swept back from his face and his smooth brow was gathered in a frown. The white shirt he wore was collarless, dipping low to the shadow of his chest, and loose enough to lend him the appearance of a brooding long-ago hero. She'd never seen him look more handsome.

He nodded out to the bay. 'We did a lot of sailing

when I was younger. There's not an inch of these waters we haven't been to at one time or another, the three of us—my mother and father and me.'

'Is there any sport you *don't* do?' she asked.

It was a flippant comment, and she almost regretted it, but his mood was slipping into serious waters and she still didn't want to navigate them. It was as if he was building up to say something. And she wasn't quite ready to hear it.

Even if they both walked away from today, they would be forced back together many times in the future. What kind of relationship would they have? One with hot sex and then flights in opposite directions? Or would he cut it dead and dread the thought of seeing her again? File her under 'No Further Action'.

Heart flipping and stomach churning, she forced a bright smile. They had to have a serious talk. She'd been pushing for it since this morning, but now that the moment was here she didn't want to spoil things. She wanted to keep the illusion going a little longer.

'Well? You swim...you play rugby. You box...'

He was looking steadily at her. He raised an eyebrow. 'I don't do ballet,' he said.

She caught the momentary flash of fun in his eyes and smiled back. 'Our child will. Especially if he's a boy. It'll be the making of him.'

'Now, that's an interesting thought.' He smiled. 'And will you be one of those overbearing mothers, berating the coach, or whatever they're called, because Matty Junior didn't get picked for the role of Sugar Plum Fairy?'

'You mean the ballet master,' she corrected him. 'And, yes, very probably. Don't tell me you won't be shouting at Little Miss Ruby from the touchline? What's good for the goose...'

'I can see we're going to have some interesting times ahead,' he replied, but it was quietly said, as if he was lost in other thoughts.

He touched his glass with his finger. There it was—his sign that he was ready to speak.

Well, all right. It had to come at some point.

She put down her knife and fork and waited for him to start. The restaurant was quiet, save for the sounds of the touch of silverware on china and muted conversation in the very best French. But still he remained silent, staring at the leaves on his plate.

'Not eating anything?' she asked, nodding to his untouched food. 'Or drinking? Don't you want any wine? You don't need to hold back on my account.'

'No. I've given up alcohol,' he said, and the ghost of his smile slid and died.

'For what? For health reasons? You're the healthiest guy I know. Surely a little wine won't do you any harm?'

He shook his head. 'There's a lot about me that you don't know. And you probably need to know if we're going to go into this thing together.'

Her ears pricked up at the word 'thing'. Her heart swelled with fear and hope in equal measures. And it was then, in that moment, that she realised that more than anything else she wanted to spend more time with him. Not just parenting time, but real time. Friends time and lovers time.

But he was a man who didn't commit. And she would never, ever beg any man for anything.

'My father had a difficult relationship with alcohol...'

He was staring at nothing, touching his glass again. The light from the candle flickered, daubing his face with ochre shadows, hollowing and saddening his features.

'I didn't know how difficult it was until he died.

He could go for weeks, months, without it, but when he got the taste he couldn't stop. It was like a demon inside, him making him drink until he had drunk everything dry.'

'Your poor mother,' was all she could say, suddenly imagining a young Mrs Rossini, her face troubled with pain.

He nodded absently at that. 'My mother could do nothing when he got like that—he didn't even know who she was. But he battled it. He went to rehab clinics. Three times. He took it head-on and he sorted himself out. We're fighters, me and him—you know?' he said, spearing her with a sudden look in the half-light.

She didn't know what to do with that look. She didn't know what he was saying—was he reassuring her? Warning her?

'But then the bank got into trouble and started losing clients. He didn't know why at the time, and for months he held it together...'

His face changed, saddened, and he dropped his head. It was as if her heart was being squeezed. To see such a man, so virile and strong and—kind...

She reached across the table for his hand, instinctively, and he looked up with surprise.

'But you're not like that,' she said, and then cautiously, 'Are you?'

'No, I'm not,' he said, and he drew his hand away and sat up straight, giving her a look right in the eyes. 'And I'm not going to risk it happening to me either. If I go down, the whole thing sinks. Banca Casa di Rossini is two hundred years old. And we're still struggling to recover from the sabotage that happened all those years ago.'

'I thought your bank was flourishing? You have all

these things—a jet and a boat and… Are you saying you're not…rich?'

It was the worst thing in the world to say. She sounded callous and selfish, but how could she avoid it?

He looked sharply at her. 'I am very rich and I intend to stay that way. I have responsibilities. As well as this baby I have my mother and my family name. The bank, the people who work for me. There's a merger almost on the table and I won't let anything get in the way of that.'

'I don't doubt you for a minute,' she said quietly. 'But what could go wrong? Are you saying that our baby is going to get in the way of your merger?'

'You saw those recent pictures in the press—us together, and me with other women—pictures from the past ten years? That was set up by someone who wants to discredit me and make me look like some kind of sex addict. Now, with you pregnant, they'll try to dig up even more dirt. And old Arturo isn't going to get into bed with a philandering sex addict.'

She sat back, her mind racing. 'Who's behind this?'

He shook his head and frowned. 'It's a long story. A guy called Claudio Calvaneo. My father's business partner.

His fingers clasped the glass tightly and he looked up at her, and it was such a penetrating look that she was held there, transfixed in his gaze.

'I'm going to need your help, Ruby.'

'To do what? This is way out of my league.'

He shook his head. 'The merger has to be handled with kid gloves. I've already had a first meeting and we're going to meet again very soon. All being well, there will be even more meetings in the coming months.'

She scanned his eyes as her brain raced to keep up

with him, but his face was set in that expressionless cast of rock again.

'Arturo's already seen you with me—thanks to Claudio's smear—and the minute there's a whisper that you're pregnant the whole thing could come down like a house of cards unless we have our story sorted.'

'You need to spell this out for me. I'm not really following.'

'He needs to see me as a serious guy, if he's going to entrust his company to me—someone who's sober and sincere about life and money. I can't be the kind of guy who gets a woman pregnant and then doesn't do the right thing. His bank means as much to him as Casa di Rossini does to us. More. It's the child he never had.'

The restaurant was now completely silent. Everyone had retired to other rooms and only a lone waiter moved through the space with a tray of glasses. Matteo's eyes tracked him as he exited, and then swung round to her, pinning her with his stare.

'I want him to think that we are more than just a casual fling. I want him to think that we are committed to one another, building a life together.'

'By "building a life" you mean…?'

'Totally committed to one another and our child. Marriage.'

'*Marriage?*' she blurted, and half-laughed, caught out by shock. 'Marriage—as in…?'

'I know what I'm asking of you is above and beyond—we barely know one another. But you're carrying my child. And I'm fighting for my life here—for many lives. This merger will see the bank in great financial shape—no one will need to worry about money again.'

He was up now, on his feet, leaning towards her. His shirt fell open, revealing a glimpse of his chest, and his scent hung like warm velvet on a cold night, wrapping around her, drawing her in.

'This isn't just for my future. It's for our child too.'

She shook her head in disbelief. This was too much to take in.

He was so close she could see tiny amber flecks in his eyes and the sleek lines of the eyelashes that encased them. His thick brown brows were knit in anticipation.

'I know I'm throwing this at you—asking you to take me on trust...'

'I can't get my head round this. You need to give me time to think.'

'There isn't any time. We have to do it *now*.'

'But how would it work? Not that I'm saying I will, but—'

He dropped to his knee and held her hands. 'I've worked it out. It's perfect. We can be married before the end of the week. Tiny, private—we can release a picture and take a few days' honeymoon, and then we'll head to Arturo's villa next weekend. You'll absolutely charm him. All his doubts will be gone.'

'But *marriage*,' she said. 'It's—massive. It's not something you can pretend, or turn off like a tap. What happens after next weekend? When I go back to London and you go back to work? There's no way we can keep it a secret then.'

'I'm not worried about after—that'll sort itself out. Whatever you want to do—I'm with you. But this is the single most important event of my professional career. This way the bank will be intact—not just for me, and our baby, but for his or her children too. Casa di Rossini will go on for years. My family will be secure.'

He was going so fast, was flying with ideas. She had to stop and think and be sure. She couldn't make the wrong choice now. It was the hugest decision of her life. Everything from here on in, every future step, hung on this moment.

'But there are other ways to be secure—and our child might not *want* to be a private banker. What then?'

He looked at her as if she was completely mad, as if she'd spoken in a different language, and she saw that he had no concept of anything other than his way of life. It was ingrained so deeply within him that all other choices were completely moot. And he wanted to drag her into it too.

She thought about her own path, how deeply she had been prepared to plough her own furrow, blinkered and refusing to see any other way.

'Matteo, maybe—just maybe—this should be left to fate to decide. You've been trying so hard for so long and maybe—'

'I can't leave this to fate. Not until I've tried every single thing I can do. And this—you being pregnant. I thought it was a disaster, but now I think it might just be the best thing for all of us.'

She narrowed her eyes. 'What do you mean?'

'I mean that having this added responsibility has made me even more focused. I thought Dad was going to live for another thirty years or more. I knew I was probably going to take charge—it was always hanging over me—but it seemed way off in the distance. Even when he died I really struggled to accept that this was my life now. But you…the baby. I know how my world has to be. I have to make this work. Don't you see?'

She opened her mouth but he shook his head and walked away, and there, framed in the restaurant window, he looked so terribly alone, set apart in his own tormented world.

And she had walked right into the middle of it. Could she leave him alone with this? She needed him as much as he needed her. Maybe even more. But this—this went beyond anything she had imagined.

Her head hurt as she tried to think. But her heart was sure. Even if it had been trampled in the process. Because how could she keep herself safe from falling in love with him? It was already be too late...

'What exactly do you need me to do next weekend?'

He spun around from the window. And suddenly he looked warrior-proud, invincible.

'Act like you love me.'

She felt a savage squeeze to her heart as his words made her gasp, and her eyes burned hot with tears. She bit her lip, forced her chin to steady. She kept her face to the floor, desperately clawing back her composure, furious at her own weakness.

He was totally oblivious. He moved closer still. Energy rolled off him in waves. She crossed her arms over her body, rubbed her fingers on her bare flesh.

'It doesn't have to be true, Ruby. I'm not asking for the world. But when you came to see me you wanted to force me to acknowledge the situation. You wanted me to give you cast-iron guarantees that I would play my part. Well, now I am prepared to admit that I will. I will give you way more than you wanted.'

'I only ever wanted one thing in my life,' she said, 'I only ever wanted my career and you need to know that that is still what I want. You're not seeing *my* needs in all this.'

He shook his head and moved right in front of her. The rest of the room—the view of the gardens through the half-closed roman blinds, the masts of the yachts and their white blooming sails, the world beyond—was blocked out. It was hard to think, to remember who she was and what she was, when he was so close.

'Ruby, you can have everything. *Everything.* Don't you want to marry me?'

'I'm not saying no, but does it have to be this way?' she pleaded. 'Do we have to be married to convince Arturo that you're the right person to take this merger forward? People have children together and live apart all the time.'

'He's very religious—for him there's no other way to raise a child but in wedlock, under the eyes of God.'

'But we would be living a lie—isn't that worse?'

'To give our child the stability it needs is *worse*? We'll sign a pre-nup. You'll get a house and a car and an income. As soon as the merger is secure we can decide what happens next. Where you live and what you do. A nanny. My name. All of that.'

His words were cold, transactional, black and white. There was no emotion or love or kindness or care. His heart was invested in his bank, in his dead father's memory, in a future that he didn't even want for himself.

And now she was a part of it too.

As she stared out at the balmy summer Côte D'Azur evening a chill of loneliness spread over her as damp and dark as all those nights in that frozen Croydon flat. The spectre was still there, whispering in her ear that she might *think* she had it all worked out, she might be *imagining* some shiny new future. But money didn't kill loneliness. Oh, no. She couldn't buy her way out this. It was only love that could do that.

Love that she feared and craved in equal measures. Love that had been like a forbidden fruit—just out of reach. The fleeting glimpse of her mother's smile, the squeeze of a passing hug. Those momentary touches that had spread sunlight through her and then been washed away, because there had never been enough to go round.

So she'd turned to the rapture of an audience and the warm delight of an aching body that performed perfection for them and the chance that maybe some day in that sea of faces, her father would call out her name Because that kept the sunshine there that little bit longer.

And now she wanted more. She wanted to feel Matteo's love. She wanted to love and be loved in return. Marry him, live with him, have a child with him. Dance. And maybe, just maybe, be a good mum…

She wanted to know how it felt to be loved for herself. Not for her smile, or her long dark hair, or her clever body. She wanted to be loved for being *Ruby*.

CHAPTER FIFTEEN

HE LET THE car window slide slowly down, then cut the engine. Warm, humid air pushed against his face and he reached for his collar, tugged the knot of his tie loose and flicked at the top button until it popped open.

Suits. He still hated wearing them and couldn't accept that he'd become one. Still never properly saw himself as that type. He'd hated being made to wear one as a teenager. Being choked in the suffocating confines of grey gabardine had *not* been his idea of a good time.

And he'd managed to avoid wearing them right up until his father's funeral. By then there had been no choice—and how much worse could it have been anyway? He'd started learning to fill his father's shoes before the hard, lumpy earth was scattered on his coffin, and he was still learning. Still a work in progress.

He got out and stretched his legs. The drive up from London had been sweet and smooth, and he was just in the mood for a little wander round the lake and then up to the house where the British Ballet held their summer school. And where his beautiful wife-to-be would be waiting to meet him.

He lifted his jacket from the back seat, slung it over his shoulder and began to move along the driveway to-

wards the patch of blue lake, lying flat and still like a
bright blue eye in a green face.

A flurry of girls just like a little Ruby flew past him
down the sweep of stone steps, hair scraped back in
buns and slim as flamingos. He tried to work out their
age. Six? Seven? He had very little idea when it came
to things like that. He had very little idea about children at all, but after years of regarding them as something he could barely tolerate, the idea of a little Ruby
to cherish almost felled him at the knees.

He couldn't imagine anything sweeter. To think that
his child would be born innocent, helpless and dependent on him, was almost drowning out every other waking thought. He felt like a warrior for this unborn child.
He would do anything and everything he could for the
little bundle of soft bones and tiny developing organs
he had seen on the scan with Ruby yesterday.

His little girl.

For years he'd positioned himself as a confirmed
bachelor. How he'd scoffed at other men, scorned
their happy family weekend stories, derided the dot-
ing daddy photographs in their wallets. He'd been su-
perior to all that. He'd never get caught out. He was
too damn smart.

But when he'd seen that image…

Life would never be the same again. He was sure
of that. He only wished he could be so sure of Ruby.

He'd watched her at the scan, lying on the bed. As the
consultant had put the image on the screen he'd watched
her eyes flicker and widen with surprise. She'd turned
pale, and her mouth had tightened into a worried line,
her hands into fists. If he hadn't known any better he'd
have said she was terrified. But that didn't make any
sense. Women *loved* babies.

He'd tried to hold her hand, but she'd pulled it away. He'd tried again—reached out to touch her stomach—but she'd literally flinched.

He'd tried to jolly her along after the consultant had left the room, but it had seemed as if she was caught in a trance. And unable and unwilling to jump out of it.

They'd travelled back to the penthouse in a silence punctuated only by the business calls he'd had to take—calls he'd been able to do nothing about, stoking the flames of the Arturo deal, keeping the embers warm so he could pick it up again after the weekend. How could he not? And as he'd done so he had felt her moving further and further away—as if she was walking away from him in a blizzard, swallowed up into another world, hidden from sight, muffled, unreachable.

He'd insisted on the scan the moment they'd arrived back from Ile-St-Agnes. He'd thought it would bring them closer—he'd thought wrong. He'd assumed she'd move in with him immediately—but no. In the three days since they'd got back they were still working on that. She wanted to stay independent, living in her little flat until they left to be married, even though that was only in two days' time.

So all he could do was wait. And plan. And hope that in these moments when the enormity of it all reared up like a wall of men battling in a scrum—a force so physical that he felt he might be crushed, as if with one wrong move, one moment of weakness the whole thing could go—all he could do was pray. Because he'd never have the energy to fight like this again. There would never be another chance, when everything was laid out for him. It was now or never.

They were going straight from here—Birch Lodge, the beautiful old manor house set in its own grounds in the north of London, where the youngest British Ballet dancers boarded and attended lessons—to the airport, and then on to be married in private in Rome.

There would be a few guests—his closest friends, as well as his mother and David. Ruby hadn't wanted to invite anyone, and nothing he'd done to try and persuade her to talk about her father or contact her mother had succeeded.

It was a strange relationship, he had to admit. They seemed to be as distant and he and his own mother were close. But he wasn't going to judge. How could he? As long as Ruby and the baby were OK, his mother had enough love to go round.

He turned from the still, glassy lake as another flurry of movement caught his eye. This time the children were definitely older—early teens. Boys and girls. He watched them, curious to see their fresh-faced youth, their lithe, strong bodies. He probably hadn't looked much different himself once...

'Matteo!'

He looked round at the sound of her voice and there she was. And, God help him, even at thirty paces he could feel the punch of that smile like a squeeze on his heart. Because now he could read it. He could see that it wasn't full and free. It was a smile of greeting, but not of welcome. She could smile brighter and better and bolder than anyone he had ever met, but there was always something held back, something hiding behind it.

But when she really smiled—when he made love to her and she lay warm in his arms, when she forgot all about her troubles and he saw who she really was—that was when he felt as if he had pulled her back from the blizzard and brought her indoors, set her by the fire.

And he'd watch as the roses bloomed in her cheeks and the sparkle shone from her eyes.

'Hi,' he said, striding over the grass towards her, never taking his eyes from her where she stood on the top step, looking down at him.

She opened her arms wide—gracefully, hypnotically. 'Beautiful day,' she said, indicating the grounds.

'Even more beautiful now,' he said, walking right up to her and putting his arms around her, folding her to him and loving the way she melded into him so perfectly. Their bodies, so different, somehow fitted together like two halves of a whole. He placed a kiss on her cheek, and then on the other, and then, because he wanted more and he didn't care who saw, he took one from her lips.

She smiled. 'I have a reputation to maintain here, you know.'

'I know,' he said, tucking her under his arm and walking them down the steps. 'How were your classes today?'

'I'm getting to really like it. Having all those little faces staring at me, trying to help them without criticising… And the feeling when they get it right is amazing. Almost as good as dancing itself.'

'You must be a natural.'

'Oh, I'm not a natural—far from it. I just love dancing and so do they.'

Just then the crowd of little girls came rushing up the grass, back from their afternoon break. They crowded around Ruby, jumping up and down, giggling excitedly.

'Where are you going?'

'Are you coming back tomorrow?'

'Please come back and teach us again—we had so much fun.'

And then they all swarmed off, like a cloud of starlings.

'You see, you're a natural,' he said solemnly, nodding and then he squeezed her hand to underline his message. 'Just like you're going to be with our little one.'

They walked towards the car, and he felt her fingers weaken in his grip as silence descended around them again. But he wasn't going to let it take hold of her. He was going to power through. He could not afford for her to get cold feet.

'We're all set for the weekend. We'll go from here to the airport and land in Rome about seven. My mother will arrive about midnight, so you won't see her until tomorrow. Ceremony's set for eleven...'

He paused, stole a quick glance at her over the roof of the car. But her face was hidden behind huge sunglasses and her mouth gave nothing away.

'I spoke with Augusto this afternoon, too. We're expected there next Friday, by which point we'll be married...'

She was pulling her seat belt across her body with infinite care. He started the engine and nosed the car along the driveway.

'Which is just as well because it turns out Claudio is going to visit them immediately after us.'

He turned sharply to look at her, to see her reaction. There was none.

'So anything he tries to say—any dirt he tries to dish up—we'll have covered all the bases. We'll play the happiest, cutest newlyweds this side of the Apennine Mountains. And there's nothing Arturo loves more than a young Italian family and all that promises to follow. Kids and houses and happily-ever-after.'

He turned again to see her, but she had turned her head to stare out of the window.

He reached for her hand, squeezed it. 'Everything OK?'

'Yes, of course. Obviously I want to get back to work as soon as I can. Now that I'm getting into it I really don't want to go disappearing for long.'

'Obviously,' he said, turning resolutely back to face the road. 'It should all be tied up one way or the other in about ten days. That's not too long to be away, is it? It *is* your wedding, after all.'

They rolled along in silence but he could hear her thinking as clear as day.

It's not a real wedding, though, is it?

And he knew that. He knew it all the way from his overloaded brain down to the sick feeling in the pit of his stomach. What he was doing was wrong. It was wrong to make her do this. It was wrong to bind her to him like this because he wanted this merger so badly.

But, more than that, he wanted his little family.

Yes, he did.

He wanted his little girl and he wanted her mother. And he was prepared to do anything to get it—because he had to. He had to make this work. He had to move those wheels, push all those pieces into position himself.

It was the long game—and he'd been playing it his whole life. If he didn't push on with this, then what? The bank would sink into oblivion and this woman would disappear off and some other guy would marry her.

No!

He slammed the steering wheel with his open hand so suddenly that the car veered slightly off the road and Ruby turned round, alarmed.

'What's wrong?'

'I'm sorry—I didn't mean to do that.' He shook his head, furious at his lack of composure. He could not allow cracks to show. Not anger, not alcohol, nothing. 'Ruby, I really want this to work.'

'I know you do.'

'No, I mean *really*. I really want this to work. It would mean the world to me. I've never properly come out and said it, but I can't get it out of my head. You and the baby. The bank. Everything.'

'There's no reason why it shouldn't,' she said quietly. 'You've done everything you could.'

He heard the wistful tone in her voice. The note of self-sacrifice was like a soprano's aria, cutting through the crystal of his own determination. She was sacrificing everything for him and their baby. Her career was effectively over for months. All she could do was cling on to the company by teaching at the school.

And what of them? Of their relationship? It was as vulnerable and beautiful and new as the baby growing inside her. He would do anything to nurture it and bring it fully to life. He wanted to do the right thing for Ruby, but that meant doing this first. Doing his duty. Once all that was dealt with, then he could finally relax...

'You know this won't last for ever,' he said, trying to cheer her up. 'We'll come out the other side and get back on track with our lives.'

'Yes, I know.'

'I won't hold you back, Ruby. I want you to be happy too. I want both of us to get what we want out of this. Your career, the bank secure, Claudio a distant memory—all of it.'

'And you really think that your having the biggest, most successful private bank in Europe is going to make Claudio disappear? Don't you think that if the merger goes ahead he'll find even more reasons to hate you? From what you've told me about him, I think he'll make it his life's work to destroy your bank. This isn't going to make him go away—it's going to make him worse.'

Matteo frowned and shook his head as he spotted the signs for the airport and turned off.

'No,' he said, dismissing the thought. 'He'll leave well alone. And anyway—this isn't about him. This is about doing the right thing for the Rossinis. I've got to get the bank—'

'Back to where it was,' she finished for him, in a resigned voice. 'I know. I get it. I just wish *you* did.'

She'd muttered the last words under her breath, but he'd caught them. Why was she being like this? His plan was sound—solid. Why was she poking holes in the one thing that he knew was completely right?

He parked the car, cut the engine and got out. He walked round the other side to help her out, but she was on her feet and had slammed the door already.

Hearing the roar of the jets and feeling the warm summer wind whipping at his face, he followed her into the building.

'I don't expect you to see it like I do, Ruby. Nobody can know what it has been like.'

In the cool air-conditioned lobby she spun to face him. 'You were a *rugby player*, for God's sake, Matteo. You're only a banker because you were forced to be, and you're never going to be free of this until you give it up. Just give it up! You're running face-first into a wall that you've built for yourself when you should be running in the opposite direction.'

She pulled her sunglasses off as she spoke and he saw tears in her eyes and anger pinching at her mouth.

'I don't need you to marry me. I can cope perfectly well without all this. I'll get by—you don't need to give it a second thought on my account.'

'What are you talking about? When did I ever give you the impression that I don't want to do this? You've got it totally wrong. This is bigger than both of us. I don't have any choice. There *is* no choice!'

As he said the words he heard himself. But there *was* no choice. There wasn't...

'There's always a choice,' she said quietly. 'You just can't see it.'

The nose of a jet pushed into view on the Tarmac. Three uniformed staff in pristine navy and white walked past, trundling little carry-on cases. His phone buzzed in his pocket. He turned away and pulled it out.

'David,' he said. 'What's up?'

'I thought you'd want to know. Your stock has just gone up—I've heard from the Levinson Group that they've finished with Claudio's operation and they're moving back to us. And with them will come others. You're in a really strong position now to go into the final stages of negotiation with Arturo. But you'll need to come back as soon as you can to keep this moving. Can you do a dinner tonight? And some meetings on Monday? I know you wanted me to keep a few days free for your little holiday, but this is all happening now and we can't afford to miss a trick.'

'Great—of course I can. That's amazing,' he said, looking at the retreating back of Ruby, at the long pony-tail defining the perfect symmetry of her perfect body.

Her posture was graceful and proud in every movement. She smiled as she handed her passport to the ground crew, and her eyes, as they flicked to him, held that secret dark promise that he still couldn't read.

And he was going to marry her. He was going to marry that woman because he damned well wanted to have her in his life. He wanted to be with her. It made him feel good. It made him feel happy and hopeful and as if there was a point to life.

Things were coming together. A beautiful, perfect fit. He was going to pull this off. He was going to be a father.

He was going to be a husband.

CHAPTER SIXTEEN

THERE WASN'T A sound when Ruby woke for the third time, alone in the antique brass bed, swaddled in the finest cream linen sheets. She'd barely slept, but already the brightening tones of morning were pushing against the windows and seeping in through the heavy drapes. She reached an arm out to check the time on her phone. Six a.m. Five hours to go.

Five hours until her life changed irrevocably—though hadn't it changed already? Hadn't it changed the moment she'd put on that red dress, opened that bottle of beer and shared the story of Rumi's poetry on that flight from Rome to London with the most wonderful man in the world? There was no going back from that moment—because that was when she had fallen completely and hopelessly in love with him.

Nothing else and no one else would ever have induced her to step from her path—her blinkered, stubborn path that had been going nowhere other than forward into loneliness. But at least then she had known every step—she had been sure where her foot would land, where her path would eventually lead.

Now she was on some slippery path, in a changing landscape that made her feel giddy with excitement one minute and sick with dread the next. So she was marrying him—she was going to do the one thing that Lady Faye had wanted more than anything else. But they weren't marrying for love. They were marrying for the sake of a baby. And a bank.

She traced the patterns on the ceiling with her eyes. The ceiling of the room that from here on forward would be her bedroom in Rome. In a house that she would never have been able to afford as a dancer—even as the prima ballerina in one of the world's best companies. Even as a director...

From along the hallway the noises of the day started to sound. Unfamiliar voices were talking in an unfamiliar language. They hadn't seen a soul last night when they'd arrived at his home. The flight had been short but the dinner with Matteo's clients had been long—delicious, but long—and despite his apologies, and his thanks for agreeing to the last-minute change of plan, she'd felt exhausted when he'd finally slid the key in the lock of his Roman villa and they'd quietly made their way to bed.

He'd made love to her. Romantically, passionately, adoringly. And then he'd slipped off to another room for the sake of tradition—as if their marriage was somehow real. As if she was going to have something old and new, borrowed and blue too. And a father to give her away, a mother to weep, and bridesmaids to throw her bouquet to. And a happily-ever-after.

The wincing pain of self-pity cut at her, making her crush her eyes closed. Because even though she'd been in denial about her deepest wishes, now that they were finally coming true she wanted even more.

But she was here in Rome, healthy and comfortable and with more choices than she'd ever had before in her life. She could work, rest, have the baby, then go back to work, back to dance.

The only thing she couldn't do was make Matteo love her. Or make him love himself.

There was another noise now—closer, outside the door.

'*Prendo che.* I'll take that.'

She strained to listen and had just figured out that it was Coral Rossini's voice when the door was opened and in came the lady herself, carrying a tray.

Ruby sat bolt-upright, totally shocked by the interruption. She'd known she would have to see her new mother-in-law at some point—but *now*? Like *this...*?

'Good morning, Ruby!' She came right into the room, put the tray down and opened first one set of curtains, then the other. 'Sleep well?'

Ruby pulled back the sheet and tried to get out of bed.

'No, no, stay there—you have to have breakfast in bed.'

Coral Rossini picked up the tray and came over to the bed, the fresh morning light streaming in to reveal the golden glow from the African sun on her well-tended skin and eyes that were penetratingly bright and clear.

Ruby watched her warily. What was her tone going to be? Would she hate her, thinking that she had trapped her beloved son? Would she be cool and condescending? Or the same old Coral who had sparkled and charmed every other time she'd seen her?

She put the tray down and sat beside it on the bed, her gaze never shifting. 'It's your wedding day—and I'm here to look after you. But first,' she said, 'let's have a proper chat.' She poured tea from a modern silver pot, one cup each. 'Milk?' she asked.

Ruby nodded, sat up straighter, took the cup, cleared her throat and said, 'Thanks…'

'Well, I'll bet neither of us could have imagined we'd be here a few weeks ago. But here we are.'

'Coral, I want you to know that I really and truly did not mean for any of this to happen. I hope you don't think…'

The older woman sat back and looked at her carefully. 'No. I don't think. So just stop there. I have known you since you were a teenager—since Banca Casa di Rossini started to sponsor the company and I started coming to see you and all your lovely friends rehearsing and performing and pushing yourselves to the limit. I know what dancing means to you.'

Coral reached for her hand.

'I know, Ruby,' she said, quietly. 'I know your mother moved away. And I don't want to pry, but everyone needs a mother and I'll be yours, for as long as you want me to be.'

Ruby felt her throat burn and her eyes sting as she choked back the surge of emotion that gushed forth inside her. She pursed her lips hard and nodded. 'Thanks,' she said, returning the squeeze on her fingers.

'It's my pleasure. Just love my grandchild and love my son. Don't assume that they won't need you, because they will. They *will*. And we won't give up on you. We're your family now.'

Ruby stared at her. How did she know? How did this woman know that her biggest fear in the world was that they would give up on her because they'd realise, like everyone else did, that there was something unlovable about her? How could Coral open her mouth and say aloud the words that she, Ruby, couldn't even bear to think?

What was she going to do if it all fell apart?

In ten short days she'd gone from being terrified that she would be left alone to look after a baby to feeling terrified that Matteo would realise he could do it all without her.

All her life she'd been so sure that she could tough it out alone, but the moment Matteo had walked into her life nothing had felt sure any more. She'd thrown caution to the wind and slept with him, and now she was pregnant by him and getting married. Her rules and boundaries were looser than the curtains wafting in the breeze.

'I know,' Coral said, sipping her tea but never taking her eyes from her, 'that had things been different—the baby, this merger with Arturo—we might not be sitting where we are right now. But Matteo is very fond of you. I've no doubt about that. And what you're going to do today shows me that you are very fond of him too.'

Ruby stared at Coral, desperately keen to tell her just how much he meant to her…how he made her feel alive…how he understood her like no one had ever taken the trouble to do before. How he'd made her begin to feel strong and sure and confident about raising a child.

'He'll be a great dad,' she said. 'He'll do everything for the baby.'

'Exactly,' said Coral, smiling. 'That's exactly what I think too.'

They sipped their tea in silence for another moment. Then Coral spoke again.

'Family is very important to us. Your child—my grandchild—is going to be brought up in a loving family. And you, lovely, sweet Ruby, are going to be part of that loving family'

Then she lifted the cup and saucer, lifted the tray, put it down carefully on the floor and enveloped her in the firmest, surest hug. And Ruby felt something thaw in the deepest, coldest corner of her heart. She squeezed her back, sealing a heartfelt promise and knowing that another little sliver of rainbow had spread its colour in her life.

'Now, let's get you looking even more beautiful. If that's possible.'

Calvaneo Capital's London headquarters sat on the top ten floors of one of the tallest skyscrapers in Canary Wharf. The lift was fast and efficient, and already crowded with people in the uniform navy and grey of the world's financial elite. It was eight a.m. GMT. Three hours before Matteo was due to make his vows in Rome.

He was in no mood be kept waiting.

He stepped out at the fiftieth floor and made his way to the reception area. He stood out from the throng, as he always did, his hair longer, a foot taller, broader. But it wasn't just his body that set him apart today. The white rose and the morning suit raised eyebrows and smiles in his wake.

He had phoned ahead, left a message, so the shape of Claudio coming along the teak-floored, glass-walled corridor towards him was no surprise. But the sight of him still made his heart pump and his fists clench and bile rise in his throat.

'Matteo. How kind of you to drop by.'

He looked older, his skin lined, but well preserved. The hair slicked back from his face was a peppery grey, where it had once been black, and his jacket was buttoned over a paunch where before there had been a well-defined six-pack. But other than that he was exactly the same.

'This isn't a casual call, Claudio. As you can see I'm getting married later today, so I won't be long.'

He walked straight past Claudio to the doorway he'd seen him emerge from. The gold letters of his name etched in the glass confirmed it as the CEO's office. He walked right in and looked around.

It was a room for entertaining as much as business, laid out like a nineteen-twenties lounge, with overstuffed stylised furniture, beautiful objects and silver-framed photographs of the rich and the beautiful, clients and friends.

He turned around. 'For someone who's stock is spiralling out of control, you're looking remarkably calm. But then you're used to bad news, being the cause of so much of it.'

'You came all this way to tell me how calm I look? Why, thank you. You look very well too. Very handsome. Your father would be proud. I feel compelled to say that.'

Claudio spoke in Italian, the language his father had spoken to him. Matteo ignored it.

'New York closed with a ten percent decline in CC stock and London is just about to open. Tokyo will do so later. Your investors have abandoned you. You're done. By the end of the day you're not going to look so calm.'

Claudio merely shrugged. 'Again, your journey is wasted. The only pleasure is seeing you here. So much you remind me of Michele.'

'My father loved you, Claudio. My father loved you and look what you did to him.'

He hadn't known what he was going to say, had only known he needed to say something, but seeing the shock on Claudio's face he knew that he had hit the mark. Tears formed instantly in the man's eyes and his jaw clenched as he swallowed hard.

'He loved you. And my mother—and me. He was a good man who only wanted the best for all of us.'

'You didn't come here to tell me that. Why don't you say what you really want to say?'

'That I hate you? What good would that do? I've spent years doing that. Hating that you brought out a side of my dad that I never wanted to believe was true. But it was there, and maybe what you had together was beautiful once, but what you turned it into was sick and shameful, and you'll have to live with that for ever.'

'Michele was a coward…'

'He was my father,' Matteo said, launching himself across the room and grabbing Claudio by the collar in his two fists, bringing their faces inches apart. 'And my children will be brought up respecting his memory.'

Claudio was the coward. The fear was real in his eyes. Matteo shoved him away.

'Good luck in finding anyone who'll respect yours.'

CHAPTER SEVENTEEN

AT ELEVEN O'CLOCK precisely Ruby stepped from the bedroom and into the hallway. Light flooded down onto the mahogany floor...voices bubbled up from below. And panic clung to every fibre of her being.

'Go to the top of the stairs and then wait there,' whispered Coral behind her, resplendent in olive-green lace, scalloped-edged, knee-length and the perfect foil for her auburn hair.

Ruby looked at her fairy godmother-in-law, as she was beginning to think of her, and then, emboldened by her strong, unflinching presence, took the steps along to top of the stairway.

She looked at her feet in pointed cream satin shoes. Ahead a mirror showed her the image she still couldn't get used to. The dress—provided at short notice by the famous designer Giorgos, who just happened to be one of Matteo's closest friends—fitted her to perfection. Sleeveless, with a bodice cut sharply to reveal her collarbone, it dipped in a V that displayed a tiny hint of her cleavage. The empire line swelled into a tulip-shaped skirt, which ended mid-calf. Plain, simple, perfect. Her hair was piled high on her head, and a tiara of pearls held it in place.

The tiara was her 'old'—all the Rossini brides had

worn it, and Coral had taken the greatest care in settling it onto her head. Her underwear was the 'blue'—silk and lace—and the 'borrowed' was the pearl and diamond earrings from Coral, which hung in simple perfection from her lobes.

The 'new' was the tissue-wrapped stockings she'd smoothed onto her legs and held in place with a suspender belt she'd never dreamed in a million years she'd wear. But the effect was lovely. And the thought of Matteo unfastening everything later was delicious.

She clutched a tied bouquet of orchid stems and stood there at the top of the stairs, waiting while Coral skirted past her. Then, as a trio of strings started to play one of her favourite pieces by Bach, they both started to walk down.

At the bottom, in a veil of sunbeams, she made her way through a pale-carpeted corridor to the room where Matteo stood, waiting. He wore a simple dark grey morning suit, a shirt as creamy as her dress, and no tie. But a little ivory rose poked above his breast pocket. His hair was swept back from his brow and brushed his collar. He turned and his brown berry eyes beamed right into hers and his mouth burst into a warm smile.

Her heart thudded in her chest and her knees began to shake. The lump in her throat swelled and burned and tears threatened to spill from her eyes.

He saw her falter and a look swept his face. He turned round and with the full force of his body and the power of his stare drew her towards him, one step at a time.

My beautiful Ruby, he mouthed keeping his eyes trained on her. 'Absolutely beautiful,' he said aloud, when she took the final steps to him.

All she could do was nod as she took her place beside him for the wedding ceremony, barely aware of the rows of people behind and the indomitable Coral in her green dress by her side.

There were words and vows and rings, and despite no rehearsal he spoke clearly and confidently. And when he slid the solid gold band onto her finger she stared at it for a moment, almost unbelieving that it had actually happened.

Then he pulled her towards him and gazed down at her. And, oh, how she loved him—so much that she could burst. She loved his mind and his spirit. She loved his beautiful soul. She loved what he had done for her and she loved the thought of a future together with him. She could barely trust herself to hope her dream would come true. She loved him—loved every pore and nerve and fibre of his body. Only him.

He kissed her, and she told him with her lips how her heart beat only for him. And as he pulled back and smiled straight into her eyes, bathing her in warmth and tenderness, she knew he was finally going to say the words she had been longing to hear.

'Thank you,' he said. 'Thank you for making me the happiest man alive.'

Her heart flooded—but not with joy—and she fixed her smile into place. That was the moment. If he had felt love that was the moment he would have said it.

Coral rushed up to them, and then things swirled around her—from signing to smiling and posing for photographs. And the whole time she felt Matteo's arm around her shoulders or her waist, or his hand holding hers, whispers in her ear, stolen kisses.

'We'll get some pictures taken at the fountains later,' he said.

Her smile was still fixed. It was fine. This was how it was going to be. She loved him and he was happy.

'The happiest man alive.'

The most important thing was that her daughter was going to have a daddy. He was invested in their child. Coral too. She didn't need to worry.

But still that sickness spread through her—the terrifying fear that she would let them all down if she couldn't show love, be loved in return.

Matteo... What would happen when his deal went through? When he had his bank, his meetings and clients and charity benefits? When women would throw themselves at him?

He loved women. He loved sex.

He had married her, but only because he'd had to. He didn't *love* her. Not the way a husband really loved his wife.

And their daughter... What if she felt nothing for her child? What then?

She stood by his side on the terrace outside the room where they had just said their vows. In the distance the roofs of the Roman skyline spread out in a clutter of terracotta and gold all the way to the plains beyond. Flimsy white clouds trailed across the sky.

It was the perfect day to be married.

She couldn't wait for it to be over.

'Come on, Ruby, this is the happiest day of my life. You're my wife. We're going to have a baby. We're going to be happy. You're going to go back to your dancing. I can go back to sport—properly, maybe one day. We couldn't ask for more...'

He scooped her close to his body.

'Sweetheart, come on. Be happy.'

She pulled her smile as wide as it would go, made her

eyes sparkle, squeezed out a tiny chuckle. 'I couldn't be any happier. I'm just as pleased as you are. Everything is going to be great, I know.'

Suddenly his face fell. His mouth hung open unhappily. His eyes bored into hers so fiercely that she had to bite her lip and look away. He shook his head and pulled her inside, along the hallway and into a room.

'I know you. You're faking this. You're unhappy and you're making stuff up in your head. You're probably already planning how to get out of here.'

'No, I'm not,' she lied.

'Yes, you are.'

He stood there, this solid wall of man, and she knew that even if she closed her eyes she would still be able to feel him. His physical presence was like a power source for her now. She needed him so badly in order to keep going. Because if she was left on her own she would falter and fail. She couldn't leave now. She didn't have the strength any more.

'Promise me you won't go,' he said. 'Stay with me, Ruby, please. Don't take all this away. I need you.'

'I know you need me now. And I'd never abandon this after coming so far. But you won't need me for ever.'

'What are you saying?' he said, pulling her further into the room and closing the door. 'Of course I'm going to need you—our child will need both of us. Look at what we've got together. We have a brilliant relationship, we're totally compatible—we just got married, for God's sake. I know this felt like some crazy hare-brained scheme when we started, but it doesn't feel like that now, does it?'

'Come on, Matteo. If it wasn't for the baby we wouldn't be here.'

She turned away from his fierce gaze, stared past his shoulder at bookshelves full of ancient books piled high behind glass, at the dust mites that danced in the sunlight.

'Is that right?' he said softy. 'Come on. I want you to read this.'

He took her hand and walked her to the shelves. There he unlocked a glass cabinet. In it were rows of soft leather books, much slimmer than the rest. He pulled a black leather notebook from the end of the middle shelf.

'These are my journals. I've kept them since I was a kid. Occasionally I still write stuff down. This is the current one.'

He fanned the pages. Half of the book was filled with drawings and words; the other half was still empty. He looked at her and smiled. Held the book against his heart.

'You're in here,' he said.

They walked outside onto the terrace and down the steps towards the bubbling fountains. Shaded from the hot midsummer sun, they sat on a marble bench as the water sparkled in rainbows of spray all around them. He couldn't have chosen a more romantic spot, and her heart bubbled as much as the water around the stone nymphs.

'I've never let anyone read these. It's nobody's business. But this is about us, so it's yours too.'

She looked at it and recognised it as the book he'd been writing in on the boat.

He skimmed through it until he found the page he wanted. 'I wrote in this the day you told me you were pregnant. And the day after we met. And loads of other times too. Here—read.'

He opened it and handed it to her. She read what he had written in his decisive handwriting.

What a night!
   Arturo is hopefully going to land in our lap, and I discovered a love of ballet.
   OK, a love of a ballet dancer...
   Met a woman and almost fell for her. Beautiful, sensitive, sensual. I'm pretty sure I'll call her. Once Arturo is in the bag...
   First time I've felt like this in ages. Feel energised. Alive. Good times.

He took the book back, skimmed past more pages, then opened it again.

Can't get this woman out of my mind.

'So you can't pretend that this is all fake. This is the start of something wonderful.'

He looked at her with such kindness in his eyes, a kindness and warmth that she'd never seen from anyone before, and it felt like torchlight in the darkness—it felt as if she was being led in from the cold. Her heart thundered. It felt terrifying.

'You say that now, but you're hardly going to be here to be part of it. You're going to be away all the time, making deals and keeping people sweet, and pulling out the knives in your back that Claudio will be sticking in.'

He shook his head, all mirth wiped from his face like melting snow slipping into a river.

'We've still got a lot to talk about, but my days of being married to the job are over. I don't want to end up like my dad—though that wasn't just about the job.

If Claudio hadn't been so in love with him none of this would have happened.'

She stared open-mouthed. 'What do you mean, in love with him?'

'Just what I say. They were lovers. I found out after the funeral, but out of respect for Mum I haven't said anything to anyone.'

Ruby stared up at the laughing stone cherubs, their innocent cheeks plump under the streaming fountains. Her head swam with all this news. So that was what this was all about. Claudio's jealousy had been driving him all these years. And Coral had never told anyone about it. How could she tell people that her husband had been gay? That brave, spirited woman must have suffered so much. And no one had known. She was a force of nature—an inspiration. And now she was her mother-in-law, too.

'Are you saying that's what drove your father to alcohol?'

'I'm saying that my dad was mixed up. He put his whole life into the bank and his family, but there was something deeply unhappy in him, and in the end it's what's killed him. Now Claudio has just announced that he's gay—that's why some of those old clients have left him.'

'And some people can't accept that? How ridiculous. Of all the underhand things Claudio's done, he's now being punished for being himself.'

'Yes, and, much as I want to build up the bank, I don't want to schmooze with people who hate like that. So I've decided.'

She heard the words. And the silence that followed. She turned. 'You've decided what?'

'I've decided that if Arturo wants to merge, that's

fine. If he doesn't, that's also fine. Because I'm going to take the bank to market, make it public, and let someone else run it for a change. I'm not going to lose my life to it any more.'

She stared around the gardens. 'But what will you do? Are you going to go back to sport?'

He lifted her hand in his, wove their fingers together. The gold bands glinted in the sunlight.

'There are options—but that depends on you. We're going to have a baby. One of us is going to have to look after it while the other goes to work—that's how I see it. If you want to dance I'll stay home. If you want to stay home I'll go to work.'

The warm Italian afternoon was rolling on. Tall poplars swayed their ambivalence in the sunshine, this way or that way. Grass stood up in straight neat rows and the fountains bubbled contentedly. The Croydon park she'd once played in was a thousand miles from this. No gravelly play area, no graffiti walls, no mums pushing prams or sitting on benches, heads deep in their phones.

This life of sunshine was what her daughter should have—her grandmother and her father, sunshine and health. Happiness. Italy.

'You'll live here I take it…?' she said, her voice trailing off.

She couldn't speak any more, because the thought of what she would miss was choking her—her whole heart seemed to be tugging free and choking the very air from her body.

'I assumed you'd want to be based in England?' he said, turning her round.

She closed her eyes as she felt his warm, wonderful strength fold around her—her solid wall.

'Where do you want us to live? We don't need to decide right here, right now, but we're free to choose—we can be wherever we want. Ruby, we're free. *I* am free. For the past ten years I've been enslaved—as much as any of the slaves that fought in that Coliseum over there. Every day making myself do a job I didn't like, becoming a person I didn't want to be, showing disrespect to women.'

She looked up into his face and saw a brightness she'd never seen before. Hope shone from his eyes and his smile broadened widely. 'I'm so happy for you, Matteo. It must have been the hardest thing to decide, but it's the best news too.'

'I still don't think you get it, Ruby. This is the happiest day of my life. You have made me the happiest man alive. I don't care about anything else.'

He cupped her face, bent forward to kiss her, and it felt different. It felt like the most possessive, passionate branding of his love.

'Do you love me?' she heard herself say.

'Do I love you? *Yes.* I've never met a woman like you. I've never seen such passion and spirit. You've set me an example that put me to shame, and when I asked you to, you stood by me. You were prepared to do anything for me and our little family. I won't ever forget that.'

She swallowed. 'You told me to pretend I loved you. I didn't need to pretend.'

'Me neither. We've got our lives ahead of us now. We'll work out where we want to be and what I'm going to do—maybe I'll coach. Who knows? But as long as we both know that we'll put our daughter first in all we do—that's all I ask. She needs to know she's the most important thing in the world to us.'

Ruby nodded. She knew more than anyone that her life's work was going to be making her daughter know that, in every fibre of her being. She knew that her only medicine was to fill up her soul with love, not fear.

'My father...' she said. 'I've never told you—or anyone, for that matter—but I've never met him. I only know his name and his home town. Will you help me find him? I really want to contact him now.'

He tucked her close and she buried herself against him, smelled him, breathed him in, and with every second felt replete with the power of his love.

'I'm so glad you've told me that. We'll find him together. We'll work it all out together. And Coral is here for you as much as she is for me. For this one,' he said, stroking the soft curve of her stomach.

She smiled into his chest. Nodded. She finally knew. She whispered the words she now understood.

"Lovers don't finally meet someone. They're in each other all along."'

* * * *

ONE NIGHT WITH THE FORBIDDEN PRINCESS

AMANDA CINELLI

For Zara and Mia

CHAPTER ONE

'YOU WILL RECEIVE *a marriage proposal this week.'*

Olivia's ears still rang with her father's words, even as she moved through the motions of greeting the rest of the guests at the formal luncheon. It was not every day that your father informed you that you were set to marry a stranger, after all.

But, then again, her father was a king.

And the King clearly thought that the best time to impart news of this magnitude was no less than thirty seconds before he introduced her to her intended fiancé—a complete stranger. It was a wonder that she had managed to greet their guest of honour at all before she'd hurriedly made an excuse to leave.

Princesses were generally not permitted to sneak away during royal functions. Especially when that royal function concerned a very esteemed guest of honour from a faraway kingdom. Still, Olivia found herself making her way slowly across the room in search of fresh air.

'Another glass of champagne, Your Highness?'

Olivia stopped her progress and gracefully accepted the crystal flute from the waiter's hand, noticing the way his fingers trembled slightly as he tried to balance his tray. He was quite young—fresh out of school, she would bet.

'Is this your first Royal Races?' she asked, glad of the distraction while her eyes scanned the room, plotting her escape.

'It's my first day, actually. In general,' he replied.

'You are doing a wonderful job.'

She smiled, hoping her words might help to calm his nerves somewhat. It couldn't be an easy start, balancing priceless crystal while surrounded by some of Europe's wealthiest and most famous people.

'Thank you, Princess Olivia—I mean, Your Highness. Er…thank you.' He stumbled over his words, then smiled nervously, showing a mouth full of shiny metal braces.

Olivia smiled back with genuine warmth as the boy made a wobbly attempt at a bow and moved away. She sighed, taking a small sip from her glass. She would happily have spent the rest of the afternoon chatting with the teenager simply to avoid thinking of the bombshell that had just completely taken her by surprise. As if these royal functions weren't difficult enough.

The usual array of eager guests had predictably occupied her afternoon so far, with wave after wave of polite, banal conversation. Her parents, King Fabian and Queen Aurelia of Monteverre, stood at the opposite side of the long balcony surrounded by people and bodyguards. Her own personal security team stood at strategic points around her, trying and failing to blend into the crowd in their plain black suits and crisp white shirts.

The Royal Monteverre Races were infamous around the globe for their week-long parade of upper-class style and glamour. The historic racetrack was spread out below them, and thousands of guests had gathered in their finery for a day of sport and socialising.

No one's style was more closely watched than her own. Her morning had consisted of three hours being transformed by her own personal styling team. Her naturally wavy long red hair had been ironed and pressed to perfection, and her fair skin polished and highlighted in all the right places.

The public hailed her as a stunning natural beauty, but she knew the effort that went into upholding that image was far from natural at all. She was a public brand—a symbol for an entire country with her every single step followed closely by the whole world.

Even her older sister, Crown Princess Eleanor, was not given the same amount of attention. Perhaps it was because she was already married. The press took much more pleasure in the single siblings than they did in the 'taken' ones. And yet her younger sister had the excuse of her studies in London to avoid the limelight.

For the past five years Olivia had been very much at the centre of public attention—since taking her official role in palace life at twenty-one. She did not shy from the pressure—she had been trained for it after all. She knew to expect intense scrutiny. And yet there was nothing that could make her feel more alone than being surrounded by thousands of people who treated her like an ornament to be admired from afar.

A sudden crash jolted her out of her thoughts and she looked up with a groan of empathy to see that the young waiter seemed to have lost his balance and gone crashing into a nearby couple.

'You absolute imbecile!'

The roar came from an elderly duke, a close friend of her father, who seemed to have been the sole recipient of the tray's liquid contents. Shards of priceless crystal lay scattered across the floor in a pool of expensive champagne while the teenage server stood frozen with a mixture of embarrassment and fear.

'Have this clumsy idiot taken back to the schoolroom. Out of my sight!' the Duke spat, his eyes bulging as his equally outraged wife hurriedly tried to dry his sodden shirt with a napkin.

As Olivia watched with horror, a single bodyguard materialised from the crowd and took the boy roughly by the shoulders.

'Stop!' She moved forward suddenly, her body seeming to propel her towards the dramatic scene of its own volition.

'A princess should never concern herself with such matters.'

Her late grandmother's voice seemed to warn her from her subconscious. But she pushed the thought away, arriving by the boy's side and looking up at the burly guard with all the authority she could muster. A hush had fallen over the crowd around them.

'I think there is a better way of managing this, don't you?' She addressed the guard, then turned her attention to the elderly Duke and his wife. 'Duque L'Arosa, this young man is a friend of mine. I know he would appreciate your kindness on his first day of work.'

The Duke's eyes widened horribly, his face turning even more red as his much younger wife gripped his arm and snorted her disapproval. Olivia stood her ground, flashing her best royal smile as the guard immediately released the boy. The young waiter avoided her eyes as he hurriedly gathered his tray and rushed off in the direction of the kitchen.

Olivia became suddenly painfully aware of the quiet that surrounded her. Members of the Monteverrian nobility and various public and government figures all averted their eyes, no one daring to speak or whisper about a member of the royal family while she stood in their midst.

A strange sensation began to spread over her bare shoulders, and she instinctively turned her head and found herself pinned by the gaze of a man who stood a few feet away. He was remarkably tall—taller than most of the men in the room. Perhaps that was what had drawn her attention to him.

She tried to look away, feeling uncomfortable under his obvious scrutiny, but there was something about the way he looked at her. She was quite used to being stared at—she was a public figure after all. But his dark eyes seemed to demand her complete attention. It was quite inappropriate, she told herself. She should be annoyed. But even with the length of the room between them, having his eyes on her seemed to make her heart beat faster.

A strange quiver of anticipation jolted to life in her chest, making her want to close the gap between them just to hear how his voice sounded. She raised one brow in challenge and felt her heart thump as a sinful smile spread across his full mouth, making him appear all the more rakish and infinitely dangerous.

No man had ever looked at her that way before— as though she was a tasty snack he might like to sample. She shook her head at the ridiculous turn of her thoughts and forced herself to look away.

When she finally looked back he had vanished.

She steeled her jaw, nodding politely to the Duque and Duquesa before making a slow and graceful exit through the main doors. Her own personal team of guards made themselves known as she walked faster, all five of them closing in from their previous placements. She had never felt more frustrated at her newly heightened security than she did at that moment. There was no immediate threat—no need for the ridiculous new measures her father had put in place the week before.

'I'm feeling ill,' she announced to the men once they had exited into the empty corridor outside the racetrack's function room. 'Surely there is no need for all of you to accompany me into the bathroom?'

The men reacted predictably, coughing awkwardly before moving aside and allowing her to walk unchaperoned into the ladies' restroom. She searched the for an exit point, her eyes landing on a second door on the opposite side of the bathroom.

She smiled with triumph. Sometimes a little rebellion was necessary.

Roman Lazarov had never been particularly comfortable at high society functions. It had been sheer curiosity that had led him to accept the Sheikh of Zayarr's invitation to attend the Royal Races while he was already in Monteverre. Small European kingdoms were one of the few niche markets he had not yet entered with his security firm, as monarchies largely tended to keep to their own traditional models of operation. Old money aristocrats also tended to show a particular disdain towards new money Russians.

His fists tightened as he thought of the scene he had witnessed after only being in the room mere moments. Nothing made him feel closer to his own humble beginnings than watching a rich man treat his server badly. There was something particularly nasty about those who had been born to immense wealth. As though they believed the world should bend to their will and that those with less than them were somehow *worth* less as well. A sweeping generalisation, to be sure, but a painfully accurate one in his own experience.

The redhead had surprised him. She was clearly upper class—he could tell by the way she was dressed. Diamonds and rich yellow silk. He had noticed her the moment he'd entered the room. She had stood proud and untouchable near the centre, all alone, with her delicate fingers holding on to a champagne flute for dear life. And yet she had stepped forward for the servant and caused an obvious scene.

He should thank her, really. She had provided the perfect distraction for him to move on to his main purpose of business.

He would have liked nothing more than to stick around at the pretentious party and see if Lady Red lived up to his expectations. But really this brief detour to the races had been a mistake on his part. Time was of the essence when you had a royal palace to break into, after all…

The early summer afternoon was pleasant as Roman rounded the last bend on the dirt path, finally bringing the high walls of the palace into view. The overgrown abandoned hunting track wasn't the easiest route, but when you were about to break into the home of Monteverre's royal family you didn't usually use the front gate.

The forest was quiet but for the sounds of wildlife and the occasional creak of tree branches protesting as he methodically pulled them out of his way. Reaching the medieval stone wall, Roman looked up. It had to be at least five metres high and three metres thick—rather impressive and designed to be impossible to scale, especially when you weren't dressed for the occasion. He checked his smartwatch, zooming in on the small map that would guide him to the access point.

In another life Roman Lazarov had found pleasure in breaking the law. Bypassing even the most high-tech security system had been child's play for a hungry, hardened orphan with a taste for troublemaking. But in all his time in the seedy underworld of St Petersburg an actual palace had never made it onto his hit list.

That life was over now—replaced by a monumental self-made wealth that his young, hungry self could only have dreamed about. And yet here he was, his pulse quickening at the prospect of what lay ahead. The fact that this little exercise was completely above-board made it no less challenging. The palace had a guard of one hundred men and all he had was a digital blueprint of the castle tunnels and his own two hands.

The thought sent adrenaline running through his veins. God, but he had missed this feeling. When the Sheikh of Zayyar had first asked him for a favour, he had presumed it to be assembling a new security team for a foreign trip or something of that nature. Khal was in high demand these days, and his guard had been assembled almost entirely from Roman's security firm,

The Lazarov Group. But Khal's request had intrigued him—likely as it had been meant to. The challenge had been set, and Roman was determined to enjoy it.

As for whether or not he would succeed—that question had made him laugh heartily in his oldest friend's face.

Roman Lazarov never failed at anything.

The daylight made it seem almost as though he were taking a leisurely stroll rather than performing an act of espionage. He finally reached the small metal hatch in the ground that would provide the cleanest and most ridiculously obvious point of entry. An evacuation hatch, more than likely from long-ago times of war. He had hardly believed his eyes when his team had uncovered it on an old blueprint.

Although it looked rather polished and clean for a decades-old abandoned grate, he thought to himself, sliding one finger along the sun-heated metal.

A sudden sound in the quiet made Roman go completely still, instinctively holding his breath. He felt the familiar heightened awareness that came from years of experience in the security business as he listened, scanning his surroundings. Footsteps, light and fast, were coming closer. The person was of small build—possibly a child. Still, Roman couldn't be seen or this whole exercise would be blown.

Without another thought he took five long steps, shielding himself under cover of the trees.

A shape emerged from thick bushes ten feet away. The figure was petite, slim and unmistakably female. She was fast. So damned fast he saw little more than a set of bare shapely legs and a shapeless dark hooded coat before she seemed to pirouette and disappear through the hatch in the ground without any effort at all.

Roman frowned, for a moment simply replaying the image in his head. Evidently he was not the only one who had been informed of the hidden entryway. He shook off his surprise, cursing himself for hesitating as he made quick work of reaching the hatch and lowering himself.

The iron ladder was slippery with damp and led down to a smooth, square-shaped concrete tunnel beneath. Small patches of sunlight poked through ventilation ducts at regular intervals, giving some light in the otherwise pitch-blackness.

Roman stilled, listening for the sound of the woman's footsteps. She had moved quickly, but he could hear her faint steps somewhere ahead of him in the tunnel. As he began his pursuit a half-smile touched his lips. He had come here today tasked with proving the ineptitude of this palace's security, and now he would have a genuine intruder to show as proof.

This cat burglar was about to get *very* rudely interrupted.

Olivia held her shoes tightly in one hand as she slid her hand along the wall of the tunnel for support. The ground was damp and slippery under her bare feet—a fact that should have disgusted a young woman of such gentle breeding. But then she had never really understood the whole 'delicate princess' rationale. It was at times like this, after escaping palace life for even one simple hour, that she truly felt alive.

Her sudden disappearance had likely been noticed by now, and yet she did not feel any remorse. Her attendance at the international horse racing event had been aimed at the King's esteemed guest of honour, Sheikh Khalil Al Rhas of Zayyar. The man that her father had informed her she was intended to marry.

Olivia paused for a moment, tightness overcoming her throat for the second time in a few short hours. The way he had phrased it, as her 'royal duty', still rung in her ears. She was only twenty-six, for goodness' sake. She wasn't ready for this particular duty.

She had always known it was customary for her father to hold the right to arrange or refuse the marriages of his offspring, but she had hoped the day would never come when she was called upon in such an archaic fashion. But now that day was here, and the Sheikh was set to propose to her formally any day now—before he completed his trip.

Olivia pressed her forehead briefly against the stone wall. She felt cold through and through, as if she would never be warm again.

'*Drama queen.*' Cressida's mocking voice sounded in her head.

Her younger sister had always been such a calm, level-headed presence in her life. It had been five years since Cress had moved away to study in England. And not a day passed that she didn't think of her. With barely a year between them, they had always been more like twins. Cress would know exactly what to say to alleviate the unbearable tension that had taken residence in her stomach today. She was sure of it.

The tunnel was a straight path along the south boundary of the palace. It seemed like an endless mile before the staircase finally appeared. Olivia climbed it in the near darkness, relying solely on memory to make her way up to the partially hidden door in the stone wall. She pressed a slim crease, sliding open a panel and stepping through easily.

The brightness of her dressing room was a welcome shock of cream and gold after the prolonged darkness. She took a moment, breathing in the clean air, before turning to slide the secret door closed.

Olivia stilled at the sound of footsteps in the tunnel below. But that was impossible. In almost fifteen years of roaming she had never seen another soul down there. She had never even told her sisters.

She stepped back down to the small landing at the top of the steps. She braced her hands on the stone balustrade to peer down into the darkness, biting the inside of her lip. Had one of the guards followed her?

The footsteps suddenly disappeared and an eerie silence filled the stone caverns. Still she held her breath. *Eight, nine, ten...* Olivia exhaled slowly, cursing her overactive imagination. The silence of the tunnel tended to play with your mind after a while—she was clearly going insane.

She turned around to move back to the doorway to her apartment—only to be blocked by a wall of muscle. Warm muscle that smelled of sandalwood and pine.

Strong hands—definitely male—appeared like chains across her chest and turned her towards the wall. Her arms were pulled behind her and she instinctively pushed her body backwards, aiming the hardness of her skull towards her assailant's nose. Even princesses were taught self-defence.

'You have some skills, I see.'

His voice was startling in the quiet darkness. A

heavy accent made his threat even more worrying. This was most definitely *not* a palace guard.

Olivia hissed, turning away and trying in vain to pull against the bands of iron strength. She squinted in the darkness, trying to see his face, a uniform, an insignia—anything that might tell her who he was and why he was here. If she could remember anything from the Palace Guards' kidnapping talk it was one thing: *Don't say a thing.*

He pressed on what seemed to be a watch and turned a faint light downwards, lowering its beam to her over-sized black trench coat and bare feet. She had swapped her designer blazer with someone else's coat in the cloakroom before bolting. The vintage lemon cocktail dress she wore underneath was hardly ideal for going unnoticed in public.

She turned her head and caught a brief glimpse of a hard jaw and gigantic shoulders before he plunged them into darkness once more.

'You're not exactly dressed for a quick escape,' he mused.

She almost laughed at that—almost. But being held captive by a mysterious hulk of a man had kind of dampened her infamous ability to see the bright side of every situation. As far as she could see there was nothing positive that could come of being abducted, which was the only logical solution for whoever this man was. He would recognise her any moment now and the game would be up.

Perhaps they would ransom her, she thought wildly. How much was her life worth? Hopefully not too much…the kingdom was already facing complete financial ruin as it was.

She gulped hard as she felt his hand slip just under her left armpit—a strange place to grope, indeed.

'Don't! Don't you dare touch me.' She gasped, arching her body away frantically. He tightened his hold on her slightly, barely even noticing her attempts to free herself.

'You are in no danger from me,' he gritted. 'I must ensure the same can be said of you. Stand still.'

Such was the authority in his voice that she stilled herself. She held her breath as his touch moved almost mechanically to her hip. His movements were calm and purposeful as he did the same to her other side, feeling inside the pockets of her coat and underneath to slide along the indentation of her waist.

Her mind suddenly realised that he was searching for a weapon. She sucked in a breath as strong fingers brushed her ribcage, just underneath her breasts. Of all the situations in which to become excited by a man's touch, this really wasn't it. And yet her traitorous body had begun to respond to the intensity of the situation even as her heart thumped with fear.

His breathing did not alter at all, and nor did he show any signs of noticing her response. As his hand finally moved to her thigh Olivia could take no more. She kicked out. Partly in shock at his boldness, but mostly because of the discomfort of her own reaction.

She took a deep breath. 'Do you honestly believe that I'm hiding a weapon in my underwear?'

The stranger cleared his throat. 'I have known people to hide weapons in the most ludicrous places. Women especially tend towards a certain…creativity.'

'Do *not* put your hands on me again.'

He was silent for a moment, and the only sound in

the dark tunnel was that of their steady breaths mingling in the air between them.

When he spoke again his accent was more pronounced, his voice deep and intimidating. 'Tell me who you are and why you are attempting to break into the palace.'

She paused at that. So he hadn't recognised her yet. Surely if he was a kidnapper he would have come here knowing the faces of the royal family. Although it was dark, she supposed. Her choices were limited. She had no panic buttons down here—no guards within shouting distance.

She needed to get away.

She turned her head towards the door, breathing a little faster with anticipation as his shrewd gaze followed the movement and he saw the sliver of light coming through the gap.

'You managed to find a way inside, I see,' he said with surprise. 'Come on, then. Let's see what you were after, shall we?'

He held her forearm tightly, dragging her behind him up the steps and into the lavish dressing room. Her eyes adjusted quickly once again, to take in the rows and rows of her wardrobes. The room was empty, as it would be for a while, seeing as her staff presumed her to be at the races for the rest of the day.

Olivia gulped hard. She had just led an uncleared intruder right into the heart of the palace.

She took a moment to look at him for the first time in the light.

'It's you...' she breathed, realising it was the man from the racetrack.

To his credit, he also looked momentarily stunned as he took in her face in the light.

He was taller this close—almost an entire foot taller than her five feet three inches. All the self-defence classes in the world wouldn't give her a hope against such a brute. Dark hair, dark eyes and a jawline that would put Michelangelo's *David* to shame. He had a fierce beauty about him—as if he had just stepped off a battlefield somewhere—and he thrummed with vitality.

Her grandmother had always said she watched too many movies. Here she was, in very real danger, and she was romanticising her captor.

'You have taken a break from saving servants, I see.' His eyes lowered to take in the coat that covered her cocktail dress. 'You seem to be a woman of many talents.'

Olivia stayed completely silent as he spoke, knowing the more she said the more chance there was that he would put two and two together and guess her identity. She glanced to her left, searching the room for possible weapons for when the time came to run. If she could find something to kick at him, perhaps...

She looked down at her bare feet, cursing her own stupidity.

'We are in the south wing,' he mused, looking around the room. 'One of the royal apartments. How did you find out about the hidden tunnel?'

She shrugged, looking down at her feet and taking one tentative step away from him while his attention wandered.

'I saw how you slid down there. You knew exactly what you were doing. Just like you know what you are doing right now.' He grabbed her arm, stopping her progress.

She couldn't help herself then—she cursed. A filthy word in Catalan that would make her father blush if he heard her.

The stranger smiled darkly. 'We're going to get absolutely nowhere if you don't speak to me. Why are you here?' he asked again, releasing her arm and pushing her to sit down in the chair in front of her dressing table.

Exactly where she needed to be.

'I could ask you the same question,' she replied, slowly reclining backwards under the pretext of stretching her tender muscles.

'That's simple. I'm here for people like you,' he said simply, crossing his arms and staring down at her.

'People like me?' she asked breathlessly, her hand feeling blindly along the dressing table behind her for where she knew an alert button had been placed. She tried to calm her breath and prayed he would not see what she was doing. She felt a smooth round bump and pressed it quickly, holding her breath in case she needed to run.

No sirens sounded…there were no flashing lights. She moved to press it again, only to have his fingers encircle her elbow and place her hands in her lap.

'Keep your hands where I can see them.'

It was clear this wasn't going to be over any time soon.

He tilted his head to one side, looking at her in such an intense way it made her toes curl into the carpet under her feet. His eyes lowered, darkening as they swept down her legs.

The way he looked at her, the blatant male appreciation on his striking features, made something seem to uncoil in the pit of her stomach. She felt warm under his gaze and turned her face away in case she blushed.

'Whomever you think I am, I can tell you now that you are very wrong.'

His answering smile was raking, and made goosebumps break out across her arms.

The stranger bent down so that their faces were level. 'I think that, whoever you are, beautiful, you are a lot stronger and a lot more dangerous than you seem.'

CHAPTER TWO

'YOU SOUND LIKE quite the expert,' she purred, her cat-like eyes seeming to glow in her pale features.

Roman frowned. 'I can tell by your eyes that you're worried about being caught in the act, and yet you mock me.'

'You're quite arrogant and you deserve some mocking, I think,' she replied sweetly.

He fought the urge to laugh at this situation. Here he was, with a thief held captive inside the palace walls, and he was enjoying their verbal sparring too much to make a decision over what to do with her.

He couldn't simply waltz up to the King's offices and present him with this gift. Problem one being that the King was out of the palace today, along with the rest of the royal family. Problem two being that the Palace Guard had no idea he would be here today. As far as they were concerned he would be just as much a criminal as the sharp-tongued redhead who sat staring at him as though she'd like to claw his eyes out.

He would have to call Khal and tell him that their plan had encountered a minor diversion. It was no matter, really. He had identified a serious security blind spot and provided the Palace Guard with an attempted burglar to boot. All in all, quite a success.

So why did the thought of handing her over make him feel so uneasy?

He had got where he was by trusting his gut, and right now his gut was telling him that something wasn't quite right here. That this woman was not all that she seemed. Something made him pause, his brain weighing the situation up piece by piece.

'You are quite possibly the most ladylike thief I have ever encountered,' he mused. 'Do you always go barefoot on a job, or was today an exception?'

'You assume that I make a habit of this?' She glared up at him.

'Correct me, then.' He held her gaze evenly until she looked away.

'You have quite an intense stare. It's making me uneasy.'

She crossed one slim leg over the other. Roman felt his throat go dry, and looked away from the expanse of creamy smooth skin below her dress.

'I'm in the business of being observant,' he said, clearing his throat. 'You might benefit from it yourself, then maybe next time you won't get caught so easily.'

'I assume you are the almighty authority on how to break into palaces?' She raised her brows, sitting straighter in her seat.

'Seeing as you arrived here first, I disagree,' he countered.

'Oh, *now* I see. You're angry that you were beaten to the punch by a woman.' She placed both feet flat on the floor, smoothing her dress over her knees. 'This whole body-searching, intimidating act has all been one big ego-stroke for you.'

'I searched you because I am not so pig-headed as to believe that you pose no threat to me simply because of your sex.' Roman shook his head in disbelief, hating himself for rising to her bait. 'Why would you assume that the fact you are a woman has anything to do with it?'

She looked away from him then. 'Because it always does.'

'I think that's far more telling of your low opinion of men than anything else.' He raised his brows. 'Trust me, I am an expert in assessing risks. Women are not somehow physically destined to surrender to men. I have seen it first-hand. I have trained women, watched them down men twice their size without breaking a sweat.'

'You *train* women? To become…thieves?' she said with disbelief. 'Who on earth *are* you?'

Roman laughed, not bothering to correct her assumption. 'Let's just say I am the last person you wish to meet while you're on a job. Not just here, in this castle. Anywhere. I know how the criminal mind works. I have made it my business to be an expert in it.'

'So if I'm a criminal, you'll know what I am thinking right now?' Her eyes darted towards the door once more.

'I'm trying to.' Roman poised himself in case she ran. 'Just tell me what it is you're after and I can make this easier for you. Tell me your name.'

'No,' she said plainly.

Her body language was telling him that she was becoming increasingly more agitated with the situation. A flight risk if ever he'd seen one.

Even as the thought crossed his mind she jumped from the chair, her speed surprising him for a split second before he moved himself. She made it a few steps before his arms were around her waist, holding her body tightly against his as she struggled in vain.

'Please—just let me go,' she breathed.

The fear in her voice startled him, but his training had taught him not to release anyone until he had another means of restraining them.

'You are making it very difficult for me to help you here. Do you know that?' he said, holding her arms tightly to her sides and trying in vain to ignore the delicious scent of vanilla that drifted up from her hair.

'Why...? Why would you offer to help after what you think of me?'

He thought for a moment. 'Because I believe in second chances.' He spoke without thought, his answer surprising even himself. 'You always have a choice—no matter how impossible it seems.'

A strange look came over her face as their eyes locked. Her breath was coming hard and heavy against his chest but she'd stopped fighting him. Her eyes drifted away from him, settling on the distance with a mixture of resolve and deep sadness.

'I'm not who you think I am.'

Without warning a heavy weight came down behind him, followed by what he presumed to be a palace guard shouting in furious Catalan.

Roman pushed the man backwards, holding his hands up in what he hoped resembled a peaceful motion.

'I have authorisation,' he began, motioning towards the lapel of his suit jacket. 'The King knows I am here.'

Roman felt his hands being pulled behind him into handcuffs and fought the urge to laugh as he looked up into a second guard's furious face.

'You will regret this.'

He grunted at the pressure of a knee between his shoulder blades, knowing that they most likely did not speak a word of English. As his face was crushed against the carpet he looked sideways, just in time to see a pair of dainty bare feet appear by his side. Up close, he could see that a tiny hand-drawn daisy adorned each red-painted toenail.

The woman spoke in rapid-fire Catalan, her voice muted and fearful yet with a strange backbone of authority. The nearest guard nodded, uttering two words that made his body freeze.

'Si, Princesa.'

Roman crushed his face further into the carpet with disbelief and sheer dread.

He had just body-searched a damn princess.

His Majesty King Fabian of Monteverre stood up as Olivia entered the private sitting room flanked by two stony-faced members of the Royal Guard.

'Of all the days to pull one of your disappearing acts, Libby,' her father said angrily, motioning for the guards to leave them with a flick of one hand.

Her mother, elegant and perpetually silent, did not acknowledge her entry. Queen Aurelia sat poised in a high-backed chair, her eyes trained solemnly on nothing in particular.

'Where have you *been*? You were informed of the intruder hours ago,' Olivia said, breathing hard.

'And naturally you expected us to abandon the

event? Honestly, Libby...' The King frowned in disbelief, reaching down to take a sip of whisky from a thick crystal tumbler.

Her father was the only one who still called her Libby. It reminded her of being five years old and being scolded for trying to sneak chocolate from the kitchens. But she was not a child any more, and she was damned tired of being treated like one.

'I was attacked,' she said slowly. 'A man held me hostage in my own dressing room. And yet I've been left to pace my apartments completely alone for the past five hours.'

'The matter has been resolved. It was a simple misunderstanding.' King Fabian avoided his daughter's eyes. 'Best to forget the whole business.'

Olivia felt all the outrage and pent-up frustration freeze in her veins as she registered her father's words. Had he actually just told her to *forget* this afternoon? She opened her mouth, then closed it, completely at a loss as to what to say in response.

'Your absence was noticed by Sheikh Khalil,' he said, scolding, his brows drawing down as they always did when he was unimpressed.

'Well, as I have just said, I was rather busy being held against my will by a dangerous intruder.' She took a deep breath, looking briefly across to her mother's uninterested blank features before returning her furious gaze to her father. 'Have I gone mad? Or are you both completely unaffected by today's events?'

'I understand it might have been...alarming...' King Fabian began solemnly.

'"Alarming" hardly covers it.' Olivia fumed. 'Why are you both so *calm*?'

The last word came out in a disbelieving whisper. She fought a distinct urge to walk over and bang her fist on her father's chest, to knock over her mother's glass, to make them both react in some way other than with this muted nothingness.

Today's events had shaken her to her core, and yet she felt as though she were intruding on their peace with her inconvenient outrage. Surely her own father should be shocked and outraged that his daughter's safety had been at risk inside their own home. Unless... Unless he wasn't shocked at all.

'What do you mean by a misunderstanding?' she asked, not bothering to hide the challenge in her voice.

'Libby...' Her father sighed, raising a hand for her to quieten.

'Please, don't "Libby" me.' She placed one hand on her hip. 'Tell me exactly what is going on. Did you know about this man?'

The King twisted his mouth in discomfort. 'Well... not directly, no.'

'Indirectly, then. You *knew* that someone would be here today? In our home.'

King Fabian strode to the window, placing one hand on the sill and looking out in silence. 'The man you met today was Roman Lazarov, founder of The Lazarov Group, an international security firm.' Her father sighed heavily. 'He is a very close friend of Sheikh Khalil and I have been assured that he is *the* authority on high-class security operations. But after the complete muddle he made today, I'm not so sure of his expert status...'

He laughed weakly, his voice trailing off as he took in her expression of horror.

'Don't look at me that way. It was a gift from Sheikh Khalil—very thoughtful of him to want to ensure your safety, I thought.'

Olivia felt a headache begin at her temples. This was all becoming too much. She closed her eyes a moment, unable to bear her father's apparent disregard for his daughter's privacy or independence.

'No, Father. In fact I find it horribly thoughtless. And intrusive, among other things.' She felt her breath coming faster, her temper rising like a caged bird set to take flight. 'This is the last straw in a long line of things I have overlooked since you began vaguely mentioning a possible marriage. I am not a piece of livestock to be insured and fenced in, for goodness' sake.'

He sighed. 'You are overreacting.'

'No, I'm really not. Did anyone consult me before all my charity events were cancelled? Was I informed when I was assigned five new bodyguards for all trips outside the palace?' She shook her head, her knuckles straining with the tightness of her fists by her sides. 'And now this. Did you even think to ask me before you sent a bloody *mercenary* into my room? I'll never feel safe there again!'

'Lazarov was simply going to *attempt* to gain entry to your rooms. To find any weaknesses in our security. Besides, you were supposed to be at the races with your fiancé.'

The tightness in her throat intensified. 'I have not yet agreed to this marriage. Until today I had no idea that you were truly serious about it! And if this is how the Sheikh shows his concern...'

She tightened her lips, willing herself to say the

words. To tell her father that the whole deal was off. She didn't want this. *Any* of it.

King Fabian's voice lowered in warning. 'Olivia, these negotiations are months old—we have discussed why this is a necessary step.'

She blinked. *Months old?* 'For the kingdom, yes. I understand what we stand to gain from a political union.' She cleared her throat, her voice sounding all of a sudden smaller. 'But what about for *me*?'

Her father's brows rose imperiously. 'You will be serving your kingdom.'

'I don't see why I must get married to a complete stranger in order to serve Monteverre. I am doing good work with Mimi's Foundation—I am making a difference.'

'Your grandmother and her damned charities...' Fabian scowled darkly, draining the last of his whisky. 'You think teaching a handful of scrawny kids to read will change anything about our situation?'

'My grandmother taught me that charity is not always about money. It's important to nourish the youth as well as to do our best to help those in need. She was beloved by this kingdom.'

'Ah, yes, the eternally perfect Queen Miranda! My mother spent so much time on her charities she didn't even notice her country's economy crumbling beneath her feet.' His mouth twisted cruelly. 'Don't you *see*, you silly girl? We are facing financial ruin without this union.'

Olivia opened her mouth to protest, only to have her father's scowl stop her as he continued on his own personal rant.

'The Kingdom of Zayyar is overflowing with

wealth, thanks to this man. He is an economic genius. But the civic history of his country still stands in the way of true acceptance from the west. To put it bluntly, they need our political influence and we need their money.'

'Money...' Olivia bit her lip, wanting to ask just how much she was worth, considering he was essentially trading her body for cash.

'Sheikh Khalil has the capabilities to take Monteverre back to its glory days—surely you want that for your people? What good is being able to read if they have no money to feed themselves?'

She had never heard her father speak so frankly, and his eyes were red-rimmed with half-madness. Olivia knew that Monteverre was in trouble. A series of bad leadership decisions and banking crashes had left them neck-deep in debt and with many of the younger generation emigrating to greener pastures. They were bleeding, and it appeared that this Sheikh had come offering a magic bandage. At a particular cost...

'Trusting an entire country's economic future to one man's hands? That seems a bit...reckless. Surely there is another way without the marriage—?'

'No,' he cut across her, his voice a dull bark in the silent room. 'There is no going back on this. I won't hear another word.'

Her father's eyes were dark in a way she had never seen them before, as though he hadn't truly slept in months.

'Everything you have had since birth is thanks to your position. It's not like you have an actual *career* to think of—you spend most of your time looking pretty and waving. None of that would even change. Your life would continue just as it has been—only as the Sheikha of Zayyar.' He took a breath, smiling down at her as if he had just bestowed upon her some enormous gift. 'This is your *duty*, Olivia. To Monteverre. It's not about you.'

She felt his words sink into her skin like an icy breeze, setting off goose pimples down her bare arms. Did being born a Sandoval really mean surrendering every aspect of your life to the good of the kingdom?

As the second daughter she had naïvely believed that her life would be different from her older sister's. She was not first in line to rule Monteverre—she didn't bear that crushing weight of responsibility and she had always been infinitely glad of it.

'The Sheikha of Zayyar…'

Her mother's melodic voice intruded on her thoughts, sounding absurdly serene.

'Sounds like something from a film…'

'I don't even know where Zayyar is,' Olivia said numbly, almost unable to speak past the tickle of panic spreading across her throat.

'Somewhere on the Persian Gulf,' Queen Aurelia offered, twirling the liquid in her glass. 'They have a hotel shaped like a boat sail.'

'That's Dubai.' King Fabian rolled his eyes. 'Zayyar is halfway between the desert and the Arabian Sea. Gorgeous scenery—you will love it.'

'Thank you for the sales pitch, Father.' Olivia sighed, looking across to her mother, who had once again turned to gaze into the empty fireplace.

It was customary for her mother to permanently nurse a glass of the finest cognac after midday. In Olivia's memory no one had ever questioned it or raised any concern. There had always been an unspoken understanding among the Sandoval children that their mother and father each did whatever they pleased and things would always be that way. They did not welcome personal discussions.

She looked up to the ceiling, feeling the familiar sense of exhaustion that always accompanied any meeting with her parents. For that was all they ever were. Meetings.

'Sheikh Khalil simply wanted to ensure your safety, Libby. Surely you find that romantic? I know you are prone to the sentiment.'

Her father looked down at his wife, but she had drifted off, her eyes dull and unfocused as she stared into nothingness. The look on his face changed to outright disgust and he turned away, busying himself with retrieving his jacket from a chair.

Olivia's heart broke a little for her parents' fractured marriage. She had fleeting memories of a happier time, when her parents had seemed madly in love and the Kingdom of Monteverre had been a shining beacon of prosperity and culture. Now there was nothing but cold resentment and constant worry.

'Father...' Olivia took a breath, trying to calm her rapid thoughts. 'This is all happening very fast. Perhaps if I just had some more time—'

'Why do you think the Sheikh arranged this trip? He plans to propose formally this afternoon so that the announcement can be made public before he leaves.'

Olivia's breath caught, expanding her throat painfully. 'He...he can't do that...'

'Oh, yes, he can—and you will be grateful for his patience.'

His voice boomed across the room, the sudden anger in it startling her, making her back away a step.

He took a breath, deliberately softening his tone. 'Can't you see that you are a vital part in this? There is power in your position.'

'Power...' Olivia repeated weakly. Her shoulders drooped. Even her bones felt heavy. *Women are not always destined to surrender to men...* Those words—*his* words—had struck something deep within her.

Roman Lazarov.

She bit her lip hard. For a moment she had regretted her decision to have him captured. He had seemed to glow from within—a fiery protector and proclaimer of women's strength. Now she knew he was just like the rest of them. Here to ensure that her cage was kept good and tight. That she had no hope of freedom.

King Fabian tightened his lips, forcing a smile before shrugging into his navy dress jacket and fixing the diamond cufflinks at his wrists. He paused by her side, looking down at her.

'You will have a private lunch with Sheikh Khalil tomorrow.' He placed one hand on her shoulder, giving it a light squeeze. 'I know you will give him the answer he wants. I'm so proud of the beautiful woman you have become.'

Olivia closed her eyes, not wanting him to see the tears that glistened there. Her heart seemed to slow in her chest as she nodded her head in defeat, glad when he was gone, with the smell of cigar smoke wafting on the air in his wake. How could he be proud of the woman she was when she had no idea who she was herself?

'I can't do this,' she breathed, silently hoping her

mother would look up. That she would hold her and listen to her worries, then kiss her forehead and tell her everything would be okay.

But sadly she knew that would never happen. She had no memories of ever being in her mother's arms, and even if she had the woman who now sat like a living ghost in the sitting room was not truly her mother.

She stood still for a long time, letting the tears fall down her cheeks and stain the neckline of her dress. Eventually she wiped her face and turned away from the unbearable silence, walking through the long main corridors of the private suites.

As usual, the guards pretended not to notice her.

She took her time, idling through the gardens on her way back to her rooms. With a few deep breaths she calmed the tremor in her throat. It had been a long time since she had let a single tear fall—probably not since the day of her grandmother's funeral. Crying was a fruitless activity when her future had already been neatly packed up and arranged.

She sat heavily on a marble bench in the centre of the courtyard. This was her favourite part of the palace, where a low stone square fountain provided the perfect vantage point to sit and listen to the staff as they went about their daily duties. Here, partially concealed by bougainvillea and foliage, she had been privy to the most heart-stopping live-action dramas outside of television.

The fights, the wicked gossip, the passionate clandestine embraces. A reluctant smile touched her lips. She had seen it all.

Just in the past month it had been revealed that one of the upstairs maids had engaged in an affair with the head gardener's handsome son. Olivia had overheard the whole sordid situation developing—right up to the point when said housemaid had found out that her beau was also heavily involved with one of the palace florists. The ensuing slap had resounded across the courtyard and earned the young Romeo a speedy transfer outside the palace.

The housemaid had moved on quickly enough, accepting a date with a palace guard. The look of delirious happiness as she'd described their first kiss to her friends had haunted Olivia for days.

She stood restlessly, leaning against the side of the fountain. Was that look the very thing she was sacrificing by agreeing to a loveless marriage?

She frowned, drawing her hand through the water and watching the ripples spread across her own solemn reflection. Love was about falling for the wrong guy, having your heart broken and then ending up with your handsome Prince Charming—not that she had ever experienced it. But she had watched enough old movies to know it was always true love's kiss at the end that gave her that butterflies feeling in her stomach. That moment when the couple swore their undying devotion and fell into each other's arms...

She wanted to feel like that. At least once in her life.

There had been a handful of kisses in her past; she was twenty-six, after all. But never more than a brief touching of lips. The kind of men who had been permitted near her just happened to be the kind of men who got aroused at the thought of their own reputations inflating with a real-life princess on their arm. Not one of the men she'd dated had ever tried to get to know her *really*.

A prickle made its way along her skin as she thought of a certain pair of grey eyes, raking their way down her body. It was madness, the way her body had seemed to thrum deep inside just from a man's gaze. It was ridiculous.

She looked down at her forearms, seeing the gooseflesh there. Why did he have to affect her so violently when no other man had managed to inspire so much as a flicker of her attraction?

She bit the inside of her cheek with frustration and turned to begin walking back to her apartments—only to find a large male frame blocking her path.

'Good evening, Printsessa.'

CHAPTER THREE

'I SEE THEY have released you... Mr Lazarov.' The Princess straightened her shoulders defensively, moving a long silken curtain of vibrant red hair away from her face as she directed her gaze upon him.

Roman ignored the strange tightening in his stomach at the way she said his name, focusing on her pale features to better read her mood.

She seemed less colourful than he remembered—as if something had stolen the fire he had witnessed earlier in the day, both at the racetrack and afterwards.

'Once they realised their mistake they were quite accommodating. I hope you were not worried for my welfare.'

'If it were my choice I would have had you detained for the night.'

She held her chin high as she delivered the blow, but Roman saw the telltale convulsive movement in her throat as she took a breath. He leaned casually against a nearby column, raising a single brow in challenge.

Far from bowing under his scrutiny, she held his gaze evenly. 'I assume you are here to make your apology?'

Roman fought the urge to laugh. 'I'm no stranger to handcuffs, Princess.' He smiled darkly. 'It would take more than five hours in a cushy palace detainment room to force me to my knees.'

Her gaze lowered a fraction and Roman gave in to his mirth, a darkly amused smile spreading across his lips.

'I don't want you to be on your...' She shook her head, exhaling hard. She crossed her arms below her chest—a gesture likely meant in defence, but all it served to do was draw his attention to the resulting swell at the neckline of her delicate yellow dress.

'Well, you are free to go,' she said, sarcasm dripping from her tone as she gestured towards the door to the main palace.

For the first time in his life Roman was at a complete loss as to what to say. How he had not recognised that she was a royal instantly, he did not know. The woman before him seemed to exude class and sophistication in every inch of her posture. She eyed him with suspicion, her brows lowering in a mixture of challenge and defence.

He should have left the moment he had been freed, and yet he had sought her out. He had told himself he needed to apologise, but right now, remembering the honest arousal in her eyes as he'd been pressed close to her... He wasn't feeling quite so apologetic.

He stood taller, hardening his voice. 'In case you are planning another escape, the tunnel has been blocked. It is no longer passable.'

'You certainly work fast,' she said quietly, leaning back against the lip of the fountain. 'I assume the Sheikh asked you to make sure my cage was good and tight?'

'Your...cage?'

She was oblivious to his confusion. 'Of course it matters to no one that I am an adult with free will. By all means let him have the run of the palace. There will be bars installed on my bedroom windows next.'

Roman raked a hand across the shadow beginning to grow along his jaw. He allowed her to a rant a moment, before clearing his throat pointedly. 'You seem upset.'

'"Upset" does not even begin to cover it. Everything about today has been unbearable.'

Something about the faraway look in her eyes bothered him. It was as though she were on the edge of a complete meltdown, and he worried that it was his mistake that had brought her there. Perhaps there was a need for his apology after all—much as it pained him to admit it.

'Princess, I need you to understand that I am not in the habit of holding a woman against her will,' he said solemnly. 'Earlier…when I searched you…'

She looked back at him, her lashes half lowered with something dark and unspoken. 'Will you be telling your fearsome Sheikh about that, I wonder?'

'The Sheikh is not the villain you seem to think he is,' Roman said quietly, inwardly grimacing at the thought of telling his best friend how he had manhandled his future wife. 'I have never known someone as loyal and dedicated.'

'Perhaps the two of you should get married, then,' she said snidely.

'I did not expect an actual princess to be quite so… cutting.' He pressed a hand to his chest in mock injury. 'Is it any wonder I mistook you for a common thief?'

That earned him the hint of a smile from her lips.

The movement lit up her eyes ever so slightly and he felt a little triumphant that he had caused it.

Roman smirked, turning to lean against the fountain, taking care to leave a good foot and a half of space between them. It had been a long time since he had been this conscious of a woman's presence.

'You seem like quite the man of mystery, Mr Lazarov,' she said, turning to look at him briefly. 'Best friends with a sheikh…founder of an international security firm.'

'You've been researching me?'

'I only found out your name twenty minutes ago,' she said honestly. 'Does the Sheikh always fly you in for such favours?'

'No, he does not.' Roman felt the corner of his mouth tilt at her mocking. It had been a long time since a woman had been so obviously unimpressed by him. 'I have my own means of transportation for such occasions.'

'Let me guess—something small and powerful with tinted windows?'

'It is black.' His lips twisted with amusement at her jibe. 'But my yacht is hardly small. No tinted windows—I much prefer the light.'

Her gaze wandered, the smile fading from her lips as she looked away from him. 'A playboy's yacht… of course.'

'These things have not magically fallen into my lap, I assure you. I have worked hard for the lifestyle I enjoy.'

'Oh, I didn't mean…' She turned her face back towards him quickly. 'I envy you, that's all.'

He raised a brow, wondering not for the first time

what on earth was going on inside her head. 'There is an entire fleet of vessels moored in the harbour with the royal crest on their hulls. You're telling me you couldn't just choose one at will?'

'I spent years learning how to sail at school. But I have yet to go on a single trip by myself,' she said, looking up and meeting his eyes for a long moment. 'It's strange…' she began, before shaking her head and turning her face away. 'I've spoken more frankly with you today—a complete stranger—than I have with anyone in a long time.'

Roman did not know how to respond to that statement. He swallowed hard, looking ahead to where a group of housemaids walked and chatted their way across the second-floor balconies. When he finally looked back the Princess had moved from beside him.

He stood up, looking around him for a sign of where she had gone, only to see a glimpse of pale yellow silk disappearing through the archway that led to the royal apartments.

He took a step forward, then caught himself.

She was where she belonged—surrounded by guards and staff.

It was time for him to get back to his own life.

The afternoon sun was hot on his neck when Roman finally walked out onto the deck of his yacht the next day. In his line of work he was no stranger to going to sleep as the sun rose, but his restless night had little to do with work. Being handcuffed in a room by himself had given him far too much time with his own thoughts. A dangerous pastime for a man with a past like his.

Nursing a strong black coffee, he slid on dark sunglasses and sank down into a hammock chair. They would set sail for the *isla* soon enough, and he would be glad to see the back of this kingdom and all its upper-class pomp.

He surveyed the busy harbour of Puerto Reina, Monteverre's main port. Tourists and locals peppered the busy marble promenade that fronted the harbour—the Queen's Balcony, he had been told it was called. A glittering golden crown insignia was emblazoned over every sign in the town, as though the people might somehow otherwise forget that it was the crown that held the power.

Never had he met a man more blinded by his own power than His Majesty, King Fabian. Khal had insisted on them meeting two nights previously, so that the three men could discuss the situation of the Princess's security—Khal was notoriously meticulous when it came to bodyguards and security measures.

It had been clear from the outset that Roman would be treated like the commoner he was, so he had made the choice to leave, rather than sit and be spoken down to. His tolerance levels only stretched so far. It seemed His Majesty still harboured some ill will, as made apparent by the gap of five hours between the time he had been informed of the incident at the palace and the time at which he'd authorised Roman's release.

Roman's fists clenched by his sides. He was no stranger to dealing with self-important asses—he'd made a career of protecting arrogant fools with more money than sense. But it was hard to stay professionally disengaged when one of the asses in question was your best friend. Khal had never treated him as 'lesser'—he knew better. But he had not so much as made a phone call to apologise for his oversight.

His friend knew, more than anyone, what time locked in a room could do to him.

Roman tilted his head up to the sun and closed his eyes. He was not in a locked room right now. He was on his own very expensive yacht, which would be out in open water just as soon as it was refuelled. He exhaled slowly, visualising the clear blue waters of Isla Arista, his own private haven.

Moments passed before his visualisation was interrupted by a loud car horn. He opened one eye and sighed as he saw a sleek black limousine edging its way through the crowds on the main street, flanked by four Monteverrian policemen on Vespas.

The Sheikh of Zayyar did not simply take a taxi, he supposed dryly as he reached forward to drain the last of his coffee and then tilted his head back to the sunshine. When he finally looked up again Khal was standing a foot away, his face a mask of cool fury.

'It was nice of you to finally come to my rescue, *bratik*.' Roman raised a brow from his perch on the deckchair, but made no move to stand and greet his oldest friend.

Khal's mouth twisted. 'I was under the impression that the untouchable Roman Lazarov never *needed* help.'

'And *I* was under the impression that our friendship came before brown-nosing the King of Monteverre.' Roman spoke quietly, venom in every word.

Right now, looking at Khal in his perfectly pressed white royal robes, a good old-fashioned punching match didn't sound like the worst way to start his day.

Back on the streets of St Petersburg it was the way most fights were resolved. Fighting had sometimes been the only way not to starve.

Roman scowled, realising the hunger in his gut was doing nothing to help his already agitated mood and the dark memories of his past threatening his control.

'I was not aware that you had been held in custody until this morning.'

Khal interrupted his thoughts, frowning with genuine concern.

Roman tipped his head back, propping one foot lazily up on the low table in front of him. People generally afforded the almighty Sheikh of Zayyar a certain level of ceremony and pomp. But not him. He usually went out of his way to take Khal down a peg whenever they were alone.

'Oh, just five hours in a windowless room with my hands cuffed behind my back—no big deal.'

'I find it hard to sympathise, considering you'd held my future wife hostage like a common criminal,' Khal said simply.

'An interesting choice of words, *Your Highness*,' Roman snarled, derision in every syllable.

A silence fell between them—not the comfortable kind that came from years of close friendship. This was a silence filled with tension and frustration.

A friendship like theirs had no clear rules, different as they were.

Khal came from a long line of royalty—had been educated and privileged and born with power in his blood. Whereas Roman had fought for everything he owned, clawing his way out of the gutter he had been abandoned in as a child. Over the years he had refined his harsh manners and learned how to act like a gentleman, but underneath he would always bear the marks of his past. The darkness had branded him— quite literally—and that was something his friend had no experience of.

Khal cleared his throat loudly. 'You know, in ten years I don't think you've changed one bit.'

Roman ignored the barely veiled insult, shrugging as he put one leg casually across the table. 'I have a lot more money.'

'And an even bigger ego.' Khal frowned.

'Need I remind you that I came here as a favour? I did not *have* to dirty my hands for you, Khal. No matter what debts I may owe you.'

'Is that the only reason you came? And here I was thinking you cared for my happiness.' Khal's mouth tightened. 'Four years is a long time to hold on to your guilt, Lazarov.'

Roman shook his head, standing to pace to the railing that edged the upper deck. He had enough painful memories affecting his concentration today—he didn't need more reminders of the long line of blackness he left in his wake.

'I came here because you needed help, *bratik*. Nothing more.'

For the first time Khal looked weary as he rubbed a hand across his clean-shaven face. He sat down in the deckchair Roman had vacated and stared up at the clear sky above them.

'This whole situation is rapidly getting away from me. My trip was supposed to be simple and straightforward, tying everything up. And now I stand to lose everything I have staked.'

Roman frowned at his friend's unusual display of weakness. 'It will be fine. I will apologise to the Princess and smooth things over for you.'

Khal looked at him, realisation dawning on his dark features. 'You don't know? The Princess has disappeared, Roman. Half the Palace Guard is out searching for her.'

Roman froze with surprise. 'Disappeared? I just spoke with her last night.'

'You *spoke* with her?' Khal's voice raised an octave. 'What on earth would possess you to speak with her after what you'd put her through?'

'She had me put through far worse, trust me.'

'So this is even more your fault than I had originally thought?'

'Khal, I had the tunnel blocked, extra guards assigned. How on earth could she have just walked out of there?'

Khal shook his head. 'Clearly she wanted to get away badly enough to risk her own safety. What did you say to her?'

'We barely spoke two words. Mainly she insulted me and then she walked away.'

Both men were silent for a long moment, facing off in the midday heat.

'The girl is reckless,' Roman said darkly. 'Are you sure that you want to marry someone so…unpredictable?'

'My kingdom needs it. So it will be done.' Khal smoothed down the front of his robes. 'I have been heavy-handed with my approach so far. I worry that perhaps I have scared her off completely.'

'How so?'

'I ordered a stricter security regime. I needed to make sure she was protected adequately before her name was linked with mine. In case...'

Roman saw the haunted look in his friend's eyes and immediately stopped. How had he not realised before now?

He moved towards him, placing a hand heavily on his shoulder. 'Khal... I understand why you felt the need to ensure her security...believe me. But there *is* such a thing as smothering with safety.'

'We both know the risks for any woman who is by my side,' Khal said, standing to his feet.

The moment of weakness had passed and he was once again the formidable and controlled Sheikh of Zayyar. But Roman could still sense the heaviness in the air, the unspoken worries that he knew plagued his friend and had likely tortured him for the past four years.

Nothing would bring back his friend's wife. Her sudden death had shifted something in the easy friendship that had once bonded them together, and nothing would erase the pain of knowing that he hadn't been there in Khal's time of need.

Roman cleared his throat. 'I will go and find the Princess,' he said gruffly.

'No. Definitely not.' Khal turned back to him, crossing his arms. 'Your presence would only aggravate the situation further.'

'If it was my actions that caused her to rethink the engagement, then let me be the one to apologise and bring her back.' Roman pushed his hands into the pockets of his trousers, feeling the weight of his own error settle somewhere in his gut. 'This is *my* fault.'

'Yes. It is.' Khal raised one brow. 'And I hate not knowing if I can trust you to fix it.'

Roman's jaw clenched. Khal was like a brother to him—his *bratik*. The closest thing to a family member he had ever chosen for himself.

'You have trusted me with your life in the past. Are you telling me you don't think I'm capable of retrieving one errant little princess?'

'This is important to me, Roman.'

'I will bring her back. You have my word,' Roman said, meaning every syllable.

He would find the little siren and bring her back to her royal duty if it was the last thing he did.

This had been a terrible plan.

Olivia slumped down in her seat, tucking an errant strand of bright red hair back into her dark, wide floppy-brimmed hat. Because of the dark sunglasses she wore, and the rather plain white shift dress, thankfully so far nobody had looked at her twice.

Olivia sighed. Had she really been so naïve as to think that she could just check in to the next commercial flight without question? The realisation of what she had almost done suddenly paralysed her with fear. She had almost broken the law, for goodness' sake.

She was hyper aware of her surroundings, noticing every little movement of the people in the departures hall. Every time one of the airport security guards looked at her she unconsciously held her breath, waiting for the moment when they would realise who she was and unceremoniously haul her back to the palace. And to her father.

She didn't even know exactly what she was trying

to achieve here. Honestly, had she really been so immature as to think that her father would take her more seriously just because she had attempted to run away from her engagement? In reality this little stunt had done nothing but ensure that she would have even less freedom than before.

She closed her eyes, leaning her head back against the seat and wishing that she had never come up with this stupid plan. She felt the air shift to her right, a gentle breeze bringing with it an eerily familiar scent of sandalwood and pine.

'A risky choice, hiding in plain sight,' a deeply accented male voice drawled from beside her, bringing memories of strong, muscular arms and eyes like gunmetal.

Roman Lazarov lowered himself casually into the seat beside her and lazily propped one ankle on the opposite knee.

'You really didn't think this through.'

From this angle, all she could see were powerful thighs encased in designer trousers and a pair of expensive leather shoes. She exhaled slowly, realising from the sound of his voice that he must have his face turned towards her. Watching to gauge her reaction.

He was probably congratulating himself on finding her so easily, the brute.

He cleared his throat loudly, waiting for her response.

Olivia pursed her lips and kept her eyes focused straight ahead. She wondered if, perhaps if she waited long enough, he would simply disappear into thin air.

'You have ten seconds to give up your silent act before I announce your presence to this entire airport.' He spoke low, his voice a barely contained growl.

She stiffened. 'You're bluffing.'

'Look at me.'

She turned her head at his demand, hardly realising she had obeyed until it was done. His eyes were focused on her, steel-grey and glowing, just as she remembered them. His lips, so full and perfectly moulded, seemed to quirk a little at the sides as his eyes narrowed. It took a moment for her to realise he was silently laughing at her.

'I *was* bluffing.' He smiled in triumph, showing a row of perfectly aligned white teeth.

His smile was aggressively beautiful, just like the rest of him, she thought, with more than a little frustration. She noticed the rather delicious hint of dark stubble that lined his jaw. It somehow made him appear rugged and unrefined, even in his finely tailored clothing. She felt her throat go dry and silently cursed herself.

'If you're wondering how I found you, I simply followed the enormous trail of breadcrumbs you left in your wake, Printsessa.'

'Don't call me that here,' Olivia murmured. The hum of noise in the airport was loud enough, but she didn't want to draw any more attention than was needed.

He raised one brow, but nodded.

Olivia took a sharp breath, a slight tremor audible in her throat. 'If I asked you to go, and pretend you'd never found me…'

'That will never happen.' He half smiled as he spoke the words, a small indentation appearing just left of his lips.

The man had dimples, she thought wildly. That was hardly fair, was it?

Before she could react, he had reached down and grabbed the small document she had been holding tightly in her hands. As she watched, he opened it, tilting his head to one side as he read.

After a long moment he looked up, meeting her eyes with disbelief. 'You planned to use this?'

'Initially, yes. But then I thought better of it.'

'A wise choice, considering identity fraud is a very serious crime. Even for princesses.'

Olivia remained silent, staring down at the red mark on her fingers from where she had clutched the maid's passport so hard it had almost cut off her circulation.

It had been a careless plan from the start, one borne of desperation and anger. If she had got caught... The thought tightened her throat. Fraud simply wasn't something that was in her nature, luckily. Meaning that she had come no closer than eight feet from the check-in desk before she had turned on her heel and run. Leaving her sitting on this damned chair for the past two hours, frantically wondering where to go next.

Olivia shook off the ridiculous self-pity and forced herself to get a handle on her emotions. She was emotionally and physically exhausted. Any sleep she had got last night had been plagued by dreams of being trapped in tunnels with no way out, and a man's voice calling to her from the darkness. When she had finally got up this morning it had been with the grim intent of getting as far away from Monteverre as possible, and yet here she was, less than an hour's distance from the palace and already captured.

The entire plan had been stupid and impulsive from the start. Honestly, where had she really thought she would go once she'd walked out of the palace gates? She didn't even have the right to hold her own passport, for goodness' sake. Everything in her life was planned and controlled by others. She didn't even have enough freedom to run away properly.

Roman was still looking at her intently. She could feel the heat of his gaze on the side of her face, almost as though he burned her simply by being near. He made her feel as though she were on show and he was the only person in the audience. The intensity of his presence was something she simultaneously wanted to bask in and run far away from.

'I'm not running from my title.' She spoke solemnly, knowing he could never understand.

'Then what are you running from?' His voice was low and serious, and his gaze still pinned on hers with silvery intensity.

Olivia took a deep breath, knowing this conversation had to end. He was not on her side, no matter how sympathetic he pretended to be.

'It's not safe for you to be wandering alone.' His voice took on a steely edge. 'I feel responsible for your decision to leave the palace. Perhaps you felt that yesterday reflected badly on your future husband—'

Again the 'future husband' talk. Olivia stood up, feeling her blood pressure rise with sheer frustration.

Roman's hand took hold of hers, pulling her back down to a sitting position. His voice was low, somewhere near her right ear, as he spoke in chilling warning, 'Don't make any more impulsive moves, Printsessa. I might seem gentle, but I can assure you if you run from me again I might not be quite so civilised in hauling you back where you belong.'

Her heart hammered hard in her chest, and the skin along her neck and shoulders tingled and prickled with the effects of his barely veiled threat.

'My car is parked at the door. We can do this the easy way or the hard way.'

Olivia briefly considered her options—or lack thereof. Was she really prepared to risk what might happen if she resisted? The memory of his powerful arms encircling her in her dressing room sprang to her mind. For a moment she sat completely still, wondering if the frisson of electricity that coursed through her veins was one of trepidation or one of something infinitely more dangerous.

She stood, spine straight, and began walking towards the entrance. He followed, as she'd expected, his muscular frame falling into step by her side. His hand cupped her elbow, steering her out into the daylight towards a gleaming white luxury model car with privacy-tinted windows. Not the kind of car she would have expected from a new money playboy with a taste for danger.

Her silent captor slid into the driver's seat across from her, his warm, masculine scent filling the small space. He didn't look at her as he manoeuvred the car out of the airport and through the maze of roads that led to the motorway.

She covertly glanced at him from behind the safety of her sunglasses. Strong, masculine hands handled the wheel with expert ease. She noticed the top two buttons of his black shirt lay open and his sleeves had been rolled up along forearms that practically bulged with muscle. Strange black markings encircled his skin just above his shirt cuff—tribal, perhaps, but she couldn't see more than the edge.

Of *course* he had a tattoo, she thought, biting her lip as she wondered just how many he might have. And where they might be...

'You are staring. Something you'd like to say?'

His low, accented voice jolted her and she averted her eyes, looking straight ahead, curling her fingers together in her lap. 'I was simply wondering if you will be delivering me to my father or to the Sheikh.'

'So dramatic.' He sighed. 'You make it sound like you are a shipment of goods.'

'I might as well be,' she muttered under her breath. 'It's hard not to feel like a piece of livestock. Being traded from one barbarian to another.'

His hands seemed to tighten on the wheel. 'I'd prefer if you didn't use your pity party to insult my friend in that fashion. "Barbarian" is not a term he would take lightly.'

'Mr Lazarov, at this point I can't say that I particularly care.'

'I suggest that you start caring,' Roman gritted, moving the car off the motorway and towards the mountain range that separated them from the Grand Palace.

Twenty minutes in this pampered princess's company and he was tempted to stop the car and make her walk the rest of the way.

She was a puzzle, this fiery redhead. A spoilt, impulsive, dangerous puzzle, all wrapped up in one very tempting package. He would not feel guilty for being attracted to Khal's fiancée. A man would have to be blind not to see the raw sensual appeal in Olivia San-doval. But, unlike her, he had his impulses under con-trol. It was not hard to brush off attraction when he could tell that all that lay beneath her flawless skin and designer curves was a spoilt, bored little royal on the hunt for a thrill.

'Your father has asked that you be returned to the palace as soon as possible,' Roman said, noticing how her body seemed to tense at the mention of the King. 'But I feel that you and your fiancé need to speak first.'

'He is *not* my fiancé,' Olivia gritted.

'Oh, so that's what is going on here. You decided to break the engagement by running away. How very mature.'

Roman felt his jaw tighten with anger for his friend, for the future of two nations that was hanging in the balance all because of one woman.

'No, *I* haven't decided anything. That's the point!'

Roman heard the slight tremor in her voice and turned briefly to see she had her head in her hands. 'Look, if this is bridal jitters, I'm sure there's plenty of time before the wedding—'

Her head snapped up and she pinned him with the most ferocious icy blue-green gaze. 'Do you honestly think I would risk my reputation, my safety, over a little case of *bridal jitters*?'

'I only met you yesterday.' He shrugged.

It was true—he didn't know very much about her except that she had a deep-rooted mistrust of men and a mean left hook.

'This isn't something to speak about with a stranger.'

'At least you're listening...somewhat.' She sighed. 'Even if you think the worst of me.'

He said nothing, concentrating on the road as they edged around the mountain face. He could have taken the new, modern tunnel that bisected the mountain entirely. But this was a new country for him and he enjoyed the scenic routes.

Olivia lay her head back on the seat, her voice low and utterly miserable. 'How can a woman suddenly have a fiancé when she hasn't heard or even decided to accept a marriage proposal?'

'You mean… Khal didn't formally propose? This is what's upset you?'

'No. He did *not* formally propose,' she said, mocking laughter in her voice. 'I only met the Sheikh yesterday for the first time—at the races. Five minutes after my father informed me that I would be marrying him.'

CHAPTER FOUR

ROMAN FELT HIS brain stumble over her words. 'That is impossible.'

'Welcome to my life.' A deep sigh left her chest. 'Apparently Monteverre has reverted to the Middle Ages.'

'The Sheikh assured me that all the arrangements have been made. That he is simply here to make the formal announcement of your intended marriage.'

'The only arrangement that has been made is a business one. Evidently the bride was not important enough to be let in on the plans.'

She laughed once—a low, hollow sound that made Roman's gut clench.

'I'm twenty-six years old and suddenly I'm expected to tie myself to a stranger for the rest of my life.'

A tense silence fell between them and Roman took a moment to process this new information. Khal had not been honest with him. And if there was one thing that Roman Lazarov despised it was being taken for a fool. Khal had said the Princess was his future bride, leaving him with the assumption that the woman had consented to the marriage. Now, knowing that she hadn't...

Call him old-fashioned, but he believed a woman

had a right to her own freedom, her own mind. Growing up on the streets, he had seen first-hand just what happened when men decided simply to assume a woman's consent.

The Princess had called Khal a barbarian, but Roman knew that was the furthest thing from the truth. He wanted to believe that this was all a misunderstanding—that Khal had been misled by the King into believing his intended bride was a willing participant in all this. However…he knew the single-minded ruthlessness that possessed the Sheikh whenever his nation's future lay in the balance.

He had said himself that this marriage was vital to Zayyar's future. Perhaps it was vital enough to overlook a reluctant bride?

They rounded a particularly sharp bend and the road began to descend towards the lush green valley that spread out below. This country had its own particular charm—there was no denying it, he thought as he took in the glittering sea in the distance.

A small lay-by had been built into the outer curve of the road—a safe place for people to stop and take photographs while stretching their legs. Making a snap decision, Roman slowed down, manoeuvring the car into a vacant spot in the deserted lay-by and bringing them to a stop.

'What are you doing?' Olivia's brows furrowed.

'I need a moment,' he said, taking the keys with him as he stood away from the car, just in case his passenger had any ideas. The lay-by was deserted, and the road far too steep for her to get anywhere on foot.

He braced his hands on the glittering granite wall and took a moment to inhale the fresh mountain air deeply. There was something about the sight of completely unspoiled nature that deeply affected him. He had spent far too much of his youth surrounded by concrete buildings and garbage-scented air.

The sea beckoned to him in the distance. His yacht was ready to leave the moment he returned—ready to sail out into the open sea, where he would be free of this troubled royal family and their tangled web.

All he had to do was drop her off at the palace and he was home free.

Why he was hesitating all of a sudden, he did not know, but something was stopping him from completing his directive without questioning it further. He heard the car's passenger door close gently and turned to see the Princess come to a stop at the wall beside him.

'This is my favourite view in all of Monteverre,' she said. There was not a hint of sadness in her voice. It was just fact, stated without emotion.

He realised that since the moment he had held her captive in the tunnel he had not seen her resort to tears once. No one, including him, would have judged her for breaking down in the face of an unknown captor. She had a backbone of steel, and yet she had not been able to follow through with her plan to use the fraudulent passport. She clearly drew the line at breaking the law, and could not blur her own moral guidelines even in apparent desperation.

'What exactly were you hoping to achieve by running?' he asked, directing his question to the side of her face as she continued to stare out at the distance.

'I don't know.' She nipped lightly at her bottom lip. 'I just needed the chance to come to a decision myself.

Some time to weigh up my options. I have no idea what life is like away from my guards and my responsibilities, and yet here I am, expected to blindly trade one set of palace walls for another.'

He couldn't disagree with her logic.

'When I agreed to perform the security operation yesterday, I presumed that your marriage had already been arranged.' He ran a hand across his jaw, the memory of his handling of her raw and uncomfortable. 'Had I known the situation was not what it seemed I would not have agreed to it.'

She shrugged, defeat evident in the downward slope of her slim shoulders.

'I will take you to Khal. You can address your concerns to him directly. That is generally how adults resolve such situations.'

Olivia stared at him with disbelief. 'I am not a child. Despite being treated like one time and time again.' She braced her two hands on the wall, her perfectly manicured nails in stark contrast against the stone. 'I have no interest in pleading my case to a man I do not know. Besides, do you think I would have done this if I wasn't already completely sure that my voice will hold no weight in this situation?'

Roman pinched the bridge of his nose, a low growl forming in his chest. 'Damn it, I do not have time for this. I could have been halfway across the Mediterranean by now.'

She turned to him, one hand on her hip. 'I'm sorry that our political situation is such an inconvenience to your playboy lifestyle, Mr Lazarov.'

She took a step away, her shoulders squared with frustration, before she turned back to face him.

'You know what? I'm tired of this too. You may as well just take me to the Sheikh right now, so that I can reject his proposal in person. If his choice in friends is anything to go by, I'm sure I won't be missing out on too much.'

'You presume I *care* how you pampered royals resolve your issues?'

'You wouldn't be here if you didn't.'

'The only reason I am here is because you chose to be a coward rather than face the situation head-on.'

Hurt flashed in her eyes and he suddenly felt like the world's biggest heel.

'I don't know what to do,' she said honestly, her eyes meeting his with sudden vulnerability. 'I know that marrying the Sheikh is the right choice for my people. Despite what you might think, I *do* care about this kingdom—very much. If I didn't, I would have already said no.'

The silence that fell between them was thick and tension-filled, although the air was cooling down now, as the sun dropped lower in the sky and evening fell across the mountain.

She had accused him of tightening her cage yesterday, and today it couldn't be more true. The idea of pretending he hadn't found her in the first place was tempting…but no matter how much it would simplify his life he knew that a woman like her wasn't safe alone in the world. He knew more than anyone that there were far too many opportunistic criminals out there, just waiting for a chance at a high-class victim. Keeping rich people safe was his business, after all.

'I have never been out in public away from the Palace Guard for this length of time. It's nice…not being surrounded by an entourage.'

'You want a taste of freedom,' he said plainly, and the sudden realisation was like clouds parting to reveal blue sky after a storm.

'Isn't that what all runaways want?' She smiled sadly. 'But we both know how that has worked out for me so far.'

'I can't just let you walk away from me, Princess. You know that.'

He pondered the situation, despising his own need to problem-solve. Khal needed this marriage to go ahead. That was his directive here. There was no point returning the Princess only for her to reject the marriage completely. But maybe he could offer a solution that would benefit everyone involved.

Everyone except him, that was.

He frowned, hardly believing he was even entertaining the idea, but words escaped his mouth and he knew he had to trust his instinct. 'What if I could offer you a temporary freedom of sorts?' he asked slowly, watching as her face tipped up and her eyes regarded him with suspicion.

'I would ask what exactly you mean by "temporary".'

'I can offer you some time alone in which you can come to a decision about your marriage.'

'Or lack thereof?'

'Exactly.'

'How would you do that?' she asked. 'And, more importantly, *why* would you?'

'Don't worry about how—just trust that I am a man of my word. If I say you will be undisturbed then I mean it. But you would have your side of the bargain to hold up.'

'I'm listening.'

'All I ask is that you take time to consider all aspects of the union. I believe that you would be making a mistake in walking away from this engagement. Khal is a great man,' he said truthfully.

He was careful not to mention the small fact that she was a flight risk who would likely end up in real trouble if the situation wasn't contained. This was containment at its most extreme. He had somehow gone from holding a princess hostage to volunteering to take one on as his guest.

He waited while she visibly weighed up her options before him, worrying at her lower lip with her teeth. Her mouth was a dusky pink colour, he noticed. No lipstick or gloss, just pure silky rose flesh. She flashed him a glance and he quickly averted his gaze, looking back out at the view.

In that moment he instantly regretted his offer to salvage his friend's union. He had the sudden uncomfortable thought that perhaps he had just voluntarily offered to step out onto a tightrope with everything hanging in the balance.

But even as he began to regret his offer she nodded her head once, murmuring her acceptance.

And just like that the deal was done.

He had never gone back on a deal in the past, and he wouldn't be starting now. Self-doubt held no place in his life. He trusted his own self-control, his own loyalty to those he cared for. And so he walked her back to the car and dutifully avoided looking down at the swell of her curves as she sashayed in front of him.

'I still don't understand why you are doing this for me.' She looked up at him through long russet lashes, and he saw a smattering of freckles appearing high on her cheeks in the evening sun.

'Consider it a wedding gift,' he gritted, shutting the door with finality and steeling himself for the drive ahead.

Olivia stepped out on the deserted deck of the yacht and watched as they drew nearer and nearer to land. The evening was fast fading to pink as dusk approached. She wondered if maybe she should be worried that she had no idea where Roman was taking her, but really the destination itself didn't matter. So long as it was far enough away from the palace for her to be able to breathe again.

With every mile that had passed since they'd set sail from Puerto Reina harbour she had felt the unbearable tension begin to ease and a sense of sharp relief take its place. But her newfound sense of freedom still held an unpleasant tinge of guilt around the edges. As if a dark cloud was hovering somewhere in her peripheral vision, just waiting to spill over and wreak havoc on her fleeting sense of calm.

She was doing the right thing, wasn't she? Taking time away from the royal bubble in a controlled manner was the mature course of action. Despite what others might think, she knew she had a very important decision to make. This wasn't so simple as making the best choice for herself—putting the rest of her life first and repercussions be damned. She had been raised always to hold Monteverre in greater esteem than herself. To value the people more than she did her own family.

But what happened when her own family didn't seem to value her happiness at all?

Her eyes drifted across the deck to where her slim black handbag sat atop a sun lounger. Inside that bag she held all the information she had found about the foundation that her grandmother had left in her name. Information on all of the amazing work that it had carried out since her passing ten years ago.

She wasn't quite ready to share what she had uncovered with anyone just yet.

At the moment, the bottom line was clear. Her father had said that she had no alternative but to marry the Sheikh and she had agreed with him, Going against a union arranged by the King now would have very real, very severe ramifications. Either way, her life was about to change drastically.

It was no big deal, really, she thought with a slightly panicked intake of breath. Sign her life away to a loveless marriage in order to save her kingdom or have her title stripped away for ever. No big deal at all.

She closed her eyes, breathing in the cool sea air and willing her mind to slow down. She had spent two days going around and around in circles already, and the effect made her temples feel fit to burst. Was it any wonder she had made such a rash decision to run away from it all?

She exhaled slowly, opening her eyes to find that the yacht was now sailing alongside the coast of the seemingly deserted island they had been approaching. The place looked completely wild—like something from a movie. But as they rounded an outcrop of rocks she was suddenly looking at a crescent-shaped coastline formed out of ragged black rocks and golden sand. A tall white lighthouse stood on the far coast in the distance, atop a lush green cliff. And a small marina was situated at the furthest end of the bay, in the shade of the cliffs.

She gradually felt the yacht lose speed until it began the process of mooring at the end of the long white floating dock.

Roman was still nowhere to be seen, she thought as she scanned what she could see of the upper decks. The yacht was huge, and he had disappeared almost immediately after depositing her in one of the lower deck living rooms.

She was still not quite sure why he had decided to give her this time in the first place. She doubted he felt pity for her, considering his disdain for 'pampered royals', as he had so delicately labelled her. But he had seemed genuinely surprised to hear that the marriage situation was not all that it seemed.

She was not naïve enough to believe that he was on her side, but she hoped that he understood her motivations a little more at least.

Still, she would do well to remember where his loyalties lay. He was determined to see her accept Sheikh Khal's proposal—there was no doubt in her mind about that. She imagined that Roman Lazarov was not the type of man to give up on something without putting up a good fight first.

Surprisingly, the thought of debating her future with him didn't fill her with the same dread that she had felt in her father's presence the day before. She couldn't quite explain it… He spoke to her like a person, not as someone lesser. Or, worse, as a princess. He wasn't afraid to look into her eyes as he spoke, unlike most others who met her.

He had listened to her today. She would never let him know how much that had meant to her. He was not a friend—she knew that. But maybe he didn't have to be her enemy.

As though conjured by her thoughts, Roman suddenly emerged from a door to her right, speaking to someone on the phone in a deep, throaty language she presumed to be his native Russian. He had made no move to interact with her in the hours since they had set sail from Monteverre.

He looked tired, she noticed, and yet his dark shirt and trousers barely held a single crease. She, on the other hand, was rumpled and in dire need of a shower and a full night of sleep. She smoothed the front of her dress self-consciously and turned herself to face him, shoulders held high.

He ended the call with one click and took a moment to tilt his face up to the view of the vibrant overgrown landscape around them. For a moment the harsh lines around his mouth relaxed and his eyes seemed to glow silver in the evening light. She realised with surprise that the look on his face was something very close to contentment. She'd not yet seen him with anything but hostility in his features, and she had to admit the man had very inviting lips when he wasn't smirking or insulting her.

'We still have a short drive from here,' he said, taking a quick look at his watch and motioning for the single cabin porter to take care of their luggage. 'I hope you don't get motion sickness.'

Before she could question that statement, he gestured for her to follow him down the steps onto the

whitewashed boards of the marina. She practically had
to run to catch up with him.

'Where are we?' she asked, her short legs struggling
to keep up with his long strides.

'My very own island paradise,' he said simply, not
bothering to slow down until they'd reached a dirt road
at the end of the dock. Roman stopped beside a small,
open-sided white Jeep and turned to face her, one hand
braced lazily on the mud-spattered door frame as he
held it open for her.

'Jump in, Princess.' His lips quirked.

That was a challenge if ever she'd heard one. He
likely expected her to throw a fit of pique, demanding
transportation that better befitted her station.

She smiled sweetly, holding up her white skirt to
protect it from the worst of the dirt, and hoisted herself up into the cab without complaint. Within minutes
the engine was roaring loudly and a cloud of dust flew
around them as they began a steady climb up the cliffs.

'When you said you could guarantee privacy, I
didn't realise you meant to maroon me on a desert
island.' She forced an easy tone, trying to hide the
breathlessness from her voice.

He didn't immediately respond, so she filled the silence by commenting on the views of the coast below
as they drove higher and higher, weaving in and out of
the treeline. As they bounced over a particularly rough
stretch of terrain her shoulder was jammed hard against
the window and she let out a little squeak of alarm.

She turned to see that he was smirking once more.
She fought the sudden, irrational urge to punch him
in the bicep.

'Judging by the transportation, am I to expect a rustic mud hut for my stay?' She gripped her seatbelt with all her might, her resolve slipping fast.

'I'm not here to act as your tour guide.' He shrugged, uninterested, his jaw tightening as he shifted gears and the terrain seemed to level out. 'I'll be sure to have your tent inspected for cockroaches, at least.'

She had never actually slept in a tent. It would be a drastic change from her usual surroundings, but she rather thought she might enjoy the novelty.

Just as she turned to say this to him she caught sight of something sparkling in the distance. The land began to slope downwards towards the lower terrain again, revealing a spectacular side view of a very large, very sleek, modern villa.

As they descended a short driveway Olivia felt her breath catch at the view that spread out before them. She could see the entire island from this vantage point. The evening sky was tinged pink and orange as the sun sank lower and lower towards the jade-green sea.

'Wow...' she breathed, her awestruck brain not quite able to form anything more eloquent after the stunning visual onslaught.

A small white-haired man appeared at the door as they stepped out of the car. He looked immediately to Roman with raised brows.

'You did not mention a guest, sir,' he said, his smile forced and pointed.

'Jorge, how many times do I have to tell you not to call me sir just because we are in company?' Roman grunted.

'It's more professional.' Jorge shrugged, trying and failing to keep his voice low.

'You are *far* from professional.' Roman smirked,

clapping the other man on the shoulder with friendly familiarity. 'Ridiculously capable and efficient? Of course. But not professional in the least. That's why I hired you.'

The two men looked back to see Olivia watching the odd exchange with interest.

'Olivia, this is my right-hand man, Jorge. He travels with me to my homes as housekeeper and chef.'

Roman seemed suddenly preoccupied as he took out his phone and clicked a few buttons.

'Show her around and set her up in the white guest room.'

Olivia frowned as he began to walk away without another word. 'You mean you won't be giving me the grand tour yourself?' she called, half joking but actually quite shocked at his blatant disregard.

A harsh laugh escaped his lips as he continued to power across the hallway, away from her. 'I am not in the hospitality business. I thought you would have noticed that by now.'

And with that he disappeared through a doorway at the end of the hall, leaving her alone with his very apologetic housekeeper.

Roman ended the call with a double-click and laid his phone down hard on the marble patio table. In almost ten years of friendship he had never heard his friend curse.

Khal had been stunned at the revelation that the Princess was being strong-armed into their union by her father. But, ever practical, he had asked if there was a chance she might go ahead with it. Roman had answered truthfully—saying that he believed the Princess was just seeking a break from the heightened security measures.

'Give her time,' he had said. 'I will ensure she returns to accept your proposal.'

Khal trusted him to guard his future bride. There wasn't another person on this earth that Roman would be doing this for. He was not a personal bodyguard. He specialised in hard security. Elite risk assessments, intruder prevention, high-tech electronic systems and such. He did not have the refined people skills that were needed to work one-on-one in this kind of setting.

And yet here he was, babysitting a runaway princess on the island that he made a point to keep free of unwelcome guests.

If he had ever been a drinker now would be an excellent time for copious amounts of alcohol in which to drown his dark mood. He leaned heavily against the glass rail that lined the balcony of his master suite, looking out at the horizon where the sun had begun to dip into the Mediterranean Sea.

A sudden splash from below caught his attention and he looked down to see a creamy silhouette cutting easily across the bottom of the pool.

She had started her holiday straight away, it seemed, he thought darkly as his fist tightened on the rail.

Her head and bare shoulders broke the surface of the water as she reached the infinity ledge. Her red hair was dark and heavy on her shoulders; she hadn't bothered to tie it up. She leaned against the side of the pool, pale shoulders glistening with moisture above a bright red one-piece bathing suit. He could see the outline of long, slim legs under the water.

Roman felt the darkness inside him roar to life.

He wanted her.

He growled to himself, turning away from the tantalising view with a jaw that suddenly felt like iron. He stalked across his suite into the large white and chrome bathroom. The large floor-to-ceiling mirror showed his frustration in high definition. His pupils were dark, his nostrils flared with anger as he began unbuttoning his shirt.

It had been a while since he had been with anyone—that was all this was. His body was reacting to its recent deprivation in the most primal way possible. He had never been good at denying himself something he wanted with this kind of intensity.

A more emotionally charged person might say it had something to do with a childhood full of being denied, he thought darkly. *He* knew better. It was simply a part of him—a part of how he was put together. It was what drove him to the heights of success, always wanting more.

All he knew was that his wealth had brought along with it the delicious ability to gratify his every whim instantly. Whether it was a new car or a beautiful woman, he always got what he wanted with minimal effort.

But not her.

She was not his to think about, to look at, to covet.

He was long past his days as a thief, he thought dryly as he divested himself of the rest of his clothing and stepped under the white-hot spray of the shower, feeling the heat seep into his taut shoulder muscles and down his back.

Another man might have opted for a cold spray, but he had spent too much of his life in the cold. He had the best hot shower that money could buy and damn it, he would use it. Even if it only spurred on the heat inside him.

He was unsure whether he was angry with his friend for trusting him so blindly or angry that he did not fully trust himself. He was a sophisticated man, well capable of resisting flimsy attractions. And yet he felt a need to keep some distance between himself and the fiery-haired Olivia, with her sharp wit and unpredictable nature.

He had built his fortune on trusting his own instincts, and everything about Olivia Sandoval signalled danger.

CHAPTER FIVE

As was usual when he stayed on Isla Arista, Roman had instructed Jorge to prepare an evening meal to be served on the terrace. The scent of aromatic rosemary chicken filled his nostrils as he stepped outside and his stomach growled in anticipation.

Olivia already sat at the table, waiting for him. He was surprised to see she had not changed after her swim; instead she was wrapped in an oversized white terry-cloth robe from the pool cabana. One bare foot peeked out from where it was tucked under her. His stomach tightened at the sight of a single red-painted toenail.

'I see you are taking your holiday quite literally,' he said, taking the seat opposite her at the long marble table.

She looked down at his crisp white shirt and uncertainty flickered across her features, followed closely by embarrassment. 'Your housekeeper said it was just a quick meal. I wasn't aware that we would eat together,' she said, standing to her feet.

'Sit down,' he said and sighed.

But she vehemently shook her head, promising to be just a few minutes as she hurried away through the terrace doors at lightning speed. He fought the urge to laugh. How ironic that out of both of them it was the member of royalty who felt unfit for polite company.

True to her word, she returned less than ten minutes later. He was relieved to see that she hadn't opted for another dress, and amused that once again she wore white. The simple white linen trousers hugged her curves just as sinfully as the dress had, but thankfully she had chosen a rather sober white button-down blouse that covered her up almost to her chin.

Still, her slim shoulders were completely bare, showing off her perfect alabaster skin. He consciously lowered his gaze, to focus on filling their water glasses.

He made no move to speak. He was tired and hungry and in no mood to make her feel at ease. In fact it was better that she wasn't completely comfortable. That would make two of them.

Ever the efficient host, Jorge soon had the table filled with delicious freshly cooked dishes. Roman loaded his plate with tender chicken, garlic-roasted baby potatoes and seasonal grilled vegetables. No matter where they were in the world—New York, Moscow or this tiny remote island—his housekeeper always managed to find the freshest ingredients. He really should give him another raise...

Roman ate as he always did—until he was completely satisfied. Which usually meant two servings, at least, and then washing his meal down with a single glass of wine from his favourite regional *cantina*.

'Where on earth do you put all that food?'

Roman looked up to see Olivia watching him with open fascination, her fork still toying with the same handful of potatoes she had spooned onto her plate ten minutes previously.

'In my stomach,' he said, keeping his tone neutral. 'You had better follow suit or risk offending the chef.'

'We are not *all* graced with fast metabolisms.' She smiled tightly, putting down her fork and dabbing the corners of her mouth delicately.

'I exercise hard so that I can eat well. Good food is there to be enjoyed.' He fought annoyance as she sat back, clearly done with her food.

'The meal was wonderful—thank you.'

'If you say so, Printsessa,' he said, with just a hint of irony, considering she had barely eaten more than a child's portion. At least she didn't seem to be downing the wine to compensate for her self-imposed starvation.

'Why do you call me that?' she asked. 'I presume it's Russian? Printsessa?'

'My apologies. Do you harbour a preference for the term your subjects use? Your Highness, perhaps?'

She frowned. 'Do you enjoy mocking people for no reason?'

'I enjoy nothing of this situation, Olivia.' He exaggerated the syllables of her name with deliberate slowness and watched with satisfaction as she visibly swallowed.

'I don't understand,' she said, sitting forward, a frown forming between perfectly shaped russet brows. '*You* are the one who offered to bring me here, remember? Nobody forced you to do that. We are practically strangers, and yet you have been nothing but rude and downright hostile since the moment we met.'

'I offered to bring you here so that you would stop running away like a teenager,' he gritted. 'This is not a holiday. And I am not here to entertain a pampered royal seeking one last thrill ride before marriage.'

Her blue-green eyes narrowed with some of the fire he remembered from her dressing room the day before. 'You have made a lot of assumptions about my character in the past twenty-four hours.'

'Like it or not, right now you are in *my* charge. If I am making assumptions, it's because I can.'

'You think you know who I am? Please—enlighten me.' She sat back, crossing one slim leg over the other.

Roman watched the movement, his pulse quickening slightly as his eyes followed the curve of her thigh down to the slim silver-heeled sandals on her feet. 'I do not pretend to know who you are—nothing quite so philosophical.'

He leaned back in his chair, stretching one arm behind his neck. She followed the movement, eyelashes lowered.

'I know your type well enough,' Roman said darkly, and his mind surprised him by conjuring up an image of a familiar face. A pair of blue eyes that had haunted him for almost two decades.

His night of imprisonment must have affected him worse than he thought. The cold sweat from being handcuffed still seemed to coat his skin like dirt, even after the hot shower and plentiful meal.

Thoughts of his past were not a common occurrence these days. Thoughts of Sofiya even less common.

He cleared his throat, irritated at himself and his momentary lapse in keeping his own demons at bay. 'You are young, beautiful and privileged, frustrated with the strict rules designed to protect you. So you go out in search of adventure. A little danger to shake up the monotony.'

'So I'm just another spoilt brat looking for a bit of fun? Is that it?'

Roman shrugged noncommittally, draining the last of his wine. 'You are telling me this *isn't* about rebellion?' he asked, knowing he had hit a nerve when her eyes darted away from his to look out at the inky darkness of the sea in the distance.

'You know, insulting me and my motivation is hardly going to send me running back to accept your friend's proposal.'

'The only reason you feel insulted is because you are likely used to always hearing what you want to hear.'

Olivia sighed, leaning her head back for a moment and pinching the bridge of her nose. 'I am simply taking a brief reprieve before making one of the most important decisions of my life. No big deal, really.'

'I hate to tell you, but that's just a fancy way of saying you're running away.' He couldn't help but smirk.

'So you have me all figured out, then?' She crossed her arms over her chest, meeting his eyes head-on. 'It must be nice, being so untouchable and faultless.'

Roman shrugged. 'It is not my fault that you dislike being told the truth.'

'What I *dislike*, Mr Lazarov, is that you find it so easy to shove all my class into one pile, simply because we were born with money.' She exhaled heavily. 'In my opinion, that says far more about you than it does me.'

'Is that so?'

'Yes, *it is*. I may have been born into wealth, but that does not automatically take away the fact that I am human.' She stood up, pacing to the stone ledge of the terrace before turning back to him. 'You know nothing of my life—just as I know nothing of yours.'

Roman watched as she looked out at the distant black waves for a moment, with that same faraway look in her eyes that he had seen the night before. He almost felt guilty for goading her.

He cleared his throat loudly. 'We are getting off-track here. This is about repairing your trust in Sheikh Khal.' He sat a little straighter and laid one leg over his knee. 'Not that it will pose much difficulty. Khal is a good man.'

'I appreciate the vote of confidence,' she said, her voice rasping slightly. 'But I believe the point of this time away is for me to come to a decision alone.'

'No one knows him better than I do. Allow me to put your mind at ease.'

'You are not my friend. And I would do well to re-member that. I am taking advantage of some time to clear my head—nothing more. I won't speak of this marriage business with you again.'

Roman raised a brow in question, getting to his feet and walking to stand beside her. '"Business…" An in-teresting word choice.'

She shrugged one slim shoulder, still looking away from him. 'It's the reality.'

'It is a very complex arrangement, from what I know—it's not just about *you*.'

It was as though he were reading straight from a script her father had written. The sudden reminder of her di-lemma settled painfully like a dead weight in between Olivia's shoulders. She was so tense she could scream. She had barely slept in the past twenty-four hours, and that coupled with being in this man's presence made every nerve in her body feel completely on edge.

She felt her throat tighten. 'I may be more sheltered than your average twenty-six-year-old woman, but I know what kind of situation I am in.' She cleared her throat, steeling herself. She would *not* show weakness. 'It's *never* been about me—that's the point.'

'Are you telling me you feel you truly have no choice in the matter?' he asked, a sudden seriousness entering his eyes. 'Because a woman being forced into marriage is something I know Khal would never condone. Nor would I.'

Olivia looked up, taking in his broad stance and the furrow between his brows. Logically, she knew that his concern was for his friend, and not for the inconvenient charge he had been landed with. But for a moment she imagined what it might be like to have that kind of protectiveness completely to herself. She imagined that when a man like Roman cared for a woman he would do it fiercely—no prisoners taken. It seemed that he brought intensity into all aspects of his life.

She shook off the fanciful thoughts, suddenly hyper aware of his broad presence looming mere feet away from her. The warm headiness of his cologne teased her nostrils on the night air. His was the kind of scent that made a girl want to stand closer, to breathe it in. It was dangerous, that smell. It made her want to do dangerous things.

'Your silence doesn't exactly give me any insight.' He leaned back on the stone ledge so that he faced her, his grey eyes strangely dark and unreadable in the warm light of the outdoor lamps.

Olivia sighed, shrugging one shoulder with practised indifference. How could she tell him that the only alternative she had to this marriage was to walk away and lose everything she had grown up to value?

'I am not going to be handcuffed and frogmarched up the aisle, if that's what you mean.'

He raised a brow. 'But there would be consequences if you refused?'

She nodded once, unable to stand still in the face of his intense gaze and unwilling to discuss those consequences with a man who'd made it clear he was firmly on the opposite side. She might have escaped her father's imperious presence, but it seemed she had simply swapped one judgemental know-it-all male for another.

She suddenly felt more alone than ever. Her restless feet took her to the end of the terrace, where the stone tiles gave way to soft, spongy grass.

'I can't remember the last time I walked barefoot in the grass,' she said, more to herself than him, and she took a few tentative steps and sighed with appreciation.

One look back showed her that he was still watching her with that same unreadable expression. It was as though he were trying to categorise her, to pin down exactly what he needed to do to fix the very problem of her.

He had said the Sheikh trusted him to problem-solve. That was all she was to him—a problem. It seemed that was all she was to everyone these days, unless she shut her mouth and did what she was told.

'Olivia, come back from there.' Roman's voice boomed from behind her. 'This time of night it's—'

'You know, I think I can make that decision for myself,' she said, cutting him off mid-speech. It was rude, but she was too irritated to care. 'If I want to walk in the grass, I will. I don't need someone to manage every second of my day.'

She took a few more steps across the grass, putting some space between herself and the surprised, strangely amused smirk that had suddenly spread across his face.

'Suit yourself,' he said quietly, looking down at the expensive watch on his wrist. 'But you're going to regret changing out of that bathing suit.'

She frowned at the cryptic statement, turning to face him. Just as she opened her mouth to question that statement the heavens seemed to open above her. Thick droplets of ice-cold rain fell hard and heavy onto her face, making her gasp as the cold spray got heavier and heavier, spreading through her clothing and down her neck and spine.

She was instantly wet through, and her mind took at least ten seconds before telling her to sprint back towards the house. After a few feet the rain suddenly stopped, and she was left looking into Roman's laughing face.

'I would have warned you about the sprinklers,' he said, crossing his arms. 'But I didn't want to manage your day too much.'

She gasped as the cool night air hit her sodden skin. She looked down at her wet clothes and, to her surprise, felt hysterical laughter bubble up her throat.

Roman frowned, also with surprise, 'What? No angry tirade about my appalling lack of consideration?'

'I'm done with being angry today.' She shook her head. 'If I don't laugh right now I might cry. And I make a point of never doing that.'

She leaned to one side, laughing once more as she

began to squeeze the water from her hair. A sudden wicked urge grabbed her, and before she could stop herself she pooled the excess liquid in the palm of her hand and threw it in his direction, watching as it landed with a satisfying splash directly in his face.

'I'm sorry,' she said quickly, trying to curb her laughter as she took in his thunderous expression.

He took a step towards her and she felt her breath catch.

'You can't throw the first punch and then retreat with an apology.' His voice was dark and silky on the night air. 'You sell yourself short. That was an excellent aim.'

'I'm not sorry, then.' She smirked, realising with a sudden jolt that she was flirting with him. And that he was flirting back.

The way he was looking at her coupled with the silent darkness of the night surrounding them made her almost imagine that this was a different moment in time entirely. That they weren't just strangers forced into each other's company by circumstance.

She imagined normal people laughed like this and poked fun at one another without fear of making a faux pas. It felt good, being normal.

'You've got quite a wild temper hidden underneath all those royal manners.' He took another step closer.

'I manage to keep it in check most of the time.'

'But not around me.' It was a statement, not a question.

'Don't flatter yourself.' She smiled nervously.

He stood little more than a foot away now, his warm scent clouding around her. She was wet and bedraggled, but she didn't want to leave just yet. She didn't want to end this—whatever it was that was passing between them. After a day filled with confrontation and being on the defensive, it was nice to lose the serious tone—even if for a brief moment.

She crossed her arms under her breasts, feeling the cold air prickle her skin into gooseflesh.

'*Khristos*, why didn't you say you were freezing?'

He reached out to touch her arm, the movement shocking them both as their eyes met in the half-darkness. It was a touch too far. They both knew it. And yet his hand stayed, gripping the soft skin just above her elbow. She shivered again, and this time it was nothing to do with the chill.

She noticed his expression darken suddenly. The air between them filled with a strange sizzling energy and his fingers flexed against her skin just a fraction.

She realised his gaze had moved below her chin. Self-consciously she looked down—and felt the air rush from her lungs in one long drawn-out breath.

Her white blouse.

She might as well be standing in front of him completely naked for all the coverage the wet piece of fabric was offering her. Of *course* tonight had to be the night when, in her haste to dress, she had decided a bra wasn't necessary. And of *course* the cool breeze had resulted in both taut peaks standing proudly to attention.

'Oh, God...'

She took in another breath, silently willing herself to laugh it off, but her mind stumbled clumsily over itself as she took in the obvious heat in his gaze. His eyes were dark and heavy-lidded as they lifted to meet hers. There was no mistaking it now. The silent strum of sensual heat that thrummed in the air between them.

It was a strange feeling—wanting to hide from the intensity of his gaze and bask in it all at the same time. He made her feel warm in places she hadn't known she could feel heat. It was as though her body was silently begging her to move towards him.

What would she do if he suddenly closed the gap between them and laid his lips hungrily on hers? Would he taste as sinfully good as he smelled?

She could suddenly think of nothing else.

What felt like hours passed, when really it was a matter of minutes. All the while his hand remained where it was, scorching her skin. Branding her.

When he finally turned his face away she fought the urge to step closer. To take the moment back. But then she followed his gaze and spied the housekeeper, quietly tidying their dinner dishes away nearby, with all the practised quietness of a professional.

She took one deliberate step away and crossed her arms over her chest, covering herself. His hand fell to his side and the haze of open lust disappeared from his features almost as quickly as it had come.

She wondered how he managed to look both furious and guilt-ridden at the same time. What would have happened if she had given in to that impulse and simply leaned forward to close the gap between them?

As though he'd heard her thoughts, a furrow appeared on his brow. He cleared his throat loudly, turning back to his housekeeper without another glance in her direction. 'Grab a towel for Miss Sandoval before she freezes.'

His cold, uncaring tone only added to the sudden chill that spread through her.

Without saying goodnight, or even looking in her direction, Roman disappeared through the terrace doors, leaving her standing alone, confused and embarrassed in her sodden clothes.

The walls of his master suite were bathed in a cold powder-blue light when Roman awoke. As usual he had not dreamed, but sleep had taken much longer than usual to claim him. And even then it had been fitful and broken at best. It was as though his entire body had thrummed with an intense nervous energy that refused to allow him any real rest.

Never one to remain in bed once his eyes had opened, Roman stood and threw on his jogging shorts.

In less than five minutes he was stretching on the steps that led to the beach. Within another ten he had completed two laps of the mile-long sandy inlet and worked up a healthy sweat. He ran barefoot on the damp sand until his chest heaved and his muscles burned with effort. And then he ran some more.

Usually a good run was enough to rid him of any thoughts strong enough to affect his sleep. A self-inflicted punishment of sorts, for those times when he knew his mind had begun to grow weak and was in need of strengthening. A weak mind had no place in his life—not when so many relied on his razor-sharp instincts to protect their homes and indeed their lives.

He prided himself on always being able to separate his personal and professional life—especially when it came to affairs with women. Lust never clouded his judgement.

The women he pursued were usually professional workaholics, just like him. Women who were sophisticated in and out of the bedroom and who weren't looking for sweet nothings to be whispered in their ear once they had scratched their mutual itch.

He had a feeling a sheltered young princess wouldn't be quite so worldly when it came to no-strings sex.

He picked up speed as he chastised himself for even entertaining the thought of a no-strings affair with Olivia. Guilt settled heavily in his chest as he thought of the night before, of the thoughts that had run through his brain as he had openly ogled his best friend's intended bride. *Stupid, weak fool.* The words flew by along with his breath as he exhausted his body with a final punishing sprint.

He had always believed that he deserved punishment for the multitude of sins he had committed in his youth. That no matter how complacent he grew in his wealth, in his power and success, there was always a darkness in him just waiting to ruin everything. It was beginning to seem that Olivia had been sent into his life to tempt that darkness to the fore. To tease him with her elegant curves and squeaky-clean nature.

He had a certain code for how he lived his life— certain people he did not betray and certain things he did not do. A rule book, of sorts, that kept him on the straight and narrow when the impulsive bastard inside him threatened to rise to the surface.

Khristos...

He exhaled hard. He had never been more tempted to break his own rules than in these past two days. Olivia reminded him of one of those perfect, luscious cakes that had always been on display behind the glass of his local bakery as a child. He had stood outside in the cold, salivating over the idea of breaking through that glass and claiming the treat for himself. But at that stage in his life his innocent boyhood self had innately known that would have been the wrong thing to do.

The Roman Lazarov of the present day did not have that luxury. Telling himself to walk away last night had been like standing in front of that bakery window all over again—hungry and frustrated, but unable to do a damn thing but fantasise about how the icing would taste in his mouth.

A delicious torture.

With his breath hard and even, he turned to the horizon and watched as the first flickers of pink and orange began to colour the dawn sky.

One of his favourite things about Isla Arista was the unspoilt view of both the sunrise and sunset from various points on the island. In those few dark months after the tragedy in Zayyar he had often spent an entire day walking here. He could completely circumnavigate the island in a few short hours because he knew the right tracks to take. It was an island of many personalities—smooth and habitable in some places, but fiercely wild and impassable in others.

He turned to begin walking back up to the villa, stopping as he spied a familiar feminine silhouette emerge from the open glass doors onto the terrace.

Olivia had been unashamedly watching Roman's progress up and down the beach with interest. It had been impossble not to stare at his broad, muscular form as he powered up and down the sand with seeming effortlessness.

She had debated hiding in her room all day, and avoiding breakfast with him altogether, but she'd decided that was something the *old* Olivia would do.

She was done with avoiding conflict and simply daydreaming of what she might say if she had the bravery in certain situations. She would sit across the table from him this morning and she would show him how completely unaffected she was by what had happened last night. Or almost happened, rather.

Aside from wanting to prove a point to herself, she had to admit that she desperately wanted to speak with him again. He was so unlike any man she had ever known. It was addictive, talking to him.

She had possibly taken slightly more time than usual in washing and preparing her hair, so that it fell in soft waves around her face. And so what if she had tried on three of the five dresses in her suitcase before committing to one?

The pale pink linen day dress was perhaps a little much for breakfast, but the way it nipped in at the waist and flowed out softly to her knees made her feel feminine and confident. And besides, she was simply taking pleasure in choosing her own outfit without a styling team surrounding her.

After twenty minutes of waiting, her stomach rumbling, with a beautiful display of fresh fruit and pastries spread out before her on the breakfast table, Jorge informed her that Mr Lazarov would be working all day and had decided it was easier to eat in his office.

She told herself that she wasn't bothered in the least as she poured herself coffee from the French press and nibbled on a piece of melon. She didn't care that he had chosen to avoid her. It was better, really. There was no one here to goad her, to push her to think about things she wanted to avoid. No all too perceptive slate-grey eyes watching her, making her skin prickle.

Eventually she gave in to the tantalising breakfast display and grabbed a large sugar-frosted croissant, smearing it liberally with butter and strawberry marmalade. The sticky sweet treat was like heaven itself as she washed it down with the fragrant gourmet coffee. Pastry was firmly on her list of *never* foods.

Regret was inevitable, and it washed over her as she self-consciously smoothed her dress against her stomach. Another result of the life she led was the constant pressure to stay slim, to stay as beautiful as possible in order to live up to her persona.

She had always harboured a soul-deep envy of her sisters and their seeming lack of pressure to play a part for the public. As the oldest, Eleanor was to be Queen one day—a position she took very seriously. She was naturally rake-thin, and always immaculately dressed, but the only media pressure *she* had to deal with was speculation on when she would start producing little heirs of her own.

Cressida was rarely, if ever, seen in the media. As a respected researcher in her field, she had somehow been allowed to study and live an almost civilian lifestyle in London, with only the barest minimum security detail.

Olivia sighed. The only skills *she* had were those best suited to what she was already doing, along with the uncanny ability to daydream herself out of any situation.

She had always adored the more dramatic movies—the ones where the heroine went through hell in order to get her happy ending. Maybe this was her punishment for refusing to adapt fully to real life?

Now, the information that lay inside that folder up in

her room had the potential to change her life. To give her a little of the freedom she had longed for, for the past ten years. But, as with every choice, there would be some fall-out. And that fall-out would affect the people of her kingdom for many years to come.

Roman had said that she was spoilt and selfish. If that were true then she would have simply walked away from her place in the royal family as soon as she'd legally become an adult. Or when she had been made aware of her private inheritance three years ago.

It was her 'Get Out of Jail Free' card—a golden ticket to civilian life. But she was a royal of the realm at heart, and her father knew that. Hence why he so easily used her own loyal nature against her and made sure that she knew the consequences of her actions if she were to defy him.

She knew her father spoke the truth when he said that this marriage had the potential to solve all of Monteverre's problems.

Could she really be the person to stand in the way of that?

CHAPTER SIX

OLIVIA SAT UP quickly in the bed, feeling a sharp pain shoot through her neck. In her exhausted state she must have fallen asleep with her head propped on one arm. A quick look in the mirror showed that not only was her hair an unsightly nest, but she also bore a hot red patch on her left cheek from her uncomfortable position.

She stood up and walked to windows. A silvery moon had risen high above the bay below, casting pretty shadows all along the gardens that surrounded the villa. It was certainly past dinner time, she imagined, but still her eyes widened as the clock showed it was almost midnight.

Disorientated and groggy, she quickly ran a brush through her hair before making her way downstairs.

The villa seemed to be completely empty, and devoid of all human presence. The air was cool out on the terrace, and she half wished she had thought to take a sweater. From her vantage point she had a spectacular view of the glass-fronted villa in all its warm, glowing glory. At night, somehow the place seemed even more beautiful than it was during the day. Soft lighting warmed the space from within and made it look like a wall of glowing amber stone.

The garden was lit up with small spherical lights that appeared to float in mid-air. Tall, thick shrubbery blocked her view of the moon and its hypnotising glow on the waves. She was filled with energy, and suddenly wanted nothing more than a brisk walk along the moonlit beach.

As she made her way towards the edge of the lights she paused, briefly wondering if it was wise to venture away from the villa. The island was completely private, so she felt she was in no real danger so long as she kept to the well-lit parts. But that didn't mean that her brooding guard would take kindly to her exploring without permission...

That thought was immediately banished once she remembered how her host had effectively barricaded himself in his office for the day. She hadn't so much as caught a glimpse of him since seeing him running on the beach.

Her arms instinctively wrapped around her midriff, shielding herself from both the cool breeze and her thoughts as she made her way down the steps to the beach. Who the hell did he think he was anyway? Did he think that she would shadow him around? Begging for his attention?

She had much more pressing things on her mind than brooding Russians with ridiculously inflated egos.

The steps at the back of the house were steeper than she had anticipated. The drive up in the Jeep had not truly given her an appreciation of how high up the house was perched above the marina. She momentarily considered turning back, but stubbornness and curiosity made her keep moving. There was a safety rail on each side, and small lamps to light the way—it was not truly dangerous.

The soles of her sandals slid suddenly against the stone surface, making her gasp as she teetered forward precariously. The world seemed to shift for a split second before she clambered back, grabbing the rail for dear life.

She slid off her sandals, abandoning them on the steps. Her bare feet gave much better grip for the rest of the way down, and soon she reached the very bottom. The sand was cold and damp under her toes but the midnight air was balmy. She took a moment to stop and simply bask in the utter stillness of it all.

It reminded her of the warm nights her family had spent out on the terrace at their summer estate. The beautiful countryside manor in the southern peninsula of Monteverre was the setting of most of her fondest childhood memories. Back in the days when her grandmother had reigned over the kingdom as Queen and her father had simply been the young, handsome heir to the throne.

There had been no palace for the three young Princesses—no twenty-four-hour bodyguards. Her grandmother had ensured they were given as normal a childhood as possible, considering the circumstances.

And even as father had grown ever more reckless, and her mother had retreated into her brandy glass, Mimi had been there. Until all of a sudden she hadn't.

Olivia shivered, taking a few long strides across the sand until she reached the long whitewashed jetty of the small marina that she had arrived at. It looked different in the semi-dark, with only a few lamps illuminating the shadows. Roman's sleek yacht was a dark shadow in the distance. The moonlight glowed against its polished glass body, smooth, severe and striking— rather like the man himself, she thought.

The marina also housed a handful of other vessels. A couple of top-of-the-range speedboats—likely for sporting use—a small rescue dinghy, and the one that had caught her eye the moment she had disembarked the day before: a magnificent vintage sailboat.

In the dark, it was hard to see any of the fine detailing. She reached out, running her hand along the smooth silver lettering emblazoned just above the waterline.

'"*Sofiya*",' she said out loud. 'Just who are you named after, I wonder?'

'That is none of your business.'

The deep voice boomed from behind her, startling her enough to make her lose her footing and fall hard against the side of the boat. She fell for what seemed like minutes rather than milliseconds, before strong arms grabbed her around the waist and lifted her swiftly upright.

'Planning a midnight escape?' Roman asked, his accent both intimidating and strangely welcoming after the prolonged silence of her day.

'You…you startled me,' she breathed hard, her voice little more than a breathy whisper.

His hands were still on her waist, the heat of him seeping through the material of her dress. She reached down, covering his hands with her own for a moment before pushing them away and taking a tentative half-step back.

The loss of heat was instant. Her skin prickled with tiny bumps, as though calling his touch back.

'If you insist on sneaking around outside in the dark, I might rethink the terms of your stay here.'

'The *terms*? I assumed I had been abandoned to my own devices.'

'Fine, then. Let's get this straight. You will only leave the house in daylight hours, and you will clear it with me first.'

'You expect me to just sit around all day and go insane from my own thoughts?' She half laughed. 'This is an island—where could I even go?'

'I have learnt not to underestimate you.'

He crossed his arms and for the first time she noticed he wore only a dark-coloured sleeveless workout shirt and cut-off shorts. Her eyes took in the bulging muscles that lined his shoulders, his lean, hard biceps and strong forearms. Her gaze wandered once again to the strange black band that stretched around his left arm, just under the elbow. The design seemed intricate, but she quickly looked back up to his face, aware she had been gawking.

'Are we clear?' he asked, scowling down at her from his impressive height.

Olivia fought the urge to roll her eyes at him in all his perpetually sardonic glory. She had a feeling this was what it would be like to have a surly, unimpressed guardian angel following her every move.

In this light he certainly looked the part. The glow of the moon emphasised his harsh features, making him even more darkly attractive. But good looks and incredibly broad shoulders would never account for a severe lack of sense of humour. Did the man *ever* smile?

'Are you like this all the time or just around me?'

she asked, turning on her heel and walking away from him, back towards the sand.

'Oh, you're telling me how I am now?' He fell easily into step beside her, mild amusement on his voice. 'Please enlighten me.'

'You are controlling. And rude.' She said, counting off on her fingers. 'Judgmental, intimidating, far too serious—'

'You are accusing *me* of being rude?' He clutched a hand to his chest as though mortally wounded.

Olivia stopped just short of where the wooden planks gave way to hard sand and turned to face him in the dim light of the spherical lamps that lined the small marina. 'You've just instructed me that I cannot leave the house without your permission.'

He smirked, reaching out to stop her when she made to move away with irritation.

She crossed her arms and met his eyes, determined to have this conversation like an adult.

'Olivia, closely controlled security is only required if there is a risk of the client putting themselves in danger. Unfortunately for me, in your case, that means, yes, it's needed.' He sighed. 'And I am not prepared to shadow you around this island simply to provide you with a more enjoyable experience.'

'Are you telling me I'm under house arrest just because you're determined not to spend any time alone with me?' she said with disbelief.

'I don't think it would be the best idea,' he said plainly. 'For obvious reasons.'

She watched him silently for a moment, wondering if he was actually openly referring to the chemistry between them. 'Are you really so unable to control a flimsy attraction?' she asked bravely, shocked at the words coming from her own mouth.

His eyes widened. 'I'm a grown man, Olivia. Older than you by almost a decade.'

'I fail to see what age has to do with it.'

He stepped forward, a dangerous glint in his slate-grey eyes. 'I'm not a mindless teenager who can be waylaid by a set of curves.'

'Well, then, what's the problem?' She shrugged one shoulder, fully committed to her act now, even as her insides quaked. 'I'm not about to jump your bones, and you've made it clear that you are far too mature to do anything quite so...*primal.*'

He smiled the kind of smile that screamed danger as he allowed his gaze to take her in slowly from her head down to her bare toes. 'Primal? Is that what you'd call it?'

She gulped.

He noticed.

Roman took a single step forward, closing the gap between them so that they stood almost toe to toe. 'I'd like to wager that you've never jumped anyone's bones in your life, Printsessa.'

'I'm not about to divulge that kind of information to you.' She tried her best to keep up her confident act but he'd rattled her. He knew it too.

Cursing her lack of practice in these things, she turned as nonchalantly as possible and began walking back towards the villa, hoping she'd simply seem bored or tired.

'I did not mean to offend you.' His voice drifted from behind her as she began climbing the steep steps.

'I'm sure you are perfectly capable of jumping my bones.'

'Don't flatter yourself,' she breathed, aware that she was barely a quarter of the way up and already feeling winded from the incline.

She hadn't eaten nearly enough today to fuel this kind of exertion, and tiny spots had begun to appear at the edges of her vision. She paused, holding on to the rail for a moment as she caught her breath.

'Problem?' he asked, coming to a stop beside her.

He was barely even breathing heavily, the great brute.

She shook her head, not wanting to admit that she had been moping around the villa for most of the day and had refused Jorge's offers of lunch and dinner.

Standing up straight, she continued to climb, begging the gods of never-ending stairs to have mercy on her. Eventually she reached the top—and not a moment too soon. She caught one glimpse of the amber lights of the villa before her ears began to pop and her legs started to shake.

Roman instantly noticed the change in her demeanour. 'Was the climb *really* so tough?' he asked, half mocking.

She groaned, moving to the grass and half sitting half falling onto her rear end with an unceremonious grunt as the world tilted around her.

'You look as though you are about to be ill.' He crouched in front of her, the mocking tone completely vanished from his voice. 'Olivia?'

'I need some water,' she managed to rasp, looking up at the blurred outline of his face. 'Just a little light-headed.'

* * *

Roman took one look at Olivia's pale features and cursed under his breath. 'When did you last eat?' he asked, a mixture of anger and concern filling him as her eyes darted away from him with embarrassment.

'Just give me a moment to catch my breath.'

'No, you need a damned sandwich and some common sense,' he gritted. 'Can you walk?'

She nodded—far too quickly. Her eyes were still unfocused and her face pale as moonlight. Still, to her stubborn credit she rose to her feet and attempted two whole steps before her legs buckled and she tipped into his waiting arms.

'This is mortifying!' she groaned, her face mashed against his chest.

Roman ignored the all too welcome sensation of having her slim figure pressed against him. With a deep breath he lifted her against his shoulder and closed the distance between them and the villa.

Once inside, he deposited her roughly onto the bench in the kitchen and set about preparing a cold meat sandwich on crusty white bread and a tall glass of ice-cold orange juice.

She sipped at the juice with gusto, and a hint of colour reappeared in her cheeks after a moment as she nibbled on the crust of the bread.

'You eat like a rabbit,' he commented, when after five minutes she hadn't taken more than a series of tiny bites.

'I eat enough.' She shrugged.

Roman remained silent. She was watching him closely over the rim of her orange juice glass, but did not speak until the sandwich was completely gone.

'White carbs are my weakness.' She sighed. 'You've just sent me down a path of total and utter ruination in the eyes of my stylist.'

'I'm sorry its not gluten-free, but true hunger can't afford to be picky.'

'What would *you* know of true hunger?' She raised a brow. 'You eat enough to feed a small army.'

'I grew accustomed to eating as much as I could fit in once I got out of prison.' He spoke without thought, and then watched as stark realisation dawned over her delicate features. 'Old habits, I suppose.' He shrugged, instantly regretting his words.

'I never thought...' She let her voice trail off. 'I'm sorry.'

'You're sorry that I was in prison?' He leaned down, grabbing her plate and turning to deposit it in the sink. 'Don't be. I deserved every year I got. Trust me.'

'No, I'm sorry you had to experience hunger like that. I didn't think when I spoke. I was just being... snarky.'

'Don't worry about it.'

In all the years that had passed since his time in jail, he couldn't remember anyone ever commiserating with him over the hardships he must have endured. She didn't even know why he had been landed there in the first place. She knew nothing of the man he had been. No, he corrected himself, the *boy* he had been.

'You're not a bad guy,' she said quietly.

Roman looked up, unable to conceal his surprise at her words.

'I mean, obviously I've only known you a couple of days...' She shrugged her shoulders, heat lightly warming her cheeks. 'But a bad guy wouldn't have brought me here to begin with. He wouldn't be making sandwiches at one in the morning to stop me from fainting like a helpless damsel.'

'Don't paint me as some hero, Olivia.' He shook his head. 'You have no idea how far that is from the truth.'

She made to continue talking, but he'd suddenly had enough. He put a hand up, silencing her. 'I've had a long day, and I'd appreciate it if you considered what I said about obeying my rules tomorrow.'

'I'll consider it.'

She shrugged, then walked past him into the hallway and began ascending the stairs, effectively robbing him of the chance to walk away first.

'That didn't sound like a yes.' He sighed, trying and failing to avoid the delectable sight of her shapely bare calves below the hemline of her dress.

'That's because it wasn't one.'

She disappeared from his view.

Olivia shielded her eyes as her hair whipped around her. The wind was like razor blades at this altitude, but the hour-long hike had definitely been worth it. She braced herself, taking one step out onto the balcony of the lighthouse. Heights had never really been an issue for her, but then again she had never been alone on a ledge in coastal winds before.

But all fear was forgotten once she stepped out and felt the sun spread across her face, warming her through.

There was nothing but ocean ahead of her for miles. She turned and caught her breath. She could see the entire island in all its glowing emerald glory. A heavy sigh escaped her lips and she leaned her elbows against the metal railing.

The villa was little more than a pea-sized white blur from here, partially hidden in the trees far over to the north. Likely Roman was still holed up in his office there, determined to spend as little time in her company as possible.

She had almost been tempted to go and ask him to show her the lighthouse. She had walked boldly up to his office door and stood poised, ready to knock. But then she had remembered his face as he'd called her Princess. The patronising tone as he had all but called her a child in need of supervision. She had not actually agreed to his terms, so technically she wasn't breaking any promises.

The hike had been just what she'd needed to shake off the extra energy that had plagued her all morning. She had made a point of eating a good wholesome breakfast before setting off, not wanting to make the same mistake as she had the night before. Now her thighs burned from exertion and her cheeks were warm and she finally felt as if she was *doing* something. And the best part of all was that she was entirely alone.

A harsh male roar caught her by surprise and her hand almost slipped on the railing. She looked down, wide-eyed, and caught sight of Roman powering across the plane at the base of the lighthouse, angry determination in his posture as he stopped and looked up at her.

He shouted something entirely inaudible, his voice fighting against the noise of the wind and the waves below. Olivia couldn't help it—she laughed. The smile that erupted on her lips made him scowl even more as he powered ahead once more and disappeared through the door beneath her.

There were at least three storeys between them, made up of one long winding staircase, and yet it seemed like barely a minute passed before she heard him step out onto the platform behind her.

'What the hell do you think you're doing up here?' he growled.

Olivia turned to look at him over her shoulder. 'I'm enjoying the view.'

'Oh, of course. Of *course* you'd have to perch yourself fifty feet in the air. You couldn't just stand on the deck below like a normal person.'

'The door was unlocked and I've never seen the inside of a lighthouse before.' She shrugged, holding onto the railing to pull herself up. 'It's not half as quaint as I'd imagined.'

She turned to face Roman, seeing his look of cold rage turn quickly to disbelief.

'This isn't a game, Olivia,' he said darkly. 'What if you'd fallen?'

'I'm quite capable of using stairs without supervision.' She stood tall, wishing he wouldn't keep looking at her that way. 'Please, just…stop treating me like a child.'

'Well, then, stop acting like one!' He raised his voice.

She sidestepped him, neatly sliding through the doorway and starting down the steps at a rapid pace.

He followed quickly behind her.

'You are the most reckless, difficult client I have ever had.' Roman stalked behind her, his voice still holding that dark edge.

'Because I wanted to explore a little?' She paused, turning to look back at him. 'This entire island is more secure than the royal vaults. You knew exactly where I was—as evidenced by the fact that you are *here*.'

'I was at least ten minutes behind you.'

'You are seriously overreacting, and I would like to know why.'

He met her eyes easily, his height making him tower above her even more than usual. 'I'm reacting as anyone would if they found the woman they are supposed to be protecting dangling her legs from a fifty-foot balcony.'

'It would hardly be your fault if I fell, would it?' She shrugged, turning back to continue down the steps. 'I'm sure your beloved Khal would find a replacement princess eventually.'

Strong hands encased her shoulders, effectively barring her from moving. Roman moved around her so they stood face to face.

She was almost completely level with him on the step below. The expression on his face completely took her breath away.

'Do you honestly have a death wish?' He grasped her shoulders tightly, his eyes blazing with real, deep concern.

'I... No, of course not.' She turned her face away from him, only for him to turn it right back.

His fingers were hot and hard against her cheek, and this close she was surrounded by the warm, delicious aroma of him that she had come to recognise so well.

'Your eyes tell me a different story.'

'Isn't that against the rules? Looking into my eyes?'

Was that her voice? That husky murmur? She could

feel her heart hammering hard and slow in her chest. It was as though the simple act of being near him sent her vitals into chaos.

'I've always hated rules.'

His mouth tightened, and tension spread through his hands and up his arms so that they felt like bands of iron on her shoulders rather than flesh and bone.

She bit her bottom lip as shivers spread down her arms. Roman's eyes lowered to take in the movement, his pupils darkening as he pressed his lips together hard. She thought he might kiss her. He certainly looked as though he wanted to.

But she saw the moment that something changed in his eyes—something that made his mouth harden and his eyes shift away from her once more.

For one crazy moment she wondered what it might be like to lean across and kiss all that tension from his mouth. To just take a wild leap and not care about the consequences.

And then all of a sudden she was doing it.

She closed the gap between them and laid her mouth against his, feeling his shocked intake of breath as their lips connected and her breasts pressed flush against the hard, strong plane of his chest.

He was going to hell.

There were no two ways about it.

Roman felt something inside him roar to life the moment Olivia's lips gently touched his, her feather-light caresses against his mouth almost completely undoing him. His hands found their way to her hair, releasing the clasp that held it wound at the nape of her neck.

He was letting this happen.

More than that, he wanted it so badly it made him ache.

She gave just as good as she got, her hands travelling over his shoulders and down his waist. Sharp fingernails grasped his hips just above his jeans. The sensation sent pulses of heat southwards and he felt himself grow hard against his zip.

The fleeting thought of stopping the madness came and went quickly as Olivia moved against him, her abdomen in direct contact with his erection. Far from being shocked or appalled, she kissed him even harder.

Their breath mingled into one frantic cloud of white-hot need. He kissed a trail down her neck, his hands sweeping deftly to the front closures of her blouse. With each satisfying click he was treated to a delicious sliver of creamy soft skin and the smallest glimpse of white lace.

Her breasts were small and firm, perfectly rounded and straining against the lace fabric of her bra. With one hand he reached behind her, undoing the clasp.

She exhaled long and slow, biting her lip as he pulled the garment away and lowered his mouth to her breast. Her skin tasted like a smooth ripe peach, the softness unbelievable against his tongue.

As he drew one peak into his mouth she hissed out a breath. 'Roman…' she breathed in awe.

Her fingers wound through his hair, anchoring him to her as he explored one taut peak and then gave ample attention to the other.

Their position on the steps made things difficult. It would be so easy to carry her down to the landing below and take her hard and fast on the floor. He could tell she was ready for him by the way she moaned at the slightest touch. She was his for the taking…

Except, she wasn't, was she?

The thought stilled him, stopping his body mid-motion.

She wasn't his.

Roman stepped away from her as though he'd been burned. His breath escaped his nostrils in harsh bursts as his body screamed in protest. He cursed out loud, his voice echoing in the cavernous space as he realised what he had been doing. What his body was still deeply invested in doing.

Olivia fell back at an uncomfortable angle, her breasts still bared to him. She looked up, confused and flushed.

'That shouldn't have happened,' he breathed, bracing his back against the cold wall and forcing himself to look away from the tantalising curves on display.

In his peripheral vision he saw Olivia stiffen, her hands quickly moving to cover herself. A prolonged silence ensued as he turned his back and listened while she frantically tried to button up her blouse and calm her breathing. When he finally turned around it was to find her gone—back up the stairs to the top of the lighthouse.

He followed, stepping out soundlessly onto the narrow balcony alongside her.

'Olivia…' he began, exhaling on a long sigh.

'Whatever you are about to say, just *don't*,' she said, her voice tight with recrimination and something else—regret, perhaps?

'It won't happen again, between us,' he said, almost as though he were trying to convince himself along with her. 'It was a mistake, bringing you here at all. This just proves what I already knew.'

'And that is?'

'That you are incapable of controlling your impulses.'

'And *you* are the most arrogant man I have ever met.' She turned to face him. 'Are you actually trying to blame *me* for this?' she asked. 'I may have kissed you first, but at least I'm emotionally mature enough to admit it was because I wanted it.'

'Excuse me?'

'*I wanted it.*' She spoke slowly and deliberately, her eyes blazing emerald in the brightness of the mid-afternoon sun. 'I wanted to know how it would feel, being kissed by you. To get under that wall of stone you surround yourself with. And I may be unpractised in these things, but I know that you wanted it too.'

His mind caught on one single word she had uttered. *Unpractised.* He coughed on the sharp intake of breath that filled his lungs.

Olivia's eyes widened, her face rapidly warming with embarrassment. 'I simply meant that I'm not accustomed to making the first move,' she said quickly, her eyes wide with mortification.

'*Chert voz'mi,*' Roman cursed under his breath, suddenly despising his own ability to see through to the truth. 'You have never had a lover, have you?'

He watched as her shoulders tensed and she tightened her grip on the rail in front of her. She hid her face from him but he could read the signs in her body. Surprise rapidly turned to self-defence. She didn't speak, but she didn't have to. He already knew he was right.

She was a virgin.

As if there weren't enough reasons already for this attraction to be the worst kind of wrong...

He turned, bracing one hand on the balcony rail and gripping it with all his might. 'Have you any idea what kind of game you are playing?' he gritted.

'I was not playing a game.' She turned her face to him, her shoulders stiff and unyielding.

'How would you even *know* what you were doing?' he said harshly. Anger raged in him—towards her, towards himself. He felt as if he was drowning in it. 'What did you think? That you could use me as a damned test run? Lose your virginity with the rough and tumble ex-con before I sent you back to your royal fiancé's bed?'

Her eyes narrowed, her fist flying out to thump him squarely in the middle of his chest. 'How dare you?'

He grabbed her hand in his fist, stopping her movement and inadvertently pulling her closer to him.

'You are angry at me because it is the truth. You think you are attracted to me? You don't even *know* me. You're attracted to my lack of refinement, Olivia. You see me as some big, uncivilised fool who you can charm with your delicate skin and innocent eye-flutters.' He shook his head, his mouth hardening into a cruel line.

'I don't think of you that way.'

'Well, maybe you should start. I might come from the gutter, but that doesn't mean I make a habit of living like a street thug. I do not sleep with virgins or with other men's fiancées. I have morals, Olivia.'

'What? And I don't? I am not engaged. I have done nothing wrong here.'

'You are as good as spoken for,' he ground out.

She looked up at him. Eyes that moments ago had been blue-black with desire were now wide and blazing

with anger. 'I will *never* be spoken for. Never again.'
A tremor passed through her throat. 'I am not another
man's property, to be protected and transported.'

'You are going back to the palace as soon as possible.'

'Roman, is it so hard to believe that I am just as
overwhelmed as you?'

'Don't flatter yourself, Princess,' he said cruelly. 'It
would take a lot more than an innocent's clumsy kisses
to overwhelm *me*.'

Her face fell and he knew he had gone too far.

But she was already turning to walk out through the
door. 'If you don't mind, I'd like to walk back alone.'

He made to walk after her but stopped, thinking it
might be best if they both had some time to calm down.

'Fine. You can take the time to prepare your explanation. I will deliver you to your fiancé tonight.'

CHAPTER SEVEN

OLIVIA REGRETTED STEALING Roman's boat almost as soon as she had set off, but stubbornness kept her from turning back. As the wind pulled her hair around her face and the salty air filled her lungs she felt the awful tension inside her loosen a fraction.

She hated him.

Every single word that Roman had thrown at her had swum around in her head as she had hiked across the craggy woodland towards the villa. His indignant accusations. His refusal to see the truth in their situation. He seemed determined to power through any argument she had.

It was the thought of his final words that had cemented her decision to change course and hightail it for the marina. *'I will deliver you to your fiancé tonight.'*

She gripped the wheel even tighter, steering the boat as the mainland drew nearer on the horizon. The distance between Isla Arista and the small mainland town of Puerto Arista was a mere fifteen minutes, but as the small dock came into view she contemplated turning around.

What *was* it about her breaking the law when she was around this man? Once again she had proved him right by giving in to an emotional impulse without a thought for the consequences.

Still, pride kept her from doing the intelligent thing and returning with her tail between her legs. She busied herself with mooring and disembarking safely, taking pleasure in the manual work.

She had always enjoyed her national sport—there was something quite peaceful about letting her mind wander as she followed through all the steps.

This small speedboat was much more streamlined and modern than the complex sporting sailboats she was used to, so before she knew it she was climbing the limestone steps up from the dock and emerging into a busy little Spanish village. Thankfully she had worn large sunglasses and a floppy-brimmed hat on her hike, to protect her from the sun, both of which now helpfully concealed her face from possible recognition.

The streets were cobbled and sloped upwards towards the impressive white cliffs that dominated the landscape. A long row of whitewashed houses and shops lined the seafront, with terracotta roofs and vibrantly coloured windows. The village was small, and seemed almost pristine in its appearance.

It was quiet. There was none of the hustle and bustle of the coastal spots in Monteverre. It was like stepping into a well-kept secret. People smiled as they walked past, shopkeepers tipped their sunhats in her direction. No one approached her or called her name. No one cared.

It was a revelation.

After she had walked to the top of the hill and back down her stomach began to growl. The thought of returning to the island—to Roman—filled her with trepidation. Without a second thought she walked into a nearby café and eyed the delicious selection of hand-made pastries and freshly cut fruit. The smell of warm butter and melted chocolate permeated the air and made her stomach flip.

Yes, this was exactly what she needed.

'Can I help you, miss?' A middle-aged man smiled jovially from behind the counter, his white apron smeared with powdered sugar.

Olivia smiled in response, really enjoying not being recognised. 'Yes—what's good here?'

'It's all good, of course.' He laughed. 'We have a special on today: three *magdalenas* for the price of two.'

Olivia looked down at the elegant golden-brown pastries and instantly felt her stomach drop.

She had no money.

With a murmured excuse she practically ran from the shop, embarrassment fuelling her as she walked swiftly down the hill back towards the marina. She stopped on the promenade, taking a seat on a bench that overlooked the small inlet.

As her breathing slowed, a heavy sadness replaced her embarrassment. She had no idea how to prepare for living in the real world. For all her thoughts of leaving her bubble and making a difference, the reality was that she had absolutely no idea how to function outside the privilege of royal life.

Her father had been right.

She had told herself that she would find a way to become the woman she wanted to be outside of her parents' expectations and royal obligations. She had believed she could fulfil the vision her grandmother had had for the foundation alone. But she didn't have a business mind—she didn't have that kind of common sense or leadership skill. She certainly didn't have the kind of innate intelligence and passion that could support her, as her siblings did.

Maybe she was delusional. Maybe her father was right and she should stick to where her strengths lay. Just another Sandoval princess, destined to stand and smile by her husband's side.

But one thing was for sure: she was *not* what Roman had accused her of being. She had not seen him as some sort of base creature to use for her own amusement. The thought that he saw her as someone capable of such cruelty…it bothered her.

She ambled towards the marina with the intention of returning and paused, watching as a familiar sailboat moored itself next to her smaller vessel. The name *Sofiya* was emblazoned across its hull.

Roman jumped down athletically onto the boards of the jetty before striding purposefully in her direction.

She turned away quickly, not quite ready for the confrontation she knew was bound to happen. He was likely furious, and he had every right to be. But she had hoped for more time to compose herself before the inevitable. Even now, the memory of his hands on her bare skin made her short of breath.

She shook off the heated thoughts, walking along the promenade at a brisk pace.

A man was walking towards her—the man from the pastry shop, she realised suddenly. He was walking quite fast and had a slightly odd expression on his face. Olivia paused, feeling suddenly very exposed on the empty promenade. As he neared her he reached into his jacket, his large hand fumbling for something in his breast pocket.

A loud growl erupted from somewhere over her left shoulder. Roman was running past her in a matter of seconds, moving to stand in front of the older man with ferocious agility and strength. His large body manoeuvred the man to the ground and he shouted to Olivia to move away. She could hear the man calling out underneath him—a strange muffled cry of one word, over and over.

Finally Roman moved from his position and the other man managed to gasp. 'Camera! Camera!'

Olivia spied the small black object that lay shattered near Roman's left knee. She rushed forward. 'Roman, it's just a camera!' She gasped, tugging at his sleeve for his to remove his body from the man. 'Roman, please stand up. He's not dangerous,' she urged, pulling at his shoulder.

Roman looked into the blue-green depths of Olivia's eyes and something inside him shifted. All at once he became aware of the man's fleshy paunch beside his knee. The roar of the waves hitting the promenade to his left. He could hear Olivia's panicked tone and his own fiercely ragged breathing.

Khristos, it had happened again.

He stood to his feet, looking away from where his unsuspecting, seemingly innocent victim had stood up and shuffled away. The roaring in his ears was deafening, the hammering in his chest making him feel as though he might pass out.

Without thinking of the lack of logic in his actions, he grabbed Olivia roughly by the wrist, ignoring her protests. Eventually she gave in and allowed him to lead her down to where his sailboat lay in wait. Within moments they were on board, and he closed the door of the spacious interior saloon with a harsh exhalation of breath.

'Sit down,' he commanded, watching confusion enter into her eyes.

'Roman, what on earth—?'

'Just sit down,' he repeated harshly, his breath still raw and uneven in his chest as he fought to control the ridiculous racing of his treacherous mind.

Sofiya.

His mind whirled against the onslaught of terrible memories threatening to overcome him as his sister's face broke through to his consciousness. As if in slow motion he could see the life leave her baby-blue eyes as the bullet tore through her body, silencing her scream.

He shook his head, swallowing past the dryness of fear in his throat.

Olivia moved in front of him, concern in her wide eyes as she placed her hands on his chest.

'You're shaking,' she said softly, in the kind of placating tone one used when trying to soothe a wild animal. 'Has this happened before?'

Her warm hands on his chest both irritated and calmed him. 'Don't push me, Olivia,' he warned. 'I don't want to hurt you, too.'

'You won't hurt me, Roman.'

She shook her head just a fraction, her innocent eyes so wide and confused it made him want to growl with frustration and bask in her concern all at once.

'Let me help you,' she whispered, moving her hand uncertainly to rest on his face.

The touch of her soft, feminine hands on his skin undid him completely.

He leaned forward, capturing her words roughly with his mouth, showing her just why she needed to run from him.

Her lips were soft against his, trying in vain to offer him comfort even as he plundered and deepened the kiss. He wound one hand around the back of her neck and twisted the fine silk of her hair in his hands. His rough touch anchored her to him while his other hand bunched into a tight fist by his side.

This was wrong, he told himself. He was using her in the aftermath of his own weakness, losing himself in her, and it was so wrong he hated himself. She was innocent to situations like this, he reminded himself, talking himself down from his own madness. She deserved better than this—than him.

He moved to away an inch and she looked up at him, lust clouding her vision.

'I can't keep my hands off of you,' he gritted, running his fingers down one side of her face and wincing as he noticed the small patch of blood staining the front of her dress.

Logic told him that the blood was likely from his own cut knuckles, but the sight of her pale skin next to the red smear was enough to sober him just for a moment. He tried to fish though the haze of his memory but drew up nothing but blankness.

'Roman, I need to know what happened back there.' She spoke slowly, as though afraid she might set him off again.

'I don't want to talk right now.' He shook his head,

pulling himself away from the heat of her, inch by inch, even as his body screamed in protest.

It was colder without her in his arms, but safer.

'Talk to me,' she said simply.

'I'm not good at talking, Olivia.' He turned to sit heavily on the leather sofa of the saloon. 'Guns trigger something inside me. Even the *thought* of guns, apparently.' He laughed cruelly.

'There was no gun, Roman,' she said. 'No danger.'

He stood, his anger boiling over to the surface. 'You think I don't *know* that?' he asked. 'But in that moment, when my mind goes there...'

'You are powerless to stop it?' she offered helpfully.

Powerless. God, how he hated that term. Was there anything in the world more terrifying than being out of control of your own mind and body, even if only for a few moments?

Olivia moved to sit beside him, her thigh brushing his on the small settee.

'You can talk about it with me, if it helps,' she offered.

'We are not all built for flowery conversations and sharing our dreams.'

Her eyes dropped and he realised he was doing it again—being needlessly cruel.

'None of this would have happened if you hadn't run off with my damn boat,' he continued, seemingly unable to stop himself.

'You deserved it,' she said harshly.

'For trying to protect your reputation?' he said incredulously.

'I don't think my reputation has a thing to do with it, Roman. You attacked a stranger, dragged me back here like the hounds of hell were chasing you and then you kissed me like your life depended on it.'

She met his eyes without hesitation.

'I kissed you to shut you up,' he argued, turning towards the bridge that housed the control panel so they could get the hell out of here and he could find some space.

'Now who's running away?' she challenged.

'You'd prefer to wait around until local law enforcement arrives to question us both?' he said darkly. 'I didn't even stop to see if I had hurt him.'

'He was fine—just shaken. You don't remember *any* of it?' She frowned. 'I got the chance to apologise quickly before you pulled me away.'

'If you think an apology is enough to stop him from pressing charges…'

'I told him that you were just a jealous lover.' She winced, half smiling with embarrassment.

Roman took a moment to look at her, and the situation suddenly replayed in his mind like a bad movie. He pursed his lips and then, before he knew it, dark laughter erupted from his chest.

Olivia smiled, also seeing the humour in their situation, and soon she was laughing too. She had a great laugh, he thought to himself as they both returned to silence after a moment.

'Thank you,' he said, looking deeply into her eyes for a moment.

He wasn't accustomed to thanking anyone for anything quite so personal; he made a point of not needing anyone enough to necessitate heartfelt apologies. But this woman had lied for him—protected him in a way. After he had treated her horribly.

It was a strange feeling—one he didn't want to examine too closely. For now, the ability to laugh it off was a novelty in itself.

Olivia nodded once—a graceful acceptance.

He took a step away from her, looking out at the harbour around them. It was late; the sky was already in full darkness around them. He suddenly did not want to return to the island—to the silence of the villa and the self-imposed exile he had placed himself in.

'Are you hungry?' he asked hopefully.

Simply named Faro, the small restaurant was partly built into the rocks that stood proudly at the tip of the peninsula. Olivia felt butterflies in her stomach as Roman's hand encircled hers, helping her down the steep steps to the low wooden door of the entrance.

'It doesn't look like much from the outside, but I assure you it's the best paella in all of Spain.'

'I'll take your word for it.'

She smiled, following him into a small hallway. Roman led the way down a corridor and out onto a large terrace that overlooked the coast as far as the eye could see. Warm glowing lanterns adorned the walls and brightened the space, making it seem like the terrace at the back of someone's home rather than a restaurant.

The overall effect was so welcoming she felt instantly at ease, all her tension from the afternoon leaving her shoulders as the waiter led them to a table on the very edge of the space. A man rushed over to take Roman's hand and clap him on the back. The pair began conversing in perfect English, and Roman ordered bottle of red wine.

When it came, Olivia took a sip of her wine, thanking the waiter and looking out across the bay. They were so close to the water she could see the waves crashing into the rocks below them. The after-effects of the day made her forehead tighten painfully.

Roman seemed determined to avoid the subject of their kiss entirely.

Both kisses.

She shivered at the memory of his rough handling after he had all but dragged her back to his boat. He had been completely raw and out of control, and yet she had felt nothing but excitement. Maybe he was right—maybe she *was* just looking for a taste of danger. Maybe she was naïve for not fearing him.

He had made one thing clear: he did not trust her. She desperately wanted to ask him about the incident on the promenade—find out why a man who ran a company of armed bodyguards would have such a deep issue with guns. But maybe she was a fool for worrying about him when he'd continuously told her she was no more than a job to him.

She had told him that she was a virgin and he had made it clear that the fact only cemented his view of her as being completely untouchable. She had never resented her own pesky innocence more than at that moment. When had he stopped being just a glowering bodyguard and become the object of all her fantasies?

She swallowed hard past the dryness in her throat as Roman sat down across from her and apologised for the interruption. After checking with her first, he ordered them both a light starter followed by the chef's special paella.

Once the waiter had taken their order they were

left completely alone. The moment of uncomfortable silence was not lost on Olivia. She cleared her throat, making a show of looking up at the vaulted ceiling that partially covered the open terrace.

'You seem to know the staff quite well,' she offered.

'It's been five years, I believe, since I started coming here for lunch every day when I was overseeing building work on my island.'

'They seem to like you.'

'The chef—he is also the owner. And the waiters are his sons.' He smiled, looking over at the young men bustling around the small restaurant. 'The first day I found this place, my architect brought me for lunch. The owner, Pedro, had an argument with his oldest boy and the kid ran off, leaving him with a pile of dishes and a line of hungry guests. I rolled up my sleeves and offered to help.'

'Not many people would do that.'

'Not many princesses would do what you did at that racetrack.' Roman shrugged, sitting back as their bread and gazpacho were laid out on their table.

Olivia couldn't mask her surprise at his mention of the incident with the young waiter and the champagne. 'That afternoon seems like a lifetime ago.'

He nodded. 'Perhaps we are both destined for the sainthood?'

She smiled. 'If you are hoping to convince me that you are not entirely heartless, it's working.'

'I might not have the benevolent influence of a royal, but I'm not afraid to get my hands dirty.' He shrugged again. 'Charity isn't always about money.'

'That's...' She shook her head, frowning at the memory of her argument with her father. Of those very words that she had spoken so vehemently. And here was Roman, echoing them as though it were simply a fact.

'Is something wrong?' he asked, frowning.

She shook her head, ignoring the painful throb in her chest at hearing his words.

She took another sip of wine, clearing the fullness from her throat. 'I adore my work in the community...' Olivia sighed, unable to hide the wistfulness that crept into her voice. 'I swear it's the only time I feel like I'm doing something worthwhile with my life.'

'That sounds like a vocation,' he said, sipping from his own glass. 'And yet you don't sound fulfilled.'

She shook her head. 'This might surprise you, but princesses don't have much sway when it comes to promoting new education laws or increasing expenditure on public schooling.' She sighed again. 'Since the crackdown on my security I've missed several important events. Perhaps the children won't even have noticed. Perhaps I'm only helping *myself* by going out there, boosting my own self-importance. Maybe I'm just an egomaniac.'

'I highly doubt that,' he said, all seriousness. 'This bothers you? Your lack of power?'

'Of course it does. How would *you* feel if you had people holding you back from living your own life at every step?'

A strange look passed over his face, disappearing just as quickly.

'I can only do so much.' She shrugged. 'Potential future innovators of my kingdom are sitting in homeless shelters and all I am allowed to do lately is hold charity balls. It means absolutely *nothing*.'

'Your work means more to those children than you could ever know.'

'How can you know that?'

Roman was quiet for a long time, his hands held tight in front of him. Then, 'I've lived that life. A long time ago, now. But you never forget.' He forced a smile, draining his glass. 'I know that a stranger's kindness means more to a homeless child than you would ever believe.'

Olivia took in the tightness on his features, the guarded emotions in his dark steel-grey eyes. 'Roman, I had no idea…'

'My past is not something that I like to relive. I just want you to know that your work has value. I owe much of my success to men and women I never even knew. They received no thanks, no rewards. I never understood such selfless giving—it was not something I had grown up to feel. Never doubt such honest goodness, Olivia.'

'I am sorry that you had such a difficult upbringing.'

'I'm not. It made me who I am today. But I am not arrogant enough to forget that the world would be an awful place if it was only filled with cynical men like me.'

Olivia understood him then—a little more than before, at least. 'You're not so bad.'

He laughed. 'You don't know the half of it.'

'Tell me, then,' she said quickly. 'Tell me whatever it is you think is so awful about yourself and let me be the judge.'

'Mine is not the kind of story you tell over paella and wine.' The laughter died from his voice, making it clear that the topic was not open for further discussion.

Their main course was laid in front of them, providing a welcome distraction. The food was delicious, and yet as Olivia watched Roman eat she couldn't help but imagine him as a young boy. Thin and hungry... helpless. It was a jarring thought—one that filled her throat with emotion.

She hated to think of anyone suffering through such hardship—especially considering the luxury she had been born into. It had never sat well with her, the enormous divide between the wealthy and the poverty-stricken. She had always felt a weight on her shoulders and an obligation to do her part.

'That was delicious,' she said, forcing a smile as the waiter came to clear their plates and replenish their wine glasses.

'I hope this meal has done something to make up for my behaviour so far,' he said, lowering his glass and looking at her. Sincerity darkened his eyes as he held her gaze. 'For some reason the idea that you see me as cold and cruel bothers me.'

'I don't think you are cold at all,' she said, in all seriousness. 'I think that's just what you prefer people to believe.'

The night had grown cold by the time they embarked at the Puerto Arista harbour and set sail for the short trip back to the island.

Olivia apologised once again for the fact that they had had to abandon his luxury speedboat, but Roman assured her it was fine. They fell into silence as he concentrated on moving the boat along the harbour safely towards open water, each of them deep in thought.

A spark in the sky behind them startled her, and she turned back just in time to see an explosion of red and blue lights erupt into the perfect black sky.

'It must be midnight,' Roman said from behind her.

She could feel him lower their speed and allow the boat to drift slightly.

'This firework display is not one to be missed, trust me.'

'There's no need to stop just for my benefit,' she said quickly.

'Consider it part two of my apology.'

He guided her to the sun deck and pulled two cushions from the built-in sofa, laying them on the cold tiled floor. It was slippery with mist, and just a little chilly, but as a cascade of golden lights began to spread across the inky black sky she knew she wouldn't have changed the night for anything.

After the final booming red spinning wheels had faded into the air, she turned to see he was watching her intently. She took in the heat in his gaze and knew he was battling with the aftermath of that kiss just as she was. She had never wanted to be kissed again more in her life.

'We should be getting back,' he rasped, his eyes not leaving hers.

'I'm really tired of doing what I *should* do all the time.' She licked her lips, silently urging him to give in one more time to the madness between them.

'Olivia…' He shook his head a fraction, lowering his eyes from hers.

She reached out to lay her hand just under the collar of his shirt, knowing she was being brazen but needing to do *something*. To show him in definite terms what her mind was struggling to convey with words.

He took her hand in his, lowered it back to her lap. 'You're not the only one who has to live by the rules,' he said quietly. 'Sometimes they are there to stop us from getting in too deep where we don't belong.'

'I am a grown woman, Roman. If I decide to take a leap into something unknown, you'd better be sure that I've got my reasons.'

'You might *think* you know what you want—'

Olivia stood quickly, looking down at him. 'I told you that I won't be spoken for again,' she warned him, feeling her temper bubble to the surface as she alternated between wanting to hit him and wanting to beg him to take her into his arms.

'Speak, then,' he said plainly, sitting back to look up at her. 'What is it that you want?'

'It's more what I *don't* want,' she said. 'Being here— away from the bubble of royal life—being with you...' She took a breath, urging the words out, needing to say them even if he simply walked away.

Roman shook his head, not giving her a chance to continue as he jumped to his feet and moved back downstairs to start up the engine once more.

The rest of their journey back to the island was silent and tense, unspoken words heavy in the air between them. She wanted to ask him if he still planned to take her back to the palace tomorrow. If he still believed that she should go ahead with the marriage.

The Jeep ride was bumpy, and all too quickly they were standing in the dim empty hallway of the villa. Jorge must have closed up for the night and headed off to his quarters on the opposite side of the island.

'Goodnight, Olivia.'

Roman's voice was dark and final as he made to walk away from her.

'Wait,' she said quietly. 'I've realised something.'

He turned around, crossing his arms over his chest as he waited for her to speak.

Olivia cleared her throat, suddenly feeling very much on show. 'I've realised that I don't want to walk away from my kingdom, and if marrying a stranger is the way to keep it safe then perhaps that's what needs to be done.'

She took a deep breath, wondering if that was relief or disappointment that flickered momentarily across his features. She couldn't tell in the dim hallway.

'You are quite the sacrificial lamb,' he said quietly, with not a hint of emotion in his tone. 'So you plan to return to the palace and accept the marriage?'

'I've decided to return, yes. And face the situation like an adult, at least.' She met his eyes, challenging him in the darkness. 'But I can't fully commit to the marriage knowing there is one thing I have yet to experience in life.'

'I thought you ran away because there were *many* things you hadn't experienced?' he said, sarcasm dripping from his tone.

'There is only one that truly matters to me. I cannot agree to an arranged marriage without allowing myself to experience one of the things I truly have control over.'

His gaze was pure heat as he moistened his lips with one smooth flick of his tongue. She felt heat spread down through her veins and pool in her stomach. If a simple look could make her feel this way, she needed to know what else he could make her feel. It was suddenly the only thing she wanted.

'I want my first time with a man to be on *my* terms, with someone who wants me just as badly as I want him.'

CHAPTER EIGHT

IN HIS MIND Roman simply gathered her into his arms and carried her up to his suite as fast as his legs could take him. Surely this was far more torture than one man was expected to endure? But in reality he remained silent for a long moment, his throat dry as his mind fought to sort between loyalty and lust.

She was offering herself to him on a silver platter.

'You think you can separate sex from love?' he said softly.

'If the sex is good enough.' She shrugged one delicate shoulder, biting her lower lip gently as though embarrassed by her own words.

She couldn't even say the word without blushing and she wanted to fall into bed with him. He took one step towards her, then another, until they were almost toe to toe.

'Men like me don't make love, Olivia,' he said darkly. 'They don't make empty promises just to play into some fantasy.'

She gulped, looking up at him through hooded lashes. 'What if I don't want the fantasy?'

'I have a thousand fantasies I could tell you about,' he whispered. 'Each one more risqué and physically demanding than the last. I would have you naked in my bed quicker than you could beg me to take you. Is that what you want me to say?'

'I...' Her voice trailed off, her eyes wide with uncertainty.

Roman let one finger trace the curve of her shoulder. 'You're not ready for me, Princess,' he said cruelly. 'You need a man who is going to whisper sweet nothings in your ear and make sugar-coated promises. I'm not that man.'

Roman braced his hand on the door of his suite and laid his forehead against the wood—hard.

Loyalty be damned. He wanted nothing more than to break down every door between them and take her like the unrefined street thug that he was.

But she was a virgin. She was not his to take.

Even as his mind thought the words his fist tightened in protest.

He took another deep, rattling breath, feeling the stale air of the room fill his lungs to bursting point.

She was not his.

With more force than necessary he turned and swung open the door to the terrace, silently thanking his housekeeper for placing his guest in the opposite wing of the villa. What would Olivia think of him now? Standing out in the night air, trying desperately to calm his raging libido like a scorned youth?

He looked across to where the light shone out from her rooms.

No. He shook his head, turning to vault down the stone steps in the direction of the pool. He had made his decision, just as she had made hers. And by God he would live with it.

The night was surprisingly mild, with barely a breath of breeze blowing in from the bay. The moon was full and high in the sky, casting a silvery glow on the water of the pool.

He took no time in stripping down and diving in, shock coursing through him as the cold water encased his skin, penetrating through to his very core. The pool was deep and he pushed himself to his limit, waiting as long as possible before breaking the surface.

As the balmy air refilled his lungs he saw the unmistakable silhouette of Olivia, standing near the water's edge.

Roman stood, so that the water reached his waist, very aware that he was completely nude in the water. His heart beat slow and hard in his chest. They were silent for a long moment, his eyes never leaving hers.

'You decided to take a late-night swim,' she said, her voice strangely husky in the dim light.

'And you followed me.'

She moved to the entry steps of the pool, dipping one toe in before stepping down ankle-deep in the water.

He noticed for the first time that her legs and feet were bare, that she wore a thin robe that stopped just above her knee. He wondered if she had anything underneath. He felt an ache in his gut, so deep, and he knew right then that he would move heaven and earth to have her out of that robe and in his arms.

He moved forward in the water, closer to her with every breath.

'I decided I couldn't leave here tomorrow without

knowing more about those fantasies,' she said, her voice carrying across the space between them loud and clear.

Her hands moved to the tie of her robe and Roman paused, feeling the breath freeze in his lungs as he simultaneously willed her to stop and to keep going.

'How much more?' he asked, his voice husky as it echoed off the pool walls.

'Everything,' she said, her eyes never leaving his.

Roman took another step and watched as Olivia's eyes dropped to where the water level now completely exposed him to her. Her eyes darkened as she looked, and looked, before finally dragging her gaze back up to meet his. What he saw there ignited a fire in his blood. Raw desire darkened her eyes and coloured her cheeks as she undid the tie of her robe.

The white silk slid from her skin and darkened as it touched the water, leaving nothing between them but space. He was within arm's length of her now, unconsciously moving towards her. But he stilled at the sight of her, completely nude and offered to him like the living statue of a goddess. Her skin glowed under the moonlight. Every perfect curve of her body was on display in high definition and it was a revelation.

She stood still for a moment, before modesty got the better of her and she self-consciously moved one hand to shield her most intimate parts from his hungry gaze.

Roman closed the distance between them in a single movement, encircling her waist with his hands and pulling her with him into the water. With her body partially hidden, she relaxed in his arms and pressed herself tightly against him.

'I changed my mind too,' Roman said throatily, his mouth tracing a path along the exposed curve of her neck.

Her hands refused to stay clasped at his neck, instead preferring to explore the muscles of his back and down his waist.

She bit her lip seductively, removing her nails from where they had pinched quite roughly. 'I have wanted to do that for quite a while now.'

'Oh, so we are making up for lost time?' He gathered her higher, to his chest, wrapping one of her legs around his waist before doing the same with the other and pressing her back against the wall of the pool. 'In that case...'

Olivia groaned at the sensation of having Roman's lean, hard body cradled between her thighs, and his mouth captured hers in a kiss filled with barely restrained want. She could feel the heat of his chest pressing against hers and silently prayed for him to kiss her there again. As if he'd heard her plea, he broke the kiss and began trailing a path down her neck. By the time his mouth reached her breast, her breath was coming in short bursts. His mouth, hot and sinful, captured the entire rosy peak and tortured her with slow, languorous circles.

She began writhing against him as his free hand cupped her bottom and squeezed hard. The pleasure that rocketed through her was like being shot with lightning, and suddenly it was not her mind but her body that knew exactly what she wanted and just where she wanted him.

Her hips rolled against him and she moved herself lower, startled as she felt the hardness of his erection press erotically against her skin.

'Slow down,' he whispered, nipping the skin of her ear with gentle pressure.

'I don't think I can,' she breathed, moving against him, silently urging him to move against her. To place himself against her.

She tried to be embarrassed at her wanton response, but found she was quite past caring. Roman held her hips tightly in his hands, effectively stopping her movements. She looked up to find his dark eyes trained on her face and his jaw tight with restraint.

'That is possibly the most beautiful torture I could experience,' he breathed, leaning forward to gently nip her bottom lip with his teeth. 'But I want this to be good for you.'

'It feels pretty good so far.' She licked the curve of his lower lip, her gut clenching as he pressed the full length of himself against her in one quick slide.

'Olivia... I'm so hard right now that taking you fast and furious against this wall is *not* a good idea.'

He moved again, letting the tip of his erection slide against her sensitive throbbing flesh.

'Oh...' She moaned low in her throat as he moved, making slow, aching circles over just the right spot. 'Roman...don't stop.'

She closed her eyes, tilting her head back as his mouth found her breast once more. The double effect of his touch made her heart jump into overdrive and she could feel her pulse thrumming hard, as though it tried to escape her skin.

He urged her on in a mixture of English and Russian, his low, husky words sending her soaring higher and higher until she swore she could take no more. She dug her fingernails deep into his shoulders, wanting him to stop but wanting him to keep going for ever. It was like being trapped in her own personal hurricane—being swept up into a power so much stronger than herself.

When she finally found her release Roman was right there to catch her and hold her as she fell back down to earth. Heat spread out across her body, sending electricity right down to the tips of her toes. She opened her eyes and realised she was being lifted out of the water as her skin came into contact with the cold lip of the pool.

The contact was brief, as Roman lifted himself out and gathered her up into his arms as though she weighed nothing at all. It was strange, allowing him to carry her naked across the terrace. They were completely alone on the island, so privacy was guaranteed, and as she looked up at him she realised the feeling she had was not one of nervousness but one of anticipation.

He carried her easily up the stairs to his master suite. She had barely taken in the cool grey sheets on the gigantic bed when she felt her anticipation quickly intensify to mild panic. He was advancing on her now, his perfect muscular torso glowing in the light of a single lamp as he lowered himself over her and cupped her face with one hand.

As his lips lowered to touch hers she turned her cheek, grimacing when she realised what she had done.

'Is everything okay?' he whispered from above her, one hand trailing down her shoulder in a slow, sensual path. 'Are you…rethinking this?'

'No,' she said quickly, noting his features soften with relief. 'No, I'm definitely not rethinking *any* of this.'

'Relax,' he murmured, kissing a path down between

the valley of her breasts. 'This is one of those fantasies I was telling you about.'

'It is?'

She lay back, staring up at the ceiling and willing herself to calm down. His mouth was doing a very good job of distracting her. That was until she realised just where those lips were headed. She tensed, reaching down for him just as his lips began to trace a path below her navel.

'This is *my* fantasy, remember?' he said, gripping her wrists and holding them by her sides. 'And I haven't even got to the good part yet.'

'Roman...you can't honestly—'

'Do you trust me?' he asked, his eyes dark with passion as his lips pressed gentle kisses along the inside of her thigh.

Olivia watched him kiss her, watched him draw closer to the centre of her, and felt herself nod once. She did trust him. Completely.

The nerves fell away with each gentle kiss on her skin and her eyes never left him, watching as he drew his tongue slowly against the centre of her sex. Her back arched and her eyes fluttered closed for a moment. When she looked back down his eyes were on her, dark and possessive, as he moved his hands to spread her wide and kiss her even deeper.

Her head sank back against the pillows as her body was enveloped in wave after wave of hot, wet pleasure. She reached down and knitted her fingers through his hair, anchoring him to the spot that felt most intense. He growled his appreciation, sliding one finger inside her in a slow rhythm.

'Oh... Roman...' She gasped at the feeling of delicious fullness, hardly believing it when he added a second digit to join the first without breaking rhythm.

Just as she began to feel that pressure mounting once more he removed his mouth, sliding up her body in one fluid movement. He reached across to the nightstand, grabbing a small foil packet and sheathing himself with lightning speed.

'I can't wait another second. This time I want to be inside you when you come,' he rasped, his voice half demand, half question as he met her eyes in the dim glowing light.

She spread her legs wide, silently answering his question with her body.

She could feel the tension in his shoulders as he positioned himself at her entrance, slick and ready from his expert attentions. His breathing hitched as he entered her with exaggerated slowness. Olivia raised her legs to encircle his waist, showing him that she was ready. That she wanted to feel him inside her for the first time.

The feeling of fullness was so intense she almost begged him to stop. After a moment she wanted to ask if there was much more of him to go.

There was.

She breathed deep as the sensation became uncomfortable, and was vaguely aware of Roman's voice intruding on her thoughts.

'I'm hurting you,' he said, deeply concerned, and began to withdraw from her.

Olivia held him with her thighs, keeping them connected as her body adjusted to his sizeable girth. 'Now it's your turn to be patient,' she breathed.

She tested her hips once, then twice, in a slow rolling movement. What had begun as a dull sting of pressure soon gave way to a more pleasurable pulse of heat.

Roman's breath hissed from between his teeth as she moved against him, but he remained exaggeratedly still above her.

'Does that feel good for you?' Olivia asked, taking in his tense jaw and serious expression as she tightened her innermost muscles, feeling the delicious hardness of him buried inside her.

Roman lowered his face into the crook of her neck, groaning low in his throat as though he was in pain. 'Oh, yes. Oh, God, yes.'

Olivia smiled, moving against him and feeling his breathing quicken in response. Suddenly he moved over her, his body arching slowly to press more firmly against her. She looked up into his eyes and somehow knew just what he needed.

He moved her thighs high on his waist, spreading her wide so that he could thrust right to the hilt. She gasped in pleasure, her hands on his chest as he braced himself on his forearms above her. His rhythm was deep and purposeful as he moved over her. He was powerful and entirely lost in his own pleasure.

Release reached them both at the same time, crashing down in wave after wave of pleasure. Olivia closed her eyes as the last of the ripples flowed through her, feeling the mattress move as Roman lay himself down heavily beside her.

CHAPTER NINE

ROMAN LAY STILL for a long time, his brain working overtime to fight through the heavy fog that always came after orgasm. This was different—heavier, somehow. He had never experienced a climax so intense.

Thoughts of why he should not feel so relaxed threatened the edges of his consciousness but he fought them off. He would analyse the repercussions of what they had just done in the morning, for now he thoroughly intended to repeat the experience just as soon as she was able.

He turned on his side, looking down at her where she lay curled on her side. Her eyes were closed, and for a moment he wondered if she was asleep, but then her lashes fluttered open and he was pinned by that blue-green gaze. Her hair had come undone at some stage, and its long lengths were spread across his sombre grey pillows in all their vibrant red glory. If possible, it looked even redder in that moment.

He reached out, taking a strand in his hands and running his fingers along the length of it. He was suddenly overcome by the realisation that it had been her first time and he had almost taken her in the swimming pool. Thankfully his brain hadn't been too far gone to realise that she deserved an actual bed for such a delicate moment, and that they needed to use protection. He *never* forgot to take precautions.

'I hope that was…satisfactory?' He smiled, a glow of male pride in his chest as he took in the slow smile that spread across her face.

'I never even dreamed that it could be so…' she began, shaking her head. 'Earth-shattering.'

'It isn't always that way.'

He ran a finger down the valley of her breasts, watching the play of light on her flawless skin. He had only just finished making love to her and he yet he couldn't stop touching her.

'I'm glad my first time was with you,' she said softly.

Roman stilled, taking in the look of deep emotion in her eyes. Knowing his own personal warning bells should be ringing at full blast. She was not experienced enough to separate the physical side of what they had just shared from her emotional reaction. And yet even as he told himself to remind her of his rules he found that he himself was having a hard time abiding by them.

He fought the urge to lean in, to kiss her mouth and lay a trail of kisses down her neck. He frowned. Such actions were dangerously close to tenderness. He was not a tender lover—to a virgin or not.

But he cared what she thought of him, that she'd enjoyed her first time—that was entirely normal, wasn't it?

Maybe that was the problem. He had nothing to compare it to, having steered clear of virgins up to now. He had never enjoyed the idea of being a woman's first, of having that much pressure on the act. But now, knowing he was the only one to have touched her, been inside her, heard her scream out in her orgasm…

He wanted more.

It was a dangerous madness, feeling like this. He had always prided himself on remaining detached and aloof from the women he chose to spend time with. They knew he wasn't in it for commitment. They got what they needed and left his bed satisfied as a result.

Olivia sighed deeply and moved so that she lay against his side. Her hand stroked up the inside of his wrist to his elbow and he looked down to see her curiously tracing the thick black band of ink that encircled his forearm.

He didn't think of the tattoo often—it was usually covered up and out of sight. But every now and then he found himself looking at it, thinking of the man who'd branded him, of the *life* that had branded him. And yet he had never had it removed.

'It's a gang tattoo,' he offered, not knowing why he suddenly felt the urge to explain. 'Not my own personal choice of design.'

Her lips formed a delicate little O as her fingers stilled over him. 'From your time in prison?' she asked quietly.

'Long before prison.'

A silence fell between them. Roman wondered if perhaps she was regretting her choice of lover after his revelation, but after a moment she sat up on her elbow, pinning him with her gaze.

'This gang—did they use guns a lot? Is that where your fear stems from?'

Roman frowned, laying his head back against the

pillows as he remembered the events of the day before in painful detail. 'No. That's not where it comes from.'

She seemed suddenly self-conscious. 'I'm sorry if this isn't exactly pillow-talk material. I know you are probably the kind of guy who doesn't like to talk afterwards.'

'I don't,' he said honestly. 'But I can compromise.' He turned smoothly onto his side, so that they were face to face. 'You can ask me *one* question about my past and I will answer it—truthfully.'

Her eyelashes lowered momentarily. 'Who is Sofiya?'

Roman was silent for a moment. Then, 'Sofiya was my little sister,' he said. 'She died a long time ago.'

'Oh, I'm sorry.' Olivia's brow deepened into a frown. 'She must have been very young.'

'Sixteen.' He shrugged. 'It's in the past. Almost twenty years ago.'

'Grief doesn't care about time.' The corners of her lips tilted down sadly. 'My grandmother was buried ten years ago and I still visit her grave often.'

'I have never visited Sofiya's resting place,' Roman said, surprised at how easily the words spilled from him. 'Her parents despised me.'

Olivia sat up slightly. '*Her* parents? Not yours?'

'We were both abandoned by our birth mother at a very young age. Sofiya was a tiny blonde cherub with big blue eyes. She was adopted very quickly. I was not.'

'Oh…' She sat up slightly, looking down at him with concern.

He hated the feeling of being so vulnerable, and yet somehow he was unable to stop the words from coming once they'd started. 'Unlike my sister, I wasn't the most appealing child. I always had too much to say. It became a part of me to cause as much trouble as I could manage.'

He frowned, remembering the uncontrollable rage that had filled him as a child. He had broken toys, furniture—even bones on a few occasions.

'I was fuelled by anger and hatred. I was kept at the orphanage until I grew too big to contain. After I ran away for the third time they stopped trying to bring me back.'

'That is when you became homeless?'

Roman nodded. But the truth was he had never known a home. The only difference was that once he'd left the orphanage he'd had the added struggle of finding a safe place to sleep at night.

'I can't imagine how that was for a young boy.'

'I was thirteen—practically a man.' A low, harsh laugh escaped his lips as he thought of his gangly young self, so cocky and self-assured. 'When the local thugs saw the size of me they asked me to run errands. I didn't mind that they were criminals. They took me in…gave me a warm bed. One of the guys even bought me shoes.'

His chest tightened at the memory. He had worn those shoes until his feet had burst out of them. Then he had gone out and stolen himself a brand-new pair.

'I was thin and fast. They used me to climb through windows and vents and such on jobs. I felt very important.'

Olivia was quiet as he spoke on, telling her of his ascent into the criminal gangs of St Petersburg. To her credit, she did not react in any way other than to ask a question or to clarify a point. She just listened.

She listened when he told her of Alexi—the father of 'the brotherhood', as he'd called it. She nodded as he told her how, when he had grown broader and stronger, he had advanced to being a part of the main crew. They'd held up banks, intercepted cash in transit and generally just taken whatever they wanted. More than once he felt the old shame seep in, threatening to silence him, but she urged him on.

'This Alexi guy...he sounds dangerous,' she said softly, tracing a small circle on his chest as she watched him.

Roman thought for a moment of the man who had simultaneously given him everything and then torn his life to pieces.

'I wanted nothing more than for Alexi to be proud of me. He was the only dominant male figure I had ever known. It made me feel needed, validated—I don't know.' He shook his head, uncomfortable with the conversation all of a sudden. He didn't like to think of Alexi, of the hold he had once had on him.

'I think that was only natural. You were easily groomed—an easy target. You were vulnerable and he exploited that.'

'I never truly relaxed into the so-called brotherhood, and Alexi could see that. I had seen how quickly some of their drunken brawls escalated and I made a point to always stay sober. More than once he questioned my loyalty using violence.'

'Is *that* where your issue with guns stems from?' she asked quietly.

Roman frowned, realising he had gone off on a tangent. How had he kept on speaking for this length of time? Usually talking of the brotherhood and its fearless leader was enough to send him into silence for days, but something about Olivia had kept him talking...opening up.

Unwelcome memories assaulted his brain. Memories of the last night he had seen Alexi. Of the blood and the outrage and that pair of terrified, lifeless, baby-blue eyes.

Suddenly he couldn't talk any more. He stood up, walking to the terrace doors to look out at the night beyond. He shivered, feeling a cold that was not actually in the air but inside him. Ingrained in him.

Olivia bit her bottom lip hard as Roman remained completely silent by the doors and then watched as he walked into the bathroom, shutting the door behind him with finality. She had pushed too hard—her curiosity had been too overbearing. He was likely already planning the best way to tell her to leave.

He had made it perfectly clear that he was a one-night-only, no-snuggling type of guy—and here she was, initiating a psychotherapy session.

She lay back, throwing one arm across her face in mortification. She had just made love with this physically gifted specimen of a man and still she kept digging deeper, wanting more from him than he had warned her to expect. Trying to peek under his armour.

She angrily swung her legs over the side of the bed and stood, feeling her inner muscles throb with just the barest hint of exertion. She didn't feel too different, she thought with a frown. A little sore, perhaps, but not monumentally transformed as she had expected.

Still, it had been...utterly perfect.

Maybe it was best that it ended this way. She would

arrange to have a helicopter pick her up in the morning and that would be it. No awkward morning-after encounter, no hurt feelings. They both knew what this was, that it could be nothing more. She was completely fine with that.

But still some small naïve part of her made her linger for a moment outside the bathroom door until she heard the shower turned on. He couldn't have sent a clearer signal if he'd shouted the words *Go away!* at the top of his lungs.

The night was over.

She returned to her bedroom in darkness, not bothering to turn on any lights as she slipped in between the cool white covers and let stillness wash over her. Her mind raced, thoughts of what tomorrow might bring seeping through to her consciousness as the afterglow of her one experience of lovemaking dimmed.

Was one night of perfect lovemaking with a man of her choosing really enough to carry her through a lifetime of a loveless marriage?

As her exhausted brain admitted defeat and she drifted into half-sleep, she imagined what her wedding day might look like. Only in her mind the man at the top of the aisle was Roman. Devastating in a dark tuxedo as he took her hand and professed his eternal love for her.

All of a sudden her dream shifted to their wedding night, becoming infinitely more erotic. She sighed as he leaned in and pressed his lips to hers, the scent of him so familiar and overwhelming it was as if she could actually feel the heat of his skin pressing against her.

'You are so beautiful...'

His voice rasped near her ear, sending shivers down her spine and even lower.

Her eyes snapped open. 'Roman?'

He was draped across her, the scent of his shower fresh and warm on the air as his mouth laid a trail of kisses down the side of her neck.

'You left without giving me a chance to say goodbye,' he said, a dark glint in his eye as he moved lower to take one of her breasts into his mouth.

'You were the one who left.' She exhaled on a slow hiss as his teeth grazed her skin. 'I thought you were a one-night-only kind of guy.'

A wicked smile spread over his dark features as he poised himself over her, one hand snaking a path down her abdomen to slip between her thighs.

'The night isn't over yet, Princess.'

His kisses became more heated as his fingers took her higher and higher towards climax. Before she could completely shatter, he turned onto his back and urged her to straddle him.

'You will still be tender... I don't want to hurt you,' he rasped, his breath coming hard and fast, evidence of his arousal.

Olivia moved over him so that her breasts grazed the smattering of dark hair on his chest. She was clumsy at first, uncertain in her own movements as she poised her body over the sizeable length of him. He was rock-hard and already sheathed, waiting for her. She took a moment to slide the tip of him against her most sensitive spot, enjoying the sensation of molten heat that spread through her.

She repeated the motion a few times, wondering if he would grow impatient and take over himself. He didn't. Even as his rigid jaw showed the extent of his control he remained still, allowing her this moment of exploration.

'I'm not quite sure if I'll be any good at this,' she said uncertainly, lifting herself so that he was poised at her entrance.

'I'm right here, holding you.' He ran his large hands down her back, cupping her buttocks with possession as he guided her.

Her body stretched around him as she took him deep inside her in one smooth movement. The barest hint of discomfort faded quickly to an impatient need to roll her hips, to ride him and increase the delicious pressure she could feel with each movement.

'Is that...good?' she asked, her breath coming faster as arousal pooled and tightened inside her.

'You are driving me insane in the best possible way,' he groaned, his eyes never leaving hers. 'Don't come yet. Not until I'm right there with you.'

Olivia tried to slow down, to control her movements and somehow hold off the mounting climax that seemed ready to shatter her entire being at any second. He held her gaze, his hands gripping her hips as he began thrusting upwards slowly, in time with her.

Their rhythm was so smooth, so gentle, and yet somehow it was filled with a barely restrained madness as they both rose closer and closer to climax. Roman's breath fanned hard and fast against her cheek as she leaned forward, her breasts crushed against his chest. His hands moved up her back to hold her close, a deep primal groan escaping his lips as he slowed down even further and moved deeper inside her.

Olivia gasped at the overwhelming intensity of

being so absolutely cocooned in his strength, and then the intense friction tipped her over the edge and she fell headlong into an orgasm that seemed to ripple through every inch of her body.

As she fell she felt a tightening in her throat, and prayed he wouldn't see the sheen of moisture in her eyes as she watched him lose control entirely beneath her.

Roman kissed her neck, growling something deeply erotic in his native tongue as the muscles of his abdomen began to ripple with the force of his own orgasm.

Afterwards, as she listened to his breathing deepen with sleep, she wondered if she had ever felt closer to another human being in her entire life.

The thought made her feel sad and grateful all at once. She had got her wish, without a doubt. He had made her first time the most sensual, real experience of her life.

His long, hard body was partly covered, but she still let her gaze sweep over him in the darkness, lingering on his features. His face was transformed in sleep, the hard lines of his mouth completely relaxed. It made him seem younger...more carefree. It dawned on her that she had never seen him look at peace. Here, in sleep, Roman the great and powerful master of security, was completely vulnerable.

The thought of returning to the palace, to her own empty bed, was suddenly inconceivable. And even worse was the thought of sleeping alongside another man.

Marrying another man.

Her throat tightened painfully with the force of her emotion. Roman would not offer her any more than this night—she knew that. He was not the marrying kind, no matter what she suddenly hoped. He was not even the relationship kind.

But as she lay staring up at the play of shadows on the ceiling she knew one thing with more certainty than she had ever known anything in her life.

She would not marry the Sheikh.

When she awoke the bed was empty beside her in the early-morning light. Ignoring the sting of loss, she grabbed a white robe and stepped out onto the terrace, taking a moment simply to breathe and take in the gorgeous view of the bay spread out below.

Her hair was a nest of tangles, and she was in dire need of a shower, but for once she had no formal breakfast to attend, no official functions. She could stand here all morning if she chose, enjoying the last few hours of her freedom.

Roman would expect her to leave today, and that was perfectly understandable.

She thought of his revelations last night, the deep, dark secrets he'd shared, and wondered if he would regret sharing so much now that their night together was done.

He had told her only briefly of his life in St Petersburg. Of the orphan who had been abandoned to sleep in cold gutters, but she remembered every word in vivid detail. Every little piece of the puzzle he had revealed that made him what he was.

Roman had lived through hell itself. It was no wonder he seemed harsh. The world had hardened him from the moment he was born. He shouldn't have had a chance—and yet he had risen from his old life, determined and hungry for better. He had created his own empire without a single care for his social class or his chequered past.

He was the master of his own destiny.

Here, in the rosy glow of dawn, she felt utterly transformed simply by having known him. She laughed at her own thoughts. Romantic, indeed, or maybe simply foolish. Perhaps all virgins felt this way about their first lover?

How would he react to the news once he found out that her marriage was not going ahead? She imagined he would be frustrated with her—with himself. He would blame it all on their brief affair.

But, truly, Olivia wasn't sure her decision was completely down to their night together. On some level she had known she was not destined for a loveless marriage from the moment her father had thrust the idea upon her.

No amount of loyalty to Monteverre would outweigh the value she needed to feel in herself. Roman had made her see that, somehow.

She told herself that it didn't bother her that he was completely unaffected by their time together. She was not going to read anything into last night, and nor would she expect anything more from their liaison. He had made it very clear that he was not the kind of guy who slept with the same woman twice.

CHAPTER TEN

ROMAN HAD TOLD Jorge to take the day off, to ensure them some privacy, wanting as little intrusion as possible so that he could deal with the aftermath of their night together.

Olivia arrived down to breakfast dressed in pink. The dress had the kind of high waist and flowing, knee-length bell-shaped skirt that made her appear like something straight from a vintage movie.

She was breathtaking.

Her eyes were shuttered and her smile forced as she sat at the table across from him. The silence was heavy and uncomfortable, and his mind scrambled to find something to break the tension. In the end he accepted that there was simply nothing to say.

To his amazement, Olivia demolished two full plates of fresh fruit and a cream-drizzled pastry. She moaned as she devoured her last bite of pastry, looking up to find his eyes trained on her.

'I was hungry,' she said, a light blush on her cheeks.

'I've seen prison inmates eat with more decorum,' he found himself saying playfully. 'One night with me and you've completely forgotten how to behave like a princess.'

Her eyes widened at his mention of last night, as though he had broken some unwritten rule by acknowledging that it had happened.

She sat back in her seat, a smile crossing her lips as she met his eyes boldly. 'Whatever will my subjects think?'

Roman raised a brow. 'That you've been taken down the path to ruin by a disreputable mongrel.'

'Mongrel?' She looked both amused and shocked.

'You come from a world where breeding is everything, after all.'

'Have we suddenly become *Lady and the Tramp*?' She laughed.

'I have no idea what that is,' he said honestly, smiling at the look of horrified surprise on her face.

'I can't believe you've never seen such a classic. It's wonderful—the lady dog comes from a fancy home and gets lost, and the tramp dog saves her?'

'You are likening me to a tramp dog?' He raised one brow in disbelief. 'I'm flattered.'

'*You* likened yourself to a mongrel—not me!' she exclaimed. 'It's not *my* fault that my brain associates everything with movies.'

'Film and television were not a regular part of my childhood,' he said, disliking where this conversation was headed. 'But let me guess: they all live happily ever after at the end?'

'Yes, exactly.' She smiled.

'That's why I don't waste my time on movies. It's not reality.'

'Well, of *course* it's not reality.' She laughed. 'That's what makes them an escape.'

Roman stood, gathering their plates and placing

them less than gently into the sink. 'You spend far too much of your time escaping real life—you know that?' he said, knowing he had hit a nerve when he looked up and saw both of her hands balled into fists on the tabletop.

'You're being cruel now, and I have no idea why.'

'This is not cruelty, Olivia,' he said calmly. 'You have no idea what true cruelty is. What true hardship is, even. You dislike it when people put real life in front of you—that's your problem.'

She shook her head slowly. 'I have no idea why you're being like this right now. We were just talking about a movie.'

'Life is not like the movies, and the sooner you realise it the better!' He raised his voice, surprising himself with the force of his outburst.

Olivia stood, closing the distance between them. 'I may not have known the kind of hardship that you have experienced in your life, but that does not negate the fact that I have feelings too.'

'I thought it was clear that last night was not about feelings,' he said stiffly.

'And yet here you stand, shouting at me, when I was perfectly prepared to leave here on good terms.' She shook her head. 'It's probably best that I wait outside until my helicopter arrives.'

'You are leaving?' he said, the words tasting like sawdust in his mouth.

'I called the palace first thing this morning. They are sending someone to get me.' She nodded, moving to the table to pick up her coffee cup before returning to place it in the sink.

Even with her perfect posture and impeccably

coiffed hair she seemed quite at ease, clearing up after herself. Far from a domesticated goddess, but still not too far above herself to consider leaving the mess for him to clean.

He thought of their conversations the evening before, of her talk of charity work. She was not the pampered royal he'd accused her of being and it was high time he admitted it to himself.

It was easy to place her in that box—to see her as stuck up and untouchable. It made her less real. But here she was, the woman who had shattered something inside him with her lovemaking last night, all too real.

And all too ready to leave him.

He knew then why he was being cruel. He simply wasn't ready to give this up. To give *her* up. Not yet. And yet he knew it had already gone on too long as it was.

He was the worst kind of bastard, he thought darkly. Khal had trusted him with this—had entrusted him with the care of the woman he hoped to spend the rest of his life with. Whether the union was cold and political or not, it did not matter. He had rationalised his actions simply because their passion had been mutual. He had got lost in the novelty of feeling so utterly out of control.

Olivia deserved more than this. She deserved more than a brief fling with a man like him. And that was all he could offer her. Once the passion wore off he would only end up hurting her when he left. Roman Lazarov did not *do* relationships. He did not make declarations of love and commitment or plan lifetimes together.

In the past he had never been good at returning the things he had stolen. He refused to repeat his mistakes.

And yet the idea of Khal knowing what had happened made him balk. Not for himself, but for Olivia. She deserved his protection.

'I'm coming with you,' he said, surprising himself.

Olivia turned around, her eyes wide with confusion. 'There is no need to escort me home, noble as it seems.'

'This is not about being noble—it's about being honest with Khal.'

Guilt entered her expression at the mention of the Sheikh's name. His gut churned at the realisation that by rights he should be displaying the same emotions himself, seeing as he had spent the past twelve hours in bed with the woman his best friend hoped to marry.

'Do you honestly want us to tell him about last night?' she said with disbelief.

'I will speak to him alone. There is no need for you to see him.' He found himself saying the words—words he had meant to protect her—and yet he could tell by the dark look on her face that they had come out wrong. As usual.

'You presume that I need you to explain on my behalf.' Her gaze seemed to darken as he took a step closer to her. She stood tall. 'I am quite capable of speaking for myself.'

'Clearly you are not. Otherwise none of this would have happened.' Roman shook his head, anger at the whole ridiculous situation coursing through him.

'Feeling some remorse, I see.' She pursed her lips.

'*One* of us should. Do you simply plan to go back and accept his proposal with the heat from my bed barely gone from your skin?'

'Is that actually what you think of me? Do you even know me at *all*?' She was completely still, unnaturally still, like the eerily calm glass of the ocean before a hurricane.

'I'm trying to—God help me. But you're not making it very easy.'

'And just what will you tell him? Seeing as you've got this covered.'

'Whatever needs to be said. Bottom line: he needs to know that we have slept together. I cannot let your marriage go ahead with him in the dark.'

'Bottom line?' Olivia's eyes widened. 'You know that telling him will essentially be ending the engagement before it can even happen? Why the sudden change of heart? Two days ago you were doing everything in your power to make this union go ahead.'

'Do I truly need to explain to you what has changed?'

Olivia's eyes darkened. 'Yes. You do.'

And there it was. The gauntlet, large and heavy, hanging in the tension-charged air between them.

'You spent the night with me, Olivia,' he said. 'I took your virginity.'

'That does not qualify as an explanation.' She bit one side of her lip, taking a few paces away from him before turning back. 'You said it yourself—it was just sex.'

Roman met the unmistakable challenge in her blue-green eyes. He had not lied when he'd told her that sex was not always so intense.

'Sex is never "just sex" when it is one person's first time,' he said quietly, knowing he was being a complete coward.

'I think that is up to me to decide.'

'You wouldn't need to decide anything if I had done the right thing and walked away last night.'

'How utterly male of you to think that.' She rolled her eyes. 'Spending the night in your bed was *my* choice too, Roman. I wanted it just as much. I wanted *you*.' Olivia took a step towards him, the sunlight glowing on her Titian waves. 'You did not *take* my virginity. You can't take something that is given freely. I took last night just as much as you did.'

She looked so beautiful at that moment—all strength and feminine power. Hadn't he told her she needed to let this woman be free?

The unmistakable sound of helicopter blades in the distance intruded on the moment. Roman looked out of the windows and sure enough a scarlet-coloured chopper was coming in from the coast, the gold crest of Monteverre emblazoned along its side.

I wanted you.

Her words echoed in his mind as he analysed his own motivation for wanting to tell Khal of their night together. He knew that telling his friend would stop the engagement, knowing Khal as he did. He still wanted her. He was not fool enough to deny the fact. One night was just not enough when it came to Olivia. She was the best and the worst thing that he had ever stolen in his life, and the bastard in him wanted to keep her here until they were both truly done with each other.

Was he really that selfish? To manipulate her situation and push Khal out of the picture simply so that he could get her out of his system?

He ran one hand through the short crop of his hair, trying to make sense of his own thoughts.

'What if I told you that I plan to refuse the marriage?'

Her voice was quiet from behind him, strangely uncertain after the power of her speech moments before.

'You said yourself that your loyalty to your country is important.'

'Yes, but that was before I realised how it felt to take control of my own life for once.' She bit her bottom lip. 'Being with you…it's made me realise that I can have more. That I want more.'

'I can't give you what you want,' he said plainly, panicking at the look of open emotion on her face. 'If you plan on placing your entire future on the hope of something more between us then you are more naïve than I originally thought.'

She flinched at his harsh words and he felt like the worst kind of bastard. Hearing her speak of their time together so tenderly did strange things to his chest. As if with every word she uttered, bands grew tighter around his lungs. And it made him want to lash out with words to make her stop. To make her see him for what he was.

It was ridiculous, and immature, and yet he could no more stop himself from reacting that way than he could stop his brain from seeing guns where they didn't exist.

Olivia fought the tightness in her throat, refusing to let him see how deeply his words had cut. She met his gaze evenly. 'I will be returning to the palace alone. I trust that you will respect my privacy when it comes to last night. I should at least have the right to that from you.'

'I never said I didn't respect you,' he said harshly.

'Good. We have an understanding.'

She kept her voice even, walking over to the terrace doors to watch as the helicopter finished its landing and a familiar assistant exited the door, making her way towards the villa.

'This is goodbye, then,' she said, not wanting to turn to look at him but knowing she would regret it for ever if she didn't. She felt anger, hot and heavy, burning in her chest. 'Thank you for allowing me to be one of the many women in your bed.'

His eyes narrowed, a cynical snarl appearing on his lips. 'Indeed. I will always have the pleasure of knowing that when it comes to you I was the first.'

'You are using the past tense already—how honest of you.'

'I have been nothing but honest with you about the kind of man I am,' he said harshly.

'Last night... I just thought that things seemed different somehow. That *we* seemed different.' She spoke calmly, trying and failing to hide the hint of insecurity in her voice.

'Everything seems different in the heat of passion, Printsessa.'

The silence that followed might only have lasted a matter of seconds, but to Olivia it felt like an eternity. In her mind she willed him to say more. Even a hint that he felt something more would be enough. Had she truly imagined that last night was momentous for them both?

And then he turned from her. Every step that he took across the kitchen seemed to hammer into her heart. Dampening down any flicker of hope she might have had.

She listened as his footsteps echoed across the marble tiles. Did he pause for just a split second in the doorway or did she imagine it? For a moment she thought he had taken a breath, preparing to speak. But then his steps kept going, out into the hallway, echoing as he moved further and further away from her.

She let out a breath that she hadn't even realised she'd been holding. The air shuddered through a gap in her teeth, like a balloon deflating and making a spectacular nosedive towards the ground. It was the ultimate heartbreak...knowing she had been just another woman in his bed.

She wanted to be *the* woman. The *only* woman.

But hadn't he made it abundantly clear that he would never be that kind of man? Was she really such a clichéd, naïve little virgin that she had fallen head over heels in love with him and expected him to do the same?

Typical that there wasn't a drop of vodka on the damned boat when he needed it.

Roman threw the empty bottle down hard on the glass bar-top, feeling it crack and shatter in his hand as it hit the surface.

'*Chert voz'mi!*'

He held his hand over the sink as the first drops of blood began to fall. The cuts were not deep, just surface wounds.

'*Damn* whoever is in charge of stocking the damned bar.'

'That would be me, sir.'

Roman turned to see Jorge in the open doorway, the man's face filled with concern.

'I came to see if you want me to close up the house.'

'Do whatever you like. I won't staying around long enough to check.'

'I see that Olivia has left us,' Jorge said tentatively.

Roman lowered his voice. 'I do not want to speak about Olivia. I want to relax and enjoy the rest of my vacation on my damned boat—alone.'

'With vodka?' Jorge added.

'Yes. With vodka. Is there a problem with that?' Roman spat. 'I am a grown man and you are not my father.'

'No. No, I am not,' Jorge said, a hint of sadness in his voice. 'But you have made it clear in the past that you at least see me as a friend of sorts.'

Roman grunted, wrapping a strip of linen carelessly around his injured hand.

'Can I speak frankly with you?' Jorge asked.

'You always do.'

The older man half smiled, crossing his arms and taking a deep breath before speaking. 'I think that you are hurting right now.'

'Believe me, I've had worse in my lifetime. I'll heal.'

'I'm not talking about the cuts on your hands.'

'Neither am I.'

'The Roman I know would never concede defeat so easily. You are not the kind of stupid man who would let pride stand in the way of what he wants.'

'Just because I want something, it doesn't mean I should have it. I have learnt that lesson in the past, Jorge. She is meant for a better man than me. A *good* man.'

'She loves you.'

'No. She is in love with the *idea* of love and nothing more.'

'I watched her get into that helicopter and, believe me, I know a heartbroken woman when I see one.'

'Well, that's not my fault. I did not hide from her the man that I am.'

'The man that you are would never come railing into his liquor cabinet unless he was deeply hurt by something. Or someone.'

'Jorge, you really must add psychoanalysis to your list of skills.'

'Tell me I'm wrong,' the other man said. 'Tell me she doesn't mean anything to you and I will fill that bar with vodka and send you on your way.'

'She is nothing to me,' he said the words, willing himself to believe them. Willing himself to ignore the burning pit of anger in his stomach.

'So if Khal marries her you will stand by his side and wish them well? I can see it now. You can visit them each summer in Zayyar. If you are lucky, their children might even call you Uncle.'

Roman's eyes snapped up to meet the gaze of his all too knowing housekeeper.

'*There.* That's all the reaction I needed to see.'

'Just because I feel the marriage is the wrong choice for both of them, it doesn't mean there is something deeper going on. I know Khal, and I know he would not be happy with a woman like Olivia. She is too adventurous, too unpredictable. She wants to see the world, to be surprised by life. Not trade one palace prison for another.'

'And have you said any of this to the woman herself?'

Roman sat down on the bar stool, pulling the linen tighter on his hand and feeling the sting of pain that came with it. Jorge was right. He had not told Olivia how he felt about the marriage. Not honestly. He had spent half his time with her trying to convince her to marry Khal, and the other half trying to make her forget.

Was it really surprising that she had run from him

again at the first chance? From the start he had handled her badly.

Women like Olivia were out of his league. She was too open, too caring and kind-hearted for a cold, unfeeling bastard like him. She deserved love. She deserved the happy-ever-after that she craved. And if he couldn't give it to her himself then he would make damned sure that she had a decent chance of finding it elsewhere.

'Shall I have the boat readied for departure?' Jorge asked hopefully.

Roman nodded once, watching as his housekeeper practically skipped from the room. He really should give that man a raise, he thought darkly as he moved to look out at the waves crashing against the lighthouse in the distance.

The marriage would not go ahead—not if he had anything to do with it.

CHAPTER ELEVEN

THE FIRST THING that Roman noticed as he entered the Sheikh's penthouse hotel suite was the utter stillness of the place. A single palace guard welcomed him inside before returning to his post outside the doorway. There was no butler to accept his coat or announce his presence—in fact no one at all roamed the halls as he passed through from room to room.

He had almost given up when finally he reached a large dining room that looked out over the lush green mountainscape of Monteverre's famous rolling hills. Khal stood alone at the head of the long dining table, his back turned as he stared out at the view.

Roman cleared his throat, feeling as though he had interrupted a moment of quiet meditation and wishing he had called ahead of his arrival.

'Roman. Now, this *is* a surprise,' Khal said, surprise filtering into his dark features as recognition dawned.

But Roman had not missed the mask of dark stillness that had been on his friend's face. That look bothered him deeply, and yet he knew that if he asked his concern would be met with a stone wall.

They were much alike, he and Khal.

'I need to speak with you,' Roman started, finding the words much more difficult than he had anticipated.

Truthfully, he was unsure where to begin. He had come here, all guns blazing, ready to rock the boat and make sure this ridiculous marriage did not go ahead. But how exactly did he tell his best friend that he had not only broken a rather important promise, but that he had done it in the worst way possible? He had promised to bring the Princess back to Monteverre to take her place as Khal's future wife, and instead...

Well, instead he had found himself consumed by a passion and a need so intense it had bordered on obsession.

He had not stopped thinking of Olivia in the few hours they had been apart. Memories of her assaulted him at every turn. If he closed his eyes he could almost smell the warm vanilla scent of her hair as it had lain spread across his pillows. He could almost hear her throaty laughter. She consumed him like no other woman ever had.

In fact, it was a mark of the strength of his feelings for her that he chose *not* to fight for her.

He was not here to lay claim to her.

He was here to set her free.

Khal sat heavily in one of the high-backed chairs, putting his feet up on the marble tabletop and surveying Roman with one raised brow. 'By all means, speak.'

'The Princess is the wrong choice for your bride.' He met Khal's gaze purposefully, making sure that there was no mistaking the seriousness of his tone.

'You sound quite sure.'

'I am. And I would like you to take my concern

into account. There are things more important in life than politics.'

'Such as friendship, perhaps?' the Sheikh suggested, a strange hint of cynicism in his voice.

'I was thinking more along the lines of personal happiness.'

'I'm touched, Roman. Truly.'

'I'm trying to do the right thing here. To stop you from making a mistake that will last the rest of your life.'

'If you were doing the right thing you would be telling me the truth. You see, you need not worry about my personal happiness at all, Lazarov. Princess Olivia has already made her refusal of marriage to me quite clear.'

Roman felt his chest tighten painfully. 'Olivia? She came to you?'

'Not long before you, actually. Strangely, when she spoke of you she bore the same look on her face as you do right now when I mention her name.'

Hot guilt burned low in his stomach as his friend stood up and met his eyes with a cold detached evenness he had never witnessed before.

'I'm trying to control my temper here, Roman, because I don't want to jump to conclusions. But I'm struggling. Three months of planning. The future of two kingdoms hanging in the balance. And after a few days with you she's ready to give everything up.'

Roman remained silent for a moment, taking in the glint of barely controlled temper visible in his oldest friend's eyes. He knew he should walk away before things became any more heated. Olivia had already refused the marriage—he had no reason to be here.

But something held him rooted to the spot. In his

mind all he could picture was King Fabian, planning Olivia's life for months before informing her of her impending engagement. Using an innocent woman as a pawn in his own political games. The man was cold enough to practically sell his own daughter to the highest bidder—as though she were a commodity rather than his own flesh and blood. It made the proud, possessive street thug inside him roar to life and demand justice.

'Tell me something,' he said calmly. 'In your three months of planning did you ever think to speak to the woman herself to see if she *wanted* a political marriage?'

He watched Khal's mouth harden into a tight line as they stood toe to toe in the utterly silent dining room. There were no onlookers here, no palace guards or servants. They did not need to maintain any level of propriety. Right now they were just two men.

'I will ask *you* this question, because I deemed it inappropriate to ask the lady herself.' Khal's voice was a low whisper. 'Did you sleep with her, Roman?'

'Yes. I did,' Roman said the words harshly, feeling the air crackle with tension between them. 'And I am not going to apologise. Not to you, or to her damned father, or anybody.'

'Well, I'm glad to see you showing some remorse.'

'She is a *person*, Khal,' Roman spat. 'Not mine or yours. She can make her own damned choices—which you would know if you had ever bothered to treat her as such.'

'Right now this has nothing to do with her and *everything* to do with you,' Khal snarled, taking a step forward and jamming one finger hard against Roman's shoulder. 'You just couldn't control yourself—admit it. You wanted a woman and so you had her. Does the Princess *know* that she is just another notch on your bedpost? Or perhaps you are both just as selfish and impulsive as each other?'

Roman surged forward. Their noses were now mere inches apart. 'She is *nothing* like me,' he said coldly. 'She is kind and giving and she deserves more in a man than either of us could ever offer her.'

He paused, watching the anger drain from Khal's face as his brows furrowed with surprise. With a deep, shuddering breath he stepped away, turning to face the window.

A long moment of deathly silence passed before he heard Khal exhale slow and hard behind him, a slight whistle escaping his lips. 'I don't believe this... You are in love with her.'

Roman braced one hand on the window ledge, looking out and seeing nothing. 'Don't be a fool. You said it yourself—women have only ever served one purpose for me.'

Khal's low whistle of laughter sounded across the room. 'I never thought I'd see this day. Roman Lazarov—brought to the edge of his infamous personal control by love.'

Roman shook his head, turning to take in the look of amused wonderment on the Sheikh's dark features. 'I am not prone to the sentiment. I simply believe Olivia has been treated poorly and I want to see it made right.'

'You poor, naïve fool. Sadly, love is not something we can choose to feel or not to feel. Trust me—I know.'

'I am not like you, Khal. I am not made for family life.' He took a deep breath, knowing it was finally time to say out loud the words that he had wanted to say for a long time. 'Look at my history with protecting the women I care for. My sister, your wife… I break things. I always have. I am simply not the kind of man she needs me to be.'

The mention of his late wife was usually enough to put an end to any conversation, but Khal surprised him, standing and placing a hand heavily on his shoulder.

'It was not your fault that Priya was killed. I have told you this time and time again. Just as it was not your fault that Sofiya was killed. You cannot take on the blame for everything that goes wrong around you.'

'What about Zayyar?' Roman said, shaking his head. 'This marriage was part of your great plan and now it's all gone to crap.'

'Perhaps not,' Khal said cryptically. 'I am not completely out of options just yet. Once Olivia ran away, the King and I discussed a possible fallback plan.'

Roman was silent for a moment. 'The youngest Princess?'

Khal shrugged. 'If she is willing, so be it. If not, I will retreat and regroup—as always.'

Roman nodded, glad that all hope was not lost for the two nations.

Olivia stood in her dressing room and placed the elegant emerald tiara upon her head for the last time. She met her own eyes in the mirror with a mixture of sadness and excitement, knowing that after tonight everything would change.

And yet everything had already changed for her.

Would anyone notice that everything inside her

had undergone a massive transformation in the past few days?

With sudden momentous clarity she realised that for the first time in her life she truly didn't care. From tomorrow she would be giving up her right to succeed to the throne voluntarily, and making the leap into actually leading Mimi's Foundation. She was done with being a pretty face who smiled and waved. The time had come for her to use her own two hands to make the difference she craved.

Perhaps once all of this was over she might appreciate this moment more—the sudden power she felt as she left her suite and began to descend the grand staircase on the way to take her life back into her own hands. But at that moment she felt neither powerful nor relieved.

She had given her virginity and her heart to a man who had repeatedly warned her that he would treasure neither. She knew now that romantic souls could not simply choose to behave otherwise. She could not switch off the part of herself that yearned to feel loved, no matter how much she willed herself to.

A lifetime of training had taught her how to relax her facial muscles into a polite mask of indifference, even while emotions threatened her composure. Harsh decisions would likely need to be made, and comfort zones abandoned. But for the first time in her twenty-six years she was not worried about the unknown.

Olivia couldn't recall the grand palace ballroom ever looking more beautiful. As she descended the long staircase into the crowd of guests below she reminded herself to smile and hold herself tall and proud.

Perhaps one day in the far future she might look

back on this night and yearn for a moment like this. But even as the tug of uncertainty threatened she pushed it away. She had made her decision and the time had come to put herself first.

The Sheikh had not been half as forbidding as she had anticipated—in fact he had seemed more pensive than anything as she had carefully outlined her reasons for refusing his proposal. His gaze had seemed knowing as he had enquired about Roman's treatment of her, but perhaps that was just her own sense of guilt.

She had her own reasons for keeping her affair with Roman private. She wanted to treasure her time with him, not have it sullied by the judgement of others. Either way, she had taken her power back and it felt great. The marriage would not be going ahead.

But she was not naïve enough to think that the hardest part was over.

Even as the thought crossed her mind she looked up to see her father watching her from across the ballroom. They had not yet formally met, but by now she assumed he would have spoken with the Sheikh. He would know that she had refused the proposal and he would be planning his punishment for her supposed betrayal.

Let him plan, she thought with a solemn shake of her head. He had no control over her. Not any more.

A commotion near the entrance caught her eye and she looked up to the top of the staircase to see a man pushing past the guards to descend the steps with ease. Two Royal Zayyari guards in crisp white and purple uniforms flanked him, holding off the Monteverre palace guards with ease and forcing them to stand down.

Roman.

Her mind went completely blank as the man she loved advanced towards her, his powerful frame accentuated by a perfectly tailored tuxedo.

'What are you doing here?' she blurted, so taken off balance by his appearance that it made her insides shake.

'It's good to see you too, *milaya moya*.'

His voice was like a balm to her soul. She hadn't realised how much her silly lovesick heart had yearned to hear it again. Just one more time. It had barely been twenty-four hours since she had left Isla Arista, and yet it felt like a lifetime since she had stood in front of him. Since she had looked into his slate-grey eyes as he had broken her heart with all the practice of a pro.

He opened his mouth to speak, but was cut off by the booming voice of her father as he advanced upon them from the other side of the room.

'Guards! Get this criminal out of my palace this instant!' King Fabian was livid, his cheeks a bright puce as he came to a stop a few steps away from where Roman stood.

The ballroom seemed to have become very quiet all of a sudden, and Olivia was thankful that the room was only half full as the guests had only just started to arrive.

'King Fabian—I was hoping I would see you tonight.' Roman's eyes narrowed, his shoulders straightening with sudden purpose.

Olivia reached out as Roman took a step towards her father, her hand on his arm stilling his movements. 'This is my fight, not yours,' she said, steeling herself as she turned to her father.

'The Sheikh has said that you refused his proposal

after your little trip with this thug,' King Fabian spat. 'Judging by the lovesick puppy expression on his face, I can take a good guess as to why.'

Roman snarled, but remained dutifully silent.

'Father, I had planned to have this conversation at a better time,' she said, looking around to see that the palace guards had descended to herd the guests to the other side of the room, offering the royal family some privacy.

'There is nothing you can say to save yourself now, girl.' Her father shook his head sadly. 'I hope he's worth giving up your place in this family.'

'He has nothing to do with me giving up my place,' she said, as Roman frowned. 'Well, he does—but not in the way that you think.'

She took a deep breath, facing her father head-on.

'By giving up my right to succeed to the throne I am free of your control. That's worth more to me than being a princess ever could be.'

Roman reached out to touch her arm, 'Olivia, you don't have to do this.'

'I do. You see, my father has made more life-altering decisions on my behalf than this one.' She looked back at her father, noting his gaze darken. 'Such as when I inherited sole ownership of my grandmother's foundation ten years ago and he had me sign away my rights to him. At sixteen years old I didn't understand the repercussions. But now I do. And I know that by stepping out from under your thumb I'll get to take control of my own destiny for once and truly start helping people.'

'You can't do that.' King Fabian laughed cruelly. 'You can't simply walk away from this life.'

'I already have, Father,' she said sadly. 'I've been in

contact with external advisors over the past few months to discuss the legalities. Once I relinquish any claim I have to the throne the foundation goes back into my name alone. Just as Mimi wished it to be.'

She hated it that her own father could look at her with such open disgust simply because she had chosen to go against his wishes.

Her own personal happiness did not matter to him.

Roman's eyes had widened as he listened to the exchange but he did not speak for her again. Nor did he attempt to interrupt as Olivia finished her conversation with her father and simply turned and walked away.

He took a moment to stand toe to toe with His Majesty, King Fabian. The urge to say everything he wished to say was so intense it consumed him. But Olivia had handled the situation with all the style and grace of the Princess she truly was. There was nothing he could add that wouldn't ruin it.

And so he walked away, following the woman he loved and ignoring the slew of vulgar curses in Catalan shouted in his wake.

He followed her in the direction of the outer terrace, instructing the two Zayyari guards Khal had lent him to stand sentry by the doors and make sure they were undisturbed.

Olivia stood with her back to him, staring out at where the moonlight shone across the ornamental pond in the gardens.

He moved to her side, reaching out his hand, needing to touch her. She flinched away and something inside him flinched too, with the hurt of that small movement.

'You're angry with me…of course you are,' he said softly, silently urging her to turn to look at him.

She didn't speak. Instead she wrapped her arms around herself defensively and stared resolutely ahead.

'I came here because I wanted to save you,' he said. 'I never even entertained the possibility that you were completely capable of saving yourself.'

'I'm glad I surprised you,' she said, irony dripping from her words as she turned to face him.

'Olivia…' he breathed. 'I came here to make sure that the marriage would not go ahead. I told myself that I was doing it for *you*, to save you from making a mistake that would last a lifetime. But I know now that I was only lying to myself.'

He braced one hand on the balustrade beside her, making sure to keep some space between them.

'I have never told anyone the things that I told you about my past.' He looked away for a moment, out at the darkness of the water. 'Something about you makes me want to tell you everything. To confide in you and trust you, even though I have spent a life-time trusting no one. It scared me to death, to be quite honest.'

'Oh, Roman…' she said softly, reaching out her hand to touch him.

He raised his hand, holding her off. 'Wait just an-other moment. I've been thinking all evening about what I would say when I got here, you see.' He inhaled sharply, felt the adrenaline coursing through him. 'I've spent years—decades—blaming myself for my sister's murder at the hands of a man I trusted. She was shot right in front of me by Alexi, to teach me a lesson.'

Olivia's hands covered her mouth and tears filled her eyes. This was all going wrong, he thought. He hadn't meant to upset her—he just needed her to understand.

He stepped forward, taking her hands in his and kissing her knuckles gently. 'No, please don't cry. Anything but that.' He looked deeply into her eyes. 'I'm telling you this because I want you to understand why I'm such a cold, unlovable bastard. That monster wanted me to see love as a weakness. So he could break me down and make me easier to control. I have unknowingly let that lesson stick to me like tar for the past twenty years. I let that man's actions shape me, even from beyond the grave.'

'You are so brave to have overcome that...' She shook her head. 'To have become what you are now...'

'My success is nothing so long as I am alone,' he said simply, taking a breath and steeling himself for possible rejection.

She was utterly breathtaking, her long fiery hair backlit by the glow of the lights in the garden. The dress she wore was utter perfection in emerald silk, but truly she could have worn rags and he would have found her breathtaking. She was beautiful, it was true. But knowing her as he did now...knowing what lay below that surface beauty... It was infinitely more spectacular.

'I came here to tell you that I love you, Olivia,' he said softly, watching as his words resonated. 'I didn't know how much I needed you until I thought of seeing you on another man's arm. *Any* other man. Of watching you become his wife and have his children... I cannot bear the thought of you marrying anyone... other than me.'

* * *

Olivia's heart thumped wildly in her chest as she looked into the solemn, emotion-filled eyes of the man she loved. 'Is that a proposal?' she breathed.

'I hadn't planned on laying it all out like that so quickly,' he said uncertainly. 'I understand if I've done too much. If I've been too cold for you to ever trust me or feel the same way.'

She shook her head, a small smile forming on her lips. 'I trusted you from the moment you offered to take me away with you.'

'Foolish girl.' He smiled, uncertainty still in his eyes.

'But love...?' she said, taking a step closer and running her hand over the lapel of his suit jacket. 'That didn't come until I truly knew you. Knew the man you are underneath all the bravado and the ice. Then I fell in love with you so deeply it took my breath away.'

He finally took her into his arms. His mouth was hot and demanding on hers as his hands held her tightly against him. His embrace filled her with warmth and strength. When he finally pulled away she groaned with protest, never wanting the moment to end.

'Are you sure you want to marry me? Even though I am no longer a princess?' She let a smile seep into her words as he tipped her back in his arms.

Roman shrugged. 'I suppose it's okay to settle for a simple philanthropist as my wife.' He sighed, sweeping his hands down her sides. 'If you're okay with the fact that *I* don't run an entire kingdom?'

She pretended to consider her options for a long moment, until his hands began to move lower on her hips and he pulled her hard against him in mock warning, with playfulness and a joy that mirrored her own in his eyes.

'I love you, Roman Lazarov,' she said solemnly. 'And nothing would make me happier than becoming your wife.'

The kiss that sealed their engagement was one filled with passion and promises. Olivia sighed with soul-deep contentment as she looked up into the face of the man she loved. The man she had chosen for herself.

Her own destiny.

* * * * *

MILLS & BOON

Coming next month

THE SICILIAN'S BOUGHT CINDERELLA
Michelle Smart

'But...' Aislin couldn't form anything more than that one syllable. Dante's offer had thrown her completely.

His smile was rueful. 'My offer is simple, dolcezza. You come to the wedding with me and I give you a million euros.'

He pronounced it 'seemple', a quirk she would have found endearing if her brain hadn't frozen into a stunned snowball.

'You want to pay me to come to a wedding with you?'

'Si.' He unfolded his arms and spread his hands. 'The money will be yours. You can give as much or as little of it to your sister.'

It took a huge amount of effort to keep her voice steady. 'But you must have a heap of women you could take and not have to pay them for it.'

'None of them are suitable.'

'What does that mean?'

'I need to make an impression on someone and having you on my arm will assist in that.'

'A million dollars for one afternoon...?'

'I never said it would be for an afternoon. The celebrations will take place over the coming weekend.'

She tugged at her ponytail. 'Weekend?'

'Aislin, the groom is one of Sicily's richest men. It is a necessity that his wedding be the biggest and flashiest it can be.'

She almost laughed at the deadpan way he explained it.

She didn't need to ask who the richest man in Sicily was.

'If I'm going to accept your offer, what else do I need to know?'

'Nothing… Apart from that I will be introducing you as my fiancée.'

'What?' Aislin winced at the squeakiness of her tone.

'I require you to play the role of my fiancée.' His grin was wide with just a touch of ruefulness. The deadened, shocked look that had rung from his eyes only a few minutes before had gone. Now they sparkled with life and the effect was almost hypnotising.

She blinked the effect away.

'Why do you need a fiancée?'

'Because the father of the bride thinks going into business with me will damage his reputation.'

'How?'

'I will go through the reasons once I have your agreement on the matter. I appreciate it is a lot to take in so I'm going to leave you to sleep on it. You can give me your answer in the morning. If you're in agreement then I shall take you home with me and give you more details. We will have a few days to get to know each other and work on putting on a convincing act.'

'And if I say no?'

He shrugged. 'If you say no, then no million euros.'

Continue reading
THE SICILIAN'S BOUGHT CINDERELLA
Michelle Smart

Available next month
www.millsandboon.co.uk

COMING SOON!

We really hope you enjoyed reading this book. If you're looking for more romance, be sure to head to the shops when new books are available on

Thursday 24th January

To see which titles are coming soon, please visit

millsandboon.co.uk/nextmonth

LET'S TALK

Romance

For exclusive extracts, competitions
and special offers, find us online:

:blue_book: facebook.com/millsandboon

:bird: @MillsandBoon

:camera: @MillsandBoonUK

Get in touch on 01413 063232

For all the latest titles coming soon, visit
millsandboon.co.uk/nextmonth